Graham Ison was a soldier for five years before joining the Metropolitan Police. During his thirty-year career in Scotland Yard's Special Branch he was involved in several espionage cases and the investigation into the escape of the spy George Blake. He spent four years at 10 Downing Street as protection officer to Prime Ministers Harold Wilson and Edward Heath, and also served as second-in-command of the Diplomatic Protection Group.

Now a full-time author and after-dinner speaker, Graham Ison lives in Hampshire.

DIVISION

Graham Ison

WARNER BOOKS

A *Warner* Book

First published in Great Britain in 1996 by Warner Books

Copyright © Graham Ison 1996

The moral right of the author has been asserted.

This is a work of fiction. Characters, organisations, situations and philosophies are either the product of the author's imagination or, if real, have been used fictitiously without any intent to describe or portray their actual conduct.

A CIP catalogue record for this book is available from the
British Library.

ISBN 0 7515 1626 0

Printed and bound in Great Britain by Clays Ltd, St Ives plc

Warner Books
A Division of
Little, Brown and Company (UK)
Brettenham House
Lancaster Place
London WC2E 7EN

'The time for division is over....'

John Major, following his re-election
to the leadership of the Conservative Party,
4th July 1995.

CHAPTER ONE

It was not until the Chancellor of the Exchequer was murdered that the Prime Minister realised just how serious the situation had become.

But by then he had left it too late. Too late to deploy the military. Too late to take command of his own government. And too late to stand up to the moguls of Europe.

Although the catalyst was undoubtedly Mrs Karen Parsons of Camberwell, the troubles stemmed from the Cabinet meeting that had taken place some two years before the one that saw the untimely death of the Chancellor.

Summer had come early that year.

On the rich, green carpet of St James's Park the horse chestnut trees, now in full leaf, stood solid, their blossom moving gently in a light breeze. Flowerbeds and rockeries – carefully nurtured by an army of gardeners – were a riot of breathtaking colour. At one end of the lake, the surface of which was rippled by noisy ducks and elegant swans, stood Buckingham Palace. At the other, Scott's Italianate Foreign Office and the Palladian-style Horse Guards building created impressive studies for the countless tourists who photographed London.

Groups of Americans pursuing some aimless sightseeing

plan of their own mooned along the pathways, occasionally stopping and staring before ambling on. Little knots of
Japanese, girt with expensive photographic equipment,
were capturing everything on film and chattering excitedly
to each other. A party of Germans, disciplined into two
lines, stopped at intervals as an officious woman guide
wearing a green hat gesticulated with an umbrella as she
pointed out various landmarks, her guttural explanation
sounding like a reproof. Native Londoners, attempting to
go about their business, were quietly cursing and pushing
their bad-tempered way through. Between them all, forag-
ing and pecking, dirty pigeons strutted self-importantly. In
the distance, a military band was playing selections from
Gilbert and Sullivan. And stretched out on the grass,
oblivious to the health risks, office workers took in the sun,
the girls in daring bikinis, the men bare to the waist.

Among the more purposeful of those crossing the park
was Alec Shepherd. There was an air of the military about
him, but not overtly so, for he was no longer a soldier. Ten
years ago, he had been serving as a captain on the
directing staff at Sandhurst when he had been invited to
join the Secret Intelligence Service. His natural aptitude for
the work had brought him to notice very quickly, and
although he had spent some of his time abroad, the
Counter-Intelligence and Security Section at the headquarters building on Albert Embankment soon claimed
him for its own, and he had become an assistant to Barry
Rogers, its director. Nevertheless, Alec Shepherd was an
ordinary man, unlikely to stand out in a crowd. His dark
suit – probably about four years old – was of quiet good
quality, and his highly polished shoes were orthodox in
design. He had a full head of dark, slightly wavy hair which
was greying at the temples. He disliked briefcases and
never carried one for fear that he might inadvertently leave
it on a train, in a taxi or at a restaurant. Such papers as he
needed were stuffed into the inside pockets of his jacket,

causing it to bulge around the chest and pull slightly on the centre button. He was the sort of man women looked at with a sigh, wishing that they could have the opportunity to get close to him, but Alec Shepherd had never married even though he had had numerous girlfriends. One long-standing relationship had finally foundered months before, the lady in question being unable to accept that the man in her life would not share with her the details of what he did every day when he went to work.

Now, with one hand in his trouser pocket, he was crossing the footbridge towards Birdcage Walk. He had just been entertained to lunch at the Travellers in Pall Mall and was on his way to Scotland Yard, where he had an appointment with a senior Special Branch officer.

At nearby 10 Downing Street, the Right Honourable Robert Fairley, Prime Minister and First Lord of the Treasury, was presiding over a particularly acrimonious Cabinet meeting. It had been in session for two whole hours now and tempers had become frayed, the open windows doing little to alleviate the heat.

'The people won't stand for it.' Kenneth Sinclair, the Home Secretary, lounged in his chair and stared hard at the Prime Minister.

'The people will have to stand for it.' Fairley was starting to show his anger at the intransigence of some of his colleagues and was heartily sick of a debate that had been raging for years now. 'Our membership of the European Union does not allow for any retraction on the concept of a single currency. It was enshrined in the Maastricht Treaty, agreed at the 1996 Inter-Governmental Con-ference and endorsed by the House. Our only purpose here today is to give formal approval to the announcement of its introduction.'

'The decision to change the currency was only pushed through the House because you turned it into a vote of confidence in the government,' said Sinclair, who never lost an opportunity to embarrass the man whose chair he coveted. 'Can you imagine what it'll be like when people start trading in ECUs?' Although it had been agreed in 1995 that the new currency would be called the Euro, that decision had later been reversed and it was to be called the ECU once again.

'I would not have thought,' said the Prime Minister heavily, his patience ebbing by the minute, 'that I would have been obliged to explain it again.' He knew that Sinclair was being deliberately obstructive. 'The entire European Union is switching to a common currency on the third of March the year after next. If we do not do the same, our currency will be crucified in the international money markets. The pound will become a punch bag for anyone who cares to trade in it. There is no alternative,' he added, borrowing a phrase from a previous prime minister.

'It will be much the same as when we went decimal in the seventies,' said Alexander Crisp, the Chancellor of the Exchequer, who was becoming equally irritated by Sinclair's posturings. 'We are giving plenty of notice, nearly two years in fact. By announcing it today, we are allowing banks and the business world to absorb the idea and to make the necessary arrangements to cater for a smooth transition. There will be plenty of time to make alterations to slot machines and suchlike. It's not as if we are going to spring it on them with a few hours' notice. All we have to do now is to give formal approval to the announcement.'

Crisp had been Chancellor for two years, and it was possibly the most invidious task of his career to oversee the change from sterling to the much-despised European Currency Unit. Previous governments had sworn that it would never happen. But they had also sworn that Britain would not re-enter the Exchange Rate Mechanism from which it had withdrawn in 1992.

The present government had reneged on both those promises.

'I still say we should abandon the whole idea. If it happens there'll be chaos, and no little resentment, you mark my words. The pound has been our unit of currency for centuries, and the people won't stand for some cheap aluminium disc that doesn't even bear the Queen's head on it.' That was overstating and simplifying the case, but Sinclair was determined to discomfit both Fairley and Crisp. The starchy and faintly militaristic Crisp, Sinclair knew, also had designs on prime ministerial office, even though most members of the party regarded him as too old to be considered.

'Coinage will be much the same as it is now,' said the Chancellor. 'It will be produced in the Royal Mint. And banknotes will be printed by the government's usual suppliers.'

Sinclair ignored him. 'It's all very well saying that the people will have plenty of warning,' he said, 'but they'll shrug it off as something that will happen tomorrow, not today.'

'It won't be today,' snapped Crisp. 'It has been decided that ECU Day will be the third of March the year after next.' He repeated the date unnecessarily and glanced at the Prime Minister, who merely nodded. 'Every other nation in the European Union is changing on that day. As the Prime Minister has said, if we opt to change later – or worse still, not at all – the economy of this country will be devastated by opportunists in the international money markets. There is absolutely no way of going back on what has been agreed ...' he paused, 'and debated over and over again, both in Cabinet and in the House.'

'I think we ought to get out of Europe altogether,' said Sinclair churlishly. 'Should never have got involved in the first place.'

'Don't talk nonsense, man,' said Donald Usher, the Foreign Secretary. 'There's no surer way of bankrupting this country than to pull out of Europe.'

Sinclair scoffed. 'You mean we're not bankrupt now? With a public-sector borrowing requirement of nigh on a hundred billion, and four million unemployed?'

Usher, not wishing to be reminded of those uncomfortable and embarrassing facts, disregarded Sinclair's sarcastic commentary. 'All our trade's tied up with our continental neighbours,' Usher continued. 'We abandoned the Commonwealth years ago, so they won't want to know us. The President of Australia has made it clear that he has no intention of trading with us if it can possibly be avoided.'

'Bloody man,' muttered the President of the Board of Trade.

'Canada is in chaos,' continued Usher, 'and the independent State of Quebec is hellbent on becoming part of metropolitan France. And we've reneged on New Zealand so often that it's no surprise that they're talking about becoming a republic too. Even if we could opt out of Europe now, we'd be on our own, but there are far too many contracts and agreements in existence for us to do so. It would take us years to disentangle ourselves.'

But Sinclair refused to yield. 'It won't last,' he said. 'It can't. Every polyglot alliance ever created has ended in disarray. The Ottoman Empire, the Austro-Hungarian Empire, the British Empire—'

'The Golders Green Empire,' said the Secretary of State for Defence quietly and received a bitter glance from the Home Secretary.

'The Eastern Bloc inevitably came apart, followed by Yugoslavia,' continued Sinclair, 'and last but not least, look at what's going on in Russia.'

'Thank you for that short history lesson,' Fairley snapped, 'but it is an irreversible decision.' He slammed shut the leather-bound folder in front of him. 'Cabinet is adjourned,' he added tersely and swept from the room.

*

The Chancellor of the Exchequer's face looked out of millions of television screens. 'The Maastricht Treaty,' he began, 'which was ratified some years ago, provided for the eventual introduction of a currency common to all the member nations of the European Union. That policy was confirmed at the 1996 Inter-Governmental Conference and I have to tell you that the European Currency Unit – the ECU – will replace the pound sterling as the currency of the United Kingdom with effect from the third of March the year after next. Her Majesty's Government is giving plenty of notice in order that banks, shops and the manufacturers and users of coin machines will be prepared for what, I am sure, will be an easy transition to the new currency.'

The Chancellor paused. 'Disappearing frontiers and a world made smaller by faster travel and speedier communications have made such a step inevitable, and if we are to take our place as the trade leaders of Europe and of the world at large, it is essential that we make the change.' He took a sip of water. 'I want to reassure you all,' he continued, 'that the introduction of the ECU will not mean that your money will be worth any less.' He had been sternly advised by the PR people not to use the phrase 'the pound in your pocket'. 'The valuation has been fixed so that one ECU will be equal to eighty pence. That means,' he added unnecessarily, 'that if you have £400 in the bank, your balance will be shown as 500 ECUs from ECU Day. And *The Daily Telegraph*, for example, which now costs 60 pence will, from then on, cost you 75 Eurocents.' Crisp went on in this vein for some time, as though explaining a simple matter to a rather dim audience, most of whom, unbeknown to him, had either got up to make a pot of tea or had switched off their sets altogether before he had been speaking for thirty seconds.

The national press treated the announcement in different

ways. *The Times*, in sombre tones, attempted to assess what it would mean to the City, to the supplier and to the consumer, its editorial suggesting that the change from the pound to the ECU was, of itself, unimportant. Currency was currency, it said, whatever it was called, but it went on to condemn the change as a smoke screen to disguise the implications of an economy tied to the poorer nations of the European Union and controlled by Brussels.

The Sun, on the other hand, took a less complex and earthier view. Banner headlines proclaimed, 'FAIRLEY ABOLISHES QUEEN'S HEAD', causing many people to believe that their local pub was to be demolished. Beneath it, however, a smaller typeface clarified that bald statement by explaining, 'THE POUND TO GO'. But the paper suggested that, this time, the British people were being pushed too far. Its editorial predicted wholesale resistance to the disappearance of sterling and went on to cite the introduction of European 'funny money' as yet another example of Brussels' interference in the domestic affairs of 'our once-great nation'. A straw poll quoted 'millions' of housewives who claimed not to understand ECUs, and the paper published a sly feature article by a former chancellor of the exchequer who predicted a sharp rise in inflation when unscrupulous shopkeepers rounded up their prices to overcome an inexact revaluation of the old currency. There was a little diagram showing how the introduction of decimal currency and the later disappearance of the halfpenny had caused prices to rise steeply. And, significantly, another graph forecast what was likely to happen to prices once the ECU was introduced.

The government's hopes that the nation would accept the change peaceably if given enough warning were dashed very quickly.

Labour and Liberal-Democrat Members of Parliament – and a few Conservatives – were vociferous in their opposition to the change, conveniently overlooking the fact that many of them had been in the House at the time of Maastricht and had supported the treaty's ratification. But now they poured scorn on it, voicing their 'concern' to anyone who was prepared to listen. And plenty were. Rarely a day passed without the tabloid press publishing the views of a so-called expert, and the television channels ran near nightly interviews with politicians, many of them former ministers, that were designed to show that the country – and its inhabitants – would be poorer as a result of the pound's disappearance.

As the months between the government's announcement and ECU Day dwindled away, so the protest lobby became stronger. Ministers and backbenchers alike were inundated with correspondence, little of it in support of sterling's abolition. And Conservative MPs, mindful of the general election that would have to be held no later than two years from ECU Day, were quick to sense the mood of resistance and align themselves with it. Many held marginal constituencies, but even those who did not recalled the doctrine that there was no such thing as a safe seat: it was just that some were more marginal than others.

Although there had been mounting concern at the prospect of losing the pound sterling, the first major show of public disquiet occurred seven months after the Chancellor's appearance on television and some fourteen months prior to ECU Day.

On a cold January Sunday, thousands flocked to Trafalgar Square to hear an impressive array of politicians from all parties, but mainly from Labour, condemn the change from sterling as a madness that would be responsible for the bankruptcy of the nation and many of its people. What they conveniently overlooked, however, was that, short of leaving the European Union altogether, the British Government had no option but to accept the ruling of Brussels. And they had also forgotten that, in 1995, the then Labour leader had come out in favour of a single currency.

At long, long last people realised just how impotent their government had become now that Britain was a sub-ordinate state of a union that was becoming increasingly dominated by an unofficial, but very real, Franco-German alliance. And they meant to show their displeasure.

The police estimated that there were some 25,000 people in Trafalgar Square and were thankful for the merciful coincidence of a major international football match in Helsinki that was being televised that afternoon.

Every one of the speakers condemned the abolition of the pound. The Leader of the Opposition, Brian Kennard, was eloquent in his scathing dismissal of the government's decision. 'In the beginning,' he said, sounding more like a crusading evangelist than a politician, 'the Conservative government of Robert Fairley decided to tie our economy to that of the other nations of the European Union. That was madness enough,' he continued, 'but to add to that lunacy by abolishing the pound is a classic example of why this government is so moribund, so bereft of imagination; it has proved itself unfit to govern over and over and over again. There was no need to do away with the pound . . .' His voice dropped and he went on in tones that implied patient reason in the face of crass and hot-headed stupidity. Although every word was clear, even to those at the back, he nevertheless gave the impression of a one-to-one confidence. 'We could have kept the pound. Revalued it against the ECU if necessary, but why, why, I ask you,' his voice rose to a crescendo, 'why insult the Queen by removing Her Majesty's effigy from our banknotes and our coinage?'

Beside him, a Conservative MP whispered to his neighbour that Brian Kennard appeared suddenly to have become a royalist.

'There was no need,' Kennard went on. 'And have you

considered the cost of replacing our entire stock of coinage and all our banknotes? Who is going to pay for new price labels, new machinery, new computers to account in ECUs not pounds. You, you the British people, will pay for it all.'

'Through the nose, guv'nor!' shouted a voice from the crowd.

Kennard grinned and continued. 'It will come as no surprise to you,' he went on, 'that the Chancellor of the Exchequer declined to attend this meeting. I imagine it was because he wouldn't have had any answers to the questions I have just posed. He certainly didn't have them when I challenged him in the House.' In all fairness, the notice of the meeting given to Alexander Crisp had been much too short and his diary had been filled not only for that date but for some months ahead. But Kennard knew that he would not have attended anyway. 'The introduction of the European Currency Unit will result in prices rising sharply because unscrupulous retailers will round up their prices to increase their profits. And that will mean more businesses going bankrupt and more people out of work. Labour would never have let that happen. But our masters who sit over there' – Kennard waved a hand in the general direction of the House of Commons – 'don't seem to care. They're all right, aren't they?'

The audience loved it, frequently interrupting with shouts of encouragement.

'So, what are we to do about it, ladies and gentlemen?' continued Kennard. 'Are we just going to sit and take it while we're ripped off by profiteers? Are we?' There was a roar from the audience. 'And what is our discredited government doing? I'll tell you, ladies and gentlemen. Nothing. Apart from telling you that we're turning the corner. Well, I reckon they've turned so many corners now that they're going round in circles. And as for Europe ...' There was a groan from the audience. 'We are being messed about by Brussels from morning until night. And what does the government do? They hold up their hands and say that we're part of the European Union and that there's nothing they can do. If you did your jobs as efficiently as they've done theirs, you'd be out on your ear.'

The Special Branch of the Metropolitan Police takes a great interest in public meetings of a political nature, and part of their duties consists of keeping the Commissioner informed of such matters in order that he may effectively deploy police to prevent serious outbreaks of public disorder. Consequently, a routine report of the Trafalgar Square meeting was prepared and submitted. A Special Branch detective chief inspector read it and filed it, but not before he had sent a copy to the Security Service, still known to the media as MI5, which also has an interest in political meetings. Just in case there is a subversive organisation behind them.

The ground swell of opposition slowly grew into uncom- promising militancy. A poster campaign was launched, paid for by an anonymous dog-food millionaire. Frequent protest meetings bore a striking similarity to each other, to the extent that the police and the Security Service became convinced that somewhere a secret hand was organising the opposition on a grand scale. 'God Save the Queen', appearing on professionally printed banners, took on a new meaning.

Newspapers and television stations kept up the pressure. Rarely a day went by without some new forecast of economic doom. Spiralling inflation and snowballing unemployment were predicted; financiers and politicians poured forth millions of words prophesying disaster. Week by week the language became less restrained and more heavily sarcastic.

*

On ECU Day itself, the front page of the *Daily Mirror* was filled with large black letters: 'WELCOME TO FAIRLEY'S THIRD WORLD', and in common with most of the other daily newspapers, it published a conversion table to help its readers when they went shopping. On Friday night, countless supermarkets and stores across the country had brought in staff to change price tickets and to reprogram the computers that would convert bar codes to cater for the new currency.

It was Karen Parsons, a housewife with a minimal budget to spend, whose protestations in a South London supermarket unwittingly started a chain of events that brought the British government to its knees and destroyed several promising careers. Using the little card bearing the conversion table, she started to compare the new ECU prices of certain items with what she knew they had been in sterling the day before.

'That's not right,' she said, half to herself, and consulted the little card again. A woman standing next to her turned. 'Bloody cornflakes,' said Mrs Parsons. 'Yesterday they was one eighty-three in old money. According to this ticket they're . . .' She paused, staring at the ticket again. 'They're two ECUs and forty-one Eurocents.' She glanced back at her *Daily Mirror* conversion card. 'That's equal to one ninety-three. They've put 'em up by ten pee.'

The other woman, pausing briefly only to chastise one of her two children, pulled down a packet of porridge oats. 'Same with this, love,' she said. She peered over Mrs Parsons's shoulder. 'What's one ECU twenty-one in real money?'

'Ninety-seven pee,' said Mrs Parsons.

'That's ten pee up on yesterday an' all,' said the woman with the two children. 'They must have made a mistake.'

By now a group of women had gathered, and they began joining in the conversation. 'You ought to have a look at the fruit,' said one of them. 'Apples is up by ten pee a pound, and they're them bloody rotten French ones an' all. My mum said this happened when they went decimal.'

It was at that moment that an assistant manager was unfortunate enough to appear on the scene. 'Is there a problem, ladies?' he enquired innocently.

'Yes, there bleedin' is,' said Mrs Parsons. 'You've cocked up all the prices, that's what. And they're all in your favour, an' all.'

'I can assure you, madam, they've all been very thoroughly checked against the head-office computers. They are correct.'

'Don't you "madam" me,' said Mrs Parsons angrily. 'I can do bleedin' arithmetic, and these new prices ain't right.'

The assistant manager's reply, that it was a head-office decision, did nothing to appease the irate Karen Parsons, and the unfortunate man was quickly surrounded by other furious women quoting similarly inflated prices.

'Well, you know what you can do with your new prices, don't you, mister?' said Karen Parsons, and started to sweep the shelves clear of stock.

'What do you think you're doing?' shrieked the alarmed manager. But Karen Parsons was promptly joined by the other housewives, and within minutes they were throwing tins of food, fresh vegetables and fruit, meat, bread and cleaning materials to the floor. Moving like a pillaging army, they had wrecked the store before the first police, hastily summoned by an assistant, started to arrive on the scene.

But they were ill equipped and lacking in the resolve required to deal with violent women on the rampage, who overturned tills, smashed expensive computer equipment and wrenched bar-code scanners out of their sockets and threw them around. From the far end of the store came the sound of breaking glass as the first of many trolleys was propelled through the plate-glass windows. Others, determined that the weekly chore of shopping should not be in vain, started to load their trolleys with the produce that now lay about the floor. The checkout assistants, for the most part housewives themselves, did nothing to stop the mass exodus as the looting women pushed their trolleys determinedly towards the car park.

Half an hour after opening its doors, the wrecked supermarket had closed for business, leaving just a handful of police officers to guard against further looting and burglar alarms ringing ineffectually in the cold March morning.

The following day, *The Mail on Sunday* described the incident as the first ECU riot. They were not wrong.

CHAPTER TWO

The assault on the South London supermarket that had been led by Mrs Karen Parsons was widely reported. Too late, the owners realised that to allow television cameras freedom to film the damage merely served to incite the public at large to destroy more of their property. And by the time an emergency board meeting had brought prices back down to the proper conversion rate, other branches and other chains across the country had been attacked. The excuse that a computer error had inadvertently increased the prices by the equivalent of ten pence all round was met with hollow laughter and unvarnished allegations of fraud from the popular press.

In Shepperton, to the southwest of London, an incensed group of new-age travellers wrecked a filling station they believed had overpriced their petrol. Old lorries, converted buses and a tractor were driven across the forecourt, smashing down pumps and canopies, and a truck was reversed into the shop, destroying the stock. Finally, whether by accident or design, the petrol that flowed around the station was ignited, the resulting explosion shattering dozens of windows in nearby houses and causing the death of two of the itinerants.

In places as far apart as Plymouth, Norwich, Liverpool,

Newcastle, Dundee and Ullapool, shops suspected of using the conversion to ECUs as an excuse for increasing their prices were attacked.

Violent demonstrations in Edinburgh, Manchester, Coventry and Portsmouth left hundreds injured, and the police suddenly realised that they were very close to being unable to contain the situation. But with the realisation there came a nagging suspicion that in many cases the new currency was being used as an excuse for widespread vandalism. The police, being the front line of authority, as usual bore the brunt of it.

Virginia Crosby lived in Windridge, a few miles south of the centre of Woking in Surrey. Every morning her husband Tim, who commanded the 27th Royal Hussars, would drive to the barracks and Virginia would be left to her own devices until he returned at about six o'clock.

Most of the people who envied her did not realise what a lonely existence it was without children, a deficiency that she and her husband had been trying to rectify all their married lives. In Germany, from whence the regiment had recently returned, she had made many friends, both British and German, but the regimental spirit was less evident now that they were back home. She visited other officers' wives from time to time and busied herself with the occasional welfare problems of the soldiers' wives and families, which she, like every other colonel's wife, saw as her duty. But it still left a lot of spare time.

At about half past nine on a chilly January morning, some two months before the introduction of the ECU, Virginia was telephoned by Amanda Strong, the wife of HQ Squadron's commander, who suggested a game of badminton. 'I'll pick you up,' Amanda said.

'No, don't do that,' Virginia replied. 'I'll jog across. It's not far, and I could do with loosening up. We can drive to the club from your place.'

Virginia changed into her kit and a tracksuit before grabbing her racket and a tube of shuttlecocks and setting out across Windridge Common to where Amanda lived. Virginia was a tall, good-looking woman, some thirty years of age, and very fit. She started to run across the deserted common, reckoning on completing the short distance to Amanda Strong's house in about ten minutes.

When she was about halfway there, she was suddenly confronted by a man who emerged from some bushes. He looked to be about twenty-eight, roughly dressed in filthy jeans and a blue shirt, over which he wore a tattered sweater with holes in it. His brown hair was gathered in a ponytail, and there was an earring in the lobe of his left ear.

Virginia ignored him, avoiding eye contact lest it should give him some excuse for starting a conversation. She diverted slightly from her chosen path in order not to go too near him but, intent upon a confrontation, he too changed course and stopped in front of her.

Virginia sidestepped him, but the man moved again so that he was in front of her once more. There was something menacing, evil, about him that frightened her. She stopped, briefly, and turning, began to run back in the direction from which she had come.

In less than six yards, the man had caught up with her. Then he was on her, seizing her around the neck from behind, tearing at her tracksuit. She cried out, screaming loudly, and tried to break away. The man pulled her round and she was conscious of his foul-smelling breath as he put his face close to hers. He put a hand into the waistband of her tracksuit trousers and started to drag them down. She clawed at his face, feebly attempting to strike him with her badminton racket. But he was too strong for her. He wrenched the racket from her grasp and threw it aside before grabbing her wrists and forcing her to the ground. She kicked and struggled, screamed and shouted, but the common was deserted. Leaning over her, he tore at her trousers with a maniacal frenzy. Virginia grabbed him between the legs and squeezed hard but he merely grunted. She twisted sharply away, taking advantage of the momentary lessening of his grip and struggled to her feet, trying desperately to escape. Then she fell again, hampered by her shorts, now around her knees, and the tracksuit trousers around her ankles. Again the man caught hold of her and tore off the remainder of her clothing. She fought like a wildcat as he hit her across the face again and again. Barely conscious, she was aware of him forcing her legs apart. And then she saw the knife, the weak January sunlight glinting on its blade as it rose and then fell. She was conscious of agonising pains in her stomach and her breasts as he struck her repeatedly. And then oblivion. Virginia Crosby was dead. The man had not spoken a single word.

After half an hour, during which time Virginia had not appeared, Amanda Strong began to get worried. Telephoning and getting no reply, she left a note on her front door telling Virginia to wait there for her, and drove around the common to her friend's house. Virginia's car was in the drive and the house was locked up. But there was no sign of Virginia.

The police began by searching the common. It did not take long. Virginia's mutilated body was found partly hidden in some bushes. The detective in charge of the murder enquiry described it as a frenzied attack, the actions of a madman.

In Guildford, on the Saturday night following the murder of Virginia Crosby, a man of twenty-nine was arrested for hitting a policeman who had remonstrated with him about his rowdiness. At first the policeman had believed that the man, a rough-looking fellow with a three-day growth of beard and unkempt hair, was drunk. But when he was eventually forced into a police van and taken to the station, he was found to be high on crack and to have a quantity of it in his possession.

The custody sergeant sent for the police surgeon immediately and, aided by the constable who had arrested the man, placed the prisoner in a cell to await the doctor's arrival.

Just before the cell door was closed, the prisoner spoke. 'It was me what done for that bird down Windridge,' he said, as though in a trance.

Unfortunately the confession was not tape-recorded, although it was made in the presence of two police officers.

The detective inspector was called out at once and, when the divisional surgeon had given the all clear, questioned the prisoner. The man was clearly familiar with Windridge Common, where Virginia Crosby had met her end, and even though he refused to repeat his admission that he had actually murdered the woman, the detective inspector's instinct told him that the man was a very strong suspect.

The detective superintendent in overall charge of the murder enquiry was sent for, and he too questioned the man. The interviews with the inspector and with the superintendent were both recorded and the provisions of the Police and Criminal Evidence Act fully complied with. Despite the prisoner's refusal to repeat his confession, the detective superintendent charged him with the murder of Virginia Crosby.

In the days following the death of his wife, Colonel Tim Crosby suffered a mixture of immense grief and impassioned anger at the futility of it all. He had been constantly reminded of the murder by frequent references to it on television and in the national and local press and, in a vain attempt to put it from his mind, he had thrown himself wholeheartedly into his work. There was not a great deal to do in barracks, but at least he was surrounded by soldiers, and the day-to-day routine of the army was a form of distraction.

But then came the second blow. The detective superintendent in charge of the murder enquiry was shown into Crosby's office one Monday morning, exactly two weeks after the discovery of Virginia Crosby's body. 'I'm afraid there isn't going to be a trial, Colonel,' he said apologetically.

Crosby stared at the superintendent, open-mouthed. 'Why the hell not?' he demanded angrily. 'You've got a man in custody, haven't you?'

'I'm afraid that the Crown Prosecution Service won't go for it,' said the superintendent. 'It seems there's less than a fifty-one per cent chance of securing a conviction.' He lowered his voice. 'They always deny that that's their policy but, believe me, I've seen enough jobs thrown out to know that's the way it is. They decided that there was no chance of securing a conviction because the admission was made while the prisoner was under the influence of drugs and the DNA test was inconclusive.'

'Is that it then?' Crosby stared at the policeman, stark disbelief plain on his face.

The superintendent shrugged. 'Murder cases always stay open, as you know, Colonel, and the police will continue to investigate the matter, but to be perfectly honest with you, I doubt that we'll have any luck. Between you and me, I'm convinced that he was the man.'

'And what about the drugs?' snapped Crosby. 'Are these precious lawyers going to throw that out too?'

'He was cautioned for that offence, Colonel.' The superintendent stood up and proffered his hand. 'I'm sorry, but there's nothing more I can do,' he said wearily.

'Thank you for coming to tell me, Superintendent,' said Crosby flatly and shook hands with him. Despite his anger and his grief, he knew it was not the superintendent's fault.

But when the policeman had left, he stood up and stared savagely out of the window at an armoured car making its way slowly across his line of vision, his fists clenching and unclenching in near uncontrollable fury.

Shortly after the visit of the detective superintendent, the coroner released Virginia Crosby's body for burial.

The funeral was a torment. A gentle rain fell across the bleak cemetery, and Virginia's open grave was marked by a little forest of umbrellas. The piles of earth on either side of the pit made it seem like a miniature battlefield, and the shabby overcoats and frayed top hats of the undertaker's men did nothing to alleviate the mourners' despair at her passing.

Hunched in his service greatcoat, Crosby stood apart, a lonely figure of grief, his face impassive as he stared into space and listened to the chaplain's sonorous recitation of the burial service.

Virginia's father, old and stooped beyond his years and leaning heavily on his walking stick, had insisted on attending the service, and stood in the drizzle as his daughter's coffin was lowered into its last resting place. He glanced briefly at his son-in-law, who was saluting rigidly, and then walked slowly away, supported by Crosby's blonde-haired and upright widowed mother, two figures belonging to a class that regarded it as unseemly to display any emotion.

The officers of the regiment had come out of a sense of duty and adjourned afterwards to the mess to relieve the tension of the tragedy that had so affected their colonel.

When it was all over, Crosby went home to an empty house and attempted to pick up the pieces of a life that only a few weeks earlier had seemed so full of hope and promise.

In the days following the funeral, Colonel Crosby descended

into a mood of morose, suppressed anger. The police refused to divulge the identity of the man whom they believed to be Virginia Crosby's murderer, so Crosby visited the offices of the Crown Prosecution Service at Woking Road in Guildford.

When eventually he was seen by a solicitor who said that he had charge of the office, Crosby demanded an explanation.

'We have to weigh the pros and cons,' said the lawyer soothingly. 'There is the question of government money, and if we regard a case as unlikely to succeed at the Crown Court, then we are justified in declining to prosecute.'

'Justified?' Crosby shouted the word. 'What sort of excuse is that? My wife was savagely murdered in broad daylight by a man who admitted to the killing and you say that you're justified in doing nothing about it. Do you call that justice?'

'I'm afraid that an admission made under the influence of drugs – and there is evidence that the man was under such influence – would carry no weight. The judge would almost certainly rule it inadmissible.' The solicitor paused. 'I can understand your anguish, Mr Crosby—'

'It's *Colonel* Crosby,' said Crosby angrily, 'and you can have no conception of my anguish. I shall take out a private prosecution.'

The solicitor smiled sympathetically. 'I'm afraid that wouldn't do any good, Colonel,' he said. 'You see the Director of Public Prosecutions is empowered to take over any private prosecution for murder and, in this case, he would offer no evidence. So it would be a pointless exercise.'

Over the ensuing weeks, Crosby wrote countless, often intemperate, letters to his Member of Parliament, to the Home Secretary and even to the Prime Minister, in which he complained bitterly of the indifference of a government that seemed more concerned with the welfare of criminals than of their victims. But the few bland responses he received, signed in each case by a civil servant, only exacerbated his bitterness and confirmed the government's indifference. Crosby wrote to the Attorney-General and the Lord Chancellor. Their replies were along the same lines as the others, each expressing sympathy but explaining that it was not possible to interfere with decisions of the Crown Prosecution Service.

Crosby wrote again to the Attorney-General, a somewhat discourteous letter this time, pointing out that as the law officer responsible for the Crown Prosecution Service he was supposedly paid to ensure that justice was done. The Attorney's reply merely repeated what he had said previously.

Finally Crosby went to the House of Commons and demanded to see him. A waiter, immaculate in white tie and tails, took the card and sent it in. But the Attorney declined to come out of the Chamber.

Crosby lost his temper. 'My wife's been murdered!' he shouted. 'And I want something done about it!'

'I'm sorry, sir,' said the waiter, 'but there's nothing that I can do if the Attorney won't come out.'

'That's typical!' shouted Crosby, getting angrier by the minute. 'It wasn't your wife, was it?'

Two policemen approached. 'Come along now, sir,' said one of them. 'You'll achieve nothing by misbehaving.'

'Don't you tell me how to behave,' said Crosby. He turned to other members of the public in the Central Lobby and started to harangue them in loud tones about the murder of his wife.

But by now he was becoming incoherent and the police removed him, first to the police room and finally to the street.

For weeks afterwards, Crosby was inconsolable. He suddenly found that all purpose in life had been swept away. And he was angry. Angry that a system of justice to which the drug addict in Guildford had practically surrendered should have allowed him to walk free. Crosby would sit in his office for hours, moody and contemplative, thinking back over the happy years he had spent with his late wife.

Not that there was, in all honesty, a great deal for Crosby to do in barracks. In common with most of the army on a home posting in peacetime, the 27th Royal Hussars tended to run itself, capably supervised by the warrant officers and sergeants. Crosby rapidly lost interest. He started to make mistakes, mistakes that in most cases were corrected by the second-in-command or the adjutant without Crosby's knowledge. He began to lose weight, and there was a lacklustre appearance about him, even though his batman made sure that his uniform and accoutrements were always properly cared for.

Slowly there arose a serious concern about his mental health, but nothing was said to anyone outside the regimental family, and a young officer who jokingly mentioned *The Caine Mutiny* was given a severe dressing-down by his squadron leader.

Some officers invited Crosby to dinner but, after a while, they gave up. Crosby's sullen presence at their tables, coupled with his diatribes about the criminal justice system, became, frankly, rather boring.

But they were agreed on one thing. Since the death of Virginia Crosby, their colonel had become an introverted, resentful and bitter man.

At Wellington Barracks in London's Birdcage Walk, the commanding officer of the First Battalion of the Grenadier Guards walked past Captain the Honourable Imogen Cresswell's open office door, paused and retraced his steps. 'Oh, Imogen, spare me a moment, if you would.'

'Yes, sir.' Imogen stood up and followed the CO down the corridor to his office.

'Sit down.'

For a moment or two the colonel stood at the window and looked down at the square, casting a critical eye over a squad of guardsmen who had recently joined the battalion from the depot at Pirbright. Incongruously dressed in bearskins, khaki pullovers and trousers, they were being rehearsed for Queen's Guard duty by a drill-sergeant. As the colonel watched, a guardsman lost his footing and fell, his rifle clattering across the gravelled surface of the parade ground. The drill-sergeant let forth a string of colourful abuse as he berated the unfortunate soldier.

'Dear me,' said the colonel, managing to inject eloquent criticism into the two words, 'they're going to have to do better than that.' He turned and seated himself behind his desk. 'The Chief of the General Staff is seeking a staff officer, Imogen,' he said suddenly and fingered the solitary sheet of paper that was in the centre of his otherwise bare desk. 'Not unnaturally, he has asked the Grenadier Guards if they have a suitable officer.' He smiled bleakly. 'I must say, it's a first-class opportunity for any young officer.'

Imogen was puzzled by the colonel's affability. Ever since joining the battalion four years ago, she had experienced a hostility among most of the officers, and the colonel in particular. The idea of having a woman officer in the Grenadier Guards had been anathema to them. 'Do you think I'm qualified for the post, sir?' she asked.

'Oh, undoubtedly, Imogen, undoubtedly,' said the colonel keenly and paused, leaning forward. 'Well, do you think you might like to be considered?'

'What does it involve, sir?'

'An informal interview with the CGS, I should think, and if he likes the look of you, you'll get the job.'

'I meant what does the job involve, sir?'

The colonel raised his eyebrows. 'As I understand it, not very much. More of a social sinecure, I imagine. A case of being there when the CGS wants something. I should think you'd be ideally suited.' And to that back-handed compliment, he added, 'Of course, Sir Simon Macey is a former Royal Tank Regiment officer.' The colonel could be very scathing when the mood took him.

'Well, if you think I ought to apply, sir ...' It was a wonderful chance for Imogen to escape the cloying atmosphere of a Guards battalion without actually leaving the regiment.

'You're prepared to let your name go forward then?'

'Yes, sir, I am.'

The office into which Imogen was shown at the Ministry of Defence was occupied by a young major.

'Oh, hello,' he said, standing up and holding out his hand, 'I'm Jack Gray, Royal Engineers. You must be Imogen Cresswell.'

'Yes, sir.'

Gray waved a deprecating hand at her salute. 'Don't go in for that sort of formality too much here,' he murmured. 'You've come to see the boss, I take it. Oh, do sit down.'

'Yes, that's right.' Imogen smiled.

Gray studied the young woman carefully. 'So you're after my job, are you?' he asked.

'I was advised to apply for it,' said Imogen stiffly. She glanced around the office. Gray's desk was piled high with files, as was another unoccupied desk adjacent to it.

Gray chuckled at her anxious expression. 'Don't be put off by all the bumph,' he said. 'It's always like that on a Monday morning, but we've got a damned good staff sarn't-major called Watkins. He takes care of it all. Makes sure we deal with the right stuff and bins the rest. Well, I think he does. Never see it again, anyhow.' The sapper major gave a careless laugh. 'The boss'll see you in a moment. He's just taking a phone call.' He glanced at the light on the base of his telephone.

'Are there many of us up for interview?' asked Imogen.

'Don't think so,' said Gray. 'I imagine he took one look at your photograph and decided there and then. But don't tell him I said so.' He glanced at his phone again as the light went out and stood up. 'Ready?' He paused. 'Give him as good as you get, Imogen. He's not a bad old stick.'

Imogen stood nervously outside the door of the Chief of the General Staff's office, feeling like a schoolgirl who had been summoned by the headmistress. She smoothed her skirt once more and gave the hem of her tunic a final tug.

Gray knocked at the door and threw it open. 'Captain Cresswell, sir,' he said.

Imogen moved gracefully and self-confidently across the room, unaware that she was exuding an indefinable quality that immediately attracted the CGS. She was slender and long-legged, and her long blonde hair was immaculately coiffed into a French roll. 'Good morning, sir.'

'Good morning.' General Sir Simon Macey rose from behind his desk and walked around it, extending a hand. 'So you're the famous Imogen Cresswell who got herself into the Grenadiers, eh? You're quite a celebrity, aren't you?' He appraised the girl with penetrating pale-blue eyes. 'Any regrets?'

Imogen hesitated before taking the man's hand. 'Some, sir.' She returned the general's gaze, taking in the neatly trimmed moustache, the full head of stylishly cut hair with only a hint of grey at the temples, the firm jaw and the strong fingers.

'Why did you do it?' asked Macey, inviting her to sit down in one of the armchairs with a wave of his hand. 'Why the Guards?' He noticed a hint of some light floral perfume as she settled herself.

'The impetuousness of youth, I suppose,' said Imogen. Her face twitched into a smile that was almost mocking, and which revealed teeth that were white and even. She sat down and arranged her skirt. 'And a rather silly determination to achieve something that no other woman had.'

'Well you certainly ruffled a few feathers in the process. I had all manner of chaps making informal approaches to me to stop it, you know. I was Adjutant-General at the time.'

'Really?' Imogen gazed directly at him with expressive eyes that were a rich hazel. She had sensed the opposition right from the day she had submitted her application, but Macey's statement surprised her. When eventually she had arrived at the battalion, she had been shunned by most of the officers but had put that down to being a new ensign. 'When I went for the interview with the regimental colonel, I certainly got the impression that he thought it was a huge joke. At least to start with. He actually asked me if I was doing it for a bet.'

Macey threw back his head and laughed. 'He's a bit of a stick-in-the-mud, is Simkins. Typical guardsman, if you'll forgive me for saying so. Of course the Prince of Wales had a lot to do with it, you know,' he added.

'What?' Imogen could not disguise her astonishment and wondered what possible influence the heir to the throne, who was, anyway, Colonel of the Welsh Guards, could have had on her commissioning into the Grenadiers.

Macey nodded. 'As you know, he's been very critical of the Guards Division's failure to recruit black soldiers. Has always said that they're much too selective. I'm told that the appointment of a woman officer in the Grenadiers was regarded as a bit of a sop to his views. Sort of going half way, if you see what I mean.'

'Not exactly, sir.' Imogen contained her irritation at being cast into the same sort of minority group as black soldiers. 'But it was quite apparent that I wasn't welcome.'

'That's a pity.' Macey leaned across to his desk and took a file from it. He opened it on his knees and studied it for a moment. 'You passed out of RMAS in the top twenty I see.'

Imogen nodded. That had probably been half the trouble. The regimental colonel had undoubtedly expected her not to pass out of either the Brigade Squad at Pirbright or Sandhurst. In fact her determination to succeed had carried her through both with distinction. And she had been helped greatly by her tactics tutor, an infantry captain called Alec Shepherd, who had told her that he admired her guts.

'And the daughter of a life peer.' Macey smiled as if to soften what seemed like a patronising comment. 'Good degree at Oxford,' he murmured as he picked out the salient points of Imogen's personal history. 'Honours in law at Somerville.'

'Yes, sir.'

'And you're quite a sportswoman, I see.'

'I was a blue in both tennis and swimming.' Imogen felt as if she was going through her recruitment interview all over again.

'What did they give you to do in the battalion, Captain Cresswell?' Macey glanced up, an enquiring expression on his face.

'They created a post specially for me, sir,' said Imogen drily. 'They made me second assistant adjutant. It was a nothing job really, but I did it for four years. The colonel said I couldn't do public duties because there was no recognised ceremonial uniform for a woman Guards officer and I'd look ridiculous in a bearskin.' She took a chance on the CGS having a sense of humour. 'Of course, there were all the usual jokes about how much better I'd look in a bare skin than a bearskin.' Macey glanced at her, smiling, and Imogen got the impression that he agreed with her brother officers' point of view. 'But that was before my promotion.' She paused to offer an unnecessary explanation. 'My commission was antedated because of my degree, you see.'

Macey nodded. 'But since I got my captaincy, I seem to have become something of a liability. They can't leave me in the same post because the assistant adjutant is only a lieutenant. One of the company commanders suggested that I should go out recruiting. He said that I would be bound to pull in a few volunteers.'

Macey nodded and thought to himself that the company commander was probably right in his assumption. 'So you decided to escape by applying for this post as my ADC?' He raised an eyebrow and studied the woman afresh. His first impression of her had been one of warmth and friendliness; there was certainly no sign of shyness, and she reacted to his probing with spirit. Added to which, Imogen Cresswell was a beautiful woman. Her hands, resting loosely in her lap, were elegant, the nails manicured and carefully varnished, and she had obviously given some skilful and painstaking attention to her make-up.

'Oh no, sir, not at all. It seemed to me to be a job where I could make use of my talents.' Too late, Imogen realised that her responses made it look as though her only interest in the post for which Macey was interviewing her was to escape from the battalion.

'And what talents would they be?' Macey smiled and leaned back in his chair.

'I mix easily,' began Imogen, 'and I'm fully conversant with staff and admin work—'

Macey held up his hand. 'I'm sure you're well qualified,' he said, 'or your CO wouldn't have recommended you.' Apart from which, every officer he had ever interviewed over the years had trotted out a similar list of their capabilities. 'Your father was a trade unionist, wasn't he?' he asked suddenly.

'I thought you would have known that from your examination of my file, sir,' said Imogen, forcing a smile. Since arriving in Macey's office, she had noticed how often he had glanced at her legs. Her feminine instincts told her that he was probably a womaniser, and she was not certain that she wanted to work for him.

'I'm sorry,' said Macey and looked as though he meant it. 'I'm beginning to sound like one of those interviewers at RCB.'

Imogen opened her hands in a meaningless gesture. She remembered very clearly the searching questions of the president of the Regular Commissions Board and his undisguised hostility to her father's former occupation. 'My father was playing a part, as most of us do, I suppose,' she said. 'He was a supporter of the Labour Party because it would have been professional suicide not to be, but he loved the good things in life. He was a keen collector of works of art, too.'

'What sort of art?' Macey put his head on one side and looked at the girl quizzically.

'Oh, nothing in particular. There was no method to his acquisitions. He just liked beautiful things.'

'I take it, from the way you're speaking of him, that he's dead.'

'He died just before I passed out from RMAS.' It had been the greatest disappointment of Imogen's life that, two weeks before the commissioning parade – which he had been looking forward to attending – her father had succumbed to a heart attack. Although opposed to his daughter's choice of career, Lord Cresswell had supported her fully once he had realised that he was not to get his own way. He had always hoped that she would become a barrister – he called it having a licence to print money – but she had been adamant about the army, partly because of the range of sporting activities it offered.

'I'm sorry,' said Macey. 'So, life in the battalion's not been too easy for you.' He reverted to their previous conversation.

'That's putting it mildly, sir,' said Imogen. 'It's been absolute hell. It's not quite so bad now I've got my

captaincy, but the first few years or so were . . .' She paused
reflectively. 'As a matter of fact, I'd more than once
considered resigning my commission.'

'Good God!' said Macey, genuinely surprised that anyone could contemplate leaving the army. 'But why?'

'I really didn't think I could stand the boorish behaviour
of my fellow officers a minute longer.' Imogen smiled, but
not at the general. 'I always thought that officers in the
Guards would behave like gentlemen' – Macey snorted, but
said nothing – 'but they really are quite insufferable at
times. Do you know, when I first joined the battalion, one
drunken ensign actually tried to persuade me to have sex
with him on the billiard table in the mess on the day of the
Queen's Birthday Parade. Said it was one of the time-
honoured traditions of the regiment.'

'Good Lord!' murmured Macey. 'That's damned bad
form, even if he was joking. What did you say to him?'

'I used a few choice words I'd learned from my father.'
She smiled. 'Not the language of an officer and a lady, I
suppose, but it seemed to have the desired effect. As a
matter of fact, I suggested that he did it with one of the
other officers.'

Macey chuckled at that. 'You could have applied for
another regiment, I suppose.'

'That would have been admitting defeat, sir.' Imogen
snapped out her reply.

'Wouldn't resigning your commission have amounted
to the same thing, though?'

'If I'm to stay in the army, sir, it'll be in my chosen
regiment and nowhere else.' Imogen met the CGS's gaze
but was not sure how to interpret his smile.

Three days later, Imogen's colonel sent for her.

'Good morning, sir.' Imogen stood to attention in front
of the CO's desk.

'It seems that the Chief of the General Staff's taken a

shine to you, Imogen. You've got the job.' The colonel stood
up and shook her hand. 'Congratulations. It's a great
opportunity. I'm sure you'll never look back.' In reality he
hoped that she'd never *come* back.

'Thank you, sir.' But Imogen knew that her commanding officer's enthusiasm was the result of the CGS having
solved a particularly ticklish problem for him, that of what
to do with an unwanted woman officer now that she was
a captain.

It was raining on the March morning when Imogen
Cresswell set out from Wellington Barracks to take up her
new appointment. She had taken one look at the leaden
sky and ordered a staff car to take her to the Ministry of
Defence building in Whitehall. It was not that she was
averse to inclement weather – in fact, she enjoyed walking
in the rain – but today her appearance had to be beyond
criticism for her first official meeting with her new boss.

'Captain Cresswell's here, sir,' said Staff Sergeant-Major
Watkins.

'Ah, good. Show her in, Mr Watkins.' General Sir Simon
Macey stood up and walked towards the door of his office.

'Good morning, sir.' Imogen Cresswell paused on the
threshold and saluted.

'Imogen, good to see you again.' Macey shook hands.
'Come in and sit down, and I'll try to tell you what we get up
to here.' He walked across to a sideboard. 'Cup of coffee?'

'Thank you, sir.'

'Sugar and milk?'

'Neither, thank you, sir.'

Macey turned and smiled at the slim-figured girl.
'Incidentally, you'll have plenty of time for sport here. To be
perfectly honest, we're not terribly pushed, except when
there's a panic on, but that doesn't happen very often.' He
placed Imogen's coffee on his desk near to where she was
sitting. 'Where do you swim?'

'At the barracks, sir. It's not a bad pool, as a matter of fact, but I do get tired of leering men.'

Macey made a sour expression. 'I think we can do better than that,' he said. 'I'm a member of the Royal Automobile Club in Pall Mall. It's handy for the MOD, and I can probably fix it for you to use the pool there. Best in Europe, so I'm told.'

'Thank you, sir.' Imogen sensed that she was being patronised because she was a woman but disguised her feelings.

'Now, about the job,' continued Macey. 'You're a staff officer, but the post is dignified with the title of aide-de-camp.' For the next few minutes he outlined the functions of his office and what he expected of his new assistant, half apologetically explaining that it really consisted of being a jack-of-all-trades. 'Or in your case a Jill,' he said, smiling. 'And you'll need plenty of initiative,' he went on. 'You'll have gathered that the office of Chief of the General Staff is a very political one. Most of the time you'll be dealing with ministers and civil servants. The only soldiers we see are each other. Anyhow, your predecessor, Jack Gray, will be here for a month or two, so you'll have quite a decent handover period. Now about your uniform. You're improperly dressed.'

Imogen glanced down at her service dress. 'Is there something wrong with it, sir?' She knew perfectly well that she was immaculately turned out.

Macey laughed. 'Yes,' he said. 'Firstly, put up major's crowns – it's a temporary promotion, but it goes with the job – and then hang your uniform in your wardrobe. We always work in plain clothes here, apart from the occasional outing for things like the Sovereign's Parade at Sandhurst or the Queen's Birthday Parade. And plain clothes doesn't necessarily mean a severely cut business suit, either. We need a bit of glamour about the place to brighten it up.'

*

Life for Imogen Cresswell on General Sir Simon Macey's staff was a thousand times better than it had been when she was serving with the battalion. Macey had kept his promise of arranging for her to swim at the Royal Automobile Club and she was there most weekday mornings before breakfast. She had followed his advice about her clothes, too, and wore either a dress or a blouse and skirt. Invariably, her blonde hair was worn loose.

On the tenth day in her new appointment, Imogen was surprised to receive a formal invitation from Lady Macey inviting her to dinner on the Saturday 'to say farewell to Major Jack Gray' and to stay for the weekend.

'You got Elizabeth's invitation, I take it?' Macey enquired casually later in the day.

'Yes, sir, thank you, but I didn't realise that Jack was going so soon.'

Macey smiled. 'Why not?' he said. 'You seem to have got a grasp of the job very quickly, but the chap he's taking over from in Washington has broken his leg, damned fool, and the ambassador wants a replacement now.'

Lady Macey spent as little of her time as possible in the official living quarters assigned to the Chief of the General Staff at Admiralty Arch. For most of her life she had dwelt in army hirings and had no intention of doing so any longer. Now that her husband was a general with a good chance of becoming a field marshal – and possibly a peer – she was determined to make a permanent home. And live in it.

Imogen Cresswell was impressed by the Maceys' house at Esher. It was a large, modern dwelling in a private road and was surrounded by gardens that were well tended and immaculate. And she was equally impressed by her chief's wife.

'How lovely to meet you, Imogen.' Lady Macey held out

both her hands in greeting. She was wearing white
trousers with a gold blouse, and her short blonde hair was
flecked with grey. 'Corporal Braker will get your bags in
and park your car round the back somewhere. Come along
in and let me get you a drink,' she said, leading Imogen
into the drawing room. 'Jack Gray arrived about ten
minutes ago and Simon should be down any minute now.'
She smiled and shrugged her shoulders. 'You'll have to
excuse me,' she continued, 'I should have got changed ages
ago, but I've been talking to the gardener about a new bed
I want him to put in. I can't help interfering, you know.'
In the drawing room, she indicated a settee with a flourish.
'Now where's Jack gone?' she asked, looking around. 'Oh,
I suppose Simon's dragged him off somewhere. Never
mind. Are you interested in gardens, Imogen? No, I
suppose not. Simon says you live at Wellington Barracks.
That must be pretty awful. When we were in Hong Kong,
years ago now, we were ... Oh, just listen to me, always
chattering on. Now, what are you going to drink?'

When General Macey eventually appeared with Jack
Gray, it was inevitable that the conversation should turn to
talk of the army.

'Oh hell,' said Elizabeth Macey, finishing her drink and
putting her glass down, 'I'm going to get changed.'

The four of them sat down to dinner at eight o'clock.
Corporal Braker, who seemed to be responsible for everything in the house, served at table. The food was imag-
inative and well prepared; Imogen got the impression that
the hidden chef would not dare to serve anything but a
perfect meal.

When coffee was about to be served, Lady Macey stood
up. 'I know you're a soldier too,' she said to Imogen, 'but
I don't suppose you'll want to stay here drinking brandy
and smoking cigars with these two. Let's go next door and
leave them to it.'

In the drawing room, Lady Macey rang the bell and the

ubiquitous Corporal Braker appeared with a tray of coffee and a whisky decanter. 'The usual, m'lady?' he asked.

'Of course, Corporal Braker, but see what Major Cresswell wants first.' Elizabeth Macey turned to Imogen. 'I always have a Scotch and water, but there's anything you want. Personally I can't stand the sort of genteel stuff that women are supposed to drink, but there's Drambuie, Chartreuse, Benedictine and so on, if you want.' It was fairly evident that Lady Macey had no high regard for anything but hard liquor.

Imogen smiled. 'I'll have a brandy, if I may, Corporal Braker,' she said.

'Very good, ma'am.' Braker poured Imogen's drink and presented it to her on a silver salver. Then he started to serve the coffee.

'Oh don't fuss with that, Braker,' said Lady Macey, 'I'll do it.'

'Very good, m'lady,' said Braker and made for the door.

'He's very well trained,' said Lady Macey in a mischievous whisper, 'but I can't help feeling he's more frightened of me than he is of the general. He's been everywhere with us, and quite frankly I don't know how we'll get on without·him when we retire. Now . . .' She half turned in her seat and looked searchingly at Imogen. 'Has Simon made a pass at you yet?'

'A pass, Lady Macey?' The mere thought that the Chief of the General Staff could have designs on her shocked Imogen nearly as much as the fact that his wife had posed the question so directly.

'For goodness' sake call me Elizabeth,' said Lady Macey. 'The general's in the army, but I'm not.' She picked up a plate of handmade chocolates and offered them to Imogen. 'Now then, has he?'

'No, of course not. He's been very kind to me, but—'

'Of course he has,' said Lady Macey, 'that's the first move. But I know my husband. Always had an eye for a pretty girl, and you're an extremely attractive young woman. Incidentally, how did he find you?' she asked and, with a guilty smile, popped another chocolate into her mouth.

'I was advised to apply for the post by my own colonel. Then I had an interview with General Macey.'

Lady Macey appraised Imogen once more and nodded knowingly. 'Yes, and that would have been that,' she said. 'Oh well.' Her expression turned to one of resignation. 'Just watch him, that's all. He's got a roving eye, even though I've told him he's too old for that sort of thing now.' She smiled at Imogen. 'Don't look so surprised, my dear,' she said. 'It wouldn't be the first time, but he always comes back. Just don't listen to any promises, that's all.'

Imogen was amazed at Lady Macey's nonchalance but felt guilty nonetheless. 'I can assure you that nothing I've done—'

Elizabeth laid a hand on Imogen's arm. 'Don't be embarrassed,' she said. 'Most men are like that. I don't know how much experience you've had – of married men, I mean – but he's no different from the rest.' She smiled at some inner thought of her husband's waywardness. 'But there's another side to his character, too. He can be very testy, petulant almost, when things aren't going his way. And that applies as much to his job as to women. I know that sounds as though I'm trying to set you against him, but it's not meant to. Just remember that he can work himself up into a foul mood at times; he doesn't usually mean anything by it. But don't you let him get away with it. If I hear he's not treating you properly, I shall have a word with him.' She stood up. 'Well,' she said, 'I'm going to have another drink. How about you?'

Alec Shepherd closed the door of his flat in Palace Street, Westminster, walked through to the sitting room and took off his jacket. When Annabel Webb had shared his life, he had always looked forward to having a drink with her when he got in, even if it was late at night. But he was disinclined to drink on his own and, after a moment or two, wandered through to the small kitchen and made himself a cup of tea. Then he flicked the switch on his Ansaphone and listened to the two or three mundane messages it had recorded.

Returning to the kitchen, he opened the fridge and took out the sealed bag of prepared continental salad leaves which he had bought earlier from the food hall at the Army and Navy Stores and put them in a bowl. The rump steak he put on a plate to bring it to room temperature. He poured a pot of low-fat crème fraîche into a bowl and mixed it with a crushed clove of garlic and a teaspoonful of crushed green peppercorns before leaving it for the flavours to blend. Finally he opened a bottle of Bardolino and left it to breathe on the sideboard in the sitting room. Annabel had always cautioned him about the dangers that could befall single men who did not eat properly.

He walked through to the bedroom and glanced wryly at the silk scarf that still hung over the dressing-table mirror. Annabel had forgotten it when she had left, and he had been waiting for a suitable opportunity to return it. But the weeks had stretched into months, and he had learned that she had moved in with someone else and there were rumours of marriage. Now the scarf served merely as a painful reminder of happier days. He stripped off his clothes and walked into the shower room. For ten minutes, he stood under the stinging needlepoints of hot water and thought, yet again, about his career. Since joining the Secret Intelligence Service, the whole pattern of world events had changed substantially the traditional targets of the service. Although he and his colleagues still kept a passing eye on the Russians, they tended to concentrate more on the Iraqis and the Argentinians, even though the latter were probably no longer a threat.

Returning to the bedroom, he towelled himself dry and, still naked, walked back to the sitting room. He poured a glass of wine, his previous good intention about not drinking alone banished, and took it back with him while he dressed.

While the steak was cooking he made the dressing for the salad, putting garlic-flavoured white wine vinegar, chopped fresh herbs and a tablespoonful of walnut oil into a screw-topped jam jar and shaking it vigorously. Finally he heated the ingredients of the sauce in a pan, put the meal together and sat down in front of the television to eat it.

Two days later Alec Shepherd and Gus Salmon were seated at a corner table in the subterranean restaurant at the Tate Gallery, a short stroll from the headquarters of the Security Service further along Millbank. Gus Salmon was an SIS officer too but for the last six months had been seconded to the Security Service, liaising between the two organisations. It was a routine assignment; there was always a Six officer at Five.

'What's the feeling up the road about the riots, Gus?' Shepherd broke a bread roll and put butter on it.

'They're collecting paper like mad,' said Salmon.

'What sort of paper?'

'They've asked every Special Branch in the country to look into the possibility of foreign involvement. Apparently the Metropolitan SB has already reported that some members of the British National Party have been seen at one or two of these shindigs.'

'Not surprised,' said Shepherd. 'And I daresay that Militant, the Socialist Workers' Party and all the other rent-a-mob crowd are there too.'

'They're not too worried about that,' said Salmon, tasting the wine and nodding to the waitress. 'It's the fact that the BNP have brought some of their friends with them.'

'Such as?'

'Special Branch picked up that some of the people at these disturbances came from Nazi-style organisations in Europe. Lille, Frankfurt and Dixmude to be precise. Although why Dixmude, God alone knows.'

'It's a rallying point for fascists,' said Shepherd casually, as though Salmon should have known. 'Can't remember why specifically, but there's some sort of memorial there that the right wing regards as a shrine. Who's looking after the desk? Anyone we know?'

'A young filly called Emma Bancroft,' said Salmon. 'She's an absolute stunner, but still carried away with the glamour of being in intelligence.' He emphasised the last word and grinned. Both he and Shepherd had met people who believed themselves to be budding James Bonds, but they were old enough to know better.

CHAPTER THREE

Detective Superintendent John Cavendish of Special Branch had been saddled with the job of examining reports from the uniform branch about the riots in the Metropolitan Police District that had been raging now for some three weeks. Then he would prepare a synopsis of those reports and send it, via the head of Special Branch, to the Commissioner, Sir Lionel Cork. What at first had been a weekly submission had now become a daily event.

Cavendish also headed a team of Special Branch officers who were attempting to discover whether there was any centralised direction to what had become, in the weeks since the introduction of the ECU, a series of well-organised and apparently coordinated attacks on shops, warehouses and garages. There had also been attacks on banks and other financial institutions, and one or two small, rather amateurish bombs had been detonated, but far more serious than that were the less flamboyant but deadlier attacks on Lloyds of London, the Stock Exchange and leading banks. They had been the victims of sabotage to their mainframe computers – and their backup systems – resulting in the electronic theft of several million ECUs.

At the headquarters of the Security Service, Emma Bancroft, the desk officer in F Branch who had been

assigned to the task of collating reports from Special
Branches around the country, would read the reports and
prepare a summary for her director. F Branch, officially
responsible for monitoring the activities of extremist political parties, had had little to do since the demise of the
Communist Party. But it also took an interest in the British
National Party and allied organisations and, upon the basis
of the flimsy evidence that they and their European
counterparts had been involved in the disturbances, the
Director F came to the rash conclusion that there was an
international plot to destabilise the economy.

When Sir Philip Hocking, the Director-General of the
Security Service, reported those fears to his political boss,
the Home Secretary, Kenneth Sinclair was dismissive and
accused the DG of imagining conspiracies where none
existed.

'First and foremost, Sir Philip,' said Sinclair, 'public
disorder is a matter for the police, not the Security
Service—'

'But Home Secretary—' Hocking was about to explain
the role of the Security Service.

Sinclair held up his hand. 'Let me finish, Sir Philip,' he
said. 'There is no conspiracy. I know that you chaps across
at Millbank would like to see some deep-rooted plot behind
all this, but what we have is simply one or two malcontents
determined to embarrass the government because we've
introduced the ECU as the standard currency. It's like the
poll tax all over again. A number of opportunists have
jumped on the bandwagon intent on creating trouble.' He
waved a hand in the air as if to waft away the problems.
'It's always the same in this country. Vandals and other
feckless troublemakers will seize upon any chance they are
given to cause mayhem in the streets. You should know.
Look at the number of people who get involved in
industrial disputes or political demonstrations, even factory farming and motorways, who are not in the least

interested in the cause. It's the old rent-a-mob routine, nothing more. I suggest, Sir Philip, that you go back to Millbank and forget all about it. The police will sort it out.' He paused. 'And none of this is to go beyond your office. Is that quite clear?'

A somewhat chastened Director-General returned to his office and told the director of F Branch not to waste any more time on the conspiracy theory. Both the DG and the director of F Branch knew that it was a political decision and that there was no point in pursuing the matter further.

Consequently, young Emma Bancroft was left in charge of the ever-increasing pile of paper. And, in an attempt to reduce the flow of reports, she advised Detective Superintendent Cavendish at Special Branch that there was no great point in sending any more as she had been told that her service was no longer interested. But she was a rather immature young woman and had yet to learn that discretion was, or should be, implicit in her profession.

For his part, the Home Secretary informed the Prime Minister that the Director-General of the Security Service had been put firmly in his place. And he further assured the Prime Minister that the standing arrangement for the free exchange of intelligence with other EU states would not benefit from any flimsy reports about attempts to destabilise the economy.

A day or two later, Alec Shepherd paid another of his routine visits to Special Branch and spoke to Cavendish. Although public disorder in London, or anywhere in the United Kingdom for that matter, was no concern of the Secret Intelligence Service, Shepherd possessed the natural curiosity of any intelligence officer.

'Got your hands pretty full at the moment, I gather, John.'

'Yes and no,' said Cavendish. 'I hear that the DG of Five

has been told by the Home Secretary that it's all in his imagination, Alec. Got a bit of a bollocking, so I'm told.'

Shepherd glanced sharply at Cavendish. 'Where did you hear that, John?' he asked.

Cavendish tapped the side of his nose. 'We have our sources too, you know,' he said and grinned. 'Anyhow, it seems his view is that a few outbreaks of disorder don't amount to a conspiracy and that's that.' He laughed and ran his thumb down a pile of reports on his desk. 'A few,' he remarked cynically.

'What's going on over at Millbank then?' asked Shepherd. He knew that Gus Salmon would keep him up to date, but intelligence officers always liked to have what they called collateral for their information.

'Your guess is as good as mine,' said Cavendish, 'but I get the distinct impression that politics have got in the way of factual reporting. Any suggestion that there's a conspiracy to destabilise the government is anathema to them. I think that the Cabinet's worried sick about the effect it will have on the country's standing in the European Union and they're trying to keep it under wraps.' He went on to give Shepherd a summary of events to date. 'And that's only London. My colleagues in the provinces are facing much the same sort of problem.'

Barry Rogers, MI6's Director of Counter-Intelligence and Security, entered Shepherd's office without knocking and sat down in an armchair, spreading his legs out untidily. 'What's happening at the Yard then?' he asked. He pulled his pipe from his pocket and filled it, slowly. Then he felt for his matches, trying several pockets before he located them. Rogers had always shunned the use of a lighter, despite his family having given him several at birthdays and Christmas.

'I dropped in on John Cavendish,' said Shepherd, gazing mildly at his chief.

'And?' Rogers blew smoke in the air, waved his match until it expired and dropped it in the ashtray. Shepherd did not smoke, but kept the ashtray on his desk to cater for Rogers' frequent visits. 'Is that fresh?' Rogers glanced across at the coffee machine in the corner.

'Probably.' Shepherd walked over to the side table and poured two cups. 'These ECU disturbances, as the Home Secretary calls them . . .' he began as he sat down again.

'What about them?'

'I gather from what Cavendish was saying that the Security Service has more or less washed its hands of them. They've told Special Branch not to send any more reports.'

Rogers paused to fiddle with his pipe once more. 'Did he say why?'

'Yes,' said Shepherd and went on to tell his boss about the rebuff that the Director-General of the Security Service had received at the hands of the Home Secretary.

'I heard about that,' said Rogers, who was renowned in SIS for having informants in many hostile places. And he tended to regard the Security Service as hostile. 'Trouble is the government aren't taking it seriously. I hate to admit that Five might be right, Alec, but I think they may have a point. Perhaps I ought to persuade the Chief to let us look into it.'

Shepherd gave his boss a cynical glance. 'Do you really believe that, or are you just trying to get in on the act?' he asked.

Rogers had the good grace to grin. 'I hope *you* never become Chief,' he said. 'At least not in my time. You're a bloody sight more sceptical than he is.'

'Am I?' asked Shepherd. 'Or is it that he doesn't always say what he's thinking?'

'To be honest with you, I don't think that a handful of fascist yobbos poses a threat. It certainly doesn't amount to foreign influence, and that may be why the Home Secretary won't countenance the idea. It was a bloody silly thing for Five to suggest, when you come to think of it. But just because there's no sabre-rattling going on, it doesn't mean that France and Germany aren't harbouring unfriendly thoughts. After all, economic destruction is a damned sight easier than going to war, and a bloody sight cheaper. Now take these riots . . .' Rogers laid down his pipe and took a sip of coffee. 'They've been happening all over the place.' He stood up and walked across to a map of the British Isles that hung on Shepherd's wall. 'Here, here and here. And here and here.' He poked at the map with a podgy forefinger, reading out the names of Edinburgh, Darlington, Stoke, Cambridge and Southampton as he did so. 'And that was all on one day.' He sat down again and relit his pipe. 'But the boffins at Five are sitting on their fat arses feeding rubbishy bits of paper to the Home Secretary, who merely says, in that lofty way of his, "Oh, don't worry yourself, Mr DG. It'll all blow over." But frankly, Alec, I don't think it will.'

'But that still doesn't make it our job. Not yet.'

'If we wait until it is our job, it'll be too bloody late to do anything about it.'

'But even then, we're not empowered to act in the UK—'

'Don't lecture me about what we can and cannot do, Alec,' said Rogers with a rare flash of temper. 'I'm telling you that if someone doesn't take a bloody interest, we'll come apart at the seams. We'll wake up one morning to find that this country's no longer ours. We certainly will if the European Union and bloody Brussels have their way,' he added in a barely audible mutter. 'Now I don't know what's going on in those plush offices of MI5 in Millbank, but I have a shrewd suspicion that Kenneth Sinclair has conned them into thinking that it's all of no great moment. I don't know why, but it's obviously something political. If I was a betting man, I'd say that the PM has put the dampers on everything. You see, Alec, this damned ECU thing has got to succeed. They can't backtrack on it now, and anyway the European Union wouldn't let us get away with it. They'd chuck us out and then we'd be finished.' He drank the remainder of his coffee at a gulp and banged the cup down noisily on its saucer. 'And that might be just what they want. Now can you see what I'm getting at? The French and the Germans picked a date for this monetary unity that would be propitious for *them*, not for us. Come to think of it, no damn date would have been propitious for us. But having launched us on the slippery slope, suppose they decide to destabilise the country by starting a vast protest movement. That's what our revered sister service ought to have been telling the Home Secretary. They should have had the nous to project such a possibility years ago, the idiots. But just imagine for a moment that that's what the Krauts and the Frogs had decided to do. Once they've brought us to our knees with internal strife – expensive internal strife – we'll be too busy picking up the pieces, and the bill, to compete with them. Well, what do you say to that, young Shepherd?'

'An interesting speculation, Barry,' said Shepherd mildly, 'but there's not a shred of evidence to support it.'

'Not yet,' said Rogers and smiled.

So did Shepherd. Rogers had been in the SIS for so long that his instincts invariably turned out to be right.

But Rogers' instincts and the thoughts that he had expressed aloud prompted him to tell Shepherd of another piece of information that had recently come to his ears. 'General Sir Simon Macey,' he said.

For a moment or two, Shepherd looked puzzled. 'Chief of the General Staff, isn't he?'

'Yes,' said Rogers. 'Bit of a leg-over merchant.'

'Really?' Shepherd glanced at the pile of paper in his in-tray and sighed. When Rogers was in one of his talkative moods there was no hope of getting any work done. 'Does that have some significance, Barry?'

'Might have,' said Rogers reflectively. 'Does the name Imogen Cresswell mean anything to you?'

'Yes, it does, as a matter of fact,' said Shepherd slowly. He knew that Rogers' occasional ramblings often turned out to be quite pertinent to whatever they were discussing, but he didn't know what possible relevance the attractive blonde he had known at Sandhurst could have.

'Good-looking young woman by all accounts.'

'What the hell's she got to do with anything, Barry?' asked Shepherd.

'Probably nothing,' said Rogers, 'but he's just taken her on as his ADC, and he does have form for a bit on the side.'

'I still don't see what—'

Rogers appeared not to notice Shepherd's interruption. 'When he was a lieutenant-general in command of a corps in Germany, he was having it off with a girl called Annelise Strigel, the daughter of General Max Strigel, but it's only just come out. Might be worth your reading his docket.'

'Do you mean we've got a file on the Chief of the General Staff?' Shepherd sounded incredulous.

'Why not? After all, a CGS who's a womaniser might become a liability. From a security point of view.'

'Even so, Barry, I don't really see what this has to do with your theories about a Franco-German alliance intent on destroying our economy.'

'Straws in the wind, my boy, straws in the wind,' said Rogers mysteriously. 'There's quite a lot of information on file about Strigel, too. He has been quite closely associated with the *Nationaldemokratische Partei Deutschlands* in recent years. According to our source, he seemed to take a mite more than an official interest.'

'I should think that quite a few German generals have an interest in extreme right-wing groups,' said Shepherd mildly. 'They miss the resounding thump of jackboots.'

'Exactly so. And Strigel and Macey were great friends when Macey was over there. More than just a professional

relationship but, as I said just now, Macey was giving
Strigel's daughter a seeing to.'

'Oh, for God's sake, Barry. You're not suggesting that
Macey's a fascist, are you? For all you know, he may have
been the one who passed this information to us.'

'He wasn't,' said Rogers firmly. 'It might just be worth
bearing in mind, that's all.'

Shepherd smiled; he clearly had no intention of taking
Rogers' theorising seriously. 'I don't think you need to
worry about Imogen Cresswell, Barry,' he said. 'She's got
her head screwed on the right way, believe me. She's not
going to jeopardise a career she fought bloody hard for by
having an affair with the CGS. You know the way the army
works. She'd be the loser and Macey'd come out of it
smelling of roses.'

'Maybe,' said Rogers gravely. 'But it might be worth
getting alongside her.' He tapped his pipe out in Shepherd's
ashtray and stood up. 'Better let you get on with some
work,' he added, and strolled out of the office.

Although Alec Shepherd now knew where Imogen Cresswell worked, he had no intention of contacting her there
and had arranged for a number of surveillance officers to
find out more about her. Within five days they had reported
that she was a regular early-morning swimmer at the
Royal Automobile Club. Now Shepherd stood at the edge of
the pool wondering whether it had been such a good idea
to plan his accidental meeting with her there.

There were several people swimming; he quickly spotted
Imogen, in a black one-piece, ploughing up and down with
a relentlessly energetic crawl. When she reached his end of
the pool, she stood up, took off her goggles and mounted
the steps. She paused to unpin her hair and then ran her
fingers through it flicking it away from the nape of her
neck.

'The last time I saw a girl swimming like that was in the

pool at Sandhurst,' said Shepherd with a grin as he surveyed the good-looking blonde. 'Imogen Cresswell, isn't it?'

Imogen turned. 'Alec Shepherd. How lovely to see you.' She picked up a towel and draped it around her shoulders. 'What on earth are you doing here?'

'I'm a member, but what's your excuse? I suppose your husband's a member?' Shepherd looked quizzically at the girl.

Imogen shook her head. 'I'm not married,' she said. 'And I hope that you're not one of the members who doesn't like seeing women here at all. I heard one of them complaining this morning that he'd found a long hair in the pool.'

Shepherd laughed. 'Then you must have an influential friend,' he said.

'The Chief of the General Staff, if you must know.'

'Yes, well it had to be something like that, knowing you. Are you still with the battalion?'

'No, I'm General Macey's ADC.'

'Are you indeed?' Shepherd feigned surprise. 'And I suppose you're a captain.'

'No, a major. And what about you? You must be a colonel by now.'

But Shepherd did not answer her question. 'How did you get that job then?' he asked.

'My colonel suggested I applied. Went up for the interview and got it.'

'Well done,' said Shepherd. 'I always knew you'd do well, Imogen. Look, we must have a lot to talk about. How about a spot of breakfast when you're dressed?'

'Sorry, I've got to get to the office. You know how it is.' Imogen wrapped the towel more firmly around her and shivered.

'Of course. I shouldn't keep you here talking. You must be getting cold. Have a drink with me one evening then?'

'I'd like that. Thank you.' Imogen assumed that Shepherd was still in the army and was cynical enough to think that he had only invited her for a drink because she was now ADC to the Chief of the General Staff and that it would be useful for him to have friends in high places. She was not to learn the real reason for some time.

From their first meeting at Sandhurst, she had been aware that Shepherd was attracted to her, but he had not allowed that to interfere with their professional relationship. In fact he had been extremely encouraging in her efforts to secure a commission in the Grenadier Guards and had given her the extra coaching that had enabled her to obtain a good pass in the final round of examinations. Since then, they had not met. Even so, it was more out of curiosity than a desire to see him again that she had accepted the invitation.

'Good,' said Shepherd. 'I'll give you a ring. At least I know where to find you.'

Sir Richard Dancer had been head of the Secret Intelligence Service for seven years. He was a career intelligence man who, during his slow climb to the top of his profession, had served in various parts of the world, had mastered one or two languages and had acquired a great deal of information about all manner of curious things that would be difficult to place in any of the disciplines at Oxford University, where he had graduated in Modern Greats more than thirty years previously. He was of medium height, invariably wore a dark suit, and had a pointed face and brushed back sparse grey hair which combined to give him the intellectual appearance of the professor of philosophy he had once hoped to become.

He was known to the staff as C, but the debate continued whether this followed a tradition set by the first head of the service, Mansfield Cumming, or whether it stood simply for 'Chief'.

This morning, Dancer sat at his desk, a cup of black coffee to one side, and glanced cursorily through the contents of his in-tray. That done, he took from his drawer a report that had attracted his attention when it had arrived the previous afternoon and read it again.

He took a sip of coffee and then stood up. Turning to the window, he eased apart two slats of the Venetian blind and stared out.

It was no easy task being head of SIS. In theory, he reported to the Secretary of State for Foreign and Commonwealth Affairs in much the same way as his Security Service counterpart reported to the Home Secretary and, indeed, as the Whitehall mandarins – the heads of the great departments of state – each reported to his own political master.

But Dancer had never seen himself as a mandarin, and he often envied the permanent secretaries their facility for passing difficult problems to their ministers.

But the SIS was different. The normal channels did not operate in the same way here. The gatherers of intelligence could not afford to be selective. It was all or nothing; political judgement did not enter into it. Dancer thought, once again, of the little-known verse from 'Genesis' that those in the trade often bandied about: 'Ye are spies; to see the nakedness of the land ye are come.' He had last used it in a signal to the Director-General of the Security Service, encoded and classified secret, when an off-duty MI5 officer had been arrested for peeping through the windows of a nurses' home in South London last year.

The sudden buzzing of the intercom startled him and he moved quickly to flick down the switch. 'Yes?'

'Mr Rogers is here, sir,' said the voice of Dancer's secretary.

'Send him in.'

Barry Rogers closed the door behind him and advanced on Dancer's desk. 'Morning, sir.'

'This is really nothing to do with us, Barry.' Dancer pointed at the report. 'Oh, er, do sit down.'

'Thank you.' Rogers lowered his heavy frame into the armchair opposite Dancer's desk and relaxed. As the Director of the Counter-Intelligence and Security Section, Rogers was not only the most trusted of all the directors but also the one who knew just about everything that went on in the service.

'Our sister service seems to have it well in hand,' said Dancer. The officers of SIS always referred to the Security Service in that way.

'Matter of opinion, sir,' said Rogers. 'Seems to me that they're not really taking it seriously. They've got a young girl called Emma Bancroft overseeing it. Struck me that a more professional approach is called for.'

'Why?' Dancer had an unnerving habit of asking direct, and usually unanswerable, questions.

But Rogers, who had been a member of SIS for almost as long as C himself, was not put off by Dancer's bluntness. 'Dammit, sir, there are serious disturbances – personally, I'd call them riots – occurring all over the country, and the government's reaction is one of apparent indifference. We've all heard broadcasts by Sinclair, the Home Secretary, and he seems to take the attitude that it'll all blow over, given time.'

'Perhaps it will,' said Dancer. 'But we've got to have a reason for interfering in something outside our brief.'

Rogers nodded. 'We don't know the extent to which foreign influence is being brought to bear in an attempt to destabilise the government, sir.' Dancer smiled at his justification of the SIS taking an interest. They both knew that officially the Secret Intelligence Service was only permitted to garner intelligence abroad, not at home.

'You'll have to do better than that, Barry.'

Rogers fidgeted with the arm of his chair. 'We've taken an interest in things before without much of an excuse,' he said. 'It's not a light-hearted comment when I say that there could be a foreign influence present in these disturbances. After all, it would make sense. France and Germany – France in particular – never wanted us in the Common Market in the first place. But now that we're there, they've a heaven-sent opportunity to destroy our economy. Let's face it, both the French and the Germans have tried to beat us on the battlefield and failed. Our trouble is that we're good fighters when we're pushed, but we never take the economy seriously. It seems to me that there is an unofficial Franco-German alliance that has woken up to the fact that if they are to become masters of Europe, it has to be done through trade and the economy. They know they can't beat us in war.'

Dancer pursed his lips and gazed at his subordinate, wondering if he was joking, but decided, eventually, that he was not. 'There may be some substance to what you say, Barry,' he said, 'but I think it's a little far-fetched.'

'From what I hear from my friends in our sister service, sir,' said Rogers, 'the Home Secretary refuses to accept the evidence that their DG is putting in front of him. It's fairly obvious that the ECU business started the disturbances, but now there is an element of anarchy that, paradoxically, is too well organised to be dismissed. A forest fire can sweep across the land, but when there are several outbreaks in different places at the same time, it is reasonable to suspect arson.'

Dancer smiled. 'You're very philosophical this morning, Barry,' he said. 'All right, look into it, but keep it within your own section. And tread carefully. I would rather not have a complaint from across the way.' He waved a hand loosely in the direction of the Security Service headquarters.

The worst eruption in the escalating cycle of violence occurred in London exactly two weeks after the introduc-

tion of the single currency. Five hundred workers from a
factory in Dagenham had been laid off and, in some
distorted way blaming the introduction of the ECU for their
plight, embarked upon an orgy of destruction. Arriving by
tube at Leicester Square, they marched to Piccadilly Circus,
smashing shop windows indiscriminately on the way.

Quick to take advantage of the situation, Militant, a
virulent left-wing organisation, marshalled their supporters by telephone; as most were unemployed and available,
first arrivals were soon joined by hooting mobs bearing
placards complaining about the introduction of the ECU.
Most bore the unoriginal slogan: 'Bring Back the Pound'.

Although Scotland Yard had been alerted by the railway
police to the influx of large numbers of angry workers
making no secret of their intentions, they were, nonetheless, caught unawares by this sudden disturbance and only
belatedly summoned enough reserves to deal with it. For
three hours the centre of the capital was filled with the
sound of police sirens as reinforcements were brought in
from outlying divisions and senior officers, unaccustomed
to disorder in the mornings, struggled to bring the riot
under control.

It was after two o'clock by the time the last of the rioters
had either been dispersed or arrested. The police operation
had not been helped by the large number of office workers
out for lunch who though at first had seen the riot as an
entertaining diversion in their otherwise dull day had then
been terrified by it as they were caught up in its ugly
violence. By the time it was all over, twenty-five people –
innocent shop assistants and office workers, tourists and
rioters – had been admitted to hospital.

The following day, a group of senior officers convened at
Scotland Yard to discuss how best to counter the increasing
number of riots. Theoretically each police force could call
for reinforcements from its neighbours and although the
system had been put under some strain in past years,

notably during the miners' strike and the poll tax riots, it was now in danger of total collapse. Outbreaks of violence resulting from the introduction of the ECU had placed such exhausting demands on most English and Welsh police forces that they were unable to contain their own problems, let alone assist anyone else. Neither was Scotland exempt. Riots had broken out in Ayr, Glasgow and Stirling. And in Aberdeen, where the collapse of the oil boom had taken a devastating toll on local businessmen, who were unable to cope with the huge loss of trade, the Lord Provost's office had been sacked and then set ablaze.

As if that was not enough, a more sinister note had been struck in the last week or two and, inevitably, it was this that became the main topic of the conference. Twenty or thirty cases of vigilante revenge had occurred, retribution wrought on individuals who had either been treated leniently by the law or had escaped its clutches altogether. In each of these cases – and they were as far apart as Cornwall and Cumbria – the mysterious letters PEG had appeared on front doors, walls, scratched on cars and, in one case, carved into the victim himself.

'What's the latest on this Protection of England Group business?' asked the Assistant Commissioner responsible for the investigation of crime in the metropolis, who was presiding over the meeting. He glanced at the Assistant Chief Constable of Hampshire. 'I hear that you had a murder last night,' he said.

'Well, early this morning, to be accurate, sir,' said the Hampshire officer in matter-of-fact tones. 'A man called Eric Wilkins was acquitted at the Old Bailey yesterday of sexually abusing one of his common-law wife's teenage children. The girl subsequently committed suicide, you may recall.' He glanced around the conference table and received several nods of acknowledgement. 'It seems that at about three this morning a group of men broke into his house – he lived in a village not far from Basingstoke –

dragged him outside and hanged him from a tree. The irony is that he was tried at the Bailey because it was thought that he wouldn't get a fair trial at Winchester Crown Court. There was a lot of local feeling about the case.'

'Obviously,' murmured the Assistant Commissioner.

'Police were called to the body by a milkman at about six this morning. There was a placard round the victim's neck which said that the "punishment" had been carried out by PEG. And a local radio station later received an anonymous telephone call which said that, and I quote, "the Protection of England Group carried out retribution for injustice."'

'We've had several similar incidents,' said the Assistant Chief Constable of the West Midlands, 'but to date, nothing fatal. I suspect, though, that it's only a matter of time.'

'So have we,' said the ACC from Wiltshire.

'Mr Knight?' The Assistant Commissioner glanced at a commander from the Public Order Branch of the Metropolitan Police.

'There was the incident of the rape-case judge, sir,' said Knight. 'A group of men apparently angry at his leniency towards a convicted rapist – he'd given him eighteen months – broke into the judge's house late at night and raped his wife. At the trial, the judge had more or less blamed the victim for dressing provocatively. Said that she was as much to blame as the rapist. Anyhow, the judge's house was wrecked and the letters PEG were scratched into the front door and sprayed on the walls. Then there was the seventy-two-year-old widow in Battersea. She was robbed by a couple of young yobbos, who got off with a community service order. The parents of the two kids, both from a council estate in Battersea, had their houses wrecked, and the fathers were beaten up for not keeping control of their children. Again the letters PEG appeared on the walls.'

'You had some trouble too, didn't you?' The Assistant Commissioner turned to the ACC of Cambridge.

'Ours was a bit of everthing, really,' said the ACC cheerfully. 'Mainly discontentment with Europe and the ECU. The day before yesterday the city's traders went on the rampage. As far as I could establish, they were having a go at the market traders who, they reckoned, didn't pay uniform business rate and weren't subject to the same stringent hygiene regulations as them. One man who was arrested blamed the "hygiene Gestapo".' The ACC grinned. 'But then we were always a bit different in Cambridge.'

'Much damage?' asked the Assistant Commissioner.

The Assistant Chief Constable shuffled the papers on the table in front of him. 'Practically all the windows in the city centre went, and a pub close to the market was burned down. The marketplace itself was like a battlefield; stalls smashed and set on fire. As for injuries . . .' The ACC pursed his lips and turned a couple of pages. 'Fifty-eight members of the public admitted to hospital, most with minor injuries but four detained as serious. Five police officers, one serious. And two firemen.' He pushed his briefing notes to one side. 'Yesterday we were invaded by the media, intent on filming the damage. And once it was shown on television, it probably contributed to the further outbreaks in Kettering, Exeter and York.'

'Ray?' The Assistant Commissioner glanced at Ray Harvey, the commander in charge of the Metropolitan Special Branch. Harvey was responsible for, among other things, all investigations into subversion likely to affect public order in the capital.

'To begin at the beginning, sir,' said Harvey, opening a file on the table in front of him, 'a fair number of ECU rioters have been before the courts and have been dealt with severely, many of them receiving custodial sentences. In one case, four years.' He glanced up. 'That was for affray. Deserved though those sentences may be, according

to my officers on the ground it's caused considerable
discontent, not only because of the widespread opposition
to the ECU but also because the sentences arising out of the
rioting frequently outweighed sentences for serious crime.
Mr Knight mentioned the rapist given eighteen months
and the two youths made the subject of community service
orders for robbery with violence and aggravated burglary.
But if a man protests against the ECU, he's likely to get six
months. As for the so-called Protection of England Group,'
the commander continued, 'it gives the appearance of
being one organisation, but if it is, it's a very big one.
Several of the incidents have taken place at roughly the
same time and at opposite ends of the country. The press
are trying to make it sound as though it's one huge set-up,
but I've got doubts about that. Looks as though someone
came up with the idea and a hell of a lot of other people
have latched on to it.' The Special Branch chief shook his
head. 'Sounds like newspaper guesswork to me,' he added.
'But just before this meeting, Press Bureau was speaking to
one paper who said that they'd also had a call purporting
to come from this PEG claiming responsibility for Wilkins'
death.'

'Doesn't mean a thing, sir,' said the Hampshire ACC. 'I
think Special Branch are right; it's a copycat affair. Anyone
can make a claim like that.'

'We're monitoring the situation closely, sir,' said the
Special Branch commander, 'although the Security Service
doesn't seem all that interested. The problem, as far as
police are concerned, is that none of the victims is prepared
to talk.'

The other assistant chief constables nodded their heads
in agreement. In common with their Metropolitan Police
colleagues, they had not been surprised to find that none
of the victims was willing to say anything, much less to
make a statement or give evidence. In every case – apart
from the rape of the judge's wife – information had come

not from the victim but from neighbours who had heard a disturbance. But even that was strange. Police had not been alerted until well after the attackers had left the area.

The senior officers were agreed on one point, however, a point voiced by the Assistant Chief Constable of Wiltshire. 'Someone had better tell the Home Secretary, sir,' he said to the Assistant Commissioner, 'that the electorate appears to be unhappy, not only about ECUs but also about so-called justice in this country. Because if he doesn't wake up to it soon, he's going to have a lot more of this on his hands.'

'This is very interesting, Jamie,' said Colonel Crosby as his adjutant entered his office.

'What's that, Colonel?'

'This report in the paper . . .' Crosby waved a hand over the copy of *The Times* that was spread across his desk. 'It's about a group of vigilantes, I suppose you'd call them, who have been mounting attacks on criminals that they think have been let off lightly by the courts.'

'Oh, yes, I read something about that. The Protection of England Group, they're calling themselves.'

Crosby folded the newspaper and put it in his out-tray. 'What have you got for me this morning, Jamie?'

Captain Makepeace smiled and placed a slim folder on the colonel's desk. 'Two troopers from B Squadron arrested by the military police for drunkenness on Saturday night in Aldershot town centre, Colonel. Been remanded for punishment by their squadron leader.'

Crosby groaned. 'Pity they aren't being dealt with by the civilian courts,' he said acidly. 'They'd be let off.'

There was a sharp double tap of boots as the regimental sergeant-major appeared in the doorway of Crosby's office and saluted. 'Commanding officer's orders present and correct, sir,' he said.

CHAPTER FOUR

Ironically the seeds of Macey's fall from grace were sewn by his wife. Imogen Cresswell had been deeply worried that Elizabeth had mentioned Macey's waywardness so early in their acquaintanceship and believed she was being politely warned off. It had confirmed Imogen's suspicions that the general had taken her on to his staff because he was attracted to her and not because she was capable of doing the job. Although she had no intention of becoming emotionally involved with Macey, she could not help feeling that she was being watched by his wife and was prepared for some sort of philandering approach from him. As a result she now displayed a certain coldness towards him, fuelled by a fear that the natural intimacy frequently existing in such a close working relationship might be misinterpreted as a sign of availability.

The first of those fears manifested itself on the Thursday following her weekend in Esher. Macey had asked Imogen if she would stay late to assist him in the drafting of a policy document for the Secretary of State, and it was eight o'clock by the time the work was finished.

'I'm most grateful for your help, Imogen,' said Macey. 'I hope it didn't upset any of your arrangements.'

'Not at all, sir. I had nothing planned.'

Macey looked thoughtfully at the girl. 'Well the least I can do is buy you supper,' he said.

'You really don't have to do that, sir,' said Imogen. 'I expected to work long hours when I came here.'

Macey shook his head and smiled. 'Least I can do,' he said again. He walked to the window and peered down into Whitehall. 'It's a lovely evening. Shall we walk?'

'Certainly, sir.'

'Splendid. Perhaps you'd tell my driver that he can go home. If we go out of the back door, we can stroll along the Embankment.'

And in that way, thought Imogen, *you will deprive your driver of an item of gossip that he would love to relate to his colleagues downstairs.*

Macey selected a discreet restaurant off the Strand and ordered a bottle of white wine to drink while they were poring over the menu. 'It's funny to think you're a Guards major,' he said, suddenly looking up. 'You don't look a bit like one.'

Imogen glanced up from the menu and smiled. 'I take that to be a compliment, sir,' she said.

Macey left it at that, for the moment. 'You've not mentioned leave since you've been with me,' he said. 'Is there somewhere you usually go?'

'I've been to Klosters a few times,' said Imogen. 'I enjoy skiing.'

'Do you go regularly?'

'As often as I can afford to, yes.'

'And the summer? What do you do for a summer holiday?'

Imogen closed the menu and folded her hands on top of it. She wondered whether Macey was about to suggest that they went somewhere together or whether he was merely expressing a genuine interest in the welfare of a sub-ordinate. 'I was thinking of taking my car across to France and just touring around for a bit,' she said.

'Good idea,' said Macey. 'Got anywhere in particular that you're thinking of making for?'

'No. Just see where I end up, I suppose.'

The arrival of the waiter stopped that line of conversation, and with the appearance of the first course, Macey turned the talk to military matters. Making frank, and not always complimentary, comments about certain senior members of the General Staff, he listed their shortcomings in a way she thought no general ever would, at least not to a junior officer. She, in turn, launched into an attack on, of all people, the Orderly Room Quartermaster-Sergeant, the warrant officer who was chief clerk of the battalion she had recently left. She told Macey of the ORQMS's sniffy snobbishness at having to defer to a woman and how he was punctilious in all his dealings with her, always standing to attention and calling her 'ma'am' in a way that only guardsmen can make sound like an insult. And she also told Macey of overhearing the occasional comments of other officers, about their not knowing what the army was coming to, in a clear allusion to her own presence in the battalion.

'Are you happier now that you're at the MOD?' asked Macey when the coffee and the Cognac arrived.

'Much, thank you, sir.'

'You don't miss the ceremonial?'

Imogen took a sip of brandy and smiled. 'If you recall our conversation at my interview, General,' she said, 'the battalion wouldn't let me play at that sort of thing.'

'Oh, yes, of course,' said Macey, laughing. 'They'd rather have their ladies in bare skins than bearskins. Incidentally, now that we're off duty, why don't you call me Simon?'

In the circumstances, the invitation did not surprise Imogen, although it made her feel uncomfortable. Her time at Sandhurst, and with the battalion, had made her very conscious of military protocol. She had certainly never visualised a situation where a general would suggest that she use his Christian name. Even in the mess, only officers below the colonel were on first-name terms.

'I think I should tell you, Imogen,' said Macey suddenly, 'that I find you very attractive, and to be perfectly honest, that was the real reason why I wanted you on my staff. After all, I took you on spec, so to speak. I had no idea whether you'd be any good as a staff officer, but as it turned out, you're very good. And that's a bonus.'

'Thank you.' Imogen replied in restrained tones, but inwardly she was seething at his arrogance.

'However, if you find the situation in any way awkward or unacceptable – I am after all, much older than you – then I shall quite understand if you tell me that you want a transfer back to your battalion.' He smiled and placed his hand on top of hers.

Imogen tensed slightly. Macey knew how much she had hated her time on regimental duties, and it was ungallant of him to offer her the stark choice of staying as his plaything – she was in no doubt about that – or returning to the misery of the Grenadiers' male-chauvinist environment. Macey was mature and, although she knew him to be in his mid-fifties, retained the athletic and youthful bearing of a much younger man. On the Sunday morning of her weekend in Esher they had played a hard game of tennis and Imogen had only just managed to beat him, despite her prowess at the game. At times she found it difficult to believe that he was the Chief of the General Staff, and her boss. But, beneath all that, to a perceptive woman like Imogen, neither his rank nor the appointment he held could disguise the fact that he shared with many other men a weakness for a pretty woman. But Macey's overtures were doomed from the outset; she did not find him attractive.

'I suppose Elizabeth warned you about me, did she?'

Macey smiled and, still keeping his hand on Imogen's, reached out for his brandy with the other.

'Yes, she did.' Now that Macey had taken the initiative in setting aside their professional relationship, Imogen felt that she could be more open. 'She said that you were a womaniser.'

Macey tipped his head back and laughed. 'Yes, she would,' he said. 'We've been married for twenty-seven years, but she still doesn't really understand me.'

'Ah!' said Imogen, 'I wondered when you would say that.'

'What?'

'You're not the first married man I've been involved with—'

'Really?' Macey looked surprised. He had made the mistake of thinking that his ADC looked too demure ever to have had an affair, or even a relationship with an eligible bachelor.

'And sooner or later they all trot out that tired old excuse that their wives don't understand them. It really is rather hackneyed, you know.'

'Oh hell!' said Macey. 'I've made a bit of a fool of myself, haven't I?'

'No more than most men of your age, I imagine.' Imogen had no intention of letting him off too lightly.

'And now you're going to get up and walk out of here and look at me reproachfully in the office tomorrow, I suppose.' Macey realised that not only had he embarrassed Imogen but had, very likely, made her position as his ADC virtually untenable.

Imogen slid her hand out from beneath Macey's and picked up her glass. 'When I've finished my brandy. If that's all right with you, *General*. You see, I have a fiancé.'

'Oh!' Macey seemed surprised at that. 'What regiment?'

'He's a first secretary at the British High Commission in

India.' In fact, they had recently split up, but Imogen was furious that Macey should assume him to be a soldier, as if no one else could possibly be suitable.

'Good God! You mean he's a—'

'Yes, General, he's a diplomat.' Imogen stressed the last word, but the implication was lost on Macey. In fact Alistair Buchanan's posting, from the Foreign Office in London to Delhi, had brought an end to their relationship. He had suggested that she resign from the army, marry him and go to India. Imogen had refused. 'I actually liked Elizabeth a lot,' she continued. 'We got on extremely well, and I think she understands you rather better than you realise.'

'I hope you'll forgive me, Imogen.' Macey stood up. 'I'll have them call a taxi for you.'

'Don't bother, General. I'd rather walk.'

Sir Simon Macey was already at work when Imogen arrived next morning, and the first she saw of him was when he appeared at the communicating door between their respective offices.

'This damned file's all to hell, Imogen.' Macey half threw the offending docket on to her desk. 'For God's sake get someone to sort it out, will you?' he said and stormed back to his office, muttering something about the army having gone to pot.

Imogen stood up. 'Yes, sir,' she said to Macey's retreating back. She was irritated by his rudeness but thankful that he had made no reference to his half-hearted attempt to seduce her the previous evening. The last thing she wanted was any sort of postmortem, and she had spent a wakeful night anguishing about what she should do if he made further romantic overtures. In the ordinary course of events, she could have forgiven any man for making a pass at her – even one old enough to be her father – but she could not forgive Macey's arrogant disregard of the fact that their disparity in rank had made it highly embarrassing for her. It was, to use his own expression, damned bad form. And it left in her a feeling of intense resentment.

The widely publicised lynching of Eric Wilkins in Hampshire set a pattern quickly followed by others. What had at first appeared to be a burglary in Windsor was actually more sinister. The man who lived in the house was known to the police and had been acquitted of rape – for the second time in his criminal career – only three days previously because his victim was too distressed by her ordeal to give evidence. His house had been methodically wrecked, and the front door bore the letters PEG in red paint. But the rapist did not see them. He was in hospital, suffering from horrific injuries to his sexual organs.

During the ensuing days, disparate groups of vigilantes, assuming the mantle of the shadowy Protection of England Group, singled out a further five cases which they believed to be deserving of their attention, and in each case a controlled retribution had been exacted.

A man of twenty-seven who had mounted an unprovoked attack on a policewoman in Leytonstone, during which she had been stabbed, had claimed at his trial that he had been high on drugs. But after he had agreed to attend a clinic specialising in drug addiction, he had been given a sentence of six months' imprisonment, suspended for two years. Later that day, he was the victim of a savage beating that resulted in his being in hospital for several weeks. And for the rest of his life he would be reminded of that night whenever he gazed down at the pinkish scar tissue where the letters PEG had been torn into his chest with a blunt screwdriver.

Some of the retribution was less violent than that, though. After a clergyman had appeared in court charged with indecent assault on a number of children, he had been bailed, and the press had been warned not to publish his name for fear of identifying the children involved. But next morning, the curate had found painted in foot-high letters, halfway up the bell tower of his church, his name and the information that he was a child molester.

The Right Honourable Kenneth Sinclair seated himself in the Westminster television studio and looked at the camera with a suitably grave expression.

'Home Secretary, the people of this nation are becoming increasingly concerned at the mounting violence that is spreading through the whole country like wildfire, and they are asking what you propose to do about it.' The interviewer brushed a hand across his clipboard.

'I am as anxious as they are, Paul,' said Kenneth Sinclair blandly, 'that the present wave of inexplicable violence should be stemmed as a matter of urgency. I realise – of course I realise – that many people are, er, unhappy at being out of work. And as for the ECU, well, the people will soon get used to it, as they got used to decimal currency.' He smiled reassuringly. 'But as the Chancellor said only yesterday, we are turning the corner of the recession. The large-scale unemployment that we have witnessed recently is only a blip. This country, I assure you, is poised on the brink not only of recovery but of great prosperity.'

'But aren't you rather missing the point, Home Secretary?' asked the interviewer. 'It's not only unemployment, is it? And it's not only dissatisfaction with the imposition of the ECU. There have been other outbreaks of a different character. For instance, the organisation calling itself the Protection of England Group has claimed responsibility for a substantial number of attacks on those they see as having been let off lightly by the courts. Isn't it time to safeguard the victim rather than to protect the criminal?'

'Spending on the police has risen by more than thirty

per cent in real terms since this government took office,' said the Home Secretary, as usual avoiding the question and taking refuge in statistics. 'And certainty of arrest is a far greater deterrent than long sentences.' The Home Secretary gave the camera a patronising smile.

'What are your feelings about the series of posters that appeared in London this morning, Home Secretary?' The interviewer suddenly changed tack.

'Er, posters?' The Home Secretary looked uncomfortable and wondered how he could safely terminate the interview without making it too obvious that he had been caught out.

'Yes, Home Secretary. I saw one opposite the headquarters of ITN and another, so I'm told, is on a hoarding at Victoria Station. But reports are coming in that they have been sighted all over the capital. They read, "If you are a criminal, vote Conservative. If you are a victim, emigrate."'

'Oh those,' said Sinclair, airily attempting to disguise the fact that he knew nothing whatever about such posters. 'I don't comment on that sort of nonsense, I'm afraid.' Inwardly he was furious that he had not been briefed about what most people, his Cabinet colleagues included, would regard as a slap in the face for the Home Office. 'The matter is being investigated by the police, and it would be most improper for me to say anything at this stage.' He was determined that some Home Office official would bear the brunt of his anger for having failed to make his master aware of this scurrilous propaganda, just as he was equally certain that the police *would* investigate the matter. The Home Secretary did not enjoy being caught out by television people.

'But are you not concerned at the undercurrent of feeling that has prompted such protestations, Home Secretary, and the violence that is erupting as a result of people taking the law into their own hands?' The interviewer sensed that he had Sinclair on the run and was not prepared to let him escape too lightly.

Kenneth Sinclair switched on his patronising smile yet again. 'I'm afraid that many of these sporadic outbreaks are merely excuses for violence and vandalism,' he said.

'Would you call the lynching of Eric Wilkins a sporadic outbreak of violence? That makes the point, surely?'

'Most unfortunate,' murmured the Home Secretary, 'shocking in fact, but the police assure me that an early arrest is likely.'

'And are the police going to be able to cope with these outbreaks of violence, Home Secretary? They're fairly widespread and are now on an almost daily basis.'

'Of course the police can cope,' snapped Sinclair. 'There is a system operated by chief constables for mutual aid between the various forces, and I would remind you that there are nearly a hundred and fifty thousand police officers in this country.'

'But a hundred resigned yesterday, Home Secretary, and a hundred the day before. Last month some five hundred left the force.' The interviewer had guessed at the figures and had also guessed that Sinclair didn't know them, although he knew that the Home Office was alarmed at the increasing rate of police resignations. 'Can you be sure that the police will be able to cope? Won't you have to call in the army?'

'Certainly not,' said the Home Secretary with unusual asperity. 'What we are seeing here are a few isolated incidents of civil disturbance. It's not a military matter at all.'

'Like Northern Ireland wasn't, you mean,' said the interviewer before turning quickly to the camera and adding, 'This is Paul Sorrell for ITN at Westminster.'

Robert Fairley had been Prime Minister for three years and had survived the last general election with a majority of ten. Not for the first time, he was balancing on the political knife-edge of trying to be all things to all people.

'Well, Kenneth, what about these disturbances over the ECU or whatever they are?' asked Fairley in the grating voice that irritated not only his Cabinet colleagues but his wife also. 'If you're not careful, they're going to engulf your police force.' He always described it as 'Sinclair's police force' when things were going wrong.

'The Commissioner of the Metropolitan Police is convinced that it's political,' said Sinclair. 'He seems to think that it's some deep-rooted plot to overthrow the government.'

'It'd have to be a bit better organised than this rabble seems to be.' Fairley laughed. 'Do *you* think it's political?' he asked.

'Certainly not.'

'If I were in your position, Kenneth, I'd convene a meeting of all the chief constables and lay it on the line for them. They're only a bunch of bloody policemen, for God's sake. Send for the buggers and get a hold of them. I want this resolved, and I want it resolved quickly.'

'I can assure you that the situation is being contained, Prime Minister,' said Sinclair smoothly.

'Contained?' Fairley waved a hand in the direction of a pile of newspapers on a side table in his study. 'You do read the papers, I suppose?' he asked acidly.

'One can't always rely on Press reports—'

'Don't give me that old Macmillan line about it all being something got up by the press. You're Home Secretary and it's your responsibility, Kenneth. I want to know what you're doing about it. You do realise, I suppose, that this could lose us the next election.'

Sinclair held up a placating hand. 'Good heavens,' he said, 'it'll all be over long before that.'

'I should hope so, because if it isn't, you'll be out of a job. Long before that.'

'The Association of Chief Police Officers has asked me to consider employing the military to assist, Prime Minister.' Sinclair advanced the idea quietly. He had some sympathy with the police, for whom he was politically responsible, and believed that it would be necessary to deploy the army sooner rather than later. But his public utterances obliged him to observe the decision of the Cabinet, which, in this case, had been forced on it by a Prime Minister who refused adamantly to sanction the use of troops. After nearly ninety years, the fiction that Winston Churchill had actually deployed tanks against the miners of Tonypandy still hung like a pall over the Conservative benches. But Sinclair had to try.

'I'm glad you discounted the use of the military in that interview with Sorrell,' said Fairley, by way of dismissing what he believed was the Home Secretary's solution, rather than that of the police, to the increasing incidents of disorder.

'That was my official view, but we may have to consider it,' said the Home Secretary mildly.

'There'll be no question of that.' Fairley lifted his chin as he growled his response and then changed the subject with alarming suddenness. 'And another thing. What about these resignations from the police? What's that all about?'

'I am assured by chief constables that it's been exaggerated out of all proportion.' But Sinclair knew that it was serious and had hoped to resolve the situation before Fairley got to learn of it. Unfortunately Paul Sorrell had thrown it into that damned interview.

'Spare me the crap, Kenneth,' said Fairley. 'You're not addressing the Police Federation now, you know. Don't try and pull the wool over my eyes.' Then he shot another probing question at the beleaguered Home Secretary. 'What about the Security Service? What are they doing, peering up their arses and hoping for a renewal of the Cold War?'

Sinclair always found Fairley's occasional lapses into coarseness distasteful. 'It's hardly their job, Prime Minister,' he said.

'You're the political head of the Security Service, Kenneth,' said Fairley menacingly, 'and their job is whatever you tell them it is. But if you feel it's beyond you ...' He left the sentence threateningly unfinished.

'That's easier said than done, Prime Minister. It's a question of their charter.' Sinclair struggled on. He knew that when Fairley seized on something that annoyed him – and the Security Service most certainly did – there was little one could do to placate him, certainly not with sensible, reasoned argument.

'Charter be damned,' snapped Fairley. 'And what's all this bloody rubbish about posters? I got the distinct impression that Paul Sorrell caught you with your trousers down.' His anger diminished and his face assumed an amused and quizzical expression.

Sinclair ignored the insult and proffered a sheet of paper to the Prime Minister. 'That is a list of sites where they have been exhibited, Prime Minister,' he said.

Fairley ignored the document. 'And who's responsible?' he asked. 'Our friends in the Labour Party?'

'Not so,' said Sinclair. 'Police enquiries have indicated that—'

'Police enquiries, did you say?' Fairley looked sharply at the Home Secretary. 'Why have the police been involved? We might not agree with the sentiments these posters express, but there's nothing criminal about them. I should have thought that the police had quite enough to do at the moment.'

'Initial thoughts were that they were in some way connected with this Protection of England Group, Prime Minister ...' Sinclair paused. 'And were therefore seditious.'

'Balls!' said Fairley. 'The police say that PEG isn't a real organisation. They're small groups of vigilantes who've cottoned on to what one lot of thugs decided to call themselves. Where did these posters come from anyway? Did your policemen tell you that?'

'All the hoardings – and there are about fifty of them – were taken legitimately and paid for.'

'By whom?' Again a bitingly incisive question.

The Home Secretary looked down at his notes, but not because he did not know the answer. 'The sites were apparently hired by a man calling himself Eric Wilkins, Prime Minister.'

'And who's he?'

'It's the name of the man who was acquitted of sexual offences against his common-law wife's daughter and who was lynched by this so-called Protection of England Group,' said the Home Secretary softly.

The Prime Minister laughed. 'If I were you, Kenneth,' he said, 'I would forget all about it. And tell your policemen to forget about it too.'

It was not often that Sir Lionel Cork, the Commissioner of the Metropolitan Police, saw the chairman of the Metropolitan branch of the Police Federation on an informal basis. In fact he rarely saw anyone on an informal basis, but he was keen to know more of the threat of mass resignations, rumours of which had recently filtered through to him.

'Take a seat, Mr Rankin.' Unlike his predecessor, Cork could not bring himself to address a constable – even the most senior Federation representative in the force – by his first name. Neither did he invite him to sit in one of the armchairs grouped in the corner where he and his more senior visitors would relax to take coffee. Cork remained behind his desk, and Rankin sat down on the hard-backed chair in front of it.

'Good morning, Sir Lionel,' said Rankin pointedly and

then lapsed into silence. It was not that he was apprehensive in the presence of the Commissioner – he had too
much negotiating experience behind him to be overawed
by anyone in the force – but was playing Cork at his own
game. The Commissioner was a cold fish and had a
tendency to listen rather than speak. It was a device that
had frequently forced even very senior officers into breaking the silence and saying something foolish.

The two, Cork and Rankin, stared at each other for some
seconds before Cork eventually spoke. 'Does it appear that
the force is taking your advice, Mr Rankin?' he asked. One
of Cork's predecessors had taken to calling the Metropolitan Police a service, but Cork would have none of it and
almost the first action he took following his appointment
was to direct that the Metropolitan Police would, once
more, be known as 'the force'.

'What advice is that, sir?' Rankin could be as obdurate
as the Commissioner when he felt like it.

'That officers of the federated ranks should complete
resignation forms and that they would be held by you
pending some unified action?'

'Yes, they are, sir.'

'Many?' Cork made it sound casual, like an enquiry into
how many raffle tickets had been sold for a police charity.

Rankin nodded. 'A substantial number, sir.'

'How many do you describe as substantial, Mr Rankin?'

Rankin stared out of the window as if mentally calcu-
lating, even though he had the figures at his fingertips. 'By
five o'clock yesterday afternoon some seventeen thousand
forms had been received at Limehouse, sir.'

'As many as that, eh?' Cork tried to keep the surprise,
and indeed the shock, out of his voice. He stared at Rankin,
waiting for some comment, but none was forthcoming.
Rankin had no intention of excusing the actions of his
members, and eventually Cork was forced into speaking
again. 'Do you really think that this is a wise course of

action? If it goes ahead, it will leave London denuded of police.'

'I'm well aware of that, sir,' said Rankin, 'and I should like to emphasise that the Federation has no argument with you. Personally, that is. But my member ire heartily sick of the way they have been treated by the government over the last few years. It's made a mockery of rent allowance, it's kicked the Edmund Davies agreement on pay into touch, it's prevented officers from protecting themselves adequately and, finally, the Sheehy Enquiry took away what few benefits they had left.' Despite the assurances of a previous Home Secretary that most of Sheehy's recommendations would be shelved, they had nonetheless been introduced piecemeal over the succeeding years. 'And that's only the tip of the iceberg,' Rankin added.

Cork had been Commissioner for long enough – and a policeman for long enough – to know that once the chairman of the Metropolitan Police Federation started making a political speech, there was little point in continuing any argument. 'I think you should know that there is a body of opinion in the Crown Prosecution Service that this action might be construed as a conspiracy.' In fact Cork had not consulted the CPS and did not believe that they would recommend prosecutions even if he did, but he thought it worth floating the idea nonetheless.

But Rankin was not to be cowed. 'The Federation's legal advisers think otherwise, sir,' he said.

The Commissioner tried another tack. 'You do realise, I hope, Mr Rankin, that the resignation of an officer can only take effect with my consent, and if I refuse to accede to an officer's request to resign, he is lawfully obliged to stay.'

Rankin nodded. He had known it would come to this. 'If you want my personal opinion, sir,' he said, 'I think that would create more problems than it would solve.'

'Is that a threat, Mr Rankin?'

'Not at all, sir. It's just an observation. We're both policemen and we know how policemen's minds work. Let's just say that the rate of sickness could rise dramatically. To a very much higher level than it's reached already.'

The disturbance started simply enough. About nine thousand rioters besieged the central police station in Chester and freed a twenty-five-year-old man who had been charged with the murder of a girl of six whom he had first brutally raped. The self-appointed leader of this mob explained to the inspector in charge of the police station that the crowd had no argument with him personally and politely requested him to release his prisoner. The inspector declined but, having insufficient manpower to prevent an attack, he and the handful of officers defending the station were quickly overwhelmed. The prisoner was dragged into the street outside the police station and kicked to death.

The mob, fired by their initial success, then went on the rampage. The Job Centre, the Social Security Office, the offices of the Inland Revenue and, ironically, the local offices of the Crown Prosecution Service, fell victim to the now inflamed rioters.

The noise of the riot was heard clearly at Alamein Barracks, south of the city, and confirmed by a news flash on the television. Concerned that the barracks might be the rioters' next target, the adjutant promptly informed the commanding officer, Lieutenant-Colonel Colin Stokes. Stokes managed to contact the police, only to be told that the situation was out of control and that he should secure the barracks against possible attack and looting. He next telephoned the magistrates' court, but there was no answer.

The First Battalion of the Cumbrian Regiment was what

the army called a 'spearhead civil disorder unit' – ready to go to any part of the world – and comprised some eight hundred men fully trained in maintaining law and order among the civilian population. But they had never visualised deploying their resources on their own doorstep.

Aware of a little-known piece of common law that set a precedent for officers commanding troops to quell a riot, Colonel Stokes immediately paraded the battalion. The armoury was opened, and some of the soldiers were issued with rifles and fifty rounds of small-arms ammunition each, while others were equipped with riot guns and plastic baton rounds.

The battalion intelligence officer was sent up in the unit's helicopter, carried out a reconnaissance sweep over the city, and reported that the rioters were now moving south in Bridge Street, apparently intent on attacking the offices of Cheshire County Council. This suited Colonel Stokes admirably, and he promptly deployed his battalion across Handbridge and into the grounds of County Hall.

It came as a surprise to the rioters, when they reached County Hall, to find their way blocked by two ranks of armed soldiers and, behind them, a row of riot vehicles.

'Pay attention,' said Stokes through the public-address system mounted on one of the vehicles. 'You are to disperse forthwith.' The mob, shouting and jeering, continued to move towards the troops and started to hurl bricks and stones and anything else they could lay hands on. 'If you do not stop, I shall order my men to open fire with baton rounds.' This was no light decision, but Stokes had been convinced by his intelligence officer's report that the city was in the grip of the mob and that innocent lives might well be at risk. Stokes had, therefore, made the decision to put down the riot no matter what the cost.

A fresh barrage of bricks, stones and pieces of paving stone started to rain down on the military, and several injured soldiers were dragged away by their comrades.

Behind them, sergeants warned the troops to remain steady.

'Baton rounds,' ordered Colonel Stokes.

A volley of plastic bullets hit the road in front of the rioters, causing them to skip and dance out of the way, but most stood firm, even advanced a few feet, taunting and abusing the soldiers and hurling more missiles. Most of them had seen such tactics in televised reports of similar events in various parts of the world, but so far they were unaware of the painful, even fatal, effects of a plastic bullet. Television's weekly fare of fictional violence left most impressionable people with the belief that you could shoot at someone without harming him; few, if any, had personal experience of the devastating effects of a gunshot wound.

'If you do not disperse, I shall use live ammunition,' announced the colonel.

This statement was greeted with jeers and catcalls by the unbelieving rioters, and more missiles.

Then, to his amazement, Colonel Stokes saw two rioters, each armed with a pistol, taking aim at his men. 'Fire live rounds as directed by your officers,' he ordered.

Two subalterns sped along the ranks, each tapping certain of their soldiers on the back and pointing out a particular rioter. It had long been apparent – in places as far apart as India, Malaya, Hong Kong and Aden – that firing over the heads of rioters merely produced among them the belief that the army did not mean business.

There was a rattle of small-arms fire, and five of the leading rioters fell to the ground, including the two men with the pistols. The mob stopped, so suddenly that some of those at the rear cannoned into those at the front, throwing them forward and causing the military to believe that the first volley had been ineffective. Again, the platoon commanders pointed out individual rioters, and again aimed shots were fired, this time bringing three more of them to the ground.

That was enough. The rioters turned and started running, dispersing in all directions. The fight had gone out of them. For the moment.

CHAPTER FIVE

That evening saw a meeting of four senior officers in the Chief of the General Staff's office. The blinds were drawn and the only light came from a standard lamp to one side of the group, who were seated in armchairs. In the CGS's high-backed chair, which had been moved near to them, was Imogen Cresswell, notebook to hand.

General Sir Simon Macey toyed briefly with the report that rested on his knee. 'Well, gentlemen, now what?' he asked, glancing at the others. 'Are we going to get a lot of flak about this?'

Major-General Charles Turner, the Director of Army Legal Services, smoothed a hand over his knee. 'The common law sets a precedent for officers commanding troops to take independent action in the event of insurrection, sir,' he said. 'Not that that will prevent a political uproar. What it does mean, of course,' he added drily, 'is that the government will probably attempt to get a quick bill through the House at the earliest opportunity to negate it.'

'But in the meantime, do we issue an order forbidding officers to quell riots?' asked General Sir Lawrence Dane, the Adjutant-General.

The third general at the meeting, Sir Arthur Aston, was

the GOC Land Command. 'Can't do that,' he said. 'It would be unlawful.'

'How so?' asked Macey.

'You can't give an order to an officer or soldier telling him not to comply with the law,' said Turner, the army lawyer. 'Well, you can, but if he chooses not to comply with that order, you can't charge him with disobedience. Best thing's not to bother.'

The Chief of the General Staff regarded the Director of Army Legal Services with a frown. 'That's all very well,' he said, 'but we can't have officers taking it into their heads to put troops out on the streets to take the occasional pot shot at rioters. I mean to say, we didn't allow that sort of thing in Northern Ireland, did we?'

'No, sir, we didn't,' said Turner. 'But there was different legislation in the province at that time, specifically geared to deal with terrorism. It's not the same, you see.'

'Not the same?' said Dane acidly. 'You could have fooled me, Charles.'

'This is a civil disorder situation, sir, I agree,' said Turner, unwilling to be overawed by the three full generals. 'But the army was in Ulster for over twenty-five years. Procedures had been established for dealing with almost any situation. The present scale of rioting is unprecedented on the mainland ... at least in recent years. I shouldn't think there's been anything like it since the Gordon Riots.'

'I don't think that history is going to help us very much here,' said Macey mildly. 'And it certainly won't help Colonel Stokes.'

'Not necessarily,' said Turner, who was beginning to enjoy his role as a sort of military attorney-general. 'The Gordon Riots established that the military need not await the orders of a magistrate before quelling a riot. Rioting is a felony, well, an arrestable offence now, and the army has ample powers, as do all citizens, to act under common law.' He paused. 'Indeed they have an obligation to act in the suppression of riots,' he added.

'Thank you,' said Macey, 'but I, for one, do not relish the prospect of citing a nineteenth-century precedent when I'm trying to justify to the Prime Minister the death of two rioters in Chester in the late twentieth century.'

'Eighteenth, sir,' said Turner.

'I beg your pardon?'

'The Gordon Riots occurred in 1780, sir.'

'Yes, well, whenever,' said Macey. 'I'm afraid I don't have such esoteric facts at my fingertips.'

'Nor did I, General,' said Turner with a grin, 'until I looked it up.'

The Chief of the General Staff had the good grace to smile. 'Be that as it may,' he said, 'the point is, what are we going to do about the present situation?'

Aston, the commander of all troops in England, Wales and Scotland, leaned forward, an earnest expression on his face. 'It seems to me,' he said slowly, 'that Her Majesty's Government has lost control of the situation and the civil police are unable to put down the rioting. People are being dragged from their homes and murdered on the streets—'

'But they—' Macey attempted to interrupt.

'I know what you're going to say, Simon.' Aston held up a hand. 'They may well be guilty of serious offences that the courts have been inhibited from dealing with effectively by the very law they're supposed to be upholding, but that does not justify what amounts to sentence without trial. The alleged murderer who was himself murdered in Chester is a classic example.' He leaned back again. 'After all, just because the police arrested him doesn't necessarily mean that he's guilty.' He paused momentarily. 'The police have been known to make mistakes in the past.'

'What are you suggesting, Arthur?' Macey asked.

'Given that the army has a responsibility to restore order,' said Aston, 'or indeed, as Charles has said, an obligation, then we must exercise some central direction, otherwise we'll have no idea what's going on. We cannot have officers – or their soldiers, for that matter – just taking the law into their own hands. If they do, they become as guilty of lawlessness as the rioters themselves. It's as simple as that.'

'I wish to God it were,' said Macey with a sigh. 'It will mean drafting an order of the day, with Charles's help, and sending it to all units.' He glanced across at his ADC. 'I hope you've made notes of all this, Imogen,' he said abruptly.

'Yes, sir.' Imogen matched Macey's rudeness with aloofness, but he appeared not to notice.

'Good,' said Macey. 'Get a confidential clerk to type them up, under your supervision. No copies, just the original. And classify it secret. Understood?' He turned back to the three other officers with an almost disdainful dismissal of the girl he had so recently made a pass at.

'Yes, sir,' said Imogen coldly, standing up and making for the door. She felt a bitter hostility towards Macey and was beginning to wonder if she was any better off on his staff than she had been with the battalion at Wellington Barracks. This was certainly not the sort of thing she had imagined she would be doing as his ADC. And she didn't much like the way things were going, either in the office or in her private life.

She had read law at university and military law at Sandhurst, but she was unhappy at the tone of the conference to which she had been privy. It was one thing for the army to suppress a riot as Colonel Stokes had done in Chester, but quite another when the General Staff talked of making contingency plans to counter future outbreaks.

She had known, too, that Macey was occasionally irascible, but she had been amazed at his recent display of arrogance towards her and shuddered at the thought of his making another attempt to seduce her.

When the typed copy of her notes was returned to her,

she made a photocopy, folded it and tucked it inside her dress.

In her quarters at Wellington Barracks, Imogen took out the photocopies she had made of the minutes of that evening's meeting of the General Staff and spread them on the table. They were curled and slightly damp from the hour or so they had been tucked uncomfortably inside her bra, and she smoothed them out. For some time she stared at them, wondering what in hell had possessed her to take the risk of bringing secret documents out of the MOD; she knew that if she had been caught she would have been in serious trouble. But now the problem arose of what to do with them. She could hardly tear them up and leave them in the wastepaper basket for an orderly to find, neither could she take them back to Whitehall thereby increasing the risk. After a moment's thought, she picked up her copy of Queen's Regulations – which she frequently carried to and from her office – and folded the documents neatly between its pages before placing it on the bookshelf. If they were discovered, she could claim that they had been brought out accidentally and must have been put in the book by someone else. It was weak, but it was the best she could think of.

The following morning's meeting of the joint chiefs of staff was a sombre affair. Graeme Kent, the Secretary of State for Defence, sat at the head of the table and glared at the four senior officers. At forty years of age, he was one of the youngest Secretaries of State ever to hold the defence portfolio, which he had done for only four months, and was still apprehensive in his dealings with the joint chiefs, mainly because they were considerably older than he and a great deal more experienced. This uneasiness was frequently disguised by a brusque, and at times quite rude, manner. Today's meeting promised to be particularly difficult, shaping up, as it was, to be his first major confrontation with the professionals in his department.

'There is absolutely no excuse for the commanding officer of a battalion of infantry to take the law into his own hands and open fire on rioters,' he began, making his own views perfectly clear and thereby hoping to influence those of the Chief of the Defence Staff and the leaders of the three armed forces.

General Sir Simon Macey smiled the sort of smile he generally reserved for keen but inexperienced junior officers. 'If law and order had prevailed, Secretary of State,' he said, 'the necessity would not have arisen in the first place. But the facts of the matter are that mobs are running wild throughout the country, looting and destroying property. Killing, even. The police cannot cope with it. Either the military must be allowed to deal with this disorder on a properly controlled basis or there will be further examples of commanding officers doing what Colonel Stokes did in Chester.'

'I'm afraid that can't be allowed to happen,' said Kent sharply, 'and I want each of you to issue orders to prevent its recurrence.'

'Unless the government passes legislation to that effect, Secretary of State, commanding officers would be under no obligation to obey such orders.' The Chief of the Defence Staff, Admiral of the Fleet Sir Godfrey Bristow, was in no mood to be browbeaten by a politician. He came from a long line of naval officers and was one of those rare men who had served more of his time afloat than ashore. He had been lucky enough to see action in an age in which there was very little of it. He had frequently said, since his appointment as CDS, that he had served under officers who were greater martinets than even the average politician knew how to be.

'Very well, gentlemen. I shall see to it that a short bill is laid before the House at the earliest opportunity that will forbid commanding officers to act without the express authority of the judiciary.' Kent tapped the table gently with his hand as if to emphasise his political authority.

'Is that wise?' Macey's mild response barely veiled his sarcasm. 'Would the general public not see that as caving in to the mob? The only complaints about what occurred in Chester have come from the usual malcontents in Parliament, who always complain when the government attempts to deal with lawlessness—'

'I find that remark offensive, Sir Simon,' snapped Kent.

Macey ignored the Secretary of State's petulant interruption. 'And, of course,' he continued, 'the tired old civil rights campaigners, who seem to think that everyone should be allowed to do exactly as he pleases.'

'The politics of the matter are no concern of yours, Sir Simon,' said Kent angrily. 'Nor any of you,' he added, allowing his severe gaze to travel round the table. Already he could feel himself losing control of the meeting. 'Your task is simply to command the armed forces, and I have to say that you're not doing a very good job at the moment.'

'Perhaps you'd like us all to resign then, Secretary of State,' said Air Chief Marshal Gilbert, the Chief of the Air Staff. Beside him, Admiral Sir Peter Ainsworth, the Chief of Naval Staff, smiled. This argument was really nothing to do with the Royal Navy.

Kent's gaze travelled once more around the faces of the joint chiefs of staff. He saw no dissent to Gilbert's suggestion. 'I wouldn't want you to make any hasty decisions, gentlemen,' he said, hurriedly retreating from his aggressive stand. He knew that such an unprecedented course of action would reflect adversely upon his own career and would be very difficult to explain to the Prime Minister. 'I'm sure you must see that the government is in a very difficult position at the moment.'

'You've only yourselves to blame for that,' said Macey, 'and right now you can't afford to alienate the armed forces. They may turn out to be your only hope. Face it, Secretary of State, the police are in disarray. They're resigning by the hundreds because the government and the courts are not backing them. They've almost given up arresting people because the Crown Prosecution Service frequently refuses to take proceedings. And if the police force cannot contain outbreaks of violence – which is happening quite often now – they're obliged to withdraw. At the moment, they have no chance of getting reinforcements from anywhere. Every police force is fully committed. They don't have the men to spare to help their neighbours. Sooner or later you're going to have to employ the military.'

'That is a matter for the Prime Minister,' said Kent curtly, 'and I have to tell you that he is implacably opposed to the idea.'

Macey grinned insolently at the youthful minister. 'In that case,' he said, 'I suggest you tell him of our disquiet. We expect you, as Secretary of State, to support the armed forces, not to criticise what we are lawfully doing.'

'How dare you!' Kent was red in the face now. Never before had he been challenged so blatantly. Accustomed to demolishing amateur hecklers with consummate ease, he now found himself faced by men who knew their own business thoroughly and were not afraid to argue with him from a standpoint outside his own knowledge and experience. Too late, he realised that his officials had been less than thorough in the preparation of the brief they had given him.

'Soldiers are citizens too, you know,' Macey continued relentlessly, 'and they will not stand by and see property destroyed and innocent people losing their livelihood and, in some cases, their lives because the government is too pusillanimous to act. Apart from anything else, they're not in the best of moods since the announcement of further cuts in the armed forces.'

'That's a bloody insolent remark to make, General.' Kent was furious that this mere soldier was lecturing him on affairs of state. 'It is your job – each of you – to ensure that the armed forces comply with the wishes and policies of Her Majesty's Government. And its orders too.'

'If you'll forgive me for saying so,' said Macey, not wishing to be forgiven at all, 'you don't know what the hell you're talking about. You have no direct authority over members of the armed forces. You're responsible for policy. The interpretation of that policy and its transmission to the officers and other ranks under our command is our responsibility, and ours alone.' He took a cigarette from the open case in front of him and felt in his pocket for his lighter. 'I can only speak for the army, of course,' he went on, 'but they're very angry at the moment. They certainly aren't amenable to complying with the wishes of a government in which they no longer have any faith.' He lit his cigarette and puffed smoke in the air.

'I beg your pardon—?' spluttered Kent.

'This government,' continued Macey in level tones, 'has consistently alienated all the people it could reasonably regard as its supporters. The armed forces, the police, the professional classes, businessmen, home owners, landowners. The socialists have come out of it rather well, I think. In fact, I would say that the best thing that ever happened to the workshy and criminal elements of this country was the election of a Conservative government.'

The Secretary of State for Defence stood up, his fists clenched. He knew he was losing the argument but was powerless to turn it in his favour. 'I will not tolerate this,' he said. 'I am not obliged to listen to your fascist outpourings, nor will I. I shall report this entire conversation to the Prime Minister.'

'We will do that, Secretary of State,' said Bristow mildly as he and the other three rose from their seats. 'We are exercising our right to see him ourselves. At the earliest opportunity.'

'During the course of a riot in Chester yesterday,' said the Prime Minister, 'soldiers of the First Battalion of the Cumbrian Regiment opened fire, killing two rioters and injuring six. The two who were killed were subsequently found to have been armed.' Then he sat down, relieved. At five feet seven tall, and slightly built, he was not an imposing figure at the despatch box.

The House erupted. Not because the Prime Minister's statement was news to them – television had made sure it was not – but because he had been so brief, dismissive almost. There was no apparent regret and no explanation. And the House did not like being treated in such a cavalier fashion. Practically every member seated on the Opposition side of the House rose, intent on catching the Speaker's eye, but they all knew it would be the Leader of the Opposition who was called.

'Mr Brian Kennard!' cried the Speaker.

'Is the Prime Minister aware that the troops opened fire without any authority from a magistrate and that they had not, in fact, been asked to aid the civil power?' It was not often these days that the Right Honourable Brian Kennard had an opportunity to discomfit the smug Robert Fairley.

'Amritsar!' shouted an amateur historian from the back benches of the Labour Party.

'Bloody Sunday!' yelled another Labourite.

The Prime Minister rose again. 'The commanding officer of the Cumbrians perceived that a riot was taking place,' he began, 'and there was evidence that the rioters possessed firearms. Right Honourable and Honourable Members will be aware that a man was abducted from the police station and beaten to death outside in the street. Much of the centre of the city of Chester has been destroyed, and that destruction had already occurred when Colonel Stokes took it upon himself, quite rightly in my view—'

There was an outburst of jeering and a few shouts of 'Murderer!'

'Quite rightly in my view,' persisted the Prime Minister, 'to deploy the troops under his command. It is not only his right to do so but his bounden duty as a Queen's officer. Furthermore, I am reliably informed that he made attempts to contact both the police and magistrates. The former told him that the city was out of control and the latter could not be reached.' The Attorney-General had earlier convinced Fairley that Colonel Stokes had acted within the law. Fairley had been appalled by the Attorney's advice and now found himself in the invidious position of defending an officer whose actions he found to be anathema.

'Balls!' shouted an unknown voice.

'Order! Order!' shouted the Speaker. 'I will not have language of that sort in the Chamber, no matter what the provocation.'

'My Right Honourable friend the Home Secretary—'

'Where is he?' asked Kenneth Sinclair's shadow from the Opposition front bench.

'The Home Secretary is at present in conference with the Chief Constable of Cheshire, obtaining a full account of all that has occurred. When that report has been received, I shall be in a better position to inform the House more fully.' The Prime Minister sat down, determined to sit out the furore that was going on around him.

'The House will not be satisfied with that,' said the Leader of the Opposition. 'It seems that the army, along with a lot of the civilian population, is out of control and the House wants to know what the Prime Minister intends to do about it,' he added, banging the despatch box to emphasise his point.

But, despite cries of 'Answer!', the Prime Minister sat firm. That was all that the House was going to get from him that day.

*

'Imogen?'

'Yes.'

'It's Alec Shepherd. How are you fixed for a drink this evening?'

Imogen Cresswell hesitated and, surprised by the call, glanced at the pile of paper on her desk. She had intended to stay on until it was cleared. 'Well, I do have rather a lot on . . .'

'Leave it,' said Shepherd. 'It'll all look much easier in the morning.'

'You've convinced me. Where and when?' Imogen had forgotten Shepherd's casual invitation to a drink but was not now going to let a few scraps of paperwork stand in the way.

'The RAC's as good a place as any. Shall we say in twenty minutes? Can you make that?'

When she arrived, Shepherd was waiting in the entrance hall and pecked her on the cheek before standing back to admire her. 'I must say that you're looking more beautiful than ever. Army life obviously agrees with you.' Imogen smiled at the compliment. 'Look,' he went on, 'I know this is all going to sound a bit mysterious, but there's someone I'd like you to meet.'

'Oh! Who?' She had hoped that he was asking her for a cosy chat somewhere exclusive. But now it was beginning to sound like business.

By way of a reply, Shepherd took her arm, led her back to the street and ushered her into a waiting chauffeur-driven car. 'I'll explain on the way,' he said, 'but I assure you that it's of vital importance.'

The car turned through Marlborough Road, left into The Mall and skirted Trafalgar Square before making its way up Charing Cross Road. Somewhat bemused and disconcerted, Imogen gazed out of the car window and wondered what she was letting herself in for.

'Incidentally, I've left the army,' said Shepherd.

'Really? What are you doing now, then?'

There was a slight pause before Shepherd said, 'Working for the government. The Foreign Office actually,' he added, employing the usual euphemism.

Imogen tensed. 'What exactly is this all about, Alec?' she asked, half turning in her seat.

'Trust me, Imogen,' said Shepherd.

After about thirty minutes they arrived at a large house in North London. It lay back off the road, shielded from public gaze by a row of conifers. Instead of following the main drive, the car took them round the back of the premises, and they stopped on a cracked patio that lay between the wall of the house and an empty and dilapidated swimming pool.

'They tell me that this place used to be an absolute riot in the thirties,' said Shepherd. 'There were all sorts of disgraceful goings-on in and around that pool.' He touched Imogen's arm. 'This way.' A man stepped forward, nodded silently to Shepherd and opened a metal-framed French window.

To Imogen, the man looked menacing. 'What is this place?' she asked.

'It's part of the Foreign Office,' said Shepherd unconvincingly, 'but a damned sight more comfortable.'

Shepherd ushered her into a large and elegantly furnished sitting room. As they entered, a balding man with horn-rimmed spectacles eased himself out of one of the leather chesterfields.

'This is Barry,' said Shepherd. The SIS did not use their surnames, and Imogen was never to discover that Barry was, in fact, Barry Rogers, Director of Counter-Intelligence and Security in the service.

'Barry, this is Major Imogen Cresswell.'

Rogers grasped Imogen's hand in a firm grip. 'Get the major a drink, Alec,' he said, momentarily holding Imogen's gaze with his own.

'I'll have a gin and tonic, please,' said Imogen as she glanced around the room.

Shepherd was at the drinks cabinet already and spoke over his shoulder. 'Ice and lemon, Imogen?'

'Please.'

Shepherd handed Imogen her drink and turned to Rogers. 'Barry?'

'Scotch, no ice.'

They sat down and Rogers raised his glass. 'Your health, Major.'

Imogen took a sip of her drink and appraised the two men. Alec Shepherd she knew, or thought she did, as an attractive and attentive companion, but Barry appeared to be a cold professional of a very different calibre. 'What's this all about?' Her voice was silkily smooth, deliberately pitched to disguise the mixture of apprehension and irritation she was feeling. Her attempts during the journey to find out from Shepherd where he was taking her and why had been met with an uncharacteristic terseness. He had merely repeated that there was someone he wanted her to meet and that it was quite important. Imogen had found that unconvincing and was annoyed at being treated like a child.

'You are aide-de-camp to the Chief of the General Staff,' said Rogers without preamble.

Imogen nodded coldly.

'And your work is covered by the Official Secrets Act.' Rogers sat in the chesterfield facing Imogen. He was relaxed, with his legs crossed at the ankles and his hands resting loosely in his lap. It was an attitude of amiable menace.

'What do you mean by that?' Imogen snapped.

'Oh, I think you know.' Years of gathering intelligence, sifting it, assessing the source – indeed identifying it – had given Rogers a carapace of confidence that made inter- rogating someone like Imogen Cresswell fairly simple. Not that he underestimated the woman opposite him. He never underestimated any of his subjects. And a woman like Imogen, a trained officer whose determination had secured for her – against all the odds – a commission in one of the army's most prestigious regiments and her present appointment, had to be regarded as possessing reserves that were not immediately apparent. 'I'm just fascinated to learn your views of General Sir Simon Macey, a womaniser and an officer whose soldiers seem to be embarrassing the government. What's he up to? Planning a coup d'état, is he?'

As Rogers had intended, Imogen was stunned by his suggestion but covered her amazement with a laugh. 'How absurd,' she said. And then, with a flash of annoyance, added, 'But I do not intend to answer any of your questions until I know who you are and why you're asking them.'

'I take it that Major Cresswell does know who we represent, Alec?' Rogers glanced at his assistant.

Shepherd shook his head. 'Not specifically,' he said.

'Ah!' Rogers realigned his gaze on Imogen. 'Alec and I are members of the Secret Intelligence Service, Imogen.' In common with all the officers of the Service, he was ill-disposed towards admitting that he was a member of SIS, but sometimes it was unavoidable. 'Much of what we do in the intelligence world is, of course, secret,' he added unnecessarily, 'and we don't always move in the ways that people might expect. We're not concerned with prosecuting people, although it does sometimes come to that when we don't get any co-operation. You see, we're not playing games, Major,' he continued. 'And I should not like to think that you were in agreement with Macey and his views. That could have serious repercussions for you in the future.' He looked up at the ceiling and then back at Imogen suddenly. 'It could have very serious repercussions indeed,' he continued. 'And I'm sure that you know enough about the army, Major, to know that if they decided that you were not behaving ...' He raised his hands and then let them fall again. 'The military regime imposes penalties that can be quite severe.' He resisted the temptation to examine his fingernails: that would have been too theatrical. Instead he smiled benignly.

'What exactly are you getting at?' asked Imogen, irritated, and a little alarmed, at Rogers' seemingly pointless waffle.

Rogers smiled. 'When we were discussing this earlier,' he said, 'it seemed to us ...' He waved a hand to include Shepherd in the statement. 'It seemed to us that you may just be the woman to assist us in a little operation we have in mind.' He eased himself off the chesterfield, the leather cushion squealing as he did so, and moved to the mantelpiece. He put his hands in his pockets and leaned back slightly so that his shoulder blades were resting on the edge of the shelf.

Shepherd was sitting comfortably in his chair, watching his chief at work, and was surprised when Imogen turned and addressed him directly. 'What sort of operation?'

Before Shepherd could react, Rogers stepped forward aggressively. 'We have reason to believe that General Macey is considering exceeding his powers as Chief of the General Staff. We know that he has deliberately flouted the wishes of the Secretary of State for Defence, if not the Prime Minister, in not preventing troops from interfering in public disorder.'

'How did you know that?' demanded Imogen bluntly. 'It was only decided yesterday.'

Rogers smiled but said nothing.

'He had no power to,' said Imogen instinctively. 'What Colonel Stokes did at Chester was perfectly lawful.'

Rogers nodded. 'Lawful maybe, but politically inept. Naive in all respects. He's on dangerous ground, Major, and although there are provisions that allow soldiers the defence of claiming that they are only obeying orders, there is a limit. Colonel Stokes might find that he's already overstepped the mark.' He paused to give impact to his next statement. 'And you might also find yourself in some difficulty. Rather depends how willing an accomplice you are.'

Imogen shook her head. 'I can't believe that you're serious,' she said. She spoke slowly with no trace of emotion. She was not a woman to be scared easily. 'All I have done is obey orders and get on with my job.'

'That age-old excuse is unlikely to hold much water.'

Imogen gave an exasperated sigh. 'Believe it or not, that's the truth,' she said.

'Maybe, but who do you imagine is going to believe it?' Rogers was a restless interrogator, and his victims usually found it disconcerting, unnerving even, but that was not the reason he moved about so much. Physical movement helped him to think more clearly. He walked to the drinks cabinet and poured himself another Scotch. He pointed a questioning finger at Imogen's glass, but she shook her head. 'Once the sweet smell of revenge pervades the air, little people like you are going to be swept away.'

'Don't patronise me,' Imogen snapped at him.

Rogers ignored her. 'It means that if Macey succeeds in what we believe to be his aim,' he said, 'a vengeful government is not going to take prisoners.'

For a brief moment, the occupants of the room were still and silent, the air full of static tension.

That tension was broken by Rogers, prosaically searching his pockets for matches. 'It seems to me,' he said, 'that we are saddled with a Chief of the General Staff who's showing signs of megalomania. Bristow, the CDS, isn't the problem, you see. He's just been caught up in Macey's mad scheme. It's quite evident from what we've learned so far that Macey sees himself as some sort of future military governor. I think he's convinced himself that Fairley and a civil government will never put this country back together the way he thinks it ought to be.'

Imogen interrupted. 'Colonel Stokes puts down a riot and immediately you ascribe to General Macey some desire to take over the country. Do you really think it's that serious?'

'We have our sources, Imogen,' said Rogers, condescendingly switching to the use of her first name. He was convinced in his own mind that Macey's previous association with General Max Strigel, coupled with recent events, made the CGS a worthy target for his interest.

'You are serious, aren't you?'

'Oh yes I am,' said Rogers. 'If Macey moves any further towards what I believe to be his aim, then I think we must act. Bristow's got the rank so he must bear the responsibility. That makes him and Macey, and to a lesser extent Ainsworth and Gilbert, the Queen's enemies. And defending the Queen against her enemies is the business we're in when it comes down to it. Even if her enemy happens to be her own Chief of the General Staff.' Rogers had raised an issue of awesome magnitude, but he spoke quietly, almost reflectively, and expelled pipe smoke towards the ceiling.

'What are you saying, Barry?' Shepherd was not only surprised at his chief's candour, he was amazed at the interpretation he had put on the very little hard intelligence that had, so far, come to hand.

For her part, Imogen was silent in disbelief.

'I am asking where our loyalties lie, Alec. All of us.'

'To the state.' Shepherd made it sound like a statement, but it was really a question.

'And what is that?' Rogers answered question with question.

'The Crown, the government,' said Shepherd, floundering. 'The people?'

'Usually all three: *tria juncta in uno*.' Rogers paused to relight his pipe. 'But supposing that any one of those three starts acting against the interests of the other two. Or even the Crown and the government act against the interests of the people. The people make the state – the people *are* the state. Our job is the defence of the realm. But what do we do when that realm starts to fragment? Which bit do we defend then?'

There was a long pause before Shepherd replied. 'It must be the lawfully elected government. To do anything else would be treason, surely?' He spoke slowly, thoughtfully. '"Treason doth never prosper; what's the reason?"' he quoted.

'Yes, I know all about that,' said Rogers. 'But the government is elected by the people and at the same time does the Queen's bidding. Her directions to us come through the government. She does not, cannot, speak to us direct. Nor can she address us through the armed forces just because they decide that they are going to displace the elected government.'

'You sound like a lawyer,' said Shepherd.

'I read law at Cambridge.' Rogers spoke in an offhand way and started to stride around the room once more. 'And where does that put the Secret Intelligence Service?'

'If you'll forgive me for saying so, Barry, that surely is a question for C,' said Shepherd.

Rogers looked at him for some time. Eventually he said, 'And do you think for one moment that he isn't giving it serious consideration?'

Shepherd watched the figure of Rogers slowly pacing around the room. 'So what do we do? What exactly are you suggesting?'

Rogers placed his glass on the mantelshelf and tamped down the tobacco in his pipe with a forefinger. Then he struck a match and applied it carefully. Waving the match until the flame expired, he dropped it into an ashtray and puffed out a cloud of smoke. 'I am suggesting that we gather as much intelligence about the activities of the Chief of the General Staff as we can, Alec. And that's where Major Cresswell comes in.'

'In what way?' Imogen had been silent during Rogers' dissertation but had absorbed every word. Her brain was racing with the implications of a situation she had neither imagined nor considered. She felt at once giddy and elated by her sudden exposure to the machinations of power. The secretive way in which the CGS had forbidden the taking of notes, the instruction that nothing was to be recorded and the apparent unwillingness on his part to comply with the wishes of the government in general and the Secretary of State in particular took on a sinister and wholly new meaning, and she realised that there was more than one construction that could be put on his behaviour. She suddenly felt very naive and insecure, but she now felt justified in having kept the documents that were hidden in her quarters.

'If you're willing, Imogen' – Rogers became suddenly quite conciliatory – 'I'd like you to maintain contact with Alec and keep him informed of everything that occurs in the office of the Chief of the General Staff.' Rogers held up his hand as Imogen went to speak. 'It is your duty. You're a Queen's officer. Your loyalty is to her, not to Macey. Do you agree?'

Imogen was not sure whether Rogers was asking if she was loyal to the Queen or whether she was willing to assist. After a moment's thought, she realised that the questions were one and the same. 'Yes,' she said, and felt a rush of adrenaline course through her body.

CHAPTER SIX

On the day following her traumatic interview with Barry Rogers, Imogen went to Whitehall early, determined to clear the backlog of work that had built up over the two days since the Chester riot. But her good intentions were frustrated when, to her surprise, the door of Macey's office opened.

'Ah, Imogen, good morning,' said the CGS affably. 'I'm glad you're here. Perhaps you'd come in.'

Imogen followed Macey into his office and closed the door behind her. She was apprehensive in case he had somehow learned of her visit to the SIS safe house but dismissed the thought almost immediately. Although she had taken a strong dislike to the man Barry, she knew that he was a professional and that their meeting would have stayed secret.

'You've probably gathered that the situation is getting pretty serious, Imogen,' said Macey. 'The business in Chester has rather put us on the spot, and right now we're at loggerheads with the Secretary of State.' A bleak smile crossed his face. 'I know that you're not a secretary,' he continued, 'but I'd like you to take down this signal and supervise its despatch.'

'Very good, sir. I'll just get a pad.'

When Imogen had returned and settled herself in a chair opposite Macey's desk, he stood up and began prowling around the office. 'From the Chief of the General Staff to all formation commanders,' he began. 'Formation commanders are to brief OCs regiments and battalions that they have a duty at common law to intercede in civil disorder. Furthermore, they are to be reminded that the decision to deploy troops is personal to them and that a magistrate's authority is not required if it is deemed inexpedient for such authority to be obtained.' He sat down behind his desk again and smiled at his ADC. 'That is to be sent Emergency and classified Top Secret,' he said. 'Perhaps you'd encipher it yourself.' He paused. 'You can do that, can't you, Imogen?'

'Yes, sir,' said Imogen, closing her notebook and rising from her chair. She realised that the mysterious Barry had persuaded her to see Macey's actions in a different light and was now convinced that her decision to assist the SIS had been the right one.

The Prime Minister was somewhat disconcerted to receive a request for an urgent interview from the joint chiefs of staff, and the reason they gave – the present situation – did nothing to enlighten him as to the real cause of their disquiet. It could be cutbacks in defence spending, which included further reductions in the strength of the forces, or the miserable pay increase which had irritated men serving in a number of trouble spots, or it could be the civil unrest. Fairley had been annoyed that the chiefs had declined to give his principal private secretary an agenda, and Kent, thoroughly rattled by the mauling he had received, was unable to give a very coherent summary of their grievances.

Now, with the Defence Secretary at his left hand and the Cabinet Secretary at his right, Robert Fairley surveyed the four service chiefs sitting opposite him on the other side of the Cabinet table. 'Well, gentlemen, this is an unexpected pleasure,' he said and smiled disingenuously.

'We'll not beat about the bush, Prime Minister,' said Bristow. 'We are greatly concerned about the present situation. And General Macey is particularly worried that Colonel Stokes, the commanding officer of the First Cumbrians, is being pilloried for doing his public duty.'

'I wouldn't say that he was being pilloried,' said Fairley, 'but you will understand, Sir Godfrey, that an enquiry must be held when the military open fire on civilians in their own country.' He smoothed a hand over the top of the table. 'There are all sorts of questions that need to be answered, the main one being whether Colonel Stokes had explored all the avenues available to him before resorting to such a final and drastic course of action.'

'I don't think that you are fully aware of the situation that was facing Stokes, Prime Minister,' said Sir Simon Macey. 'I served in Ulster, as you know, and to face a violent mob – one that, I would remind you, had already killed a man – is a frightening thing. And at least two men were armed. You mentioned it in the House.'

The Prime Minister dismissed that slight complication with a wave of his hand. 'But Colonel Stokes didn't have to face them, General,' he said coldly. 'He could have stayed in his barracks and secured the perimeter, surely? He didn't have to venture into the town and interfere. Had the barracks been under attack, then that would have been a different matter altogether.'

'Are you suggesting that a responsible officer, aware that people had been murdered and seeing a city being sacked, should stand by and do nothing, Prime Minister?' Macey's chin jutted forward aggressively.

'Sir Simon, I do understand your desire to defend the actions of one of your own officers, but it is I who have to weigh the implications of his actions in the political balance. The Opposition are baying for my blood.'

'I am not defending Stokes unreasonably,' said Macey. 'If he has acted unlawfully, then I will sign the convening order for his court martial without hesitation.' The Prime Minister nodded but forbore from pointing out that if Stokes were to stand trial, it would be before a civilian court. 'But what I am saying,' continued Macey, 'is that because the government was unable to contain the situation by the use of the civil police, the army had a bounden duty to act.'

The Prime Minister smiled condescendingly. 'I envy you, Sir Simon,' he said, 'being able to look at this with a soldier's eye and with no consideration for the political ramifications. In any event, I take note of your concerns, gentlemen, but you will appreciate, I am sure, that I can offer no opinion until the enquiry into the events at Chester has been completed. In the meantime, Sir Simon, I think you will agree that it is better that Colonel Stokes is relieved of his command, temporarily at least.'

The Chief of the General Staff grunted and Sir Godfrey Bristow leaned forward, intent upon preventing the soldier from making some insubordinate remark. 'Have you reconsidered using the military on a formalised basis to assist the civil powers in putting down what comes close to being insurrection, Prime Minister?' Bristow asked mildly.

Fairley smiled. 'Oh, hardly an insurrection, Sir Godfrey,' he said. Then he looked into the middle distance before embarking upon the sort of homily with which his Cabinet colleagues were more than familiar. 'There is a danger, gentlemen,' he continued, 'that this whole business could get out of hand. One has to consider all the implications. It is not a battle to be fought. If I were to authorise the use of the military, it would merely exacerbate a situation that is far from being beyond the control of the police. Just imagine the effect of having armed troops patrolling the streets. It would be setting up targets for malcontents to snipe at. We are all familiar with what happened in Northern Ireland—'

'That only came about because of lack of purposefulness on the part of the government,' said Macey, half to himself.

The Prime Minister glanced sharply at the CGS. 'I would advise you most strongly, General,' he said, 'not to interfere in matters that are outside your brief. I can understand the frustration of the armed forces,' he continued in conciliatory tones. 'There are no longer wars to be fought, and the army in particular is looking around for a new role.' He shrugged. 'But there is no question of their interfering with the duties of the police. The police exist to maintain the Queen's peace. It is their task, and their task alone. It is not the military's.' He placed both his hands flat on the table. 'There is no question of using the military in aid of the civil power in mainland Britain,' he said.

'Then there is a danger of commanding officers acting independently, as did Colonel Stokes,' said Bristow. 'The common law is quite clear on the matter.'

'I have discussed that with the Secretary of State for Defence,' said Fairley, 'and I agree with him that the best thing would be to push a prohibiting bill through the House as quickly as possible. That would debar service officers from taking the action they see as a requirement under the existing law. And now if you'll excuse me, gentlemen . . .'

'If you'll forgive me for saying so, Prime Minister,' said Bristow, 'that seems an ill thought out course of action. And at the risk of offending you by quoting a Whig politician, it was Edmund Burke who said, "I am not determining a point of law; I am restoring tranquillity."'

'You let me worry about that, eh, Sir Godfrey?' said the Prime Minister as he stood up and walked to the door of the Cabinet Room. Dwarfed by the four service chiefs, he shook hands with each in turn.

*

Before Kent's bill could be laid before the House, another
riot broke out, this time in Kingston upon Thames. And
this time the assistant commissioner in charge of the area,
whose office happened to be in the town and who was
unaware – in strict terms of constitutional law – of what
precisely had occurred at Chester, called upon the military
himself.

He had first sought assistance from the other Metropolitan Police areas, but none of the four ACs was able to help.
The assistant commissioner responsible for Central London
had already committed his officers to the protection of
Downing Street, Parliament and Buckingham Palace and,
for that reason, had first call on the rest of the Metropolitan
Police. The response to the Kingston officer's request was
simple and to the point: 'You're on your own.'

The AC decided to take personal charge of the situation
and moved from his office in Penrhyn Road into the
command centre at Kingston Police Station, close by the
River Thames. Having called in a few officers from surrounding stations, but not daring to denude those areas
completely, he now realised that his meagre force was in
danger of being overwhelmed. For the safety of the officers
themselves, he directed those who could reach it to
withdraw to the police station. He instructed the remainder
to find places of safety, preferably in a building with a good
vantage point and ideally near a telephone in case the
personal radio system went down and to monitor the
situation to the best of their ability.

The riot had started on an estate of council flats at
Kingston Hill. A youth of fifteen, long known to be
responsible for numerous break-ins on the estate, had been
set upon and severely beaten by his exasperated neighbours. When an ambulance had arrived, the crew had
been attacked and driven back in the face of a hail of bricks
and other missiles. A police car that had sped to the scene

to support the ambulancemen had been overturned and set on fire, its crew being lucky to escape with their lives. They had retreated ignominiously and called for assistance on their personal radios, only to be told that none was available. Already other pockets of disorder had been erupting in the town centre. A mob had surged down Clarence Street, throwing anything they could find through shop windows and leaving a carpet of broken glass through the pedestrian area that ran from Eden Street almost to Kingston Bridge. In the wake of the riot, youths, women and children were looting the insecure shops of clothing, electrical equipment, television sets, video cassette recorders and computer games.

To the terror of screaming shop assistants, another mob swept through the Bentall Centre and across the road into the John Lewis department store, smashing everything it could lay hands on. And in the Norbiton area a bus was hijacked and set on fire.

The last policeman to gain the sanctuary of the police station estimated the largest of the rampaging mobs at two thousand.

Mindful of how the army in Chester had saved the police from more serious injury, the AC made several attempts to get authority to call out the military, but by now another outbreak of violence had occurred in Central London, in Whitehall and, separately, in the Regent Street and Oxford Street areas. Reports that Selfridges was ablaze were occupying the senior officers at Scotland Yard, and the troubles at Kingston came low down their list of priorities.

The nearest barracks were at Woking. It was a long way away from Kingston, but the AC could see no alternative to calling on the military for assistance. Reluctantly, he asked the communications officer to connect him with the officer in charge.

Lieutenant-Colonel Tim Crosby, the commanding officer

of the 27th Royal Hussars, listened carefully to the AC, promised to do what he could and then telephoned his own brigade commander at Aldershot. The brigadier's response was unhelpful. Reminded of Macey's signal and the law, the cavalry CO was told to use his own judgement.

With an enthusiasm he had not experienced for a long time, Crosby at last felt that he could do something to fight the system that had so callously disregarded the murder of his wife. The 27th Royal Hussars were mobilised, and within minutes Crosby was leading four squadrons of armoured cars, along with support vehicles, towards Kingston.

The roads around the police station and the nearby guildhall were filled with rioters, and most of the windows in the police station had been broken by missiles. The appearance of armoured cars speeding in from the Portsmouth Road was greeted with howls of derision and a hail of bricks and stones.

Unlike Colonel Stokes's battalion, the hussar colonel's regiment was not equipped with baton rounds. So Crosby ordered his lead armoured car to fire a few ranging shots over the heads of the rioters. The sharp rattle of the medium machine guns with which the armoured cars were equipped produced a stunned silence among the mob. Aware of what had happened in Chester, the rioters turned tail and ran but then regrouped in other parts of the town.

Ordering some of his vehicles to form a defensive line in front of the police station and moving others to the rear entrance in Kingston Hall Road, Crosby sought out the officer in charge.

The AC was seated in the front office; a woman officer was bathing a nasty cut on his forehead where he had been hit by a brick that had come through the window.

The cavalry colonel saluted. 'Tim Crosby, sir,' he said, 'commanding the 27th Royal Hussars. Come to pull your chestnuts out of the fire,' he added with a grin that didn't reach his eyes.

The AC waved the policewoman away and stood up, extending a hand. 'I can't tell you how pleased I am to see you, Colonel,' he said. 'Perhaps you'd care to come up to the command centre.' And, holding a handkerchief to his head, he led the way upstairs.

The control room staff were managing to monitor the situation quite well with the help of those police officers still hidden in various parts of the town. The AC nodded to an inspector. 'This is Colonel Crosby,' he said, indicating the soldier. 'Perhaps you'll brief him on the situation.'

Rapidly, and with the aid of a map of the area, the inspector indicated to the colonel where the mobs were now. 'They've set fire to one or two buses at the Norbiton depot,' he said, 'but other buses have been driven out into the streets. Some are being used to block Kingston Hill ...' He glanced up from the map. 'That's the main road from London. Others are being used to ram buildings.' He ran a hand through his hair. 'Whatever started it, it's degenerated into pure, unadulterated vandalism, and to be honest, there are now about a dozen groups rampaging all over the town. The last place to go was the Conservative Party's office here in Birkenhead Avenue.' He pointed at the map and then shrugged at the hopelessness of it all.

With a grin, Crosby took off his beret and pointed to the regimental motto beneath the royal cypher. '*Divide et impera,*' he said. 'Divide and rule. And with your approval, sir' – he glanced at the AC – 'that's exactly what I propose to do. I've got half a regiment of armoured cars out there, and I intend to chase these bastards all over the place until they drop.'

The AC sat down, the pain in his head becoming more severe by the minute. 'I'll leave it to you, Colonel,' he said. 'Quite frankly, I've had enough. We've been under siege for four hours now.' He glanced at the clock in confirmation. 'And we've got a bloody government that doesn't give a damn.'

'I won't argue with that,' said Crosby, and for the next hour his armoured cars swept around the centre of Kingston, dispersing the mob with all the panache of the old mounted regiment they had once been. Although all Crosby's troopers were comparatively young men, they knew their regimental history. Stories of the rout of the French at Talavera, of the Germans on the Marne, where their predecessors had fought as infantry, and the grand sweep into Tobruk in the vanguard of Montgomery's conquering army were as familiar to them as if they had taken part.

As the armoured cars drove at them, at least four laggardly rioters, failing to get out of the way in time, were struck down, one fatally, it was later learned. But by seven o'clock in the evening, the town centre, wrecked though it was, had resumed a fragile state of comparative tranquillity.

At seven o'clock the next morning, the assistant commissioner died in Kingston Hospital from a massive heart attack.

'Uproar in the House' was a headline that most of the newspapers had been employing with monotonous regularity since the start of what, with a stark lack of originality, they described as 'the Troubles'. Almost every day there were fresh disturbances, and almost every day opposition MPs were baying for the government's collective head. Government backbenchers were being quietly critical, and the government chief whip was having an increasingly difficult task marshalling his party's members through the correct lobby.

It was entirely the wrong time for Graeme Kent to lay before the House a bill that would prohibit the military from taking the sort of action in which they had now been involved on two occasions. Resistance to the bill came not only from the Labour benches but from the government's own supporters too.

Dudley Walsh, the Conservative member for Kingston and Surbiton, rose threateningly from his place on the back benches, his well-filled belly putting his shirt buttons under a great deal of strain. 'I cannot think of a less propitious moment than this for my Right Honourable friend the Secretary of State for Defence to attempt, with a sleight of hand that would do credit to the Magic Circle, to push through a bill that would prohibit the military from taking action to suppress the riots now sweeping the country. If it had not been for the 27th Royal Hussars' prompt action yesterday—'

A Labour backbencher cried, 'Shame!'

Walsh looked at him frostily. 'I suggest the Honourable Member opposite confines his remarks to subjects he knows something about,' he said.

'That should shut him up forever,' cried another Tory.

'Had it not been for the 27th Royal Hussars' prompt action yesterday,' Walsh repeated, 'there is little doubt in my mind that there would have been even greater damage than there was and that even more lives would have been lost.' There were shouts of 'Hear, Hear,' from behind Walsh. 'And I should like it put on record that this House owes a debt of gratitude to Colonel Crosby for his valiant efforts on behalf of the lawful majority of my constituents.'

There were shouts of derision from the Labour benches but the Leader of the Opposition confined himself to a sad shaking of his head.

Unabashed, Walsh went on. 'And it should not be forgotten,' he said, 'that the assistant commissioner in charge of that area of the Metropolitan Police this morning suffered a fatal heart attack, undoubtedly as a result of yesterday's disgraceful incidents.' He paused. 'Incidents that, I'm sorry to say, could have been prevented if the Home Secretary and the Defence Secretary, but above all the Prime Minister, had faced up to the fact that this country is on the brink of revolution and the military must be deployed on a formal and well-organised footing.' From his lofty position, he stared reproachfully at the back of the Prime Minister's head. Sandwiched between the Home Secretary and the Defence Secretary, the diminutive figure of Robert Fairley sat stoically indifferent to his 'friend's' vituperative attack.

Members rose to their feet on all sides, intent on catching the Speaker's eye. But it was the Defence Secretary who was called.

Despite what he believed to be a reasoned argument, Kent was unable to convince the House to pass his prohibiting bill; thirty Tories voted against it because they didn't believe in it, and the Opposition voted against it to embarrass the government. In the event, it was soundly defeated and Kent, with shouts of 'Resign!' ringing in his ears, scurried from the Chamber.

It was a badly shaken group of ministers who met later that evening at Downing Street. The members of the hastily formed Cabinet committee had been unwise enough to call themselves the Civil Defence Committee, which caused *The Times*, in an acerbic leader, to suggest that its first priority ought to be to put the Prime Minister into a deep shelter and forget about him.

'There are rumbles,' said the Home Secretary, Kenneth Sinclair, 'that you should consider resigning, Prime Minister.' Sinclair, an ebullient forty-seven-year-old whose designs on the leadership drove him to seize every available opportunity to discomfit the Prime Minister, was always careful to confine such comments to the Cabinet Room. Although he believed that he had a fair measure of support for his aspirations on the Conservative benches, he was aware that any open or premature show of untoward covetousness could damage forever his chances of reaching the highest office.

'I've no doubt,' said Fairley. He knew that Sinclair regarded himself as the heir apparent and knew also that he had some following in the party, though not as much as Sinclair thought. 'But if I go, you'll go too, Home Secretary. The House seems to regard the present unrest as the fault of your department.' The grating pitch of his voice rose a little, making him sound petulant, like a wronged school-boy.

Sinclair went on the offensive. 'I have suggested several times in the past few days, Prime Minister, that we should use troops. The more often that rioters are seen to get away with it, the greater will be the willingness of others to join in.' He pulled a large handkerchief from his pocket and mopped at his brow with it.

'Dammit, man,' said Fairley, with a rare flash of ill temper, 'Can you not see the danger in that? One of my predecessors put troops into Northern Ireland in 1969. And they were there for years. It's a recipe for disaster. No, Home Secretary, we've got to contain this thing by the use of available police. And that is your job.' He shook his head in feigned desperation. 'I sometimes wonder what goes on at the Home Office. Perhaps you allow your officials too much say. That certainly used to be the case, but I had hoped that I'd appointed a Home Secretary who would take charge of things over there.' Fairley was directing his anger at the military's independent action towards the Home Secretary, the nearest – and most convenient – target for his wrath. 'What about the Special Constabulary?'

The Home Secretary emitted a hollow laugh. 'What Special Constabulary?' he asked. 'There were fifteen thousand of them in England and Wales when this started. Now there are five thousand.'

'Why?' The Prime Minister seemed genuinely surprised at Sinclair's revelation.

'I suspect because the regular police have influenced them,' said Sinclair. 'Not directly, but they've seen the regulars resigning in shoals and they've followed suit. As for the remainder, they're refusing duty.'

'But that's . . . that's . . .'

Sinclair shook his head. 'It's not a mutiny, if that's what you were thinking, Prime Minister. Neither is it a strike. If Specials don't want to report for duty, there's nothing we can do to make them.'

'Can't we pass a bill compelling them? Embody them in the regular force?'

'Like Franco did with strikers in fascist Spain, you mean?' Sinclair regarded his leader with a sardonic smile. 'Anyway, you saw what happened to Graeme Kent's bill this afternoon.' He shot a glance of barely concealed amusement at the Defence Secretary.

'We've fallen between two stools, Prime Minister,' said Kent. 'I do implore you to consider using the military. I don't think anyone now thinks that the police can hold on for much longer. We have soldiers, many of whom served in Northern Ireland, who are more than capable of aiding the civil power. You've got to consider it most urgently.'

'I agree,' said Alexander Crisp, the Chancellor. 'How much longer are we to let things slide? The country's on the verge of anarchy, Prime Minister, and something must be done before it's too late.'

'It seems to me,' said Fairley, 'that everyone here, and indeed beyond this room, is getting things out of proportion. Admittedly there have been a few outbreaks of public disorder.' Sinclair raised his eyebrows at this masterful understatement. 'And on two of those occasions,' the Prime Minister continued, 'soldiers have reacted prematurely. The worst thing that we can be seen to be doing is panic. We must maintain a firm resolve, gentlemen. The police will contain the situation, rest assured.'

The committee regarded him in impotent silence.

The Prime Minister struck silently at the top of the table with the flat of his hand several times. 'I will not deploy troops,' he said.

By the time the meeting of the Civil Defence Committee had finished, the party in the pillared drawing room upstairs in Downing Street had been under way for some forty minutes. It had been scheduled months previously, and the Prime Minister had had no intention of being panicked into cancelling it as a result of the disorder that was now consuming much of the government's time. Not that he would have had much success in trying to do so. The reception had been arranged by his wife as a gesture of support for her favourite charity, and Fairley would have had a fight on his hands if he had tried to prevent it happening.

Now, in a dress cut too low for her husband's liking, Diana Fairley sailed round the huge room clutching a large gin and tonic and engaging the charity's directors and senior officials in animated conversation, laughing infectiously and clearly enjoying herself. It did not escape Gordon Whitmore, the Prime Minister's detective, who had placed himself strategically near the door, that she spent more time talking to the younger, good-looking men, frequently emphasising a point by laying her hand on their arm.

The Prime Minister stayed long enough to circle the room once, chatting lightly to everyone, encouraging the impressionable and abandoning those whose views he could not influence as though it was a political meeting – as to him all functions were – and, despite his problems, giving the impression that he did not have a care in the world.

Diana Fairley caught up with her husband as he was making for the door. 'You're not leaving already, Bob, surely?' she asked.

'Sorry, my dear, but I just don't have the time.'

'Well you should make it,' said Diana sharply. 'These people haven't come here to see me. They've come to see you.'

'I doubt it,' said Fairley. 'They're more interested in being able to tell their friends that they've seen the inside of Number Ten. I'm sorry, but there's a lot on. These damned soldiers are making life very difficult at the moment.'

Several times during the five days that had elapsed since her meeting with Barry Rogers, Imogen had agonised over the situation in which she now found herself. The petty squabbles and cheap remarks that had made her life in the battalion so miserable seemed now almost preferable to life on the CGS's staff.

Elizabeth Macey's warning about her husband's infidelity had been the first disturbing factor, and Imogen had been constantly on her guard against any overtures that Macey might make after his initial attempt in the restaurant near the Strand. In her saner moments, she thought perhaps that she was overreacting and searched for alternative meanings to his casual remarks. But she could not discount Macey's habit of leaning over her, a little too closely, when she was sitting at her desk, often laying a hand on her shoulder. She had tried to avoid the embarrassment this caused her by standing up whenever he came into her office – as military protocol demanded – but he had told her to remain seated 'otherwise you'll be up and down like a jack-in-a-box'.

But that was as nothing compared with the frightening task she had been set by Rogers of the SIS. It still seemed unbelievable that Alec Shepherd, of all people, had taken her to that sinister house – she still had no idea precisely where it was – and that Rogers had subjected her to a diatribe about loyalty. She felt sick at his assumption that spying on her boss would be quite acceptable to her and doubted that she could carry it off without losing her nerve. She knew very little about the SIS – the lecture at Sandhurst from one of its anonymous officers had been uninformative, to say the least – but it was enough for her to realise that if Rogers' plan went wrong, he would certainly deny ever having spoken to her. She suspected too that Shepherd would be prevented from coming to her aid.

And Shepherd was the third dimension to her distress. Feeling particularly low after breaking up with Alistair Buchanan, she had been cheered immensely by her posting to Macey's office and then meeting Shepherd again, but ironically those two factors were now the most depressing elements of her new life.

Then she thought of Macey's arrogance, and his rudeness, and determined that she would do what she could. And if Rogers' assessment of Macey's potential for treachery were true, she knew that she had no alternative.

Two men were seated at the far end of the long drawing room on the first floor of Brooks's Club in St James's Street. One of them wore an Old Etonian tie, the other that of the Royal Tank Regiment, although each was entitled to wear either. They had been at school together and had trained at Sandhurst at the same time. One was the Chief of the General Staff, the other the Chancellor of the Exchequer. But Alexander Crisp had decided that the army was not for him and, three years after passing out of the Royal Military Academy, had resigned his commission to make a career in politics.

'Your chaps have certainly stirred things up a bit, Simon,' said Crisp.

'Only doing what's required of them.' Macey was relaxed, leaning back in his chair with his legs crossed.

'The Prime Minister's absolutely furious. But he still refuses to deploy the military on a formal footing.'

'But surely to God he can see that the police can't cope with the situation. And it's going to get worse.' Macey reached across to take his whisky from the table.

'I agree, but none of us can make him understand the seriousness of what's happening. Kenneth Sinclair knows very well that the police are up against it, and so, I think, does Graeme Kent. Unfortunately the rest of the Cabinet, apart from me, seem unable to grasp just how bad it is. Actually, they probably do, they're just frightened for their own skins.'

'Kent certainly doesn't give the impression of being in favour of using troops,' said Macey.

'He can't, Simon. It's called collective Cabinet responsibility, but believe me, Kent's all for using the army now he's lost his silly little bill. But he wants to be the one to make the decision, not you. Mind you, I think he sees a bit of glory in it, being S of S for Defence. Let's be honest, there's not a lot been happening on your front recently. No wars to fight, eh? The only hope is that we'll eventually make Bob Fairley see sense.'

'What's really brought things to a head, of course, Alex, is your damned department and the ECU.'

'Not my idea,' said Crisp. 'It was agreed in principle years ago. In all honesty, I must say that Fairley had little option but to implement it. This European Union is like a bloody straitjacket. We're either in or out. And to leave would be economic suicide.'

'But can't he reverse the process? Doesn't the EU know what's happening? Surely if a case was put to them that the imposition of this currency was causing serious and widespread public disorder they'd allow us to go back to sterling? I'm no financial expert, but serious riots are bound to affect our economy sooner or later. And in turn, I suppose, the economy of the EU itself.'

'It's not that easy, Simon. It's a question of the Exchange Rate Mechanism, you see.' Crisp lowered his voice even though the only other occupants of the huge room were at the far end. 'But what worries me more is that I believe the French and the Germans are quite happy for us to tear ourselves apart economically – the so-called Franco-German alliance is an open secret in the EU – and when we're finished, they can pick up the pieces. After all, they've no chance of beating us in war. They've tried that before.'

'But why did we go back into the ERM? Frankly, I'd've thought we'd learned our lesson from the last débâcle.'

Crisp smiled the sort of smile that politicians reserve for those outside their esoteric sphere, the sort of smile that implies that no one else could possibly understand the intricacies of world affairs. 'But it's not only the ERM. Or the ECU. It's the crime rate as well. It's going up and up.'

'That's easy to deal with,' said Macey. 'All that's needed is a bit of firm resolve on the part of the government. Lock some of these buggers up for a few years and make them work their balls off instead of lounging about watching television or working out in well-equipped gyms.' He teased his moustache and then played an impatient little tattoo with his left hand on the arm of the chair.

'Maybe.' Crisp looked doubtful and lit a cigarette. 'What d'you think is likely to happen on your front, Simon?' He looked sideways at the CGS and raised an eyebrow.

'If civil disorder continues, officers commanding troops will continue to intervene whenever they consider it their duty to do so.'

'I should be careful if I were you, Simon,' said Crisp. 'I wouldn't like to see you removed from your post.'

'Wouldn't make much difference. I've told the PM, and

I've told the Defence Secretary, that I am not in a position to give orders to officers to ignore the law. And any successor they cared to appoint would tell them the same. Kent knows it, and so does Fairley. They've both acknowledged the legality of the actions of Stokes and Crosby by trying to get a prohibiting bill through the House. And they failed, as you well know.' Macey finished his whisky. 'Fairley's going to have to use the military sooner or later, and the longer he leaves it, the greater the problem's going to become. But I can't allow troops to intervene without proper support. Adequate reinforcements must be available, and if the PM doesn't sanction it, I'll have to do so myself.'

Crisp nodded. 'Well, Simon,' he said, 'you know that you can count on me to keep you informed, but I foresee grave consequences arising out of the present situation, and I just hope that you're not the one who's in the firing line when it happens. Just be careful, that's all.'

'What do you think is likely to happen, Alex?' asked Macey. 'Off the record, I mean.'

'There are rumblings on the back benches, Simon, and particularly among members of the 1922 Committee. There's an increasing wave of dissatisfaction with Fairley's leadership. Trouble is, he's got us over a barrel, in a sense.'

'How so?'

'If we make a move to change leaders now, it will be seen as a sign of disunity in the party. And there's no guarantee of success, either. Fairley's a stubborn man, and he's hinted that if we try to get rid of him he'll go to the country. His argument is that he was asked by the Queen to form a government and rather than yield to party pressure, he'll seek a dissolution. If that happens, we'll lose the election. And badly.'

'Who's the heir apparent?' Macey asked the question softly. 'Sinclair?'

'I think not,' said Crisp. 'Not one of the party's darlings, even though he thinks he has great support. They applaud him to his face, just in case by some quirk he ever became leader, but behind his back they regard him as a fool. And a liability.'

'You then?'

Crisp smiled bleakly. 'Shall we go in to lunch?' he said.

CHAPTER SEVEN

'Anything happening, Alec?' Barry Rogers strolled into Shepherd's office, kicked the door shut and dropped into a chair.

'Yes, as a matter of fact,' said Shepherd. 'Just had a call from GCHQ.'

'Oh?' Rogers pulled out his pipe and filled it. 'What did they want?'

'Surprisingly, they wanted to give us something.'

'Good God!' said Rogers, who had long been convinced that every other intelligence organisation in the country, including Government Communications Headquarters, was working against the interests of his own service.

'It seems that the Chief of the General Staff has sent out a signal ...' Shepherd picked up a sheet of paper and handed it to his director. 'Top Secret and enciphered, you'll notice.'

Rogers read through the clear copy of the signal and handed it back to Shepherd. 'What's he up to now?'

'Looks as though he's determined to put the military on the alert, doesn't it?'

Rogers spent a minute lighting his pipe. 'How long has GCHQ been monitoring MOD signals then, Alec?' he asked.

'I thought they were supposed to be on our side.'

'They haven't,' said Shepherd, grinning. 'The French have. Apparently the signal went to all units, and that included the ones in Germany. It was the *Groupement de Contrôle Radio-Électrique* that picked it up. And they copied it to the French Embassy in London. That's when GCHQ picked it up. Coming back in, so to speak.'

'Well,' said Rogers cynically, 'isn't that just amazing?' He stood up and walked towards the door, pausing when he got there. 'Why don't you contact Major Cresswell, Alec? See if she's prepared to tell you about it.'

'But what can she tell us that we don't already know, Barry?'

'Probably nothing, but you will learn whether the lovely Imogen's really prepared to help us. If she tells you about that signal, we'll know that she is.'

Shepherd grinned. 'And shall I give our man Salmon a ring at Five as well? See if that lot have heard about it?'

'Why not?'

The next morning, Alec Shepherd made a point of meeting Imogen as she left the RAC to go to the Ministry of Defence. A few days ago, she would have believed it to be a chance encounter; now she knew that SIS officers left nothing to chance.

'Well, fancy seeing you, Alec,' she said sarcastically but did not lessen her stride. 'Bit risky, contacting your spies in the open air, isn't it?'

'I only wanted to invite you to dinner,' said Shepherd, a hurt note in his voice. 'How about coming to my flat this evening? It's not far from here, in Palace Street.' He gave her the exact address.

'And what will that do for my reputation, if I'm seen visiting a gentleman's flat?' Imogen suddenly relented and flashed him a smile. 'All right,' she said. 'What time?'

*

'Gin and tonic?'

'Please. This is nice, Alec.' Imogen cast an appraising glance around Shepherd's third-floor flat and was impressed by what she saw.

'I suppose you expected me to live in the sort of sparse accommodation the army used to provide.' Shepherd grinned and handed her drink to her.

'Yes, I suppose so.'

'Well I'm not a soldier any more, and now I'm into luxury.'

'Why did you give up the army? I thought you had a glittering career ahead of you.'

'Had a better offer,' said Shepherd. 'Excuse me, must check in the kitchen.'

Imogen followed him and stood in the doorway, sipping her drink and watching him as he busied himself with sauces and saucepans. 'And is it better?'

'It'll do,' said Shepherd, unwilling to divulge any more than he had to of his job with the SIS. 'Incidentally, I hope you weren't too upset by my little escapade the other evening.'

'Frankly, Alec, I was bloody furious,' said Imogen. 'I am a soldier and I understand that you have a duty to perform, but you could have done me the courtesy of warning me what you proposed to do. You didn't have to drag me up to North London, either. All that could have been said over a drink.' She paused. 'And I didn't like your Barry one little bit.'

Shepherd looked shocked at her outburst and glanced at her nervously. 'His bark's worse than his bite,' he said lamely.

'Maybe. But you work for him. I don't.'

'I'm sorry, Imogen, really I am, but I was in a cleft stick. And as you say, he is my boss.'

'Alec . . .' Imogen spoke tentatively.

Shepherd stopped what he was doing and looked up. 'What is it?'

'Do you believe what he was saying, about General Macey plotting to overthrow the government? It all seems so far-fetched to me. After all, this is England.'

Shepherd laughed. 'Just because this is England,' he said, 'doesn't necessarily rule out the possibility of people having aspirations of that sort. Yes, I think it's a possibility.'

Imogen was silent for some moments. 'Alec, I, er ...' Again she hesitated, but Shepherd knew better than to rush her. 'I sent out a signal the other day. Macey ordered all formation commanders to advise their regimental and battalion COs that they had a duty at common law to intercede in riots and that they didn't have to wait for authority from the civil power to do so.'

'I know.' Shepherd was pleased that, despite her apparent reluctance, Imogen had decided to adopt the role of informant.

'How did you know?' Imogen sounded surprised, shocked even. The signal had been Top Secret, and she had enciphered it personally.

Shepherd grinned at the girl. 'Don't ever ask an SIS officer about his sources of information,' he said gently. 'A refusal often offends.'

They sat down to eat, and Imogen was impressed by the quality of the meal that Shepherd had prepared. 'You should have been in the Catering Corps,' she said.

'I'll treat that remark with the contempt it deserves,' said Shepherd and poured more wine into Imogen's glass.

'Alec, why is the SIS so interested in Macey?'

Shepherd looked serious. 'I'm sorry to sound so secretive,' he said, 'but I'm not at liberty to tell you. The feeling is that it might put you in an embarrassing position.'

'I'm not likely to let it slip in casual conversation with Macey,' said Imogen sharply.

'It's not that,' said Shepherd. 'I'm under strict orders as to what I can and can't tell you. It's not that I don't trust you.'

When dinner was over, they sat in armchairs and Shepherd poured brandy.

'What do you want me to do, Alec?' asked Imogen. Ever since her meeting with Barry at the safe house in North London, she had been mulling over what had been said. Her loyalty was to Macey, but this suggestion that there was something sinister in his background worried her. If he turned out to be a traitor, she would not have the slightest compunction in informing on him; that was her duty as an officer.

'Keep in touch with me and let me know what's going on. And don't ring me from the office. I know that sounds a little melodramatic, but I don't want you to put yourself in the position of having to explain a phone call if he catches you at it.' Shepherd leaned forward, an earnest expression on his face. 'Don't imagine that you're doing anything wrong, Imogen, will you? This is more serious than you know. There's a lot happening that I can't tell you about, but it's vital that we keep a careful watch on General Macey.'

Imogen opened her handbag. 'You'd better have these then,' she said and handed over a sheaf of photocopies.

Alec reached out and took the papers. 'What are they?'

'They're minutes of Macey's meeting with the Director of Army Legal Services. He told me not to make any copies, but it was that meeting that prompted the sending of the signal that you've seen.'

Shepherd unfolded the few sheets of paper, and his eyes flicked over the 'Secret' stamp at the top of the first page before he looked up to stare at Imogen. 'But this meeting was on the day before I took you to see Barry,' he said.

Imogen shrugged. 'So?'

'Well I'm damned,' said Shepherd and laughed.

*

The Commissioner of the Metropolitan Police acknowledged the salutes of the constables on duty at the main
entrance to New Scotland Yard and strode through St
James's Park Underground Station towards the Home
Office in Queen Anne's Gate. He was not looking forward
to his interview with the Home Secretary.

He made his way first to the office of Her Majesty's Chief
Inspector of Constabulary, an elderly former chief constable called Joe Wiggins. Different parts of the Home Office
building were colour coded and, not for the first time, Cork
reflected on the irony of the Police Department being
situated on a floor designated 'the grey area'.

'Morning, Joe.'

'Morning, Len.' Wiggins stood up and shook hands. The
animosity that had existed between these two – a result of
Cork getting the top job at the Yard when Wiggins thought
he was in line for it – had slowly ebbed over the past four
and a half years and had been replaced by a wary respect
for each other's abilities. And Wiggins had got his knight-
hood, which was all that had really concerned him or,
more particularly, his wife.

Wiggins glanced at the clock. 'Better go and see if
Sinclair has finished his conference, I suppose,' he said.

The two senior policemen made their way to the Home
Secretary's suite of offices and sat in the waiting room. As
usual, Sinclair was running late and it was some fifteen
minutes before Cork and Wiggins were ushered into his
presence.

'You will have heard about the setback that the government suffered, I imagine,' Sinclair began without preamble. It was unusual for the Home Secretary, superficially
a courteous man when dealing with officials, not to make
polite conversation and to offer his visitors coffee before
getting down to business. But in recent weeks he had been
attacked, over and again, in Parliament and in Cabinet,
and, in common with many politicians, was thrashing

about for someone to blame. With the present unrest, it was not difficult for him to lay the responsibility for his dilemma on the police. And now he had the two most senior policemen in the country sitting in his office.

'I suppose that it was fairly predictable in the circumstances,' said Cork unwisely.

'What was?' Sinclair snapped out his response.

'That the House would not want the military deprived of powers that allow them to intervene in public order situations, Home Secretary.' Cork had six months to run on his contract before he retired, and he did not much care any more what he said to his political boss. His only concern was that he should not be obliged to resign on a question of public order as one of his predecessors, Sir Edmund Henderson, had done last century when police reinforcements were mistakenly sent to The Mall instead of Pall Mall, where a mob was destroying gentlemen's clubs. He took comfort in the fact that resignation seemed out of fashion these days and could recall a number of senior police officers whose vicarious responsibility for the incompetence of their subordinates ought to have brought about their resignations. And as for Cabinet ministers, well Cork could think of at least four who had clung ignominiously to office in the face of storms that would have forced more honourable men out of public life, particularly Home Secretaries.

'There would be no need of military intervention if the police were containing the situation,' said Sinclair, 'as is their duty.' He glared at Cork, then at Wiggins and then back at Cork. 'And for which, I would remind you, gentlemen, they are handsomely paid.'

'They're not getting the support, Home Secretary,' said Wiggins mildly. 'You may have noticed that fewer and fewer cases are going to court, and that is because arrests are down. And of those cases that are getting to court, an unacceptable number are being thrown out.'

'Why?' Again Sinclair angrily surveyed the two police-men.

'Any number of reasons,' said Wiggins. 'Firstly, the Police and Criminal Evidence Act is a lawyer's delight. The first thing any defence counsel will do these days is pick holes in what happened at the police station. And if one comma's out of place, the job gets slung out. Then there's the Crown Prosecution Service, a bunch of incompetent lawyers who actually sit in judgement on the cases that police present to them. You've virtually replaced the judicial system with the CPS. They're the ones who decide guilt or innocence, long before the case goes in front of a magistrate.' Wiggins leaned forward, warming to his subject. 'The second-rate lawyers of this country must have offered up a prayer of thanksgiving when the CPS was formed.'

'We have to live with the system, Sir Joseph,' said Sinclair, 'like it or not.'

'We don't like it,' said Wiggins tersely, 'but the govern-ment can change it.'

Sinclair turned to the Commissioner. 'Is that your view too, Sir Lionel?'

'Yes,' said Cork. Now that Wiggins had made a stand, he saw no harm in agreeing with him. It was how he felt after all. 'The police are fighting crime with one hand tied behind their back,' he said.

'Yes, well, be that as it may,' said Sinclair dismissively, 'it doesn't answer the pressing questions of why public order has broken down or how it can be restored.'

'Oh, but it does, Home Secretary,' said Cork. 'Police officers are heartily sick of being assaulted – often seriously injured – only to see the courts impose risible sentences on their attackers. They've had enough. And there's another thing. The police, because they're sorely pressed, are being obliged to go in hard. And that, I'm afraid, alienates the older and law-abiding members of the population, to say nothing of innocent bystanders. They don't see the need for such force – don't understand it – and the result is that the police lose their sympathy. And their support. My personnel department now sends me a daily print-out of resignations from the force.' He glanced at his watch. 'As of eight o'clock this morning the total of officers who have submitted their resignations in the past twenty-four hours is three hundred, give or take a dozen.' The Home Secretary held up a hand, but Cork went on. 'There is, however, much more disquieting news than that.'

'Really?' Sinclair responded listlessly. He found it difficult to imagine that there could be worse to come.

'It has been confirmed to me, quite recently, that the Police Federation is actively soliciting all Metropolitan officers below the rank of superintendent to complete resignation forms and to lodge them with their Federation representatives.'

'What's the point of that, Sir Lionel?' The significance of what Cork had said seemed genuinely to have escaped the Home Secretary.

'The point of it, Home Secretary, is that when the federation thinks that the time is right, they will submit those resignations en masse. One month from the date that they do so, the Metropolitan Police will cease to exist.' He smiled at the Home Secretary's shocked expression. 'Save for about five hundred senior officers.' He paused. 'At which point they'll probably decide to retire.'

'Good God!' The implications of what the Commissioner was saying were so horrific that Sinclair could only wonder how the hell he was going to explain them away to the Prime Minister. He coughed. 'Is there nothing that can be done?'

'I understand that similar approaches are being made to officers in the provinces,' said Wiggins, happily turning the screw.

'But that's tantamount to a strike. A mutiny. It's illegal.

The police can't strike,' the Home Secretary gabbled. 'Something will have to be done.'

'What do you suggest, Home Secretary?' asked Wiggins and deliberately lit one of the small cheroots that he knew the fanatically antismoking minister detested. 'It certainly wouldn't be a strike. I defy even the Attorney-General to find that any offences have been committed.' Wiggins was enjoying the alarm with which the Home Secretary had been seized.

'Conspiracy!' Sinclair spat the word.

'Before the Crown Prosecution Service was born,' said Cork quietly, 'I'd certainly have given conspiracy a run. But the DPP wouldn't consider it now, even if I were so foolhardy as to ask him.'

Sinclair swung out of his chair and turned to the window, his hands stuffed into his trouser pockets. He stood like that for a minute or so before turning to face the two senior officers again. 'I have tried to persuade the Prime Minister that we need to deploy the military,' he said. 'But he won't budge.'

'I hate to say this,' said Wiggins dishonestly, 'but the ball is in your court. Len Cork and I have done all we can. It's up to the government now.'

Robert Fairley sat down behind his desk in the study on the west side of 10 Downing Street, pressed his fingertips together and regarded the Home Secretary with a pensive expression. 'I think you're allowing these policemen to get to you, Kenneth,' he said.

'I am merely relaying to you what they said, Prime Minister.' Sinclair was clearly on edge, and the politician in him had already told him that if the mass resignation of the police came to pass, his own career would be in ignominious ruins, ruins which even an unfashionable ministerial resignation would fail to revive.

'It's bluff,' said Fairley. 'You don't honestly think that,

what is it, a hundred thousand or so police officers will submit their resignations on a matter of principle?' He scoffed at the prospect. 'If they do, it'll be the first time they've ever made such a stand.'

'There was a police strike just after the First World War, Prime Minister.' Shortly after taking office, Sinclair had been shown a photograph, taken in 1919, of Downing Street packed with police strikers. Most of them had been wearing boaters, as though it were a day at the seaside. The Home Secretary had smiled at the time, but now the prospect did not seem so funny.

'I'm not surprised,' said Fairley affably. 'Their pay and conditions then were appalling. But now . . .' He spread his hands upwards. 'They are very well paid indeed. No, Kenneth, they're not going to throw all that up just because one or two of them get hurt once in a while.'

Indignantly, Sinclair slung a sheet of paper on the Prime Minister's desk. 'Those are the figures for the Metropolitan Police alone for last year,' he said angrily. 'Fourteen thousand, as near as dammit, injured on duty. That's half the force. And of those, five thousand were assaulted. That's what they're complaining about.'

'Figures,' said Fairley, pushing the sheet of paper aside without reading it. 'You know what Churchill said about statistics, don't you, Kenneth?'

'Yes, I do,' said Sinclair vehemently, 'and I also know that he didn't hesitate to use troops when the necessity arose.'

'Tonypandy is a name that I would rather see expunged from the history books,' said Fairley. 'The place, not the former Speaker,' he added with a wry grin.

Sinclair did not smile at the Prime Minister's joke. 'I wasn't thinking of Tonypandy,' he said. 'I had the siege of Sidney Street more in mind.'

'Different thing altogether.' The Prime Minister flicked absently at a biscuit crumb left over from his mid-morning coffee break and sent it scudding across the polished surface. 'Communists! The government then was dealing with an incident that almost amounted to an armed insurrection.'

'And aren't we now?' The Home Secretary felt like screaming in the face of the Prime Minister's lethargic reaction.

'Kenneth, I've been in politics a lot longer than you have.' Fairley leaned forward, linking his hands loosely on the desk top, and regarded the Home Secretary with an avuncular expression. 'And you have to learn to keep your nerve. What's happening at the moment is a series of outbreaks of public disorder. Nothing that can't be contained, given time. The worst thing that we could possibly do is panic and put in troops. I do not intend to suppress the honest working folk of this great country by the use of military force.'

'But for God's sake, Prime Minister, can you not see just how serious it is? There are people being lynched, and almost every day mobs are literally running riot in the streets. Next month we could be without a police force. When will you come to your senses, man?'

The Prime Minister looked reproachfully at the Home Secretary. 'I don't think that personal abuse will help either of us, Kenneth,' he said, 'and I repeat that I am not going to make the mistake of putting in troops.'

'I think you're making one right now, Prime Minister, in not facing up to what is happening,' said Sinclair, rising to his feet.

Robert Fairley smiled benignly. 'As Harold Wilson said, Kenneth, "If you can't stand the heat, get out of the kitchen."'

'It was Harry Truman who said it first,' said Sinclair, scoring an empty point.

'I take it you don't wish to resign then,' said Fairley with a chuckle.

*

Colonel Tim Crosby leaped on to the armoured car and surveyed his regiment. 'Gather round, lads,' he shouted. Since the Kingston riot he had become much more animated, appearing at last to have shrugged off the death of his wife. But the pain of knowing that her killer was still at liberty was something that he could not forget. And for that he blamed the pusillanimous attitude of the government towards law and order. His fellow officers had learned not to mention crime, for they knew that it would cause Crosby to launch into an angry diatribe on the subject.

The seven hundred officers and men standing in serried ranks on the parade ground looked uncertainly about them before moving forward to surround the vehicle upon which their CO was standing.

'First of all, chaps, I want to congratulate you on the first-class job you did in Kingston. Those of you who read a decent newspaper instead of drooling over some half-naked filly on page three' – a roar of laughter greeted that remark – 'will have seen that the MP for Kingston and Surbiton was fulsome in his praise in the House. Do not, however, be deluded by the rainbow behind me ...' It was a warm, sunny day and the recent downpour of rain had left the barracks with a clean, fresh smell about them. 'It's not all beer and skittles, and this morning, I'm sorry to have to tell you, we are to be punished for interfering.' A sudden hush descended on the parade ground. 'I have received orders from the Ministry of Defence that on the last day of next month the 27th Royal Hussars will be disbanded. The regiment, gentlemen, will cease to exist. They claim that it's part of the latest round of Options for Change.' And if you believe that, he thought to himself, you'll believe anything.

There was a howl of protest that even the stentorian voice of the regimental sergeant-major failed to still, and the air became blue with oaths. The phrase 'to swear like a trooper' seemed especially apposite this morning.

'I'm sorry, gentlemen,' Crosby went on, 'more sorry than you will ever know, but those are our orders. I know that I can rely upon you to see the regiment's end in an orderly and soldier-like fashion. Some of you, I regret to say, will be discharged "services no longer required", but the remainder will be found places in other regiments.' It was a particularly bitter blow for Crosby. Both his father and his grandfather had commanded the regiment, the latter having been killed doing so in the Western Desert at the battle of Mersa Matruh. Crosby looked down sadly at his men but decided that he could say no more without the risk of breaking down. 'Fall out the officers,' he said. 'Conference, officers' mess, now.' And then, glancing across at the moustached, ramrod figure of the RSM, he said, 'Carry on, sarn't-major.' Jumping down from the armoured car, he strode swiftly across the parade ground towards the mess as the regiment was brought crashing to attention behind him.

Crosby looked around at his officers. 'Sit down, gentlemen,' he said. 'Everyone got a drink?' He took a sip of his own Scotch and soda and perched on the edge of a table. 'This is a bad business, chaps,' he began. 'But it seems to be what you get for doing your duty.'

'Is there nothing that can be done, Colonel?' asked a senior major.

'I don't know, John,' said Crosby, 'but I'm going to have a damned good try. The Adjutant-General is a former Two-Seven and I've arranged to see him tomorrow. I shall plead the regiment's case, but I've a feeling it's a lost cause. And it's my fault, I'm afraid. I got us involved in politics.'

'Do you really think that that shindig at Kingston was the reason behind the disbandment order, Colonel?' asked a young cornet. The 27th Royal Hussars was an old regiment and believed in maintaining its traditions and customs, and whereas most other cavalry regiments now referred to their junior subalterns as second-lieutenants, the 27th retained the older title of cornet.

'Sure of it,' said Crosby. 'I remember reading something about General Redvers Buller when I was at the Staff College ...' He grinned at a captain who had raised an eyebrow. 'He was a general in the Boer War, Rollo, in case you missed that lecture.' There was a ripple of laughter. 'And he said something to the effect that soldiers called in aid of the civil power are always in an invidious position because whatever they do is wrong.' He took out a gunmetal case, carefully selected a cigarette and lit it. 'And if they do nothing, that's wrong as well,' he added, blowing a plume of smoke in the air.

Later on one of the cornets caught sight of his colonel standing in the foyer of the officers' mess, reading the scroll of battle honours engraved on a pewter shield that had accompanied the regiment in every theatre of its operations. It was a proud list, the names rolling off it like pages from a history book. Colonel Crosby spoke them silently as his eye scanned them: Albuhera, Badajoz, Inkerman, Ladysmith, Mons, Somme, Mersa Matruh, Salerno and Korea. And many, many more.

The building occupied by the Naval and Military Club has stood in London's Piccadilly for almost two hundred and fifty years. Originally the home of Lord Egremont, then the Duke of Cambridge and, latterly, Lord Palmerston, it is known to its members – and to countless taxi drivers – as the 'In and Out' from the signs painted on its gateposts.

It was probably the meeting of two men in this club that hastened the events of the following month. And that because one of the two chose to misinterpret what the other said.

General Sir Lawrence Dane was a tall, spare man with iron-grey hair and a guardee moustache. As a callow youth of nineteen, he had watched the adjutant at

Sandhurst riding his horse up the steps of the academy at the conclusion of the Sovereign's Parade and had then gone to London with the other newly commissioned officers of his class and got uproariously drunk. A fortnight later he had joined the 27th Royal Hussars and, for most of the next thirty-five years, had soldiered everywhere that the British Army had served. Now, six months from retirement, he was Adjutant-General, and Colonel of his old regiment.

The entrance hall of the club was gloomy after the unusually bright April sunlight outside. Dane nodded to the hall porter and strode through to the bar.

Lieutenant-Colonel Tim Crosby stood up as Dane entered and pushed out a hand. 'General Larry,' he said warmly, using the army's accepted familiar form of address. 'Good to see you again, sir. And thanks for agreeing to come.'

Dane seized the younger man's hand and appraised him, thinking how much like his late father he had grown. Dane had shared a few adventures – and a few disappointments – over the years with Crosby's father and, as single officers, they'd shared a few girls too. 'Always willing to take lunch off another Two-Seven, Tim,' he said. 'How's your mother keeping these days?'

'Fine, sir, thanks.'

'Good. And you?'

'Could be better, sir,' said Crosby, 'but my health's all right if that's what you mean.' He grinned at the general. 'Get you a drink, sir?'

The two soldiers found a table in the corner of the bar and sipped their whisky.

'Bad business, Tim,' said Dane.

'Bloody awful, General. I keep trying to tell myself that it was nothing to do with that skirmish at Kingston, but ...'

'The official line is that the disbandment of the regiment

is another round of Options for Change, Part Two, or Part Two Hundred and Two, whatever it is, but the Twenty-Seventh wasn't on the original list. Deep down I know bloody well that it's a case of the Defence Secretary being spiteful. Perhaps even the Prime Minister. Simon Macey, the CGS, has had a run-in with him over the intervention of the military, not that it got him very far.' Dane sighed. 'It's not that the army's glory seeking – heaven forbid – but we're all genuinely worried about what's happening.'

Crosby nodded. 'It seems eminently sensible that the army should be used, sir,' he said. 'Not that we want the job: aid to the civil power is not the best thing a soldier can do. In fact it's a bloody awful thing to get involved in, as those of us who served in Northern Ireland know, eh?'

'I'm afraid that the Prime Minister doesn't seem to think that the situation is serious enough yet to deploy the military, Tim,' said Dane as he and Crosby walked through to the dining room.

'The Prime Minister should have been at Kingston,' said Crosby. 'Those poor bastards of coppers were just about all in when we arrived. God knows what would have happened if their chief hadn't called us in. And the poor devil died the next morning. Not that it was any wonder, mind you.' He picked up the wine list and ran his eye down it. 'But a fat lot of good it did us,' he said, looking up at Dane once more. 'The thing that really worries me,' he went on, 'is that the government seems powerless to act. Or unwilling to do so. I can't understand it. It's patently obvious to anyone with half a brain that the police can't contain the situation. It's Ulster all over again. Or Aden, or Cyprus, or a host of other places any soldier can think of.'

Dane lowered his voice. 'I can tell you this, in confidence, Tim, that there are a number of very senior officers at the MOD who are greatly concerned. I know about the CGS's signal, but if battalion and regimental commanders continue to exercise their powers under common law to intervene in public disorder situations, sooner or later they're going to come to grief. They could be overrun or get pushed into a corner – literally – and have to fight their way out. You know as well as I do that young soldiers have to be supervised carefully, but if it gets to a point where they're up against it, I dread to think what might happen.'

'We were fortunate at Kingston,' said Crosby. 'The mob just didn't expect armoured cars, and when we started chasing them, they dispersed and made for the hills. Next time it might not be so easy, especially if infantry are involved.'

Dane nodded. 'I don't have to tell an experienced graduate of the Staff College,' he said, 'that in any military action there has to be a capability for calling up reinforcements. I have to say, and it might sound melodramatic, that there could come a time when a trap is set for the army by one of these mobs, and without recourse to additional troops some of our chaps could be killed. And that would be the spark. Can you imagine the reaction of some of the mere boys that we've got in the ranks to a situation like that?' He paused reflectively. 'And I'm not sure that young troop commanders would be able to hold them in check.' He shook his head. 'Something'll have to happen, and soon.'

Crosby signalled to the wine waiter and ordered a bottle of the house claret. 'But what, General, given that the Prime Minister has set his face against the use of military force?' he asked, facing Dane once more. 'Without exaggerating the position, it seems to me that the country is very close to anarchy.'

'Something may happen in the near future, Tim. The joint chiefs of staff have seen the PM once and, I understand, are intending to do so again. See if they can't persuade the stubborn fool. My advice to you is just to wait and see.'

'Don't have a great deal of time for that, General,' said

Crosby. 'Not with the regiment on the verge of being disbanded.' He sighed and took a sip of wine.

'How are they taking it, Tim? The regiment, I mean.'

'Badly, sir, which is what you'd expect. They want to know what can be done, if anything.' Crosby shrugged. 'I've told them that there's little hope, but they're very angry.' He leaned forward slightly. 'To be perfectly frank, General, I'm going to have a job holding them. I know all about discipline, but take the regiment away and you take away esprit de corps and you take away loyalty. It's going to be a difficult few weeks. And I'm not sure what will happen when the dismissals come through.'

'That will be done as soon as possible,' said Dane, whose branch at the Army Department of the Ministry of Defence was responsible for manpower. 'Some will have to go, obviously, but others will be remustered to other regiments.'

'I don't know which will be worse, General,' said Crosby. 'And I'm not sure that my chaps will either.'

'Something may yet happen, Tim,' said Dane mysteriously. 'I don't wish to bolster your hopes, but this thing is far from over. And when that time comes, your support and your loyalty will be paramount.'

Colonel Crosby wandered around his regiment's barracks at Woking, acknowledging salutes from time to time and occasionally stopping to talk to the men under his command. But every time he did so, the question was always the same. Officers, warrant officers, NCOs and men all wanted to know if there was a chance of saving the 27th Royal Hussars. It both saddened and angered Crosby that nothing in his conversation with General Dane had given him any hope that there might be a last-minute reprieve. All except the general's final, and enigmatic, comment, when he had said, 'This thing is far from over.' But it was not a remark that he could, in all conscience, pass on to the troops. Personally, Crosby had little hope of anything happening. It was, he had decided, just Dane's way of trying to improve morale. His own as well as Crosby's and that of the regiment.

Diana Fairley was seated in the centre of the settee. On one side of her was a thesaurus, on the other a dictionary, and on her knee *The Times* crossword.

'What are you doing?' asked Fairley as he entered the room.

'What I always do on a Saturday,' said Diana. '*The Times* crossword.'

Fairley glanced at the two books. 'That's cheating,' he said.

'Do you think the compilers don't use a dictionary and a thesaurus?' said Diana. 'Anyway, there's money involved.'

'You don't submit it, do you?' Fairley turned from the drinks table with a faintly bemused expression on his face.

'On the rare occasions I manage to finish it, yes.'

'But you're the wife of the Prime Minister. You can't go in for competitions.'

'You do,' said Diana drily. 'They're called general elections.' She put the newspaper aside and dropped the pen into her handbag. 'And I should think you'll be holding one quite soon.'

'Why do you say that?' Unbidden, Fairley handed his wife a gin and tonic.

Diana took a sip of her drink and crossed to the drinks table to add more gin. 'You drowned it,' she said, and sat down again.

'You still haven't answered the question, Diana.'

'If you're insistent that you won't give up office without a general election, then that's what you'll be doing very soon, my love. It's no good going around pretending that nothing's happening. The country's in the grip of anarchy, and you can't cope with it.'

'There have been one or two—'

'I'm not in the Cabinet, my love,' said Diana sharply, 'and I'm not in the House of Commons. I'm your wife, and you can't fool me. Sinclair's after your job, and that little toad Graeme Kent at the MOD is waiting in the wings too.' Fairley scoffed. 'Oh, you can dismiss it,' Diana went on, 'but right now you're playing into their hands. Sinclair's a cunning devil. He's telling everyone that you won't use troops but that he would if he was Prime Minister. Don't let him get away with it. Act firmly, now. Bring in the army, and the navy and the air force as well if you need to, and sort this thing out. Because if you don't we'll be packing our bags and moving out. Not that I'm particularly worried about that. As you know, I can't stand either Number Ten or Chequers.'

'I've got to do what I believe in,' said Fairley.

'Balls!' Diana dismissed his statement. 'I don't know what's happened to you, my love. You're not the man you were a few years ago. Where's the fire, the ambition, the commitment?'

'It becomes increasingly difficult when you're Prime Minister—'

'Jesus, Bob, will you stop addressing me as though I'm the party conference. Save your pompous rhetoric for the blue-rinse dowagers who have an orgasm every time you stand up to speak. Start thinking about the country again and talk to the people the way you used to, like you were the man in charge. You had fire in your belly in those days. I've seen you captivate a street-corner audience in a Labour stronghold and leave them speechless, and then we'd go back to the hotel and you'd still find time to screw me before we went down to dinner. What the hell's happened to you? Have you no guts any more, no pride?'

'It's not as easy as you think—' began Fairley lamely.

But Diana was in full flow. 'There you go again, making excuses, Bob. Can't you see the dangers, not only from what's happening in the country but from those weasels who want your job?' She crossed the room and poured herself another hefty gin and tonic. 'This is what gives me my satisfaction now,' she said, holding up the glass, 'and I hope you're proud of yourself.'

But when she turned from the drinks table, Fairley had gone, cowed by the tirade he knew he thoroughly deserved.

CHAPTER EIGHT

Sir Lionel Cork, the Commissioner of the Metropolitan Police, was a very unhappy man. He sat in his office mulling over the statistics that lay on his desk in the form of computer print-outs. He moved the sheets of paper about, but whichever way he studied them, they did not produce good news. He examined the daily return of resignations – the spectre always hanging over him of mass resignation if the Police Federation kept its promise – and noted that some of the more senior officers, inspectors and superintendents, were leaving too. The worry was that these officers were going before they had qualified for a pension, a situation not helped by the new system of allowing pensions to be transferred. And recruitment had slumped to an all-time low, thanks to the introduction of short-service engagements. Apart from the fear of attack – the alarming daily return of officers assaulted on duty was also on his desk – young men and women were not prepared to sign on for ten years and face the possibility that in their late twenties or early thirties they would be looking for a new career.

Cork slung the print-outs into his out-tray and thumbed through the report of the riot at Kingston, which had been prepared by the acting assistant commissioner, following the death of the officer in post. The stilted prose made unedifying reading: a report of a division of police completely overwhelmed by a savage mob who had virtually destroyed the centre of a busy town, together with lists of officers injured, some seriously, and a final condemnatory paragraph laying the blame for what had happened firmly upon the Commissioner. Cork re-read what the acting AC had written with mounting annoyance. That this man should write such vitriolic comments about his own chief officer was more than Cork was prepared to tolerate. He pressed the intercom button and waited.

'Sir?' said the disembodied voice of his staff officer.

'This acting AC on Southwest Area, Commander Dobson.'

'Yes, sir?'

'I want to see him. Now!'

While he was waiting for Commander Dobson to get to New Scotland Yard from Kingston, the Commissioner dialled the direct-line number of the Prime Minister's principal protection officer at Downing Street.

'Detectives' office,' said a voice.

'Is Detective Superintendent Whitmore there?' asked the Commissioner.

'Speaking.'

'This is the Commissioner.'

'Oh, really?' said Whitmore, the doubt very evident in his voice.

'Yes, it is,' said Cork sharply. 'How soon can you come and see me, Mr Whitmore?'

'I'll ring you back, sir,' said Whitmore, still convinced that he was the victim of some practical joke.

'Oh, very well,' said Cork testily.

Whitmore consulted the programme of the Prime Minister's engagements for that day and then, finding the Commissioner's extension number in the internal directory, rang him back. 'It's Questions this afternoon, sir,' he

said, satisfied at last that the Commissioner really had
called him. 'I usually go with the PM to the House, but I
could send Chief Inspector Enderby; he's my deputy.'

'No, don't do that. When do you think that you can get
over here?'

Whitmore glanced at his watch. 'The PM's got a
meeting at five o'clock, sir, here at Number Ten. He'll have
to be back for that, although such meetings are sometimes
switched to the House, and then there's nothing until a
dinner in the City at eight. That may be cancelled though.'

'Oh? Why?'

'I'm waiting for a public order report from the City of
London Special Branch, sir. If it's not safe, I'll recommend
that the PM doesn't go.'

'Right. In that case, try and get over here when you get
back from the House.'

'Yes, sir,' said Whitmore, still puzzled as to why the
Commissioner should want to see him.

'Oh, and Whitmore . . .'

'Sir?'

'Tell no one over there that you're coming to see me. No
one at all, is that understood?'

Cork was standing up when Commander Dobson entered
his office and he did not invite the acting head of Southwest
Area to sit down. Nor did he do so himself.

'I have read your report, Mr Dobson,' said Cork icily,
'and I do not like what it contains.'

'It wasn't meant to be comforting, sir,' said Dobson
truculently. 'It was sheer bloody hell down there, and if the
assistant commissioner, God rest his soul, hadn't called for
the military, I doubt if I would be here in your office today.'

'I do have enough experience of policing to know what
a riot is like, Mr Dobson,' snapped Cork, 'but it was the tone
of your last paragraph that displeased me. I will not have
officers, even officers of your rank and experience, implying

criticism of me in reports that go to the Home Office. The
fact that reserves were not available is something of which
I am well aware and something about which I could do
absolutely nothing.' The Commissioner picked up the
offending report and held it out to the commander. 'I want
this report resubmitted with the last paragraph removed.'

'I'm sorry, sir,' said Dobson. 'I'm not prepared to do
that.'

'It's a direction, not a point for discussion,' said Cork.
'Please don't force me to suspend you from duty for failing
to comply with a lawful order.'

'I am quite ready to debate the legality of that order, sir,'
said Dobson, 'but quite frankly, I'm tired of the whole
damned business.' And he unbuttoned his tunic pocket
and drew out a folded sheet of paper. 'That's my resignation, sir,' he said and placed the form firmly on the
Commissioner's desk. 'I take it that you will grant me the
privilege of going immediately.' He paused. 'I'm prepared to
forgo pay in lieu of notice.'

For the next hour Cork sat glumly behind his desk,
wondering whether the time had come for him to resign as
well. In a way he sympathised with Dobson's feelings but,
even in these trying times, senior officers had to understand that discipline must be maintained. In fact, now
more than ever. The interview that he had had with the
Home Secretary held out no hope that the Metropolitan
Police would get any assistance from outside sources.
Much as Cork abhorred the idea of deploying the military
– it had not been done since the assault on the Iranian
Embassy in 1980, and then for one specific purpose – he
could see no alternative to the use of troops. But the Prime
Minister was the sticking point. Robert Fairley had set his
face against such a solution, and there appeared to be
nothing that either Cork or the Home Secretary, or even
Parliament for that matter, could do about it.

He became more depressed the more he thought about

the appalling consequences of having his force overrun, of being unable to contain the rioting, and of being unable to fulfil their prime task of maintaining the Queen's Peace. But his bleak musings were, mercifully, interrupted by his staff officer announcing Whitmore's arrival.

Detective Superintendent Gordon Whitmore had been a prime minister's chief protection officer for five years and had asked to be allowed to stay at Number Ten until his retirement, now only seven months away. He was tall and well dressed, with a shock of white hair that made it easy for his colleagues to identify him whenever they spotted him on television, as always at the Prime Minister's side.

'Mr Whitmore, thank you for sparing the time to come and see me.' The Commissioner shook hands. 'Sit down.'

'That's quite all right, sir,' said Whitmore, amused that Cork should think that he had any choice in the matter.

Cork waited until his secretary had served tea and closed the door leading to the outer office. 'I was wondering, Mr Whitmore, if you were in a position to tell me what exactly is in the Prime Minister's mind.'

Whitmore bit back a facetious retort and brushed at the cloth of his trousers where it was stretched over his knee. 'About what, sir?'

'About the present situation.' Cork, in common with politicians, officials and other policemen, had fallen into the trap of describing the frightening wave of rioting in euphemistic phrases.

'He's concerned, sir, naturally, but he hasn't actually discussed it with me.' In truth Fairley had raised the matter with his detective on more than one occasion, but his scathing opinions said little for the reputation of either the police or the man now seated opposite Whitmore.

Cork nodded. 'I was wondering if you'd picked up any scraps of information. Discussions in the back of the car. You know the sort of thing.'

Whitmore took a sip of tea and then replaced his cup

and saucer on the coffee table with a calm that belied his inner feelings. 'I know what you mean, sir,' he said slowly, 'but any conversation that a protection officer overhears is strictly confidential. I'm sure you understand, sir, that our job would become untenable if ever there was any hint that we could not be trusted.'

Cork smiled, but there was no warmth in it. 'I do understand that, Mr Whitmore,' he said smoothly, 'and in the ordinary course of events I would not ask you to betray such confidences. But these are not ordinary days, and I would remind you that I am your Commissioner. I think that puts me in a rather different position, don't you?'

'Not really, sir,' said Whitmore, 'but perhaps you can be a little more specific.'

'Is there any hint that the Prime Minister might be changing his mind about the use of troops?'

'None whatsoever, sir,' said Whitmore. 'I'm not privy to what goes on in Cabinet, of course, but I gather that the Prime Minister's view is that the police ought to be able to contain the situation without outside help.'

'We might be able to if we had another fifty thousand officers,' said Cork sarcastically.

'I'm sorry that I'm not able to be more helpful, sir,' said Whitmore.

'Have you spoken to the officer who does duty with the Home Secretary, Mr Whitmore?'

'Almost every day, sir. The Home Secretary's practically moved into Number Ten.'

'Has he let slip anything that he's heard?'

'Protection officers do not let slip things of that nature, sir,' said Whitmore stiffly.

Cork was beginning to get a little annoyed with this superintendent. 'The Metropolitan Police are facing a very serious situation at the moment, Mr Whitmore,' he said, 'and although I understand your reticence to discuss, even with me, anything you may have heard, I think it's essential that I am in possession of all the relevant information. No matter how that information is obtained.' He paused and, seeing that Whitmore was not going to respond, added, 'However, if you feel that you're unable to assist me, then so be it.'

There was an implied threat in that last remark, but Whitmore was too old, too near retirement and too experienced, after years of service in the nearest Britain would have to a political police, to be concerned by it and he shrugged it off. During his years at Downing Street he had jousted with the most astute of politicians; by comparison, a senior police officer presented no great challenge. But inwardly he was furious that the Commissioner should have attempted to make him break the unspoken vow of silence that Whitmore and his colleagues took when they started the job of protecting members of the government. And just for the sheer hell of it, he decided to teach the Commissioner the old lesson that eavesdroppers hear no good of themselves. 'There was one thing, sir . . .'

'Yes?' Cork looked up expectantly.

'But you will appreciate, I hope, sir, that this is in the strictest confidence.'

'Of course.'

'And if it ever comes out that I told you, I will have no alternative but to deny that I ever said it.'

'Yes, yes, of course,' said Cork impatiently.

'I understand that there is talk of replacing you as Commissioner, sir,' said Whitmore.

Emma Bancroft's face was alive with excitement as she walked into the assistant director's office at the head-quarters of the Security Service at Vauxhall Cross. 'We've scored,' she said.

'Oh?' The AD took off his glasses and placed them carefully on top of the papers he had been reading.

'I've received a report from the watchers,' said Emma,

dropping casually into a chair. 'Colonel Crosby, the officer who dealt with the riot at Kingston, had lunch at the Naval and Military Club yesterday.'

'Poor fellow's got to eat,' said the AD, an amused expression on his face.

'But he had lunch with General Sir Lawrence Dane, the Adjutant-General,' said Emma triumphantly. 'They were seen to be in animated conversation for about two hours altogether.'

'So?' The AD refused to be panicked into believing that some sort of plot had been uncovered by the Security Service's A4 Branch.

'All here.' Emma placed a file on the desk.

The AD picked up his glasses and perused the contents of the slim folder with professional speed. 'So,' he said, 'Dane was in the army with Crosby's father; they were at Sandhurst together. And Dane is Colonel of Crosby's regiment.' He smiled sympathetically at the young intelligence officer. 'I'm afraid you'll have to come up with more than that to establish any sort of conspiracy, Emma,' he said.

Emma's colour rose slightly. 'I just thought that it might be of interest,' she said.

'Perhaps,' said the AD softly. 'But I don't really see any profit in wasting the watchers' time in keeping Colonel Crosby under surveillance. After all, he has done nothing unlawful or subversive. Admittedly he's got up the government's nose by his actions, but that's their problem, not ours. Take the surveillance off.'

Emma returned to her office and threw the report on the desk. Why, she wondered to herself, had she not thought of that?

Gus Salmon, the MI6 officer attached to MI5, strolled into the downstairs bar of the Royal Automobile Club and looked around.

Alec Shepherd was sitting in the corner nursing a pint of beer. 'Let me get you a drink, Gus,' he said, as Salmon approached.

'Thanks. A pint of bitter, if I may.'

'Well, what news from the funny factory?' asked Shepherd as he returned from the bar.

'Nothing much,' said Salmon, taking the head off his beer. 'Young Emma Bancroft's getting very excited because the watchers spotted Lieutenant-General Dane having lunch with Colonel Crosby, the hero of Kingston, at the In and Out.'

'Big deal,' said Shepherd, 'but I'll mention it to Barry.'

'Has the time not come for us to consider our position, sir?' asked General Sir Simon Macey, the Chief of the General Staff.

'In what way, Simon?' Admiral of the Fleet Sir Godfrey Bristow was seated at the head of the conference table that occupied one end of his office in the Ministry of Defence.

'Put simply, sir,' said Macey, 'can we any longer just stand by and watch?' It was a momentous question, and each of the chiefs of staff present was sufficiently versed in the law, criminal as well as naval and military, to know that their meeting, however carefully defended, could possibly be construed, at some future date, as a conspiracy.

'As Chief of the Defence Staff, I have a responsibility that weighs even more heavily than your own.' Bristow paused and looked gravely at the other officers. 'And I have to ask you to think very carefully about what you are saying and, indeed, what you are thinking. But one thing is becoming clear: we cannot have disparate groups of soldiers, albeit under command, interfering in public order situations on an ad hoc basis.'

'Are you about to suggest that we do something more positive, sir?' Macey's role was the most significant in the present circumstances. If the chiefs of staff decided upon a

course of action contrary to the policies of Her Majesty's
Government, it would be soldiers who were sent on to the
streets rather than sailors or airmen, and Macey would be
the officer who shouldered most of the blame for such a
decision. At least to start with. As if suddenly becoming
aware of the implications of what he had said, Macey
glanced down the table at Major Imogen Cresswell, who
had been selected, out of the four ADCs available, to record
the minutes of the meeting. 'There's no need to take notes
of this, Imogen,' he said. The woman officer smiled and
closed her notebook.

'The problem is this . . .' Again Bristow looked at each of
the other officers in turn. 'The law provides for such action,
but sooner or later troops are going to be involved in a riot
that cannot be contained without reinforcements,' he said,
unaware how precisely he was echoing the argument that
Dane had put forward to Crosby at the Naval and Military
Club. 'But we cannot order them to desist. One cannot
prevent an officer fulfilling what he sees as his role under
the law.'

'Are you suggesting that we should start anticipating
military response so that assistance is available if needed,
sir?' asked Macey. 'Indeed, to start organising it?'

'Not necessarily.' Bristow was not only weighing the
implications of the military role very carefully but safeguarding his own position as well. He glanced at Admiral
Ainsworth and Air Chief Marshal Gilbert. 'I'd be interested
in your opinions, too, gentlemen,' he said. 'If things get
worse, then both the Royal Navy and the Royal Air Force
may become involved.'

Gilbert nodded. 'We're in a cleft stick, sir,' he said. 'The
Prime Mir ˙ ter refuses to sanction the use of military force,
but commanding officers are deploying troops nonetheless
because they see a breakdown in public order. Simon quite
rightly reminded them of that responsibility in his recent
signal. And I have to say that if a squadron of the RAF

Regiment had been near to such an incident, I don't doubt that the commanding officer would have acted as the CO of the Cumbrians did, or as Colonel Crosby did at Kingston.'

'And I'm sure that any ship's company would have enjoyed getting stuck in if there'd been a punch up at Portsmouth,' said Admiral Ainsworth with a grin.

Bristow cast him a disdainful eye. 'Yes,' he said sourly. 'And doubtless with shouts of "The Navy's here".' He picked up a silver propelling pencil and toyed with it for a moment or two. 'Of course,' he said, 'the common law allows officers commanding troops to take action. But we have to consider that a strict interpretation of that law may, technically, preclude sailors and airmen on the grounds that they are not troops.'

'In other words, it's left to the army,' said Macey. 'We can organise proper responses, but the problem is going to be if the Secretary of State issues a direct order telling us not to.'

'I would argue that he doesn't have that power,' said Bristow. 'We've had this out already, and the mere fact that Graeme Kent tried to get that bill through the House – and failed – is proof enough for me that he thinks they're right in law. Even if Kent has the power to issue such an order, which I doubt, it would have no more force than if you or I had issued it, Simon.'

'I think that I've made clear that there's no doubt in my mind about the position at common law of commanding officers intervening, sir,' said Macey. 'But the deployment of troops on a large scale to take account of it might not be provided for. We'd need to ask the Director of Army Legal Services. But supposing the Secretary of State goes over our heads. What if he appeals direct to the armed forces?'

'He wouldn't dare,' said Bristow.

Imogen had telephoned Shepherd from a public call box on her way back to Wellington Barracks and told him that they needed to meet. He had apologised that he would be unable to make it until about a quarter to nine and asked her if she would mind coming to his flat again.

Although Shepherd had arrived home only a few minutes before Imogen got there, he had made time to change into casual trousers and a sweater. Imogen had changed too and was wearing a pair of jeans and an open-necked white shirt.

Shepherd handed her a gin and tonic and turned on the television before sitting down in the chair opposite her with a Scotch in his hand. 'Apparently the Defence Secretary is making a broadcast tonight,' he said. 'Might be as well to hear what he has to say.'

Graeme Kent, attempting to appear at his statesman-like best and with a grave expression on his face, looked directly at the camera. 'You will all be aware,' he began, 'that some outbreaks of public disorder have taken place in various parts of the country over the past few weeks. There have been two occasions now when the army has taken it upon itself to intervene. I have to tell you that this has merely served to exacerbate an already volatile situation. There is a misconception ...' He paused for emphasis. 'Yes, a misconception, that the army has a duty to intervene. That is not so. The part of the law upon which they rely for authority came about before the advent of the modern police force and, indeed, before more recent legislation on public order. The law is delicately defined, and often commanding officers are unaware of its finer points. The existing forces of law and order are well able to contain the present unrest, and soldiers who obey the orders of their officers to put down such disturbances could well lay themselves open to criminal proceedings. The government knows what is going on and is taking steps to deal with it. Soldiers who interfere are only making a difficult situation worse. My message to the military, therefore, is this: they should consider carefully whether the orders that they are given are, in fact, lawful orders. And that means that each soldier must question his own actions and ask himself whether what he is being ordered to do is, in itself, within the framework of the law. Because if it subsequently transpires that he took part in an unlawful act, it will be no defence to say that he was only obeying orders. Frankly, I say this: it would be better for all concerned if soldiers were to remain in their barracks.'

Shepherd stood up and switched off the television set. 'Well that should ruffle a few feathers among the military hierarchy,' he said and busied himself pouring more drinks. 'I'll bet Macey is livid.' He handed Imogen her glass and sat down again. 'And what news from the nerve centre of the British Army then?'

'There was a meeting today of the joint chiefs,' Imogen began, and went on to tell Shepherd what had been said, emphasising that she had been forbidden to take notes.

Shepherd listened carefully. 'I would have thought,' he said, 'that if it was that secret, Macey would have asked you to leave.'

Imogen smiled. 'He trusts me, Alec.'

Shepherd laughed. 'I wouldn't,' he said.

'Ah, but then you know me better than he does.' Imogen paused and adopted a serious expression. 'Although I'm not sure that I do know you. I certainly saw another side of you the other night at that house you took me to.'

Shepherd tried to make light of her lingering annoyance about the way he had almost shanghaied her. 'I was wearing my official hat,' he said defensively and forced a laugh.

'But is it really as serious as your Barry made out, Alec? I still find it hard to believe that you suspect Macey of wanting to overthrow the government.'

'You've still got doubts?' Shepherd leaned forward earnestly, cradling his glass between his hands.

'Of course I have. Until I became Macey's ADC – it's only a matter of weeks ago, but it seems like years – the only problems I had were fending off childish Guards officers and worrying about getting a partner for tennis. And now this.'

'Barry is no fool, Imogen. He's been in the Service for years and he's seen it all, all over the world. He never offers an opinion unless it's based on hard, sound intelligence. And I have to tell you that he's very concerned about Macey.'

Imogen shook her head and stared at the carpet. 'What the hell have I got myself into?' she asked, half to herself. She looked up. 'I'm worried about Macey finding out, Alec,' she said.

'Finding out what?'

'Finding out that I'm ...' Imogen paused. 'Spying on him,' she added softly. 'That's not what I thought the army would be about.'

Shepherd leaned across the space between their two chairs and laid a hand on Imogen's knee. 'Look,' he said, 'I know how hard it is—'

'Do you?' Imogen stared at him accusingly.

'Sure I do. Don't forget I was an army officer once. And when I joined the SIS I found the whole business of intelligence gathering, particularly the methods, quite distasteful. But one gets used to it and realises that it's for the greater good.'

'But you never had to spy on your boss, did you?'

'No ...' Shepherd drew the word out slowly as though doubtful. 'But I would have done if the occasion had arisen.'

'And you really think it has now?' You really think that Macey presents a threat? After all, he's only doing what most Englishmen would do if they had the power. Putting down riots and protecting ordinary people.'

Shepherd leaned back in his chair. 'If that was all, there'd be no great problem, Imogen, but we have to look beyond the actual to his motives. If, for example, he had fascist leanings then the outcome could be far more serious. You've read military history, and you know what the Germans did during the Second World War – the death camps, the summary executions, the hostage-taking, occupation of innocent countries – because they couldn't get their own way.'

'My God!' said Imogen. 'You're surely not suggesting that Simon Macey is a latter-day Adolf Hitler, are you?'

Shepherd looked apologetic, even slightly embarrassed. 'I wish I could tell you everything we know, Imogen,' he said. 'But I can't.'

'But shouldn't we wait until he makes a more positive move?' she asked.

'Like the German people waited in the late thirties, you mean? Or, for that matter, like the British government did. Fairley's not a Churchill, you know. And do you really think that the British people like being fired on by their own army? No, Imogen, I think Fairley's got the balance right. And it's the government and the people we're protecting. Macey's on the other side. Let me get you another drink.' Shepherd stood up and moved to take her glass, intent upon breaking off the conversation before he revealed too much of what the SIS knew. 'It looks as though he intends to deploy troops whether the government likes it or not, then.' He turned the discussion back to Imogen's information about that day's secret conference at the MOD. 'And obviously that's what Kent was trying to avoid by that broadcast.' He waved a hand towards the television. 'I wonder whether that was his personal view or whether he was just playing the Prime Minister's tune.'

'I thought you'd want to know about the deployment,' said Imogen.

'Mmm!' Shepherd was still deep in thought.

'Well there's no need to be so wildly enthusiastic,' said Imogen, sipping her gin.

Shepherd looked up. 'I'm sorry, Imogen. Didn't mean to be rude. I was just thinking through what you'd said. And what Kent said. Did you get the impression that Macey's the one who's making the decisions? Rather than the Chief of the Defence Staff, I mean.'

'Yes, I suppose he is. Sir Godfrey is a nice old boy but close to retirement. He's a sailor rather than a politician, and I don't think he really understands the army. He seems quite content to leave decisions like those to Simon Macey. At least for the time being.'

'Perhaps so,' said Shepherd. 'Although it's difficult to know where command finishes and advice begins at that sort of level.'

'What do you mean by that?' Imogen asked.

'What I mean is that I'm not sure to what extent the Chief of the Defence Staff can overrule any decisions taken by the CGS in purely military matters. If Macey decides to deploy troops, I don't know that Bristow is empowered to order him not to. What he can do, of course, is to inform the Secretary of State of his misgivings. If, indeed, he has any misgivings about it. Not that that would make much difference. Despite what he has just said, I don't think Kent can interfere too much in purely operational matters either.' He stood up and paced the room for a moment or two. 'Are you likely to be able to get anything out of Bristow's ADC? How well do you know him?' he asked, stopping in front of her.

'Hardly at all. We meet fairly regularly, daily almost, but he's a typical stand-offish naval officer who thinks that his service is not only senior but superior as well.'

Shepherd laughed. 'Typical comment from a woman who thinks that a man doesn't find her attractive.'

'Oh really?' said Imogen, smiling wickedly.

General Sir Simon Macey was seething about Graeme Kent's broadcast and immediately telephoned the Chief of the Defence Staff at his home. For some minutes he fulminated about Kent's presumptuousness in almost incomprehensible tones. After a while, Bristow said that they would talk about it in the morning and put the phone down.

But Macey was still bristling when he arrived at his office early the next day, and rudely ordered Imogen Cresswell to seek an immediate interview with the Secretary of State in order that he could tell him exactly what he thought of him. But Kent was in a Cabinet meeting. Which was probably as well; the delay would prevent Macey from storming into the Defence Secretary's office and submitting his resignation. And that, no doubt, was precisely what Kent would have liked to happen. Meanwhile Macey had to accept that he would be informed the moment that the Secretary of State was available.

Admiral of the Fleet Sir Godfrey Bristow, however, was in a far more ordered frame of mind when he asked the Chief of the General Staff to see him.

'Well, Simon?'

'I've asked to see the Secretary of State as soon as he's free, sir.'

Bristow smiled. 'Don't bother,' he said. 'You and I have an appointment with the Prime Minister this afternoon. I intend to make it plain to Robert Fairley that the Secretary of State for Defence has no authority to issue orders to the armed forces.'

'What about Peter Ainsworth and John Gilbert, sir?' asked Macey.

'I thought that, for a start, it might be better if just you and I saw him, Simon. There's no doubt in my mind that Kent's message was aimed at the army. And I'm not having it. I have spoken to Peter and John, however, and as they are not directly involved, at least not yet, they are willing to leave their appointments in my hands. So if the Prime Minister won't listen to reason, he can have our resignations.' Bristow looked up. 'I suppose you're willing to go along with that?'

'Yes, sir, most definitely. It was my intention to resign the moment I saw Kent.' The lie enabled Macey to appear at one with the Chief of the Defence Staff's mood.

'Good. I imagine that a threat of resignation by the joint chiefs of staff might just precipitate some political crisis. But I'm not altogether sure.'

'There is another way, sir.' Macey stood up and walked to the window. For a few seconds, he glanced down into Whitehall, at the police in riot gear and the row upon row of police tenders with steel shutters over the windscreens and unsightly cowcatchers fitted low on the front of the vehicles.

'And what is that?' Bristow spoke softly.

Still Macey stared down into the street, wondering whether to take this step from which there would be no retreat. Then he decided. Turning on his heel to face the Chief of the Defence Staff, he said, 'Perhaps the time has come for the armed forces to take over the enforcement of law and order despite the PM's opposition to it. It wouldn't be much different from what's been happening so far. Just on a grander scale.' He sat down again and smiled so that Bristow could take it as a joke if he wished.

But he didn't. 'I think all four of us have been thinking that way of late, Simon. The other two haven't said as much, but you get to know how brother officers are feeling.' Bristow stretched his arms out sideways so that the sun caught the gold braid on his sleeves. 'However, that could be construed as the first step of a coup d'état by the armed forces of the Crown, and that is unthinkable.'

Macey nodded. 'Yes, I suppose so.' Then, changing the subject slightly, 'I had a word with Lawrence Dane yesterday, sir, the Adjutant-General. Apparently he had lunch with Colonel Crosby—'

'Oh?' Bristow looked up sharply.

'Dane served with Crosby's father,' said Macey. 'In the 27th Hussars.'

'I suppose Colonel Crosby was trying to save his regiment.'

'Yes, sir, but without much hope. I think he realises that it is an act of vindictiveness on Kent's part to punish them for getting involved down at Kingston.'

'How very interesting.' Bristow ran a finger along the edge of his desk. 'Tell me, Simon, how dependable are the 27th Hussars?'

Macey looked sharply at the Chief of the Defence Staff. 'That's a strange question, sir,' he said.

'I was thinking of the mutiny of the Connaught Rangers in 1922 when I posed it,' said Bristow mildly.

'Oh, I'd forgotten that. It was a few years before the navy mutinied at Invergordon, if memory serves me correctly.' Macey's barbed comment clearly irritated Bristow. 'However,' continued the CGS, 'if you are asking whether the threat of disbandment is likely to cause them to do something rash, I can say categorically that they are loyal to the Queen. Colonel Crosby is a fine officer. He'll hold them in check.'

'Good. The last thing we want right now is a regiment going off the rails.' Bristow stood up. 'A spot of lunch, I think, Simon, then we'll tackle the Prime Minister. If he refuses to play ball, I'll convene a meeting of the four of us for, say, five o'clock. The situation is getting too serious for my liking.'

The Prime Minister was not in the best of moods. The Cabinet meeting had dragged on until past one o'clock, and the views put forward had strained the convention of collective responsibility almost to breaking point. The Home Secretary had fought, yet again, for the use of troops and had been supported by Graeme Kent, despite the latter's television appeal to the armed forces.

Robert Fairley had been extremely irritated that Kent had made the broadcast without reference to him, but Kent had argued that, as Fairley had refused to sanction the use of troops, something had to be done, and done quickly, in an attempt to prevent the independent action of colonels up and down the country.

And now, at a quarter past two, Fairley was in the Cabinet room once more, this time facing two very annoyed high-ranking service officers.

'Well, gentlemen?' asked Fairley. He sounded tired and was starting to look it.

'It's about the broadcast by the Secretary of State for Defence, Prime Minister,' began Bristow.

'Thought it might be.' Fairley tried to defuse the Chief of the Defence Staff's obvious anger by smiling.

'General Macey and I find it quite unacceptable that a Cabinet minister should go over our heads and appeal directly to soldiers to disobey the lawful orders of their officers. It practically amounted to an incitement to mutiny. The soldier's oath requires him to obey his sovereign and the generals and officers set over him.' Bristow paused, then added. 'It doesn't say anything about politicians.'

Fairley raised a placating hand. 'Gentlemen, gentlemen,' he said. 'I can understand your feelings, but Graeme Kent was merely pointing out the inherent dangers of soldiers acting ultra vires. You will know that the law is ill-defined on this matter. It is a grey area.'

'The Secretary of State for Defence obviously doesn't think so, Prime Minister,' said Macey mildly, 'or he wouldn't have tried to get a bill through the House a couple of days ago attempting to prevent the army from intervening. In any event, it has yet to be tested in the courts and until it is I am content, on the basis of legal advice, that officers, and therefore soldiers, are acting within the law.'

'I don't know how often I have to say this,' said Fairley,

'but I do not intend to use the military to suppress public disorder, neither do I intend to be blackmailed into doing so by the maverick actions of a few colonels. And that is final. The police are perfectly capable of dealing with the situation.'

'I can assure you, Prime Minister,' Macey said with studied care, 'that the police are not only fully stretched but are in danger of being overwhelmed. I have taken the trouble of seeing Colonel Crosby and getting from him a first-hand account of what took place in Kingston. The officer in charge of police in that part of London tried repeatedly to secure reinforcements both from within the Metropolitan Police and from provincial forces. When none were forthcoming, he had no alternative but to seek military assistance. Now if that's your concept of a police force dealing capably with the present situation, then I'm afraid we shall have to disagree.'

'Added to which,' said Bristow, fuelling the Prime Minister's discomfort, 'I have to tell you that the joint chiefs of staff are utterly incensed by Graeme Kent's appeal. As I said just now, it was practically an incitement to mutiny. And that is not an accusation I make lightly. It is a very serious one and cannot be excused, particularly as it comes from the Secretary of State. In fact we regard it so seriously that we are considering resigning.'

The Prime Minister gazed mildly at the Chief of the Defence Staff. 'That is a matter for you,' he said, 'but I do not intend to be coerced into making a decision contrary to my own beliefs.' For a moment he looked beyond the two service officers, out of the windows at the garden of Number Ten. 'I am sure that you have heard of an organisation called Europol, gentlemen,' he continued. 'It was set up a few years ago to exchange intelligence about criminal and terrorist matters among the police forces of the European Union. It is my intention now to further that arrangement, and I propose to appeal to France to send reinforcements of police to assist us in our problems.'

The sheer enormity of the Prime Minister's proposition shocked both Bristow and Macey into silence. The clock on Horse Guards Arch struck the half-hour and the wailing siren of an ambulance in Approach Road briefly filled the room. From beyond the double doors leading directly to the principal private secretary's office came a snatch of stifled laughter.

Eventually it was Macey, still doubting that he had heard Fairley aright, who spoke. 'Are you seriously suggesting that the arrival of a force such as the French *Compagnies Républicaines de Sécurité* will alleviate the situation, Prime Minister?' he asked. 'But far more to the point, can you imagine the reaction of the public to foreign forces on British soil? Good God, man, the entire population will be begging us to throw you out of office.'

'Really, Sir Simon!' said Fairley. 'You have totally misread the situation. The sight of a few determined gendarmes will be welcomed by every law-abiding citizen. And it will bolster the morale of the British police tremendously.'

Bristow and Macey could only gaze at him in openmouthed astonishment.

Imogen Cresswell was not the only officer at the Ministry of Defence to feel some disquiet at the events that were unfolding there and in the country at large. General Sir Lawrence Dane, the Adjutant-General, was becoming increasingly worried, and he telephoned Barry Rogers of the Secret Intelligence Service.

'I thought it was about time we had a spot of lunch,' said Dane.

'Your budget or mine?' asked Rogers.

Dane laughed. 'I think the MOD can stand you a lunch.'

'With a salary like yours, I wouldn't have thought you'd have to worry about the cost of a lunch for an impoverished civil servant,' said Rogers.

They met at one of the few restaurants in Soho that still boasted a number of private rooms. Not that they were concerned at being seen together. They were old friends and, in any event, there was nothing sinister about the Adjutant-General having a meal with a senior officer of the Secret Intelligence Service.

It was not until the meal was over, and Dane and Rogers each had a glass of brandy in front of him, that Dane broached the subject that was worrying him.

'I'm a little concerned about what's going on at the MOD, Barry.'

'I've always been concerned about what goes on at the MOD,' said Rogers mischievously and took out his pipe, scraping at the bowl before filling it with tobacco. 'What in particular?'

'It's this question of the army getting involved in civil disorder. It's none of our damned business really, but Macey's hellbent on arranging for the movement of troops to cater for future outbreaks. On the face of it, that seems sensible, but I'm sure there's more to it. There's been a bit of a row about it between him and Kent, and Macey and the other joint chiefs have even been to see Fairley.'

'So I heard,' said Rogers, puffing smoke into the air.

'Oh?' said Dane. 'And what else have you heard?'

'Nothing. Not that I'd tell you if I had.'

Dane grunted. 'You don't even disclose the colour of your toilet rolls, you chaps,' he said.

'That's true, but I'm interested in what you're saying.' Rogers paused to tamp down the tobacco in his pipe, and then looked up. 'And what *exactly* are you saying, Larry?'

'I'm concerned that the army might be getting itself into an untenable position,' said Dane. 'For centuries we've avoided any sort of involvement in affairs of state, but I think that there's a danger of our becoming embroiled now.' He lowered his voice, even though they had the room to themselves. 'To be honest, I'm more than a little worried about the way that Simon Macey is behaving.'

'Really? Going mad or something, is he?'

'You know what I mean, Barry.' Dane looked at Rogers reproachfully, even though he knew he was joking. He also knew that beneath the banter, Rogers was a very shrewd and experienced intelligence officer. 'I don't know what he's got in mind, but it seems to me that he's taking much too much of an interest in matters that are really the prerogative of the government. And the Home Office in particular. These riots have got nothing to do with the MOD. Not directly, anyhow.'

'I get the impression that the army seems to think it has a divine right to interfere.' Rogers' reply was crushing and to the point. 'But why are you telling me this, Larry?' The SIS man suddenly became serious.

'I've been a soldier all my life,' said Dane, 'and one of the things that has always attracted me about it is that we're above politics. Now I'm not so sure. We're becoming too involved, you see. And I really do believe that Macey's enjoying every minute of it. And that worries me. The difficulty is knowing what to do. The army is, to a certain extent, hidebound. Discipline still plays a very important part in everything we do. Ever since I was commissioned, I have been aware of the problem facing any officer who believes that he has been given an unlawful order. If he fails to comply he risks a court martial. But if he does obey, he takes the same risk.'

'And do you think you've been given an unlawful order, Larry?'

'Doesn't matter to me any more,' said Dane. 'If I thought that was the case, I'd tell Macey what to do. And he knows it. No, it doesn't matter a damn to me. But I'm still concerned for the reputation of the army.'

In view of their last conversation, the Director-General of

the Security Service wondered why the Home Secretary had sent for him again.

'This business of the ECU riots, Sir Philip,' Sinclair began. 'Is there anything further to report?'

'No, Home Secretary. In fact you directed me to discontinue any enquiries into the matter.' The hostility was plainly evident in Hocking's voice.

'Yes, yes, I know,' said Sinclair smoothly and then smiled. 'But knowing the Security Service, I assume that you've continued to monitor the situation.'

'I have a very junior officer collating any information that comes in,' said Hocking. 'Nothing more.'

The Home Secretary appeared to consider that statement for some time. 'And do those reports lead you to any particular conclusions, Sir Philip?'

'They are merely factual reports of those incidents that have taken place.' Hocking wondered why the subject had been raised again. 'As I reminded you just now, Home Secretary, you said previously, and quite specifically, that you wanted nothing further done.'

'So I did, so I did. But I'm thinking that I may have been somewhat precipitate in making that decision. What I'd like you to do, Sir Philip, is to cause some deeper enquiries to be made and then let me have a periodic report, say once a week, more often if necessary. And in person, if you'd be so good.'

'As you wish, Home Secretary,' Hocking replied with stiff formality.

'And I'd be grateful if those reports were limited to me. I'd prefer it if the Prime Minister is not troubled; he has enough on his plate at the moment.'

Hocking was not happy at that and said so. 'You do realise, Home Secretary, that I have a right of direct access to the Prime Minister if, in my view or his, the situation warrants it.'

'Yes, yes, of course. I understand that. I would, however,

consider it a courtesy if you spoke to me first before exercising that right. I'd hate for us to give the PM different versions of the same story. It might give the impression that you weren't quite up to the job.' Sinclair smiled.

'As you wish, Home Secretary.' Hocking knew a threat when he heard one, and the one or two hints that he had been given recently that he might succeed Sir Richard Dancer at MI6 caused him to heed it.

CHAPTER NINE

Alec Shepherd had drawn the line at yet another early-morning swimming session. Instead, when he arrived at the Royal Automobile Club at seven o'clock, he went straight to the balcony overlooking the pool and peered down until he saw Imogen in her black one-piece swimsuit. Then he returned to the foyer and waited. Half an hour later she appeared, her sports bag over her shoulder, making for the door.

'Good morning, Imogen.'

'Hello, Alec.' Imogen stopped, looking slightly surprised to see him there. 'Not swimming this morning?'

'There is a limit to what I'll do for the Service,' whispered Shepherd with a grin. 'I didn't want to ring you at the office or at the barracks, and this is the only other place where I can be sure of finding you.'

'Nobody ever said the life of a spy was easy,' said Imogen quietly and dropped her sports bag on the floor.

'I'm not a spy,' said Shepherd, equally quietly. 'Can I see you this evening?'

'Er, this evening?' Imogen paused as if mentally running through all the engagements in her diary. 'Yes, that'll be all right,' she said at last.

'Good. Will you come to the flat? Do you mind?'

Imogen sounded hesitant. 'No, I suppose that's the only place, really. Can't very well invite you to my quarters in the mess.'

'Good God no,' said Shepherd hurriedly. 'I could be compromised if I saw someone who knew me.'

Imogen surveyed him with a sour expression. 'I wasn't thinking so much of you being compromised as me,' she said. 'People do talk, you know.'

Shepherd grinned. 'All right,' he said, 'but do you think that you could do something in the meantime?'

'What?'

'Do you have access to Macey's personal records?'

'No, of course not. Have you forgotten all you ever learned in the army, Alec? General officers' records are held by the Military Secretary or the Adjutant-General. There's no way I can ever get to see them.'

'Damn!' said Shepherd and looked thoughtful. 'There's the usual anodyne stuff about him in *Who's Who*, but we need to know more. I'm particularly interested to learn as much as possible about his time in Germany.'

'How mysterious,' said Imogen, 'but can't *you* get official access to his records, Alec?'

'We could, but that would alert the Ministry of Defence to our interest. We can't afford to do that. At least not yet.'

'I do have copies of his curriculum vitae, but it's not awfully comprehensive. Is that likely to help?'

'It might. Can you bring one with you?' Shepherd already had a copy but the SIS never refused information.

'Of course, but it only gives the bare bones. If you care to tell me what this is all about, Alec, I might be able to do more.'

'I'll put you in the picture this evening.' Shepherd paused. 'As much as I can. Then you'll know what to look for.' He had, at last, got Rogers' reluctant agreement to divulge more of what concerned the SIS about Macey.

'This is getting pretty serious, isn't it?' said Imogen.

'Possibly,' said Shepherd.

When she arrived at his flat that evening, he answered the door wearing a chef's apron. 'Hello, come in,' he said, holding the door wide.

'You're looking very domesticated, Alec.' Imogen walked through into the sitting room.

'I've just knocked up a quick spaghetti Bolognese for this evening. I hope that'll be all right.' Shepherd put his head round the door of the kitchen, seeking the woman's approval.

'I hope that standards aren't slipping just because I'm becoming a regular customer.' Imogen made a pretence of appearing doubtful, but seeing his reaction said, 'Of course it is. I didn't expect to be fed, you know.' She paused. 'And stop taking me so seriously.'

'I don't,' said Shepherd and went back to the cooker. When they had finished their meal – and a bottle of Valpolicella between them – Shepherd put a brandy bottle and two glasses on the coffee table and, once Imogen had settled herself in an armchair, sat down on the sofa. After a moment's hesitation, Imogen crossed the room and sat beside him.

Shepherd said nothing and poured the brandy. 'Simon Macey was a corps commander when he was in Germany,' he began. 'He was a lieutenant-general at the time, of course.'

Imogen opened her bag and drew out several sheets of paper. 'That's a copy of his CV, but I doubt if it tells you much more than *Who's Who* does.'

'Thanks.' Shepherd took the papers and skimmed through their contents. 'Yes,' he said, 'you're right. There's not much there.'

'Why the interest in what he was doing in Germany, Alec?'

Shepherd leaned forward to pick up his brandy and took a sip before replacing it on the table. 'We, er, have received information that—' He broke off. 'It's rather—'

'Alec . . .'

Shepherd turned his head and looked at Imogen. 'Yes?'

'I am to be trusted, you know. Anything you tell me is strictly between the two of us.'

'Yes, of course.' Shepherd put a hand on Imogen's knee, only to remove it hastily when he realised what he had done. 'It's just that in my trade one gets so paranoiac about sources and secrets and security that one gets scared stiff to talk to anyone.'

'Would that include your wife . . . if you had one?'

'Yes, I suppose it would. As a matter of fact, my last girlfriend—' Shepherd stopped abruptly.

'Was she beautiful?'

'Yes, she was actually. Very.' Shepherd sensed that he had made an ungallant remark and sought to redress its insensitivity. 'Not as good-looking as you, though,' he said with a smile.

Imogen laughed. 'Good try,' she said, 'but too little, too late. Now what were you saying about Macey?'

'Ah yes, Macey. We've learned that when he was in Germany he became very friendly with a German general, a chap called Max Strigel. Ring any bells? Has Macey mentioned him at all?'

'No, he hasn't, but what's so suspicious about that? After all, we're all in NATO. One imagines that regular liaison between British and German forces would have been part of his job.'

'Yes, of course it would, but it seems that Macey and Strigel were closer than just professional colleagues. Very much closer. They met frequently on social occasions.'

'Well even that's hardly surprising,' said Imogen. 'Soldiers are very sociable people. Sometimes,' she added with a sly sideways glance at Shepherd, who failed to notice either her glance or her comment.

'Yes, I know all about that, but there have been doubts raised about Strigel. Since the reunification of Germany there has been a resurgence of fascism in certain parts of the country. He is said to have links, albeit tenuous, with the NPD.'

'What's that?'

'The *Nationaldemokratische Partei Deutschlands*.' Shepherd explained. 'It's a neo-Nazi group.'

Imogen turned sharply and studied Shepherd's face. 'How long have you known all this?' she asked.

For a moment Shepherd said nothing. It was an awkward silence. 'For some time,' he said eventually.

'Is that why you recruited me to spy on him?'

Shepherd struggled to phrase his words in a way that would neither offend Imogen nor give the impression that he was taking her for a fool. 'Our meeting at the RAC was no accident,' he began. 'I had been told that you were Macey's ADC and I, that is to say we, realised that if anyone would be able to help us, it would be you.'

Imogen was pleased that Shepherd had been so frank, but she was, as yet, unconvinced that Macey's association with General Strigel was as serious as he seemed to think. 'So the fact that Macey had a few drinks with this Strigel makes him a suspect fascist does it?' She had recovered from her initial shock, and the cynicism in her voice was now unmistakable.

'God, you're worse than my boss,' said Shepherd and laughed. 'No, it doesn't mean that at all, but we have to take account of all these things, particularly in the present climate.'

'Particularly in the present climate!' Imogen savoured the words. 'That sounds a pretty typical Secret Service phrase,' she said. 'Well if that's all there is, I think you're worrying too much. For one moment I thought you were going to tell me that he'd had an affair with Strigel's wife.' She was mocking him now.

'No, he didn't,' said Shepherd. 'But he did with Strigel's daughter.

'You're asking for permission to mount a special operation, I take it?' said the head of the SIS.

'May I speak off the record, Richard?' said Rogers. He and Dancer had been friends for long enough to allow the occasional informality.

'Of course.'

'I have received information from a well-placed inform-ant that there are factions among the senior ranks of the professionals in the Ministry of Defence – the Chief of the General Staff in particular – who could be thinking of taking advantage of the present situation. If that happens, there's got to be some stability and some support for the government because there's no telling which way our sister service will jump. Frankly, I don't think that they're taking it anything like seriously enough. And Gus Salmon, our liaison with Five, tells me that Hocking has been warned off by the Home Secretary and told only to report to him, not the PM. Looks very much as though Hocking is being leaned on.'

'How did Salmon find that out?' asked Dancer, an amused expression on his face.

'Didn't ask, but he is a trained intelligence officer,' said Rogers, and he smiled too. 'But if something goes dras-tically wrong, and it could, then someone has to be in full possession of all the facts.'

'I am not doubting what you say, Barry, but I need to assess the worth of your information, and I can't do that without knowing who you've been talking to in the Ministry of Defence.'

'Sir Lawrence Dane. The Adjutant-General.'

'I see.' Dancer's expression remained unchanged. He had been in the Service too long to be surprised by anything any more. 'But do you really believe that General

Sir Simon Macey is plotting to overthrow the government?'
He raised his head and concentrated his deep-brown eyes
on Rogers. 'Or are you suggesting that our sister service
may itself be a part of this possible conspiracy?'

'No, sir,' said Rogers, resuming his customary formality.
'What I am saying is that we ought to find out whether
there is any substance to it or not. If what I've heard from
my informant is capable of proof, then there is no telling
what the outcome may be if senior officers of the armed
forces are involved.' Rogers' recent conversation with
Dane had satisfied him that far from a conspiracy existing
between Dane and Macey, Dane was very worried about
what was happening, but he needed C's authority to look
further into the concerns that Dane had expressed. 'And of
course it may be linked with the Franco-German alliance.'

Dancer smiled. 'You really believe that, Barry?'

'Look at the evidence, sir. Long before the single
currency came about, the French and the Germans
were—'

'I do read the newspapers, as well as the cables from our
people overseas,' said Dancer, holding up a staying hand.
'Very well, Barry. Go ahead with your special operation,
but be careful not to tread on the toes of the Security
Service. It is their responsibility rather than ours, as I'm
sure you appreciate.'

'I don't think they'd notice,' said Rogers.

With the possible exception of a rusty colander, there is
nothing quite so leaky as the Whitehall machine, and
within hours of the Prime Minister having forced the
Cabinet into agreeing to his plan to call for help from the
French police, the evening papers and television news
bulletins carried details of it.

With its customary disregard for English grammar in
general and tenses in particular, the BBC informed the
nation, on the six o'clock news, that 'the Prime Minister

brings French police to Britain.' Bulletins later in the evening expanded on the fears of the British people, and political commentators were in full flood, issuing dire warnings of the consequences of what, in their view, was this latest intrusion by the European Union.

The following morning headlines screamed the news, and the tabloids, with uncharacteristic accuracy, told their readers that 'sources close to the Queen indicate that Her Majesty is unhappy about the decision'.

As Bristow and Macey had predicted, the announcement served not to quell the unrest but to exacerbate it. Robert Fairley had given the British people a common cause.

And the reaction of the British people was swift.

The captains of two British car ferries, *Davina I* and *Davina II*, manoeuvred their vessels to block the entrances to Dover Harbour and dropped anchor. And at Folkestone, Ramsgate, Portsmouth, Southampton, Harwich and Newhaven, the crews of British ships blockaded the ports.

At Heathrow, Gatwick, City, Luton and Stansted airports, air-traffic controllers went on strike, to be followed within hours by their colleagues at all other British airports.

Thousands of returning passengers found themselves marooned on car ferries in mid-Channel and in airport lounges on the mainland of Europe. The car ferries wallowed at anchor for twelve hours before turning back to their continental ports, and harassed airport staff attempted to find hotel accommodation where hardly any existed.

But by far the most serious incident occurred at Gatwick Airport, where outgoing travellers, furious that their package holidays had been put in jeopardy, rioted. All day long they had been waiting for the call that would tell them to board their flights. Apologetic announcements had been broadcast over the airport's public address system, telling only half-truths, but there were numerous journalists and television crews in the airport, and the reason for the dispute filtered through to the passengers. They were made more angry when they suspected that the airlines were trying to avoid the cost – and the practical difficulties – of accommodating their passengers in nearby hotels.

Fearful for their safety in the face of ever-increasing anger, and quite a few ugly incidents, airline staff had withdrawn to their offices and locked themselves in. The police commander, unable to secure help from either his own force or neighbouring ones, put his officers on full alert and armed as many as he had guns for. The already familiar sight of airport bobbies carrying machine guns became more sinister as families realised that those weapons could easily be turned on them.

It was at around midnight that a group of ten men, confined for hours in a gate lounge waiting to board their package-holiday flight to Orlando, Florida, and worn down by the grizzling of their children and the nagging of their wives, decided to make a stand. And a protest.

A burly plasterer from Battersea started it. Moving among the other passengers, he recruited a number of similarly irate men. 'How about we get on the bloody plane?' he said to each of them. 'Then they'll have to do something.'

In no mood to listen any longer to platitudinous announcements, the men readily agreed and the group made a concerted rush from the gate lounge towards the entrance to the Boeing 747.

A jittery young policeman, stationed in the corridor leading to the aircraft, who had been unnerved by the anger of the mob in the airport lounges earlier in the day, believed that the group of determined men was attempting to hijack the aircraft and called on them to stop. Given more time to think about it, he would have realised that none of the men was likely to be a qualified pilot and that such an enterprise had no hope of succeeding. It was more of a gesture intended to emphasise their plight – the journalists at the airport would have been delighted to record the event – but it turned into tragedy.

'Stay where you are!' shouted the policeman, tightening his grip on his Heckler and Koch semi-automatic.

The Battersea plasterer laughed and moved menacingly towards the young constable. 'Leave it out, son,' he said. 'We're going on, and that's that.'

'I'm telling you to stop,' said the policeman.

'And I'm telling you we're going on that bloody plane. We're sick and tired of being buggered about, so get out of the way, copper.'

'I won't warn you again,' said the PC, retreating towards the entrance to the aircraft.

Still the men moved closer, and suddenly the policeman fired. Whether it was panic or an accident was never determined, but what was indisputable was that seconds later two men lay dead at the entrance to the aircraft.

Meanwhile railway workers at the British end of the Channel Tunnel went on strike, but not before they had derailed several wagons a mile into each of the two main tunnels and in the service tunnel. Finally, for less than one ECU, a telephone call was made to a national newspaper falsely claiming that the derailed trains had been booby-trapped with explosives. Within an hour the approach roads to both the British and French ends of the tunnel had been brought to a standstill by traffic jams that stretched for miles.

In Central London passengers thronged the tunnel's Waterloo terminal and when the first announcements of delays were made over the public address systems, the disenchanted holiday-makers launched attacks on detach-ments of the *Police de l'Air et des Frontières*. The French border police had been stationed in England to exercise control over non-EU passengers travelling to France, the idea being to prevent delays in the tunnel itself by conducting examinations at the point of departure. Angry travellers besieged their offices, shouting abuse and hammering on the door. But the delays were not of their making.

Within hours Britain was effectively sealed off from the outside world. And any hope for the imminent arrival of the French police, who the Prime Minister thought would save his political credibility, was stillborn.

The immediate reaction of the Home Office was to ask the Defence Ministry in London to advise the French that they should attempt to fly their police in military transporters to Royal Air Force landing grounds. And that precipitated the first major crisis for Air Chief Marshal Sir John Gilbert.

'It is quite evident from our meeting with the Prime Minister,' said Sir Godfrey Bristow, 'that he does not intend to move one iota from his present entrenched position.' It was late afternoon on the day following that meeting, and it was clear that Bristow had done a lot of thinking. He also had an air of defeat about him. 'As a result, we find ourselves in some difficulty.' He looked slowly and searchingly at the faces of the other three. 'We all know what's happened at ports and airports since his ridiculous decision was announced.'

'And there's no telling what might happen if the French police actually arrive,' added Macey reflectively. 'My personal view is that we should prevent it.'

Bristow studied the Chief of the General Staff for some moments. 'Are you suggesting, Simon, that we should use military force to prevent a landing?'

'Precisely so, sir. It's a breach of this country's sovereignty. The fact that the Queen is opposed to it is good enough for me. Just because the government thinks it's a good idea doesn't make it right.' Macey paused. 'Not that

I'm convinced that the government does think that way. From what I hear, it's Fairley's idea. I'm not sure that the rest of the Cabinet is with him on this, but they daren't resist. We must act.'

'We must be very careful about all this, Simon.' Bristow looked decidedly unhappy at Macey's suggestion. 'I'm not sure that the common-law powers of commanding officers to put down disorder can be extended to resist a government decision in anticipation of such disorder. That's quite a different thing.'

'Maybe you're right, sir,' said Macey.

'I'm sure I am,' said Bristow, but he was uneasy that Macey had agreed too readily and he feared that the Chief of the General Staff might just go ahead anyway.

As if to deflect the Chief of the Defence Staff from his thoughts, Macey fingered a message form across the broad conference table. 'A movement control officer stationed at Aldershot was at Gatwick this morning, arranging – or attempting to arrange – the airlift of a draft of troops to Germany. He thought that we might be interested in a situation report of what exactly was happening there.' Macey pushed the flimsy sheet of paper towards Sir Godfrey Bristow. 'You might wish to read it, gentlemen. My personal view,' he continued, 'is that the time has come for organised response.' He leaned forward with an earnest expression on his face and sighed. 'If I were to propose that the armed forces of the Crown take over the government' – he paused and looked at each of the three chiefs of staff – 'it would probably be regarded as treason. However, I think that we must now deploy the armed forces so that they can respond to outbreaks of disorder in such a way as to ensure that they are dealt with efficiently and promptly and that there is no undue loss of life. Particularly to members of the armed forces themselves.' He paused. 'Or indeed to the French police, if they ever get here.' He paused again and chuckled.

'Perhaps we should intern the French for their own safety!'

'But is that constitutional?' Bristow ignored Macey's comment about the French police and concentrated on the suggestion about deployment of troops.

'I believe so,' said Macey mildly.

'But that is tantamount to the imposition of martial law without the consent of the government,' said Bristow aghast. 'And it could bring them down.'

Macey dismissed that proposition with a wave of the hand. 'The question I have to put to you now is whether you are with me or against me. It is your decision because what I am proposing goes way beyond our brief as chiefs of staff, but I must ask because if the situation worsens, God forbid, the navy and the air force could become involved.' He glanced around at the others. 'I believe that the RAF are already making it very difficult for the French police to be landed at any of their stations.'

'There is some misconception about that,' said the Chief of the Air Staff pedantically. 'What has actually happened is that units of the RAF Regiment have been put in position to prevent sabotage to airstrips.'

For some moments there was silence in the room, broken only by the sound of police vehicles coming and going in the street outside and the occasional orders bellowed by senior police officers to their men.

Then Macey spoke again. 'My own view,' he said, measuring his words, 'is that I owe it to the British Army to defend them against what is happening at present. The last thing we want is for soldiers to heed what the Secretary of State said on television. If that happens we could well be faced with mutinies around the country, ironically incited by him. The tragedy of it is that if some soldiers refuse to obey orders, they could be putting the lives of those who do obey at risk.'

'I suggest that we think very carefully before commit- ting ourselves to a state of affairs that could be construed

as a military takeover, gentlemen.' Bristow's tone of voice
implied that he was hoping for a retreat from the brink.
'The Prime Minister has ruled out the use of the military.
What Simon is now suggesting amounts to the same thing
but disguised as stationing reinforcements in places where
they will be available to assist those commanding officers
who intervene on a local basis. Peter?' Bristow glanced at
the Chief of Naval Staff.

'I'm with Simon, sir.'

'John?'

There was only a momentary pause before the Chief of
the Air Staff replied. 'I agree with General Macey, sir.
Something has to be done.'

The pungent smell of diesel fuel hung heavily over the
barracks at Woking as armoured cars were put through
their morning ritual of servicing and inspection. In his
office, Lieutenant-Colonel Tim Crosby pondered the telephone call he had just received from General Macey. The
Chief of the General Staff had asked Crosby to go immediately to the Ministry of Defence building in Whitehall.
Crosby had already reported, in person, his version of
events at Kingston and wondered why the general should
wish to see him again.

Donning his service dress and Sam Browne, and placing
his red hussar forage cap squarely on his head, Crosby sent
for his staff car and was driven to London.

'What are the chances, sir?'

Crosby did not have to ask his driver what chances he
was talking about. Saving the regiment was the sole topic
of conversation at the moment. 'About as good as your
chance of becoming a field marshal, I should think,
Thompson.'

'Bloody rum do, sir,' said Trooper Thompson.

'That's putting it mildly,' said Crosby.

'Going to have another go up the MOD, sir?' As Colonel

Crosby's driver, Thompson was relied upon by his mates in the motor transport section to glean the latest news on all that was happening at the top of the regiment.

Crosby knew that and often used it to his own advantage. 'You can tell the lads I'm doing my best, Thompson.'

'Yes, sir.' Thompson grinned and concentrated on the road.

It was only when Crosby arrived at the entrance to the Defence Ministry building in Horseguards Avenue that he discovered that he had become something of a celebrity. As he stepped out of his car, he was momentarily blinded by a battery of flashlights wielded by the press and television reporters who had set up a permanent presence there and this morning had the good fortune to glimpse 'the saviour of Kingston'.

'Are the army going to be used, Colonel?' shouted one hopeful as television cameras started to film Crosby's arrival. But with no response other than a broad grin and an ironic salute, the CO of the 27th Royal Hussars strode into the building and made his way to Macey's office.

'Good morning, Colonel.' Imogen Cresswell recognised Crosby from the photographs of him that had appeared in the newspapers.

'Good morning.' Crosby appraised the attractive blonde standing by the window and smiled. 'Didn't realise that General Macey had such good taste in secretaries,' he said. The last time he had visited the CGS's office Imogen Cresswell had not been there.

'I am the CGS's ADC, Colonel,' said Imogen a little frostily.

'I do apologise,' he said, holding out his hand. 'Tim Crosby, 27th Hussars. It's just that none of my officers is as attractive as you.' And he grinned.

Imogen could not help smiling. 'Imogen Cresswell,' she said. 'Grenadier Guards.'

'Good grief,' said Crosby. 'I think I'd better see General

Macey before I say something really stupid.' He turned and tapped lightly on the CGS's door.

'Morning, Tim.' The Chief of the General Staff stood up and shook hands. 'Sit down. Drink?'

'Thank you, sir. A Scotch, if I may.' Crosby settled into one of the general's armchairs and watched while Macey busied himself at his drinks cabinet.

Macey handed Crosby a chunky crystal tumbler and sat down opposite the youthful colonel. 'You saw the Secretary of State's broadcast, I take it?'

'Yes, I did, sir,' said Crosby. 'Pretty poor show, I thought.'

'We all did.' Macey took a sip of whisky. 'The CDS and I went to see the PM about it. Had a bit of a go at him, as a matter of fact.'

'Did you persuade him to change his mind, sir?'

'No, he wouldn't budge. The man's quite intransigent.' Macey stretched out his legs. 'To be perfectly honest, I don't think he really knows what's happening. Either that or he's set his face firmly against accepting that the country's on the brink of anarchy. And his latest idea of bringing French police over here to sort things out is, quite frankly, a recipe for disaster. The British won't have it, you see, Tim, and given that they're quite willing to have a go at their own police force, there'll be a blood bath if the damned Frogs do eventually turn up.'

'So what's going to happen, sir?'

Macey stood up and strolled around the room, still clutching his glass. 'I think that the military – and the navy and the air force as well – have got to the point where firm action must be taken.' He stopped and stared down at Crosby. 'We cannot just stand by and hope that it all pans out successfully. Because it won't.' He walked to the window and moved a slat of the Venetian blinds. 'No doubt you saw the police presence in Whitehall when you arrived . . .' He turned to face Crosby. 'All they're managing to do is keep the mobs away from Downing Street. Robert Fairley is sitting there, cocooned from the outside world. I understand that he's not been out for days, and I don't think they're telling him what's going on. Either that or he's refusing to believe what he hears.'

Crosby wondered when Macey was going to get to the nub of the interview and decided to prompt him. 'Are we going to get involved, sir?'

Macey carried the whisky bottle across the room and poured another measure into Crosby's glass before sitting down again behind his desk. 'Rather depends on chaps like you, Tim,' he said slowly.

'Thought it might,' said Crosby.

'What's the morale of your fellows like at the moment?'

'Just about rock bottom, sir. The adrenaline flowed at Kingston, but the moment they heard that the regiment was to be disbanded, morale went through the floor. It was bad enough when we lost the tanks and got armoured cars instead, but nothing like it is now.'

'Yes, I can imagine how they feel. Think they'd like a bit more action?'

Crosby grinned. 'Can't keep a good hussar down, sir.'

But still Macey avoided the purpose of his sending for Crosby. 'General Aston, the GOC Land Command, and I are seeing a number of formation, regimental and battalion commanders, Tim, to put a proposition to them. And it's one I am now going to put to you.' Macey took a thoughtful pull at his whisky before continuing. 'It is likely that public disorder will worsen rather than abate and if that does happen, the military must be ready to deal with it. Do you agree?'

'Absolutely, sir.' Crosby was wondering why Macey was telling him this instead of giving him an order, because that, clearly, was what he was building up to.

'Good man. Now listen carefully. General Aston and I are proposing to deploy UK Land Forces so that they are in a position to deal with further outbreaks of violence.'

'Makes sense, sir,' said Crosby.

'Perhaps. But you have to realise, Tim, that it will be in direct contravention of the wishes of both the Prime Minister and the Secretary of State for Defence. That could mean a lot of trouble for all of us.' Macey gently swirled the last of his whisky around his glass and drank it down. 'I want you to be under no illusion about that.' He stood up and walked to a slim cabinet on the wall, unlocking it to reveal a large-scale map of England.

Crosby stood up too and ran his thumb down the inside of the cross strap of his Sam Browne belt. 'I'm probably going to get the sack anyway, sir,' he said. 'Might as well go out in a blaze of glory.'

'Good. Now then, once we get everyone in position, we shall use the tactical headquarters at Northwood, but in the meantime we are starting operations from here.' He took a pin with a small red flag from the bottom of the cabinet and stuck it into the map at a point southwest of London. 'I want you to move your regiment to Richmond Park. Under canvas.' Macey turned and grinned.

'We haven't got any canvas, sir.'

'I know that, Tim. Arrangements have been made for you to collect tentage from the ordnance depot at Bramley.'

'Fine, sir,' said Crosby. 'When?'

'Soon as you like. And send a signal once you're there and fully operational. Can you manage it within twenty-four hours?'

'No, sir,' said Crosby. 'Twelve.'

When Crosby left the Ministry of Defence building, he was deep in thought and did not notice that the press and the television crews had gone. But they had. To Knightsbridge.

The explosion outside the French Embassy was shocking.

Explosives officers attached to New Scotland Yard's Anti-
Terrorist Branch later estimated that about a thousand
pounds of 'co-op mix', the lethal concoction that had been
used so successfully by the IRA, had been packed into the
van that had been left in the roadway outside the embassy
building.

The van's driver had stopped his vehicle a yard or two
beyond the traffic lights in Knightsbridge itself, although
the entrance to the embassy was just around the corner in
Albert Gate. With callous irony, he had switched on the
hazard lights and raised the bonnet. Then, whistling, and
indifferent to the congestion he had caused, he had darted
across Knightsbridge and run down William Street. Reaching the comparative safety of Lowndes Street, he had
dialled a number on his mobile phone that rang out on
another phone cunningly wired to the detonator in the
van.

With a total disregard for the lives of innocent passers-
by, the huge bomb was detonated at one o'clock precisely,
when the street was filled with lunch-time office workers
and tourists.

It was a scene of the most appalling devastation. The
split second of sudden silence that seemed to follow the
deafening explosion was broken by the falling of shattered
glass and the screams of the injured. Within minutes there
came a cacophony of sirens as ambulances, fire engines
and police reinforcements flooded into the area. Those
soldiers of the Household Cavalry who were not pacifying
their terrified horses in nearby Hyde Park Barracks ran to
the scene, intent on offering assistance.

Traffic police set up diversions as their harassed colleagues attempted to bring order to the chaos. Tapes were
snaked across side streets and would-be spectators uncer-
emoniously bundled away from the grisly scene. At Scotland Yard, at the headquarters of the ambulance service
and the fire brigade, and at half a dozen London hospitals,

major-incident procedures were put into operation.

At the scene of the explosion, regardless of the possibility that other explosive devices might be present, doctors, nurses, paramedics, ambulance crews and first-aiders moved quickly among the bodies. With a calm efficiency, those pronounced dead were labelled with the sinister letter *D* before the medics moved on to tend others for whom there might be some hope.

The side wall of the French Embassy had been reduced to a pile of rubble, hindering the rescue workers. The building was ripped open to public gaze, and desks hung drunkenly close to the edge of upstairs offices. One desk, complete with a computer display unit, suddenly fell from two floors up and crashed into the street. The two huge columns at the entrance to the embassy had been swept away together with the canopy they supported. The two iron gates into Hyde Park had been wrenched from their hinges and thrown across South Carriage Drive to land in a heap of twisted metal, enmeshing the two ornamental deer that had surmounted the gate pillars. The embassy's tattered tricolour had draped itself over a burning car and was soon consumed by the flames.

A shrill discordance of disrupted burglar alarms rang out vainly in the April sunshine that filtered through the pall of smoke and dust. The street was a sea of debris as far as the eye could see, and curtains and Venetian blinds protruded and flapped from the now glassless windows of surrounding buildings.

A young man, his left foot torn off, lay on the pavement. 'I'm all right. I'm all right,' he kept saying to the postman who was tending him. 'Look after the others.'

A once-pretty young woman, blinded by the blast, her face a mass of blood, stumbled silently amid the debris.

Much later, firemen and ambulance workers started the macabre task of removing the dead, in ominous body bags, from the shops and offices nearest the blast. And at about this time the BBC received a telephone call announcing that the atrocity was the work of the Protection of England Group. The caller stated that it was a protest against the Prime Minister's decision to call on the French police for assistance to quell the riots.

The butcher's bill, as the Home Secretary later, somewhat insensitively, put it to the Prime Minister, was two hundred and thirty-seven dead, and four hundred and two injured. Within twenty-four hours, a further eighty-four had died.

Among the dead was His Excellency Monsieur Raoul Daumier, the French ambassador. At four o'clock that afternoon Phillipe Gourmand, a second secretary at the French Embassy but the most senior of its least-wounded diplomats, delivered a formal but strong note of protest from the President of France to Donald Usher, the Foreign Secretary. But diplomatic niceties still obtained and, at the end of his visit, Gourmand shook hands with the British politician, albeit left-handed. His right arm was in a sling.

The village of Wenham in Norfolk is a delightful pastoral backwater resting in the triangle formed by Norwich, Great Yarmouth and Lowestoft. It has a church, a pub, a village shop and a few houses. The largest of these houses is called Drapers, and Robert Fairley had bought it some twenty years previously. Long before he became Prime Minister.

Diana Fairley much preferred the Norfolk house to Chequers, which she regarded as little more than an extension of Number Ten itself. On the rare occasions that her husband was with her the minimal police guard was increased and Fairley was accompanied by a group of detectives and one of the inevitable Garden Room girls – the secretariat's offices overlooked the garden at Number Ten – but they respected it as a family home and did their best to keep out of the way. At Drapers Diana felt free of the trappings of government and so spent as much of her time there as possible.

But this morning she had made a point of returning to London. 'Where is the Prime Minister?' she asked as the Downing Street doorkeeper admitted her.

'I believe he's in the study, ma'am,' said the doorkeeper and stepped towards the telephone. 'I'll find out for you.'

'Don't bother,' said Diana. 'I'll find him.' She walked across to the table upon which the visitors' book rested and opened it, scanning the last few pages. As she did so, she absent-mindedly ran her finger along the edge of the table and then examined it. Later the housekeeper was informed that the Prime Minister's wife had been doing some checking up.

Although Diana had declined the doorkeeper's offer to find out where the Prime Minister was, some arcane communication system had been activated and a messenger appeared to tell her that her husband was indeed in his study and was alone.

'Good morning, Bob.' Diana Fairley allowed the study door to close behind her and sat down in one of the armchairs.

'Diana, what brings you to London?'

'You do, my love.' Diana put her handbag on the floor beside her and casually dropped her gloves on to it.

'Oh?'

'Bob, have you taken leave of your senses?'

'I'm not quite sure what you—'

'Is it true that you're still persisting in bringing the French police over here?'

'Well, yes, but it's beginning to look increasingly hopeless, what with the blockade and the air-traffic controllers' strike. And now the RAF are—'

'Good!'

'I don't think that you fully understand what—'

'Oh I understand well enough, Bob Fairley,' said his

wife. 'Don't you realise that the French are regarded as our implacable enemies? The man in the street hates them far more than he hates the Germans—'

'Oh I don't think that's so, Diana.'

'Why do you think we've still got a station called Waterloo? And why do you think that the navy still celebrates Trafalgar Day in October each year when every naval officer raises a glass to The Immortal Memory? It's because they detest the French. No one bothers to celebrate the Battle of Alamein, and the Battle of Britain is likely to slip from the calendar once The Few have all died. But you, Bob, decide to ask the French police over here to sort out our problems. Frankly, I think you're stark, staring mad.'

'You don't understand—' began Fairley again.

'Bob, don't keep telling me that I don't understand. I understand only too well. You're the one who doesn't. Just look at what's happened. All those poor people were killed in the Knightsbridge bomb just because you came up with some hare-brained idea.'

'The Commissioner isn't convinced that there's any connection,' said Fairley lamely.

'No connection?' Diana laughed derisively. 'No connection?' she repeated. 'I think I'd better have a word with the Commissioner and put him straight on a few things. Anyway, it's immaterial what he thinks or, for that matter, what you think either. It's what the people *believe*.' She eyed the drinks cabinet but thought better of asking for a gin and tonic. 'You know damned well that you should have put the army in, but having been proved wrong, you're too pig-headed to say that you've made a mistake. Well that's not statesmanship, that's stupidity, and it's going to lose you the next election.' Diana looked around the study. 'Not that there'll be one. If you allow the French in here, you won't get rid of them in a hurry, I can tell you that.'

'Diana—'

But Diana was not going to give ground. 'And look at your pathetic performance in the House after the Chester business. And after Kingston. You should have stood up and commended the army for their action, but instead you let Kennard make mincemeat of you.' She changed her mind, swept majestically across to the drinks cabinet and poured herself a stiff gin and tonic.

'Diana, I do have an appointment—'

'The trouble with politicians ...' Diana paused and opened the ice bucket. 'There's no ice,' she said as though it typified the collapse of the government. 'The trouble with you politicians is that you don't read history. If you did, you might learn something from the mistakes of the past. Instead of which you all read PPE at university.' She drank her gin down at a gulp. 'You've got no philosophy, your politics are a disaster and you've made a hopeless mess of the economy.' She banged her glass down on the corner of her husband's desk. 'Will you be at Drapers at the weekend?' she asked.

'I don't really know,' said Fairley lamely.

'No,' said Diana, 'I didn't think you would.'

CHAPTER TEN

The inspector in charge of the Richmond Park police looked askance at the convoy of armoured cars rolling through the Kingston Gate and wondered why he had not been informed of their arrival. For a second or two, he considered the bye-law that prohibited trade vehicles from travelling through the park without a permit and wondered whether a military vehicle could, in fact, be construed as a trade vehicle. When a constable told him that the army was setting up camp close to Spankers Hill Wood, he telephoned the headquarters of the Royal Parks Constabulary at Marsham Street in Westminster. But they knew nothing about it.

Such minor administrative matters, however, were of little concern to Lieutenant-Colonel Crosby. The officer he had sent on reconnaissance some hours earlier had pinpointed the area as ideal for the regiment's purpose, being about halfway between Kingston and Sheen Gates. That it was also close to the Royal Ballet School caused the RSM, unaware that most of the school's pupils were children, to issue a stern warning to the soldiers about their behaviour.

Within hours, tents and stores marquees had been erected and armoured command vehicles were in place and operational. And a coded signal to the Ministry of

Defence told the Chief of the General Staff that the 27th Royal Hussars were ready for action.

The inspector of the park police arrived while all this was going on and looked in astonishment at the forest of canvas that had sprung up. Demanding to see the commanding officer, he was eventually shown into Crosby's command vehicle.

'I have been in touch with my superiors, sir,' said the inspector, 'and it seems that no authority has been granted for the military to move on to Royal Parks land.'

'Really?'

'What normally happens, sir,' persisted the inspector, 'is that the Ministry of Defence gets in touch with the Department of National Heritage to obtain permission, but it seems that hasn't happened on this occasion. The appropriate official at Heritage has been in touch with his opposite number at Defence and he knows nothing about it. It's all a bit odd.' The inspector stood up. 'I have therefore been directed by the department to give you official notice to move, sir,' he added pompously.

Crosby grinned. 'Thank you for your concern in this matter, Inspector,' he said. 'And, indeed, for the enquiries you've made. But the short answer is that we're here to stay.' And putting an arm round the policeman's shoulder as he steered him towards the tented canopy that covered the entrance to his vehicle, he added, 'This thing is bigger than both of us, Inspector. If I were in your boots, I wouldn't worry about it too much.'

'I have something to tell you,' said Imogen when she rang Shepherd from a public call box. 'Can we meet?'

Shepherd hesitated and then asked, 'Have you ever been to the Special Forces Club?'

'No. Where is it?'

'Not far,' said Shepherd, giving her the address. 'I'll be there at 7.30.'

One glance at Imogen's strained face as he was admitted to the lobby of the club caused Shepherd to take her arm gently, settle her in a corner of the bar and order a large drink for each of them. When she had begun to sip her gin and tonic, Alec said, 'Okay, what's going on?'

Imogen ran a finger down the outside of her glass, making little patterns in the misting. 'Orders have been given to certain units,' she said in a low monotone, 'to start redeploying so that they are better positioned to deal with civil unrest.'

'Are you certain of that?'

'Yes. Absolutely. It was from the horse's mouth.'

'I see,' said Shepherd thoughtfully. 'Can you tell me any details?'

'All I can tell you so far is that the 27th Royal Hussars have been moved to Richmond Park. Their CO is Colonel Crosby.'

There was a pause before Shepherd replied. 'And this was Macey who gave the order, was it?'

'Yes.'

'In writing?'

'I haven't seen a signal. Under normal circumstances I would have done, so I can only assume that it was arranged by word of mouth. Crosby came to see Macey, just before the Knightsbridge explosion yesterday.' Imogen held the stem of her glass between finger and thumb and turned it before taking another sip.

'Are you suggesting a connection between those two events?' Shepherd kept his voice low and his questioning incisive.

'What?'

'A connection between the mobilisation of Crosby's regiment and the explosion in Knightsbridge?'

Imogen looked at him in astonishment. 'Good heavens no, not at all,' she said.

'Do you think that any other units will be moved?'

'I don't know. That's the only one so far, but if I hear of any others I'll let you know. Macey and the other chiefs have been in conference on an almost daily basis and they've discussed deployment on more than one occasion. They're frightened that units might find themselves isolated if a mob gets out of hand. Macey even mentioned the possibility of a trap being set for the military.'

'Interesting,' said Shepherd.

Ironically it was the information that the 27th Royal Hussars had lodged itself in Richmond Park that first brought the army's widespread deployment to the notice of the Defence Secretary. Alerted by his officials that permission had not been sought, the Secretary of State for National Heritage had telephoned the Defence Secretary. Patrick Hillier's spirited defence of the park's environs was the first Graeme Kent knew about the move, and he sent for the Chief of the General Staff.

'Secretary of State?' Macey walked into Kent's office and took a seat without waiting to be invited to do so.

'What the hell's this about the 27th Hussars taking up residence in Richmond Park, General? I've just had Patrick Hillier breathing fire and brimstone down the telephone about it and I want an explanation.'

'The 27th Royal Hussars have been moved to Richmond Park so that they are better placed to deal with outbreaks of public disorder in the capital, Secretary of State,' said Macey. He leaned across and laid a sheaf of papers on Kent's desk. 'That is a list of the new dispositions of all available troops in the United Kingdom, most of which have now been moved to strategic locations.'

Kent's mouth dropped open. 'Do you mean to say, General, that despite my instructions and despite the Prime Minister's avowed intention not to use troops, you have ordered the movement of the army into places where they can actually be used?'

'Exactly so,' said Macey. 'You see, Secretary of State, I am not prepared to take the risk of soldiers being overrun simply because reinforcements are not to hand and quickly available.'

'But this is outrageous, General Macey.' Kent was clearly having some difficulty in controlling his temper. 'The Prime Minister has made it quite clear that troops are not to be used, and on television the other night I specifically told the armed forces that they were not to respond to unlawful orders.'

'What you actually did, Secretary of State, was advise soldiers to disobey the orders of their superior officers. That, in my view, amounts to incitement to disaffection.' Macey leaned back in his chair. 'And that is a criminal offence.'

'General, I will not tolerate—'

'You attempted to create a law forbidding commanding officers from intervening in civil disturbances' – Macey's cool interruption was deliberately antagonistic – 'which indicates to me, quite plainly, that you recognise and acknowledge that the existing law not only permits but requires them to intervene.'

'I think you will understand, General, that this state of affairs cannot continue. It is an unworkable arrangement when the Chief of the General Staff is at loggerheads with his Secretary of State. I feel I must insist on your resignation in the face of this . . . this insubordination.'

'Or you must resign,' said Macey mildly. He studied the flaccid face of the minister before casually adding, 'I'm afraid that my resignation is not an option. I have no doubt that there is some machinery to cater for my removal, but quite frankly I haven't bothered to look it up.'

The Secretary of State glared at the head of the army. His hands rested on his desk, fists clenched in a determined effort to prevent them from trembling with rage. 'I am not going to tolerate outright insubordination, General

Macey,' he said. 'You will shortly be informed of the name of your successor.'

Macey rose from his chair and smiled condescendingly. 'That is your prerogative, Secretary of State,' he said.

Sharon Willis was fifteen but looked considerably older and had a reputation for being a good-time girl. Her idea of a night's entertainment was to go to the Deadly Nightshade Club in Putney and dance, often until closing time. Having had a few drinks, preferably at someone else's expense, and perhaps having even smoked a joint or two, she would cadge a lift back home to the Roehampton council estate where she lived with her mother. She had never known her father, and she wasn't sure that her mother had known which of her many men friends he had been either.

On this occasion, she had got into conversation with three men, all in their middle twenties, who lived on the estate. When they had suggested going to another club, Sharon, somewhat unwisely, had accepted. What the men did not know was that, despite her apparent waywardness, Sharon Willis was still at school and, incredibly, still a virgin. Assuming her to be 'a bit of a goer', they thought they were on to what they called a good thing and instead took her to Putney Heath where, one after the other, they raped her, mistakenly assuming her screams of protest to be a feminine ploy to encourage rather than dissuade them.

When, at about nine o'clock, Sharon was dumped near the block where she lived, she staggered, sobbing hysterically, to her flat and told her mother what had happened.

Sharon's mother, well versed in the ways of self-protection and having a wariness of the police engendered by several convictions for shoplifting, declined to report the matter to them. Instead, having dragged the identity of the attackers from the distraught girl, she called on several of the neighbours.

Among the men to whom Sharon's mother appealed for assistance was a greengrocer. About thirty years of age, he was a dedicated weight trainer and amateur wrestler. And he had also had a run-in or two with the three men named as the rapists. Quickly rounding up reinforcements, the green-grocer and his accomplices smashed their way into the flat occupied by one of the men and threw him over the balcony; he died instantly from a massive fracture to the skull.

Witnessing the disturbance from their own balconies, the other two men – brothers who shared a flat with a woman – barricaded themselves in. But it was to no avail. A sledgehammer made short work of the door, and the two men were hustled downstairs while others wrecked the flat and handed the brothers' girlfriend over to the increasing number of women who were joining the throng.

While the two brothers were kicked half to death, their girlfriend was stripped naked, beaten and thrown into a stream that ran through the estate, badly cutting her back when she fell on a rusty bicycle that lay among the detritus that the stream contained.

An old age pensioner, viewing the activity from the top floor of one of the blocks, called the police.

Minutes later, a territorial support group, comprising an inspector, two sergeants and twenty constables, drove in to the estate in their Transit vans. Seeing in the police their common enemy, the mob turned on them. Bricks, pieces of paving stone and any other missiles that the rioters could lay hands on now started flying through the air, forcing the police to beat a retreat and radio for help.

But a riot in Richmond and another in Twickenham meant that the police at Roehampton found themselves in what, of late, had become an all too familiar situation. In short, they were alone.

The rioters now spilled out of the estate and made their way towards the centre of Putney, possessed of some idea to destroy the Deadly Nightshade Club. That was, after all, in the minds of the mob, the root cause of the trouble. Had not other parents found that their offspring had been admitted, under age, to that den of iniquity?

Failing in his attempts to get through on the telephone to the 27th Hussars' encampment in Richmond Park, the police superintendent, no longer caring about the legal niceties of involving the army, despatched an inspector to plead with Colonel Crosby for assistance.

Within half an hour the first armoured cars, having left Richmond Park by Roehampton Gate, were speeding along Priory Lane and the Upper Richmond Road. Minutes later the detachment rolled into Putney High Street behind the tail end of the mob, who had now set fire to the Deadly Nightshade and were smashing every shop window they came upon. Slowly the armoured cars forced their way through the savage crowd, their drivers indifferent to the occasional rioter who failed to get out of the way.

But it was then that the rioting reached a new and higher pitch of violence. A soldier, standing in the turret of his armoured car and using a loud-hailer, was shot by a man in the crowd. With nothing more than a gurgle, the young trooper slumped down into the hold of the armoured car, his loud-hailer bouncing off the side of the vehicle and falling into the road. The corporal commanding the crew pushed the trooper sideways, unaware of what had happened. But then he saw the widening patch of blood on the front of his comrade's combat suit.

'Jesus Christ! It's bloody Belfast all over again,' said the corporal, his face white, and sent an urgent radio message to his CO telling him what had happened.

Crosby immediately gave the order for hatches to be closed an ' peering through the observation slit of his armoured car, ordered his machine gunner to pick off two of the apparent leaders. When both fell dead, the remainder of the crowd started to break up and run, panic-stricken, in all directions.

At half past two in the morning the riot was over, and the police had taken charge of a scene of devastation that would cost property owners – or, more accurately, their insurers – millions of ECUs to repair.

Colonel Crosby left a brief report with the police commander and ordered his flying column to return to the camp at Richmond Park. There he would write a letter to the dead soldier's next-of-kin; he was convinced that the Prime Minister would now have to take positive action. Or someone would.

Although Imogen had seen Shepherd the previous evening, what had now come into her possession made it essential, in her view, to see him again. 'I seem to be spending all my off-duty time in your flat, Alec,' she said.

'Oh, don't apologise,' said Shepherd as he poured the woman a drink. 'I'm very grateful to you.'

'I wasn't apologising,' said Imogen with a subtle mischievousness that, for a second or two, escaped Shepherd completely.

A week ago Shepherd would have made an embarrassed excuse for misunderstanding her, but he was gradually growing accustomed to Imogen's sense of humour. 'Never mind,' he said, handing her a drink. 'It's all in a good cause.'

Imogen opened her handbag and handed Shepherd a sheaf of papers. 'That is the order of battle of the latest dispositions,' she said.

Shepherd took the papers and, sitting down next to her on the settee, began to peruse them. 'Do you think these are the final deployments?' he asked.

Imogen shrugged. 'I've no way of knowing,' she said, 'and I certainly don't know whether similar deployments have been made by the navy, the marines or the air force.'

'I'll hold on to these, if that's all right with you,' said Shepherd and when Imogen looked doubtful, he asked,

'They are gash photocopies, aren't they?'

'Yes, they are, but I wouldn't like them to go astray. There's only one place they could have come from.'

'Things don't go astray in the SIS,' said Shepherd, a trifle sharply.

'Pleased to hear it.'

'I'll take them to the office and shred them. It'll be safer than you taking them back. Might get caught, and I wouldn't want that to happen.'

'No,' said Imogen, 'you'd have to get another mole, wouldn't you?'

'That's not what's worrying me,' said Shepherd. 'I wouldn't want you to get into trouble. This is a dicey business, you know. I mean, it's all right for me, but you're the one taking the risks.'

Imogen touched his knee lightly. 'You really care, don't you, Alec?' she said.

'Must look after the staff,' mumbled Shepherd and stood up. 'Lamb chops all right?'

When the meal was over, Shepherd produced coffee and brandy, as he always did, and Imogen made a note to bring him a bottle of Cognac next time she came.

'I really do appreciate what you're doing,' said Shepherd, sitting beside her once again. 'I know it can't be easy to spy on the CGS. It rather goes against the grain of everything we learned at Sandhurst, doesn't it? But I don't want you to take any risks. Understood?' He glanced sideways and sensed, rather than saw, the vulnerability of a young woman faced with a fearsome task. Suddenly he put his arms around her shoulders and, drawing her towards him, kissed her full on the mouth.

For one brief moment, it took them both by surprise, but then Imogen responded passionately and slid her hand inside his shirt.

Shepherd was the first to break their embrace. 'Imogen, I hope you don't think that I'm—'

She placed a finger on his lips, silencing him. 'Alec,' she whispered, 'I want to.' And standing up, held out her hand.

Determined that General Sir Simon Macey could no longer be Chief of the General Staff, the Secretary of State for Defence's first task was to set about removing him from office. There were precedents, although not recent ones, and it was an issue that he would need to discuss with both the Prime Minister and the Minister of State for the Armed Forces, as well as with the legal advisers at the Defence Ministry. But so confident was he of success that he embarked immediately on the second task, that of finding Macey's successor.

On the advice of the permanent secretary, he first sent for the next senior general, Sir Arthur Aston, the GOC Land Command, and offered him the post.

'I was unaware that General Macey had resigned, Secretary of State,' said Aston stiffly. He had already learned of the row that had occurred between Kent and Macey and had no intention of helping Kent out of his predicament.

'He hasn't,' said Kent and paused, wondering how best to explain the position. 'His appointment is, er, under review. I'm afraid, General Aston, that General Macey and I have reached an impasse. It is evident that his views on the running of the army conflict so sharply with government policy that it has become impossible for both of us for him to remain.'

'I see. Well, Secretary of State, in view of the fact that my views on how the army should be run accord exactly with those of General Macey, it would be pointless for me to accept your invitation.' And with that Aston, who had not bothered to sit down, turned on his heel and left the office.

Kent next sent for Sir Lawrence Dane, the Adjutant-General, followed by the Commander-in-Chief of the British

Army in Germany and finally the Deputy Supreme Allied Commander, Europe. All refused the appointment. Kent reluctantly came to the conclusion that he would have to air the problem with Robert Fairley.

'Perhaps Macey was right, Graeme,' said Fairley when this state of affairs was reported to him. He was beginning to wonder whether advancing Kent to Cabinet rank so rapidly had been a mistake. With the decline of the Cold War and the reduced responsibilities thus devolving on the Secretary of State for Defence, it had seemed like a good idea. What Fairley had not envisaged at the time of Kent's appointment was the independent action of the army in the light of the recent unforeseen events. It was a situation that needed a strong and experienced politician, and Kent did not have those qualities.

'In what way right, Prime Minister?'

'Well if you can't control a bunch of generals – which is, after all, your job – perhaps *you* should resign.'

'Are you asking me to go, then?' Kent bristled.

'Not necessarily,' said the Prime Minister mildly and smiled. 'It's a matter for you. But I have to say, Graeme, that you've seemed a mite unhappy at Defence. Perhaps Environment might suit you better.'

'Is that a joke, Prime Minister?' Kent was beginning to feel somewhat uncomfortable under the Prime Minister's cynical gaze.

'Environment's no joke, Graeme,' said Fairley enigmatically. 'The problem, as I'm sure you will appreciate, is that to sack Macey now would cause the government some embarrassment. The desire of the generals to use the army to put down the present disturbances is a ploy on their part to find a role for themselves, as they seem to have run out of wars to fight, and I'm sorry to have to admit that there is some support for such action among the people. But—'

'In that case why don't you accede to those wishes,

Prime Minister, and put in the military?' Kent interrupted rudely. 'It's obvious to anyone with half a brain' – Fairley looked up sharply – 'that it's the only solution.'

'Graeme, I am aware that you would perhaps see some personal aggrandisement in taking over from the Home Secretary, but it's not going to happen. Not while I am Prime Minister. I sometimes wonder if, secretly, you think that General Macey is right and that I am wrong, but I can assure you that to be seen to panic in circumstances like these is a recipe for disaster. I suggest that you go back to the Ministry of Defence and begin exercising some control over these recalcitrant generals of yours.' The Prime Minister closed the file of briefing papers in front of him and stood up. 'It would please me greatly if General Macey were to resign. Perhaps he would like to spend more time with his family, Graeme. Why not offer him a peerage and a field marshal's baton? That should shut him up.'

Sir Lionel Cork was a little tired of being summoned by ministers, and his first reaction when he was asked to see the Secretary of State for National Heritage was to refuse on the grounds that he was far too busy trying to keep the peace in London; he was, after all, the Commissioner. But the Secretary of State was insistent.

The Right Honourable Patrick Hillier was a tall, skeletal man. A product of Winchester College and Balliol, he had begun his political career, some twenty-two years previously, with aspirations of one day becoming Prime Minister. He recognised that National Heritage was a singularly unimportant post and now that the younger echelons of the party had made a breakthrough, he feared that it was likely to be his last ministerial appointment before being shunted off to the House of Lords.

'Commissioner, it is so kind of you to make the time to come and see me,' Hillier began effusively. 'This is a matter which very much concerns you.'

'It is?' Cork eased himself into one of the Secretary of State's armchairs.

'We have received an application from a man called Harry Lambert who claims to be acting on behalf of the Protection of England Group. He wants permission to hold a law and order rally in Trafalgar Square on Sunday next.'

'Does he indeed?' Cork sat up slightly.

'Is this the organisation we've heard so much about recently, Sir Lionel?'

'I don't think it is an organisation as such, Secretary of State. Certainly a number of lynchings and other outbreaks of violence have been carried out under its banner, so to speak, but my Special Branch is of the view that someone coined the name as a piece of patriotic jingoism. I think that most of the rioters have used it to give the impression that it's a highly organised campaign, and this so-called law and order rally might be one such example. The Knightsbridge bombing was even claimed in their name, although my Anti-Terrorist Branch is disinclined to attribute it to any particular known organisation. I think it likely that it was some maverick group with no real interest in the state of the nation.'

'So I understand.' Hillier nodded. He had heard all this from the Home Secretary in Cabinet but was pleased to hear it confirmed by the Commissioner. He was never quite sure, these days, to what extent Kenneth Sinclair was trying to frighten the Prime Minister into taking more positive action, perhaps even into resigning to make way for Sinclair himself. 'I take it, then, Sir Lionel, that you would agree that I should refuse this application?'

Cork laughed, but there was no humour in it. 'Frankly, Secretary of State, it doesn't matter a damn whether you refuse it or not. The bald fact of the matter is that if they decide they're going to hold a rally, they'll hold it. My officers are so stretched that we would be unable to enforce a ban. Probably the best thing would be to approve the application and hope that this lot will be amenable to police directions.'

Hillier was clearly amazed at the Commissioner's reply. 'Are you saying, Sir Lionel, that you're unable to maintain order in the capital?'

For a moment or two Cork, stifling an ironic laugh, stared out of the window and thought of the cottage that he and his wife had bought in the Loire Valley and thought too, for about the hundredth time that week, that he should retire. It would be worth it just to escape from the sort of idiocy that Hillier was now displaying. Cork wondered if politicians actually read newspapers or heard any news as they were whisked around the capital in their bullet-proof Rovers. 'That's about the size of it,' he said. 'It might interest you to know, Secretary of State, that the assistant commissioner for that part of London has about five thousand officers available to him, all up. And that would mean pulling out every policeman and policewoman available. It would mean putting detectives back into uniform for the day, dragging in men from much-needed days off and denuding the outer districts of the area.' He refrained from repeating the litany of violence London had experienced over the past few days.

'But you have more officers than that in the Metropolitan Police, surely, Commissioner?' said Hillier.

'Oh certainly,' said Cork wearily, 'but I dare not move men in from the surrounding areas. It's almost as if some sophisticated intelligence organisation is at work. The moment I bring men into the centre, you can bet on riots erupting in the suburbs within the hour.' All his professional life, Cork had found himself arguing with people who thought they knew more about running a police force than he did.

Hillier stood up. 'Well I am not about to give in to the mob,' he said. 'I intend to refuse the application.'

Sir Lionel Cork stood up too and shrugged. 'On your

own head be it, Secretary of State,' he said. 'But if there's a blood bath, please don't say that I didn't warn you.' And just for the hell of it, he added, 'I suppose you've discussed this with the Home Secretary.'

News of the law and order rally in Trafalgar Square had been published in most of the tabloids and in the broadsheets. But some of the more responsible elements of the press appeared to think that things had gone far enough. In a vitriolic editorial, *The Guardian* lambasted the rally's organisers as 'the architects of an ill-conceived plan which had brought about the deaths of hundreds of innocents in Knightsbridge, and little else', even though Scotland Yard were undecided as to who had been responsible for that outrage. It went on to suggest that the only outcome of the rally on Sunday would be further death and injury, the age of peaceful protest having now long gone. There was, it concluded, no substitute for parliamentary democracy, neither would there ever be.

On the other hand, the *Daily Mirror*, ever ready to embarrass the government, saw the rally as the voice of the people and cautioned Robert Fairley to heed what they were saying. It even suggested that he should address the rally himself. But perhaps, it concluded caustically, he did not speak their language.

It was a warm Sunday with no sign of rain and although the rally had been scheduled to start at three o'clock, crowds began to assemble as early as half past twelve. By the time that those who had convened the rally arrived, the police estimated that some eighty thousand people were packed into the square and its surrounding streets. Among the crowd could be seen the banners of extremist organisations which, as ever, were taking advantage of any situation likely to result in a confrontation with the police. Morley's Hill, between South Africa House and the square itself, the road on the north side in front of the

National Gallery and the carriageway facing the side of
Canada House were all packed with people, and the police,
having no option, had diverted traffic.

A Metropolitan Police commander pushed his way
towards a little group. 'Which of you is Harry Lambert?' he
asked.

'Me.' Lambert turned to face the police chief and thrust
his hands in his pockets.

'You were advised, Mr Lambert, that permission to hold
this rally had been refused. I now have to tell you that if
you persist in going ahead with it, you will be committing
an offence and will render yourself liable to arrest.'

Lambert looked at the vast sea of faces around him.
'Then *you'd* better tell them, chief,' he said. 'Because I'm
not going to.'

'Very well,' said the commander, 'I am arresting you for
holding a public meeting in Trafalgar Square without the
permission of the Secretary of State for National Heritage,
contrary to the bye-laws.' He took a small plastic card from
his tunic pocket. 'You do not have to say anything,' he
continued in a monotone, 'but it may harm your defence
if you do not mention when questioned something which
you later rely on in court. Anything you do say may be
given in evidence.' And with that, he placed a hand on
Lambert's arm as a token of detention.

Despite the attempts of two policemen, one of Lambert's
cohorts leaped on to the plinth of Nelson's Column.
'They've arrested Harry Lambert!' he cried through his
loud-hailer. But that was as far as he got. A posse of police
clambered on to the plinth and, grabbing the man, handed
him down to their colleagues below.

There was immediate uproar as those elements of the
mob nearest to the police commander pressed more closely
around him, his two prisoners and the woefully inadequate
group of policemen and policewomen who were attempting to push their way towards Duncannon Street and the

nearby Charing Cross Police Station.

'It is a serious offence to attempt to release a prisoner—' began the commander, at which point someone knocked his cap off. 'I'm warning you,' he shouted at his unseen assailant.

'Let them go, let them go,' chanted the crowd. Then a fight broke out. In the ensuing scuffle, Lambert and his colleague were freed, and the police were punched and manhandled towards the edge of the square.

One man handed the commander his cap. 'Take a word of advice, guv'nor,' he said. 'This meeting's going ahead whether you like it or not. The worse thing you can do is to try and stop it. Anyway, you haven't got enough coppers.' He gave the commander a surly grin. 'I reckon your best bet is to stand on the sidelines and listen. You might hear something worthwhile.'

Lambert, dishevelled by the struggle but now free of constraint, leaped on to the plinth and picked up the loud-hailer. 'Ladies and gentlemen,' he began, 'you have just witnessed the law at work. They're quite prepared to arrest me for some piddling little offence while rapists, child molesters and men who beat up and rob little old ladies are allowed to walk free from the courts every day of the week. But it's us – you and me – who are their target, just for complaining. And what's their answer? They're going to bring Frog coppers over here to sort you out, that's what they're going to do. Seen 'em on the telly, have you? In leather coats, just like the Gestapo, with their tear gas and their bloody great truncheons. That's what Fairley and his mob have brought us to. But what does his government care about you, eh? I'll tell you. Nothing is what they care. If you're a murderer or a robber, you're all right, believe me. Just read the newspapers. Unemployment is rife, people are being declared redundant every day and small busi-nesses are going bust. And the greatest fraud that's ever been perpetrated is the ECU swindle. Big business is all right, but you're not. And the army is being run down so that it can't cope with the defence of the country and soldiers who have served this once-great nation are being thrown on the scrap heap. And it'll be your turn next, those of you who still have jobs.' For some time, he gabbled on in this vein, each of his pronouncements drawing cheers of encouragement from the crowd. Then came the peroration. 'The time has come,' Lambert went on, 'nay, it is long past, when we should tell this lily-livered government that what they're doing – or not doing – isn't good enough. The people of this country will not stand for it.'

The cheers were deafening and a chant of 'Action!', started by a group nearest the plinth, was taken up by the whole crowd until the noise swelled to a pitch that must have been heard in Downing Street itself. A back-bench Labour MP, who did not wholeheartedly agree with the principles expressed by Lambert but who was prepared to seize on any opportunity to attack the government, appeared beside him, intent upon making a rousing speech. But he didn't get the chance.

A man at the front of the crowd jumped on to the plinth and grabbed the loud-hailer from him. 'Harry Lambert's absolutely right,' he yelled. 'We should tell the government. And we should tell that slug Fairley.' Each of his statements was punctuated by riotous cheers and shouts of encouragement. 'And we should tell him now.' The man swept his arm round in a dramatic gesture and pointed up Whitehall. 'Let's do it!' he cried and jumped down into the crowd.

By bringing in every available officer from the divisions that comprised his area, the assistant commissioner in charge of Central London had managed to parade some four thousand police, both foot-duty and mounted. Sensing the danger instantly, the AC mustered as many of his officers as he could and ran down Whitehall to Downing Street, where he positioned his men, many of whom were in riot gear, in an attempt to afford added protection to the huge gates guarding the short road that led to the Prime Minister's residence. But the mood of the crowd was such that the police stood little or no chance of doing much more than that.

Earlier a senior officer had thrown a cordon across the north end of Whitehall in an attempt to prevent the very tactic upon which the crowd now seemed bent, but the police were immediately swept aside.

The vast mob stormed down Whitehall, completely filling the road. Lambert and his supporters, standing helplessly on the plinth, let them go. In all honesty, they could do little else. Even if they had wanted to.

Many of the rioters had armed themselves with sticks, and others had torn up paving stones which, together with an assortment of other missiles, now began to rain down on the unfortunate police.

As the mob surged down the broad street that for centuries had been associated with government, a mounted sergeant was seized by the leg and pulled from his horse to be trampled underfoot. Another, his elbow smashed by half a paving slab, spurred his horse away and tried to escape. And a hatless superintendent, attempting to marshal enough police to protect the entrance to Horse Guards, was felled by two women who hurled a crush barrier at him.

Many of the windows in shops and government buildings between Trafalgar Square and Downing Street were smashed by the crowd as they made their way southwards. Some cars, which the overstretched police had been unable to prevent from parking in the side streets, were set on fire, leaving black plumes of smoke rising vertically in the still, spring air. Opposite the Scottish Office a pub burned unchecked because the fire brigade were unable to get anywhere near it.

Suddenly the crowd parted as a dustcart, which had

been hijacked from its Pimlico depot, drove at speed, its orange beacons flashing, towards Downing Street. Police and rioters leaped from its path as the vehicle's driver, with kamikaze-like disdain for his own safety, careered into the huge gates. There was a rending of metal as the steel bowed inwards, but the gates held, leaving the vehicle enmeshed in them. The driver, bleeding profusely from a gash on his forehead, jumped from the cab and disappeared into the crowd. Several policemen attempted to pursue him, but the crowd closed around them, ensuring the driver's escape.

Eye-witness reports of the riot were conveyed by the duty officer at the Ministry of Defence to General Macey at his home in Esher. He immediately ordered that Colonel Crosby at Richmond Park, the commanding officers of the Surrey Fusiliers in Regents Park, and the Duke of York's Own in temporary accommodation in the grounds of the Royal Hospital at Chelsea be alerted. Finally he directed that the Household Division should be warned to protect Buckingham Palace and Kensington Palace. And at Windsor, every guardsman at Victoria Barracks was turned out to protect the castle, where the Queen was spending the weekend. Ten minutes later, an army helicopter landed on the lawn of General Macey's Esher home and took him to the tactical headquarters at Northwood.

The Surrey Fusiliers and the Duke of York's Own, being the troops nearest to Whitehall, arrived first, but only forty minutes ahead of Colonel Crosby's hussars in their flying column of armoured cars.

Dressed in riot gear and equipped with baton rounds, the two battalions of infantry approached the scene of the riot from Parliament Square. But the 27th Hussars had been advised by radio, during their journey to Central London, that a fairly substantial group of the rioters, tired of being repulsed by the hard-pressed police at Downing Street, had turned and made off up the Charing Cross Road. Crosby immediately ordered his armoured cars to pursue the unruly crowd and break it up.

Having learned from the lesson of the soldier who had been killed in Putney, Crosby ordered his troops to proceed 'hatches down', and they swept up Charing Cross Road at high speed, dispersing rioters and in some cases chasing them up side streets, with the occasional chatter of the medium machine guns with which their vehicles were equipped.

As darkness fell, the streets of Westminster and Soho, Regent Street and Oxford Street, were littered with debris. Shop windows had been broken and valuable stock pulled out and either stolen or abandoned on the pavements and in the roadways. Here and there, the bodies of the more seriously injured, police as well as rioters, were propped in shop doorways, and the side streets had become escape routes for the walking wounded intent on avoiding arrest. All around could be heard the sirens of the emergency services as they tried, none too successfully, to reach the several centres of the fast-fragmenting riot.

By midnight the last of the mob had been dispersed, leaving two hundred or so of their number in hospital and three in the mortuary. Of the police, one hundred and twenty-one officers had been injured, seventeen seriously. And twenty-five soldiers had suffered injuries for which they needed hospital treatment.

At Northwood, General Macey listened to the last reports of the three commanding officers and gave a grin of satisfaction. 'Now let the Prime Minister say that he doesn't need the military,' he said.

CHAPTER ELEVEN

Although the Whitehall riot had been suppressed by midnight, it continued to smoulder. At the height of the disturbance a group of some fifty men, frustrated in their attempts to reach 10 Downing Street, had repaired to St James's Park and held an impromptu meeting. Before they were dispersed by a detachment of Surrey Fusiliers, their ringleader, Bert Perkins, called on his supporters to regroup there the following morning.

They gathered at nine o'clock. The police, exhausted and depleted by the exertions and injuries of the previous day, had only a minimal presence on the streets, and no one in authority was aware of the meeting.

'There's only one answer!' shouted Perkins. 'We must get more guns.' Several of the rioters had been armed the previous day although, providentially, none had used their weapons. The advent of the single market a few years previously had severely limited the ability of Customs and Excise to prevent wholesale smuggling of handguns. Even so, in Perkins' view they did not have sufficient guns to effect their purpose.

'How?' asked a voice in the crowd.

'There's plenty in Wellington Barracks,' said Perkins, 'and all they've got is one unarmed sentry on the gate.

It'll be a piece of cake.'

Had the men not been fired by Perkins' rabble rousing and ill-considered rhetoric, and if they had stopped to think about it, they would have realised that an attempt by fifty men armed mostly with sticks to mount a raid on a barracks already alert to the possibility of such attacks was doomed to failure. But they tried nonetheless.

Led by Perkins, the mob made their way to Petty France. One of their number knocked the sentry unconscious and seized his rifle; to his astonishment, and contrary to Perkins' information, he found it to be loaded. Inspired by this initial success, the remainder of the party flooded through the gates of Wellington Barracks, some now flourishing handguns.

'Right, lads, let's find the armoury,' said Perkins. And without any idea of where it was situated, the mob set off around the barracks in search of firearms.

The guard commander had witnessed the incursion, and his first action was to hit the highly polished alarm button on the wall near his desk. Immediately, warning bells sounded throughout the barracks: in the soldiers' quarters, the officers' and sergeants' messes and in the headquarters block occupied by the commanding officer and the adjutant, as well as in the guardroom at Buckingham Palace.

It took less than a minute for the First Battalion of the Grenadier Guards, the current occupants of the barracks, to turn out to repel the attack.

Seizing their rifles – to which they had rapidly fixed their bayonets – guardsmen started to appear from all directions, and moments later the air was filled with shouted orders as the invaders were encircled. The man who had seized the sentry's rifle raised the weapon. Not waiting to ask questions, a lance-sergeant fired his rifle from the waist and shot the man dead. Another insurgent, wielding an iron bar, attempted to strike down a soldier only to be bayoneted in the stomach. Clutching his abdomen, the assailant fell to the ground and died seconds later. And a man who raised a pistol died instantly from gunshot wounds.

After less than three minutes of what the army describes as hand-to-hand fighting, during which there had never been any doubt as to who would emerge victorious, the insurgents had been quelled. Most were placed in secure accommodation under the guard of a handful of very aggressive soldiers, but at least six required hospital treatment, mostly for jaws smashed by rifle butts. Perkins' attempt to seize weapons from the British Army had failed, as it had to, and the dishevelled attackers were left in no doubt that any false moves on their part would have fatal repercussions.

The adjutant, resplendent in his frock coat, sent for the regimental sergeant-major. 'What happened, Mr Gibbons?' he asked.

'According to the drill-sarn't-in-waiting, sir,' said Gibbons, 'they said they didn't have an argument with us but they wanted weapons to attack 10 Downing Street with.'

The adjutant stroked his moustache and smiled. 'Did they indeed,' he said. 'Do we have the ringleader?'

'Yes, sir. A man called Perkins.'

'Well that, as I'm sure you know, Mr Gibbons, amounts to insurrection. In fact, given that they seized the sentry's rifle and that others were armed, it amounts to *armed* insurrection, and we were quite within our rights to resist it with whatever means available.'

'Yes, sir,' said Gibbons.

'Good. Now where is the sentry who was disarmed?'

'In close arrest, sir,' said Gibbons. 'Charged with delivering up his post. He'll appear before his company commander tomorrow morning, oh-eight-forty-five hours, sir.'

'Yes, of course,' said the adjutant and stroked his

moustache again. 'Very well.' He nodded. 'Thank you, Mr Gibbons. Carry on.'

When the RSM had left, the adjutant informed the commanding officer what had occurred. The colonel telephoned Major-General Thomas Ryder, the general officer commanding London District and the Household Division, and gave him a full report of the incident.

That same morning at the Home Office in Queen Anne's Gate, the Home Secretary listened gravely to the account of the previous day's riot, delivered in person by Sir Lionel Cork.

'A bad business, Sir Lionel.'

'Yes, Home Secretary,' said Cork, 'and I'm very grateful to you for authorising the intervention of the army. Without them it would have been a bloody sight worse.'

'I didn't authorise the use of the military,' said Sinclair angrily, 'and neither did the Prime Minister.' He took a sip of his coffee. 'I should like a report from you, Commissioner, detailing exactly what part the army took in the disturbance. I'm fairly clear in my own mind that their interference merely served to exacerbate an already volatile situation. And I sincerely hope that you will be submitting papers to the Director of Public Prosecutions.'

Cork smiled at the Home Secretary's reluctance to describe the events of the previous day as a riot, for that undoubtedly was what it had been. 'Many of the ringleaders were identified by my Special Branch,' he said, 'and I am satisfied that they will shortly be in custody. And, yes, a report will be prepared for the Crown Prosecution Service.'

Sinclair looked at Cork, wondering whether he was being facetious. 'I was thinking of the military commanders, Commissioner,' he said.

Cork stared at the Home Secretary in astonishment. 'Are you seriously suggesting that the CPS should consider prosecuting the military?'

'Certainly. There must be numerous offences that they've committed. Malicious wounding, grievous bodily harm and other minor assaults, dangerous driving. That sort of thing.' Sinclair paused dramatically. 'Murder even.'

'As I understand it, Home Secretary,' said Cork, 'the military commanders were acting within the common law, which authorises them—'

'It authorises them nothing,' said Sinclair savagely. 'And I want them dealt with according to the law. This whole thing has gone far enough, and it's time that the judiciary decided whether they were acting illegally. Then, and only then, will this whole matter be resolved.'

'In that case, I'm afraid we'll need witnesses,' said Cork. He spoke quietly, refusing to respond to Sinclair's wild assertions.

'That shouldn't be a problem, surely, Sir Lionel. There were plenty of policemen there.'

'If you think that I'll be able to find a single policeman prepared to testify against the soldiers who, in many cases, saved their lives, I'm afraid you're wrong.'

'That's scandalous,' said Sinclair. 'Do you mean that they'll refuse to give evidence? That would be a disciplinary offence.'

Cork smiled at the Home Secretary's naivety. 'It's not so much that they'll refuse, Home Secretary,' he said, 'more that their memories will be found wanting when it comes to it.'

'But—'

'You see, Home Secretary,' said Cork, 'policemen are very good at not seeing things they don't want to see. And, apart from anything else, even assuming that the CPS decides to prosecute, it would be months before any cases came to court. And by that time memories will definitely have faded.'

The Home Secretary stood up, his face suffused with anger. 'I sincerely hope that you are not being deliberately obstructive, Sir Lionel,' he said.

The Commissioner stood up also. 'I'll let you have my report as soon as possible, Home Secretary,' he said.

While the Home Secretary had been venting his wrath on the Commissioner of Police, Graeme Kent was attempting to reprimand the Chief of the General Staff. 'I understand that you ordered the deployment of a brigade of troops in the Whitehall area yesterday, Sir Simon.' Kent looked tired and drawn. He knew that he was caught between Sir Simon Macey and the Prime Minister, and it would be the latter who would be demanding an explanation, and possibly Kent's resignation.

'Yes, I did.'

'Against my express wishes and those of the Prime Minister.'

'In a military situation, political wishes do not have the weight of law, Secretary of State.'

Graeme Kent sighed. 'It is quite evident, Sir Simon, that you and I have now reached the stage where we are not going to agree on anything.' He leaned back in his chair and gripped the arms until his knuckles showed white. 'I have been authorised by the Prime Minister to tell you that he intends to recommend to the Queen that you be appointed a field marshal and elevated to the peerage.'

'Is that some sort of reward?' asked Macey sarcastically.

'No, Sir Simon, it is in exchange for your resignation as Chief of the General Staff.'

'I see.' Macey crossed his legs and gazed mildly at the Secretary of State. 'Bribery, in other words.'

Kent shrugged. 'Call it what you like.' He switched on his desk lamp to supplement the overhead lighting. The broken windows had been boarded up following the riot and all natural light had been obscured. Then he made a mistake by saying, 'The Prime Minister thinks it would look bad if you were dismissed. At the present time, that is.'

Realising his error, he added, 'However ...' and left the sentence unfinished.

'I don't particularly want to go to the Lords,' said Macey, 'at least not yet, and there are no vacancies for field marshal. As I'm sure you know, the establishment allows for eight and there are eight. And they all seem pretty healthy to me.'

'The establishment can be changed, Sir Simon,' said Kent smoothly, 'but I would rather that you *didn't* force me into dismissing you.'

'No, you wouldn't want to upset the Prime Minister, would you?' said Macey cuttingly. He frequently showed more political acumen than the Secretary of State. 'It might look like panic.'

'I propose to give you twenty-four hours to think over my offer, Sir Simon,' said Kent. 'I would hate for you to regret turning it down.'

'As you wish, Secretary of State.' General Sir Simon Macey nodded. Twenty-four hours was all he needed to make up his mind.

That breathing space, however, was to prove a dreadful error on the part of the Secretary of State for Defence. An error that was to redound violently on the heads of the Prime Minister and the rest of the Cabinet.

Macey was still in a foul mood when he returned to his office. 'Is my car ready, Imogen?' he demanded.

'Not as far as I know, sir,' Imogen replied coolly.

'For God's sake, girl, I've got a luncheon appointment at the Army and Navy.' Macey glanced ostentatiously at his watch.

'I'm sorry, sir, I didn't know that. There's nothing in your diary.'

'I know it's not in my diary, but I'm sure I told you about it,' snapped Macey. 'Well don't stand there, Major Cresswell, get to it.'

Imogen suppressed her anger and held out a sheet of

paper. 'This priority signal has just arrived from GOC London District, sir,' she said patiently. 'It contains details of an incident that occurred at Wellington Barracks an hour or so ago.'

Macey snatched the form and scanned it. 'Bloody marvellous,' he said and, handing the form back to his ADC, suddenly relented. 'Sorry I shouted, Imogen,' he said. 'Bit of a bad day.'

'I know the feeling, sir,' said Imogen wryly. 'I'll get someone to send for your driver.'

'Yes, thank you,' said Macey absently, 'and perhaps you'd ask General Aston if he would be so good as to spare me a moment at, say, two-thirty.'

When Macey and the Chancellor of the Exchequer met for lunch at the Army and Navy Club in Pall Mall, they found that some of the tables had been smashed by chunks of concrete that had been thrown through the windows during the previous day's riot. But the head waiter assured them that the kitchens were still functioning normally. 'It's business as usual, gentlemen,' he said cheerfully and showed them to a table.

Macey, still delighted at the army's success in routing Sunday's rioters, rubbed his hands together. 'And what does the Prime Minister think now, Alex?' he asked.

Alexander Crisp pushed the menu to one side and glanced briefly at the boarded up windows of the club. 'No idea,' he said.

'Really? No reaction at all?'

'I haven't seen him today, Simon, but I'm not sure that he knows what's going on anyway. I have to say that if one surveys the current situation through the eyes of the Prime Minister, one does not get a very accurate picture. Added to which Kenneth Sinclair and your man Kent seem to be playing some devious game.'

'In what way?' Macey beckoned to a waiter and then leaned back in his chair, a cynical smile on his face.

'You've seen the papers, I take it?'

'Yes,' said Macey. 'Not as much coverage as I thought there would be.'

'It's rather strange, but such reports as have appeared in the papers and on television seem to have played down the Whitehall riot. Well, not so much played it down as left out details. Usually they list the injuries to police and rioters, and damage to property. But there's none of that. And Fairley is in Downing Street, refusing to see anyone. Claims he's got meetings all day. To be frank, Simon, I think he's running scared. The situation's out of hand, but Bob Fairley has said publicly that he will not use the army and now he's frightened to go back on that undertaking.'

'Unusual for a politician,' murmured Macey.

Crisp ignored the soldier's jibe. 'Frankly, I don't think he knows what the hell to do.'

'Can't you force him out, Alex?'

The Chancellor did not dismiss that proposition immediately. 'I wish I knew of a way, Simon, but as I said the other day, this is not exactly a propitious moment for a change of leadership.'

'What would you do if you succeeded Fairley, Alex?' Macey posed the question in a casual way, as if the reply would be of no real consequence.

Crisp smiled. 'The first thing I'd do is mobilise the army. Put them on to the streets and get this mess cleared up.'

'You make it sound as though you're dealing with a dustmen's strike, Alex.'

'Not far from the truth, really. The trouble is – and this is strictly between you and me, Simon – that Sinclair and, to a lesser extent, Kent are playing politics. Each one of them is trying to score off the other and is using the civil disorder as a device with which to unseat Fairley. And each wants to succeed him. But that's not what being in government is about.'

'It's a dangerous game,' said Macey. 'At the present time anyway.'

'Meaning?' Crisp glanced quizzically at the Chief of the General Staff.

'The Whitehall riot was a damned close-run thing, Alex. Those people were within an ace of sacking 10 Downing Street. If they'd got in, there is a good chance that they'd have murdered Fairley and anyone else who was in the building.' Macey leaned forward. 'You'll have heard about the attack on Wellington Barracks this morning, I take it?'

'Yes, but not the whole story. Perhaps you can fill me in.'

With a certain relish, Macey related details of the abortive assault. 'If they had succeeded, Downing Street could have been attacked again this morning, and there's no telling what the outcome of that might have been. Fortunately the Grenadier Guards were on the alert, but we might not be so lucky next time.'

Crisp was clearly shaken by Macey's news. 'We?' he said.

'The security forces,' said Macey, coining a phrase that had been familiar to the inhabitants of Northern Ireland. 'But to let the Prime Minister be murdered might be the only way you'll get rid of him,' he added softly.

Crisp leaned back to allow the waiter to serve the soup. 'You might be right at that, Simon.' He laughed and shook his head. 'But this is a damned worrying situation.'

'There could be a way, Alex.' Macey spoke quietly, as though what he was about to propose was the sort of topic that was discussed over lunch every day.

'What way is that?' Crisp dabbed at his lips with a table napkin and waited expectantly.

'There are precedents for the army running things when the civilian government has proved to be inept.'

Crisp smiled. 'Yes, in Africa or South America, perhaps.

Even Greece. But never here, Simon. At least not since
Oliver Cromwell.'

'It's not as bizarre as it sounds, Alex,' said Macey,
breaking a bread roll. 'Try to look at it objectively. With
due respect to yourself, we have a weak government faced
with widespread public disorder. The worst we've ever
known. And the mob is getting stronger every day. Every
time they get away with something like yesterday's mayhem in Whitehall, every time another murderer is freed for
so-called lack of evidence, all the time that crime is
increasing, they get stronger still. Now if you want mob
rule, a sure way to get it is to sit back and wait. But if the
army takes charge, at least you'll know that you have
conscientious and well-organised men looking after things.
Men whose training has taught them to be calm in a crisis.'
He put butter on a piece of bread roll, but then left it on the
plate. 'You were at Sandhurst, Alex. You know the quality
of chaps they turn out.'

For a moment or two Crisp looked pensively at
Macey. 'A military government in peacetime England?' He
shook his head sadly. 'Is that what you're suggesting,
Simon?'

'No. What I'm suggesting is that if the Conservative
Party is incapable of removing a spent Prime Minister, then
someone else will have to do it for them. Better the army
than the mob. But I don't mean military government. The
army should merely be the vehicle that replaces that Prime
Minister with another Cabinet minister who can run
things. Like you, Alex.'

There was silence for some time as Crisp carefully
spooned the last of his soup. Then, taking a sip of wine, he
looked directly at Macey. 'Do you really think that things
have got that bad, Simon?'

'Yes, I do.' Macey gazed across the room as he gathered
his thoughts. 'I'm the Chief of the General Staff, Alex. I'm
not prone to making wild statements. First thing this

morning I received reports from the three commanding
officers involved in yesterday's riot, and they scared the
hell out of me. I tell you, Alex, if Fairley's not removed from
10 Downing Street very quickly, this country will dissolve
into anarchy. A way of life that has existed for centuries
will just disappear, and God alone knows what will take its
place, although we've had an insight. All the hallowed
institutions, the ancient universities, the House of Lords –
the Commons too perhaps, the MCC, Sandhurst and
certainly clubs like this' – he waved a hand around the
room for emphasis – 'will be gone forever. And you and I,
Alex, will be swept away with them.'

Again there was a long silence while Crisp dissected a
carrot. It was a silence that Macey had no intention of
interrupting.

Then, at last, Crisp looked up. 'What do you want of me
then, Simon?' he asked.

Macey placed his knife and fork together and folded his
hands in his lap. 'If it so happened that Fairley came to be
removed from office, in the interests of public order,' he
said, an earnest expression on his face, 'we would need a
minister capable of taking over from him. Neither Sinclair
nor Kent is the man; they've both shown advanced
symptoms of arrogance and ignorance. It would need the
steadying hand of a seasoned politician, someone with
democratic principles, a solid political background and
sufficient gravitas. That's you, Alex. A man of your calibre
would show the country that it had not been taken over by
a junta of colonels.'

Crisp gave a tight smile. 'I take it that by "seasoned",
you mean elderly, Simon?' he said.

'You're the same age as me, give or take a few months,'
said Macey. 'But I won't deny that you're a respected elder
statesman.'

Crisp absently flicked a crumb from the polished surface
of the table and then lined up his mat with the edge. He had

been in the House for long enough to recognise a blandishment when he heard one. 'I will not abuse the law, Simon,' he said, suddenly looking up.

Macey sensed the caution in Crisp's response, emphasising as it did the politician's doctrine of backing everything both ways. 'Of course not, Alex, my dear fellow,' he said, and smiled reassuringly. 'I am merely asking if you would be prepared to take over the leadership if anything happened to Fairley . . .' He paused. 'And, for that matter, to Sinclair and Kent who, it seems, regard themselves as the heirs apparent.'

For a long time, Crisp surveyed the cabinet pudding that the waiter had just placed in front of him. Then he plunged his spoon into it with grim determination. 'I would be prepared to do it, Simon,' he said and, looking up, repeated, 'but I'll not be involved in anything illegal.'

'Naturally,' murmured Macey, 'but there is just one thing you could keep me advised about . . .'

'Well, Arthur, what do you think?' The Chief of the General Staff sat down opposite Sir Arthur Aston and stirred his tea. 'In a sense I suppose that what I'm suggesting is a bit like the so-called Curragh mutiny.' As GOC Land Command, Aston was the officer without whose co-operation Macey's plan would be stillborn.

'Actually, it's quite the opposite of what happened at the Curragh,' said Aston who, at one stage in his career, had lectured on military history and tactics at the Staff College. 'In Ireland the government intended to use troops to quell Ulster's resistance to independence, and it was the army who didn't agree. This is the other way around.'

'Yes, well, whatever.' Macey should have known better than to quote military history to Aston. 'The point is, Arthur, that things can't be allowed to go on as they are. I'm told that Robert Fairley is sitting in Downing Street trying to pretend that all is well. I'm not sure of our Secretary of State, but I think he's just the messenger boy. It seems to me that he and Kenneth Sinclair at the Home Office are biding their time, hoping that Fairley will cut and run, and then there'll be a fight between those two for Number Ten.' It was not an accurate version of what Alexander Crisp had told Macey over lunch, but it would do for Aston.

'Does the Prime Minister know about this abysmal attempt to break into the armoury at Wellington Barracks this morning, Simon?'

'I don't know,' said Macey. 'It's interesting, though. Fits the definition of armed insurrection, of course. Apparently the ringleader admitted that they intended to seize arms to attack Number Ten. That amounts to a plot to overthrow the lawfully elected government.'

Aston nodded. 'And it seems to me that they're just going to sit there and let it happen,' he said, choosing his words carefully. 'But where does that put the army?'

'We have to do something, Arthur. As I see it, we have a duty to protect the government from mob rule.'

'I agree with you. The situation's ridiculous. It can't be allowed to continue, and if the government refuses to act, then we must. But how do we go about it?'

'Call in your formation commanders today, Arthur, and put it to them straight. The Prime Minister has set his face against military intervention. Whatever his reasoning, it's clearly a misguided decision.'

'And if the army declines to go along with us?'

Macey smiled. 'It's the Curragh all over again, Arthur. If formation commanders won't co-operate, we can't coerce them, but it might be a good idea to switch those who won't to non-operational posts.'

'Where do you want me to hold this meeting, Simon? Here at the MOD?'

'I think not, Arthur. How about Steele's Road? It's secure, and commanders can get in by helicopter if they want.'

*

Since the decimation of the British Army under Options for Change, there weren't many senior officers left, and the few who commanded those divisions and brigades remaining in England assembled in the conference room of 4 Division's Headquarters at Steele's Road, Aldershot, at eight o'clock that evening. There was an air of tense expectation. Not since the United Nations' intervention in the Gulf crisis had so many senior commanders been summoned to an urgent meeting, and they scented momentous events.

'You will all be aware, gentlemen, of the very serious situation obtaining in the country today,' began General Sir Arthur Aston. 'And although the Prime Minister seems sternly to have rejected the organised deployment of the army to suppress rioting, commanding officers are taking action in accordance with their perception of the common law. This morning, as you will know from the renewed alert-state, an attempt was made to seize arms from Wellington Barracks. You will also know that the attempt failed.' Aston paused. 'It seems that the Grenadiers take a poor view of such behaviour,' he added and received a subdued chuckle from his audience. 'But now for the serious part,' he continued. 'The CGS and I, together with other senior officers, have been monitoring the situation very carefully, and we have come to the conclusion that the government is seized with a sort of paralysis. They will not act to suppress what was, today, an attempt at armed insurrection. Now that the news about the Wellington Barracks fiasco has been made public, and given the wide availability of firearms, there is no doubt in my mind that other attempts will be made by the rabble to take up arms against the government. And, gentlemen, we have a duty to prevent armed insurrection against the Crown. As the Queen's soldiers, we cannot – we will not – stand by and let it happen.'

There was a muted mumble of agreement and one

brigadier asked, 'What are you proposing we should do about it, sir?'

'I want you to call in your battalion and regimental commanders and discover if they are willing to support the Chief of the General Staff in whatever action he decides is necessary to restore order. I need hardly say that these conferences must take place in the utmost secrecy. And I should like your answers' – Aston glanced at his watch – 'by eleven hundred hours tomorrow. That is all, gentlemen.'

At twelve noon the following day General Sir Arthur Aston strode into Macey's office. 'The message from the colonels is as we imagined, Simon,' he said, 'but couched rather cleverly, I thought.'

'Oh?' Macey took off the glasses he occasionally wore and laid them on his desk. 'I must say you've been very quick.' He peered at the small clock on his desk.

'They will continue to obey the orders of the generals and officers set over them.' Aston smiled as he repeated the soldier's oath.

'Excellent. In that case, Arthur, we shall open up the Tactical Headquarters at Northwood on a twenty-four-hour basis so that operations can be conducted from there.' Macey spent a few moments scribbling out a message and then flicked the switch on his intercom. 'Come in, Imogen, will you?'

Imogen Cresswell appeared in the doorway of the office. 'Yes, sir?'

'Get this signal off to all units, Flash and Secret. Then inform Colonel Crosby urgently that he is to meet me at Northwoc   soonest. And arrange helicopters for each of us.'

'Very good, sir,' said Imogen, attempting to conceal her anger at Macey's peremptory rudeness.

'I shall be back later, Imogen. Perhaps you'd wait until

I return. Just in case anything crops up.'

'What I'm asking you to do, Tim,' said Macey, 'probably goes beyond what I am entitled to ask of you. All I can say is we're safeguarding the Queen.'

Colonel Crosby grinned at the Chief of the General Staff. 'From the way the brigade commander avoided the real point of his little talk this morning, sir,' he said, 'I sort of got the impression that we're moving into the unknown.'

'If you wish to refuse the assignment, I shall quite understand, Tim,' said Macey. 'Incidentally,' he added, intent on pushing Crosby into making what, in his view, was the right decision, 'General Dane has just told me that you are one of the officers who is to be bowler-hatted when the regiment's disbanded.'

Crosby nodded. 'Comes as no surprise, sir,' he said. 'I have rather been bringing myself to notice of late.'

'But that is not all, Tim, I'm afraid.' Macey continued to speak softly. 'I have heard that the Home Secretary is seeking to prosecute all those soldiers who intervened in Sunday's riot.'

'What?' Crosby slumped in his chair. 'Is that some sort of joke, sir?'

'If it is, I for one fail to see the funny side of it,' said Macey. 'But the bloody man's apparently determined to stop the military from putting down disorder.'

For some seconds Crosby stared moodily at the floor. Then, his mind made up, he looked at the CGS. 'What do you want me to do, sir?' he asked.

'Come down to the TSR, Tim, and I'll explain.' Macey stood up and he and Crosby walked along the corridor and took the lift to the basement, where the CGS led the hussar colonel into the Top Secret Room, a bunker-like and windowless office that was immune from any electronic eavesdropping device known to exist. Macey took a large-scale map of the Whitehall area from a locked cabinet and spread it on a table. 'Have a look at this,' he said.

Crosby leaned forward. 'Looks familiar, sir,' he said.

Macey sat on a stool and gazed closely at Crosby as though weighing up his reliability. 'You were in Whitehall at the weekend, Tim, and you saw what a close call it was.' Crosby nodded. 'That mob,' Macey continued, 'was within a whisker of gaining entry to Number Ten. And they were encouraged by the obvious disarray of the police. Perhaps so encouraged that they'll try again.' He fidgeted restlessly. 'In fact they almost certainly will. If they tried to get into the armoury at Wellington Barracks, they mean business.' A wintry smile crossed his face. 'But the Prime Minister and the Cabinet are too stubborn to see danger when they're staring it in the face. The police are too stretched to protect them, and so we must. But to a soldier, 10 Downing Street is virtually indefensible.'

'What are you suggesting, sir?' Crosby knew, but wanted Macey to put it into words.

'For their own good, Tim, the Cabinet must be moved to somewhere safer. We cannot defend them where they are.'

'Where do you propose to put them, sir? One of the old regional seats of government?'

Macey shook his head. 'No good,' he said. 'They were all sold off after the Cold War ended. No, it will have to be somewhere else.' He glanced up from the plan of Whitehall. 'You've served in Germany, haven't you?' The CGS had examined Crosby's personal file closely and knew everything there was to know about him.

'Yes, sir.' Crosby looked puzzled. 'The regiment was at Bad Lippspringe.'

'Yes, of course,' said Macey as though it was news to him. 'Then you'll know Sennelager.'

'Like the back of my hand, sir. But is this all legal?' A brief frown crossed Crosby's face. 'I mean, couldn't our action be misinterpreted?'

'Possibly,' said Macey, 'but we must do what is best for

the country. And at the present time protecting the Queen and Her Majesty's Government seems to me to be a top priority.'

Crosby nodded slowly. 'Well, put like that, sir, I suppose there's no alternative.'

'Good. So this is the plan ...' Macey outlined what he had in mind, occasionally prodding the map with a forefinger as he emphasised salient points. 'Naturally I shall leave to you the way in which you execute the operation, Tim,' he said, standing upright. 'But I shall advise you of the exact timing.' He shook hands with the young hussar colonel. 'You'll need every minute you've got, so start preparing your operation order the moment you get back. You may get very little notice of D-day.'

On Tuesday morning, at about the time that formation commanders were reporting back to General Aston, Detective Superintendent Gordon Whitmore walked slowly down the pathway leading from the back door of 10 Downing Street, unlocked the gate and stepped out on to Horse Guards Parade. He glanced across at the waiting helicopter and surveyed the emptiness of the parade ground, devoid now of the cars that were usually allowed to park there. There must have been two hundred police ringing Horse Guards Parade, and Whitmore idly wondered what Robert Fairley's decision to go to Chequers for a couple of days must be costing the taxpayer.

'All correct, sir.' A uniformed inspector saluted Whitmore.

'Not taking any chances, I see,' said Whitmore.

'No, sir. The assistant commissioner's ordered Horse Guards and Approach Road to be closed. All you can see now are policemen. It's only to cover the PM's departure, then we can put them back to work.' The inspector spoke bitterly and glanced at his watch. 'Is the PM about ready to depart, sir?' he asked.

'Any minute now.' Whitmore glanced over his shoulder just as the Prime Minister appeared in the gateway, accompanied by David Enderby, Whitmore's deputy.

'All set, Gordon?' asked Fairley.

'Ready when you are, sir.' Whitmore pointed at the blades of the helicopter's rotor, still revolving lazily in the morning sunshine. 'Don't forget to keep your head down.'

'I've done little else these last few days, Gordon,' said the Prime Minister wearily.

By half past four that same afternoon, Robert Fairley and his detective were taking a leisurely stroll in the vast grounds of Chequers. Fairley was wearing a pair of beige trousers and an old woolly cardigan over a check shirt.

'I always find Chequers a wonderfully relaxing place, Gordon,' said the Prime Minister.

'A bit of Buckinghamshire air works miracles, sir.' Whitmore was making polite conversation. In fact he detested Chequers. It was old and it was draughty, and he had once offended the curator, the title the Chequers Trust gave the housekeeper, by suggesting that it should be pulled down and replaced by a modern dwelling.

'I'd rather be playing a round of golf, though.' Fairley glanced hopefully at his protection officer. 'But I suppose you'd veto that on the grounds of security?'

''Fraid so, sir. Ellesborough golf course is impossible to guard.' Whitmore had anticipated the Prime Minister's suggestion and had taken a run out to the golf club earlier. He had walked the course many times with Fairley but wanted to reassure himself that, in the present climate of uncertainty, it would be foolish to allow the Prime Minister to roam the fairways. Any one of the hills around the course would offer an undetectable hiding place for a determined sniper. The exposure had worried him often in the past, but now it would be little short of insanity to allow the Prime Minister to play golf there. 'I reckon we'd need three thousand troops to give even a measure of security, sir,' he added.

'Well that would do my dented image no good at all, Gordon.' The Prime Minister grinned and, reversing his walking stick, took a swipe at a dandelion. 'The press would have a field day with that. "Prime Minister refuses to use troops but plays golf surrounded by brigade of infantry." Yes, they'd love that.' He stopped and sat down on a low branch of an old oak tree. For a few minutes he scraped at the bowl of his pipe with a reamer and then filled it before handing his pouch to Whitmore. 'Have a fill,' he said.

'Any progress on the use of the French police, sir?' asked Whitmore, slowly filling his pipe with Fairley's tobacco.

'They've stymied us, Gordon. The air-traffic controllers are still on strike, and the ports are blockaded. The damned fishermen have joined in now as a protest against the French, and the navy are being very laggardly in attempting to clear a passage.'

'What about RAF stations, sir?'

'They're creating problems about giving clearance for landing, and by some strange coincidence they've taken to parking tenders and fire engines across their runways. They claim that it's some sort of security measure. Graeme Kent's spoken to the Chief of the Air Staff and he's promised to do something about it. But you know what the services are like. When they decide to stonewall, nothing gets done in a hurry.' Fairley stood up and continued his stroll. 'But when this is all over, there'll be a few heads rolling at the Ministry of Defence, I can tell you, Gordon.'

'And you're definitely not going to use troops, sir?' Whitmore eased his revolver holster into a more comfortable position and kept pace with the Prime Minister.

'No, Gordon. It's wrong, you see.' Fairley was less vehement in his response than he was with his Cabinet colleagues. 'We've got the awful example of Northern

Ireland. Troops were there for over twenty-five years, stuck in a never-ending cycle of violence, and I don't want it to happen here. Once you introduce the military into a civil disorder situation, the people causing the trouble get accustomed to their presence, and then there's no way of getting them out again.' The Prime Minister turned his head towards his detective. 'How are your people feeling about it all?'

Whitmore sighed inwardly. It was always the same. The Prime Minister imagined that his detective would be fully conversant with all that went on in each of the police forces in the country. The truth of the matter was that, being stationed at Downing Street, Whitmore knew more of what went on there than he knew about Scotland Yard, never mind the rest. But he felt that he ought to say something. 'Many more riots like the one in Whitehall the day before yesterday, sir, and the force will be on its knees. There are still about a hundred officers in hospital.'

The Prime Minister stopped dead in his tracks and turned to face Whitmore. 'How many?'

'About a hundred, sir, so I was told.'

'But that's ridiculous. The Home Secretary told me that there were three times that many, and that four policemen had been killed.'

Whitmore shook his head and then paused. In his experience it was most unwise to argue with the Prime Minister, or any politician for that matter, but Fairley had clearly been misinformed. 'There were no fatalities, sir. I saw the messages when I was across at the Yard. A hundred and twenty-one officers were injured, seventeen seriously.'

'Is that all?' said the Prime Minister, but realised immediately that his comment had sounded callous, particularly to a policeman. 'I'm sorry, Gordon, I didn't mean it to sound like that,' he added. 'That's bad enough, but the Home Secretary made out that it was far worse.'

'I can assure you that those are the correct figures, sir.'

'Are you certain, Gordon?'

'Absolutely, sir.'

'I see.' The Prime Minister poked at the ground with his stick. 'They're trying to force me into deploying the military, Gordon. And that raises another question. Why were there no details in the papers or on television, other than a general sort of coverage?'

'I'm prepared to swear by those figures, sir.' Whitmore paused to wonder why Fairley was asking him the question rather than one of his officials. He had been given the details in confidence, in case they impinged upon his task of protecting the Prime Minister, but after his interview with the Commissioner he felt no compunction about disclosing them to his principal. 'I understand that the Home Secretary ordered the Commissioner not to release any figures of injuries to the media, sir.' He spoke cautiously; this was really none of his business. 'Apparently he was fearful that it might encourage further disorder. At least that's what was said. I understand that the Home Secretary issued a DA notice too, sir.' Whitmore had been surprised at that. A DA notice was normally issued to the media only when the government wished to prevent the publication of sensitive information that might affect national security.

'A DA notice? But that's disgraceful, Gordon.' The Prime Minister turned back towards the house and then stopped again. 'Are you sure of that? About the DA notice, I mean.'

'Yes, sir. I saw a copy of it that the Press Bureau at the Yard received. I also saw a copy of the report that went to the Home Office containing details of the casualties.'

'People are trying to delude me, Gordon,' said Fairley, his face black with suppressed rage. 'They're trying to force me into deploying the military by feeding me false information, and I'm not having it. What time is it?'

Whitmore glanced at his watch. 'Just gone five, sir.'

'Time for tea, Gordon,' said the Prime Minister. 'When we get in, ask the Garden Room girl to see me straight-away, will you? I will not have colleagues distorting the facts or keeping them from me or from the public.'

The duty Garden Room girl, the secretary whose turn it had been to accompany the Prime Minister to Chequers on this occasion, had been having a bath when she was summoned urgently to the Prime Minister's presence. She appeared in the White Parlour wearing a fetching pink satin robe and clutching a shorthand notebook. 'Please excuse my dress, Prime Minister,' she said. 'I came as soon as I could, but I was having a bath.'

The Prime Minister appeared not to notice. 'Sarah, get hold of the Home Secretary and the Secretary of State for Defence, will you, please? I want them here, and I want them here this evening. And I don't care what they're doing or what they have to cancel. I'll accept no excuses. And when you've done that, tell the Cabinet Secretary to arrange a special Cabinet for . . .' He paused. 'What day is it?' he asked, as though he genuinely didn't know.

'Tuesday, Prime Minister.'

'Yes. Very well, a Cabinet for Thursday at ten o'clock.'

'Yes, Prime Minister,' said Sarah. She had never seen Robert Fairley so angry.

CHAPTER TWELVE

Macey's 'Flash' signal, mobilising all army units in the United Kingdom, had gone out shortly after Robert Fairley and his detectives had left for Chequers that morning, and within hours armed soldiers were patrolling the streets. Suddenly a pattern of behaviour that had in the past become familiar to the people of Ulster was being re-enacted on the streets of London and other major cities.

The Secretary of State for Defence was furious and sent for Macey the moment the CGS had returned from Northwood. 'Precisely what is the meaning of this, General Macey?' he asked, striding back and forth across his office.

'At the risk of repeating myself, Secretary of State,' said Macey, 'soldiers are still being deployed by commanding officers, who see such tasks as their duty and their obligation under the law. Unless the military are properly organised to deal with civil disorder, they run the risk of being overwhelmed. Unnecessary death and injury to the army could ensue. By putting the troops out and ensuring that reinforcements are available, I hope to keep casualties to a minimum.'

'Do you, General? Do you, indeed? Well I am instructing you that these soldiers are to be withdrawn to barracks immediately.' Kent was shouting now. 'Immediately, do you hear?'

'Yes, I hear you, Secretary of State, but I am not complying. You have no authority to order me to do something that is contrary to my duty under the law. There has even been an incident of armed insurrection now—'

'Rubbish!' Macey's calmness was infuriating Kent even further and his face was working with rage. 'One man seizing a rifle from a sentry at Wellington Barracks is not armed insurrection, man!' he shouted.

Macey smiled. 'You may find that the Attorney-General holds a slightly different view, Secretary of State,' he said. 'And I would point out that no less than seven handguns were seized from the insurgents.'

'Be that as it may, General—' began Kent but broke off as one of his secretaries entered the office. 'I said I wasn't to be interrupted,' he snapped, scowling at the unfortunate woman.

'There's an urgent message from the Prime Minister, Secretary of State,' she said. 'You are wanted at Chequers immediately.'

'Would you care for the use of a helicopter?' asked Macey.

By the time that Kenneth Sinclair and Graeme Kent arrived at Chequers it was past nine o'clock, and the duty stewardess conducted them quickly to the Great Parlour on the first floor of the old house.

The Prime Minister was seated in an armchair at the far end, at the head of the long table that dominated the oak-panelled room; behind him, long brown velvet curtains acted as an impressive backdrop. In the centre of the table was a vase of white carnations.

'Sit down, gentlemen,' said Fairley. 'Thank you for coming.' There was an icy tone to the courtesy. 'It has come to my notice,' he began, without preamble, 'that I was given a wholly inaccurate account of the Whitehall riot.'

His gaze settled on the Home Secretary. 'I was told that four police officers had been killed. I was told that the police suffered something in the order of three hundred casualties. I was told that, of that figure, seventy-five officers had been seriously injured and two hundred police officers were still in hospital. Those figures were a gross exaggeration of the truth.' Fairley punched out his accusations like the searing cuts of a whiplash.

The Home Secretary shifted uncomfortably in his chair.

'On top of which,' the Prime Minister continued, 'I have learned that the media were muzzled with a DA notice, an action which was not only totally inappropriate in the circumstances but a gross violation of the terms under which such notices are issued.' Fairley rested his hands on the table and linked his fingers, a grim expression of betrayal on his face. 'So explain to me, gentlemen, precisely why I have been lied to.'

'Reports of the number of injuries were very confused to start with, Prime Minister—' The Home Secretary's nervous and impulsive response was immediately interrupted.

'Not that confused.' The Prime Minister snapped. 'My detective was able to give me the full facts this afternoon, Home Secretary. Figures that he had obtained from Scotland Yard on the morning following the disturbance. Is the Home Office machine so gravely in need of overhaul that it is unable to obtain such figures, figures that the Commissioner of Police passed to your department almost immediately? Were they lost in some moribund administrative process?' The sarcasm flowed unchecked from Fairley's tight lips.

'I thought, that is, er, we thought ...' Sinclair looked desperately at Graeme Kent, vainly seeking support. 'It was thought better not to worry you with the trivia of the riot, Prime Minister—'

'Trivia?' Fairley banged the table with the flat of his hand. 'How dare you presume to keep vital information from me? If you consider this to be trivia, I dread to imagine what might strike you as important.' He rounded on Graeme Kent. 'And what about you, Secretary of State for Defence? Did you know about this?' Fairley's steely gaze seemed to bore right into Kent.

'Well, yes, Prime Minister, but I didn't regard it as my place to inform you of a Home Office matter. The protocol—'

'Protocol, fiddlesticks,' thundered Fairley. 'I know what you're doing, both of you.' He surveyed the pair petulantly. 'If you think that you can force me into deploying the military by tactics of this nature, you are very much mistaken, gentlemen.' He glared at Sinclair and Kent in turn. 'I know that each of you has prime ministerial aspirations—'

'But, Prime Minister—' Sinclair and Kent both spoke at once.

Fairley ignored the interruption. 'But there is no vacancy,' he said. 'I am not a Margaret Thatcher. There will be no forcing me out, not without my first going to the Queen and seeking a dissolution. And I do not have to tell you, gentlemen, what the result of a general election would be were it to be held now.'

'I assure you, Prime Minister—' began Sinclair, making a second attempt to put his case.

But Fairley was brooking no excuses. 'Losing the general election would mean you losing your posts in government and, in your case, Home Secretary,' – he pointed a finger at Sinclair – 'with a majority of one thousand and sixty-three, very likely your seat as well.' He derived some grim satisfaction from the expression on Sinclair's face; he knew that the Home Secretary was living to the limit of his income. 'I want you both to consider your positions carefully. In simple terms, gentlemen, you will have to decide whether you intend to support me or become backbenchers. That is the stark choice facing you both.' He paused to run his hand over the shiny surface of the table. 'I am not a vindictive man, but I will not tolerate treachery. There will be a special Cabinet thirty-six hours from now, and unless I receive assurances of your unswerving loyalty at that time, I shall reallocate your portfolios as I see fit.'

The journey from Northwood to his temporary encampment in Richmond Park earlier that day had given Lieutenant-Colonel Crosby plenty of time to think about his conversation with the CGS. What Macey had asked him to do had, at first, sounded like sheer lunacy, but after careful consideration, Crosby decided that he had nothing to lose. He no longer cared. His wife had been murdered, her killer freed by the inadequacies of the justice system, and he was on the point of redundancy. The circumstances of his ruin were solely the fault of a government which was now content to see his country collapse in anarchy. He was unsure whether depression or anger dominated his emotions.

But then he recalled General Sir Lawrence Dane's enigmatic remark, that 'something may yet happen', and felt cheered that this is what he must have meant.

Despite his encounter with the irate Secretary of State, Macey was particularly ebullient when he returned to his office following Kent's hurried departure for Chequers. Ignoring the pile of files in his in-tray, he stood behind his desk and rubbed his hands together. 'I feel like celebrating tonight, Imogen,' he said. 'Ring up and book a table at the Savoy Grill.'

'For how many, sir?' Imogen knew exactly what Macey meant but, despite her desire to remain on trusted terms with him, she still resented his attitude.

Macey sensed her hostility and immediately tried to make amends. 'I'm sorry,' he said, 'that was rather presumptuous of me. Will you join me for dinner?' He smiled disarmingly.

'Thank you very much, sir.' Imogen returned Macey's smile. 'The Chancellor of the Exchequer telephoned while you were at Northwood, sir. He asked if you would ring him back on a secure line. As a matter of urgency.'

For a moment, Macey looked disconcerted. 'Er, yes, very well,' he said. 'I'll do that now. Perhaps you'd close the door.'

Following his conversation with Alexander Crisp, Macey telephoned Lieutenant-Colonel Crosby, again on a secure line.

'It's on for the day after tomorrow, Tim,' said Macey. 'Thursday.'

'Good God, sir, it's pretty short notice.' It was not that Crosby was having second thoughts, but the logistics required to mount the operation less than two days hence were formidable to say the least, and he'd only just got back to Richmond Park.

'You've got as much intelligence as you're going to get, Tim,' said Macey. 'And you've got the element of surprise.'

The linkman in Savoy Court touched his hat as Macey and Imogen alighted from the taxi and cast a discreet but appraising eye at the young woman's figure. He knew Sir Simon Macey, and he knew perfectly well that although Imogen was young enough to be the CGS's daughter, it was most unlikely that she was.

'Good evening, General. Beautiful evening, sir.' The linkman closed the door of the cab and moved quickly across the narrow pavement to give the revolving doors a push as Imogen stepped into one of the compartments. 'Thank you, sir, have a pleasant time,' he added as he pocketed the tip that Macey had handed him.

'You seem particularly pleased with yourself this evening,' said Imogen when they were settled at their table and the waiter had brought their drinks. She took a sip of her gin and tonic and looked directly at him.

'Do I?' Macey glanced around the sparsely occupied room. Most of the tables were shared by couples, some of whom, he surmised, were married but not to each other. Then he looked back at Imogen. 'Yes, I suppose I do,' he said. 'But today has gone well. I think that we are on the verge of exciting things, my dear.'

Although she had been unable to monitor the telephone calls that Macey had made, Imogen had sensed that something dramatic was about to happen and was determined to learn what it was. 'And what exciting things are they?' she asked in an offhand way. She found it difficult to envisage anything more exciting than the signal mobilising the army, which she had sent out that afternoon.

But Macey had no intention of divulging what was planned, even to his ADC. 'It's probably better that you don't know, Imogen,' he said, casting a casual eye down the wine list. He looked up. 'The fewer people who know, the better, and in times like these, one never knows who to trust.'

'Don't you trust me, General?' Imogen disguised the frisson of fear she felt by sipping at her gin and tonic.

Macey covered her hand with his own. 'Of course I trust you, my dear,' he said. 'But I also need to protect you. That's precisely why you must be kept in the dark. For the time being.'

As soon as he had finished talking to Macey on the telephone, Crosby called a conference of his officers. 'I have today been to see the Chief of the General Staff ...' he began.

The assembled officers looked hopeful. 'Have any luck, Colonel?' asked a squadron leader.

'No, none,' said Crosby. 'And it's worse than I thought. The regiment is to be disbanded, as you know, but further decisions have been taken.' He looked around the group, knowing that he was about to lie to them, to mislead them into a course of action they might not take if he told them the truth. 'I have been given to understand that none of you, officers or soldiers, will be remustered. You will all be discharged, services no longer required.'

'Bloody hell!' said a captain. 'I say, Colonel, that's not on.'

Crosby held up a hand. 'Oh, it gets worse,' he said. 'The Commissioner of Police has told the CGS that the Home Secretary is determined to launch prosecutions against every officer and soldier who helped suppress the Kingston and Putney riots, and . . .' he paused, 'against the Cumbrian Regiment for their effort in Chester. In addition to that, I understand that papers are being prepared for the Director of Public Prosecutions with a view to proceeding against officers and soldiers who were involved in the Whitehall riots at the weekend.'

There was a stunned silence. Then a young cornet spoke. 'That's damned unfair, Colonel,' he said. 'What the hell does this bloody government want of us? We were put on offer, and at Putney one of the lads was killed.'

'That's what we're paid for, you bloody young fool,' growled the adjutant.

'Yes, I know,' mumbled the cornet, unhappy that his outburst appeared to have been misconstrued, then lapsed into embarrassed silence.

'The whole army is seething with discontent at the treatment they've received from the government,' Crosby went on, 'both from the point of view of the disbandments and from the way in which they've viewed our attempts to help keep the peace. It's a dog-in-the-manger attitude. The government won't do anything but they won't let anyone else do anything either.'

'So what now, Colonel?' asked another captain.

'We have been given an opportunity to take decisive action, gentlemen,' said Crosby. 'If we're to go, then we'll go out in a blaze of glory.' As concisely as possible, Crosby outlined the task he had been given by the Chief of the General Staff.

As his audience sat in amazed silence, he added, 'Anyone who is unwilling to support me, and the regiment, will be held here in custody until the show's over.'

At first the officers of the 27th Royal Hussars found it hard to absorb Crosby's breathtaking statement. The enormity of an operation so decisive, so unparalleled – even in the history of their illustrious regiment – had taken even the seasoned officers by surprise. For some time the group was thoughtfully silent. They avoided each other's gaze and dwelt on the personal implications of an act which if not treasonable came damned close to it. Slowly each separately concluded that they were being presented with an opportunity to break out of the impasse into which they had been forced partly by their own actions and partly by a government that was taking away their regiment, their livelihood, their very reason for being. Then the questions began.

As the Thursday meeting of the Cabinet had been specially convened, Fairley turned immediately to the reason. 'For those of you who have yet to grasp it,' he said, surveying every one of his ministers, 'I wish to make abundantly clear that we are facing grave problems. We are not being helped to overcome them by the actions of the army, but that is something I hope to resolve very shortly.' The Cabinet looked expectant, but the Prime Minister did not enlarge on how he proposed to curb the military. 'Furthermore,' he went on, 'I am extremely displeased that certain colleagues have been acting in a way that indicates to me that they are not wholeheartedly supportive of my policies. I repeat, the military will *not* be deployed in support of the civil power to suppress the present disorders.' His clenched fist hammered on the table as he emphasised each word of his statement. Having arrived on Horse Guards Parade by helicopter, Fairley was unaware that soldiers were now openly patrolling the streets. And Kent was not about to tell him. 'The French president has agreed to my request for assistance, and as soon as the French police can be landed here they will reinforce our own. In the meantime I expect each and every one of you to support me to the hilt. In the light of the misinformation with which I have been supplied, I have given an ultimatum to certain ministers.' He drummed his fingers on the table in an attempt to contain his anger. 'If I do not have an undertaking from them, and from you all ...' he paused to allow his censorious gaze to sweep round the Cabinet table, 'of your absolute loyalty, I shall not hesitate to make changes.' The Prime Minister closed the leather-bound folder on the table in front of him. 'Well, gentlemen, am I to receive your allegiance or do we start playing musical chairs?'

Oblivious of the political crisis being played out behind him, the constable on duty at the rear of Number Ten looked up sharply at the sound of military vehicles crossing the parade ground at speed. In the present climate of disorder, all manner of unusual things were occurring, so it was with a marked lack of interest that he witnessed the arrival of the army, and he was not unduly disturbed when a corporal swung open the door of his small cabin. It was not until the soldier levelled a machine pistol at him, that he realised something untoward was happening.

'Out,' said the corporal.

The policeman stepped out into the weak April sunshine and the corporal grabbed at the personal radio lying on the table beside a newspaper.

'What's on then?' asked the constable.

'Just hand over your weapon, laddie,' said the corporal.

'What's this all about?' asked the policeman, making no immediate move to comply.

'You're relieved of duty, my old son,' said the corporal. 'That's what it's all about. Now make with the pistol.'

The policeman shrugged and handed over his revolver. Then, helplessly bemused, he watched as more soldiers started to spill out of the personnel carriers that now formed a phalanx of armour covering the back wall of the gardens of 10 and 11 Downing Street and the side wall by Foreign Office Green and the Mountbatten statue. Seconds later one of the armoured personnel carriers was driven at the garden gate to Number Ten, tossing aside the steel posts as if they were skittles, smashing down the brickwork and braking to a standstill at the foot of the steps leading to the French doors of the Cabinet Room.

Minutes earlier the inspector on duty in Downing Street had been faced with two armoured personnel carriers of a distinguished cavalry regiment and a major who calmly announced that he and his men had been sent to reinforce the security.

The inspector, who always felt socially inferior to the sort of man who became an officer in the cavalry, did not demur when he heard the bogus orders convincingly passed on in the upper-class drawl of the major in tank gear. The inspector just nodded and thought to himself that no one ever told him anything. He signalled to the constable manning the wedge-shaped steel barrier set into the roadway to allow the military vehicles to pass. The huge gates, normally an extra safeguard, had not been repaired following the Whitehall riot and had been forced open, hanging at a drunken angle.

The first intimation that all was not as it should be came an instant later when the soldiers calmly disarmed the police and took their personal radios from them. Then the major commanding the detachment rang the doorbell to

Number Ten and waited until the uniformed doorkeeper opened it before leading his troops into the entrance hall.

Although he had never before set foot in the Prime Minister's official residence, the major had spent half the previous night thoroughly familiarising himself with the plans. Pausing for only a moment beneath the lantern light fitting, he directed soldiers to the drivers' room to the right of the front door, to the press office behind it and to the detectives' office in the passageway leading to the Garden Room on the floor below. As they spread themselves quickly throughout the house, the telephone switchboard on the top floor was taken over and the two women operating it removed to another room. Troopers, under the command of a sergeant, had been sent to the private office and were now preventing the private secretaries and the duty clerk from taking any action. In the small office next door to the Cabinet Room, the Prime Minister's principal private secretary and the Foreign Office secretary were ordered, somewhat peremptorily, to join their colleagues in the private office.

The Prime Minister's protection officers were quickly disarmed and downstairs in the Garden Room the staff of the secretariat, all women, who had at first been amused at the sight of the soldiers, now became alarmed as they were herded out into the corridor at gunpoint.

No one had thought to press a panic button.

The main body of the invading party had raced down the long corridor to the Cabinet Room at the back of the house. As the soldiers, their faces hidden beneath ski masks, flooded into the room, they found that the members of the Cabinet were already on their feet, alarmed at the advent of an armoured car smashing down the garden wall. Stun grenades were thrown, and before the senior members of Her Majesty's Government had recovered sufficiently to wonder what was going on, almost all of them had been secured, face down, with plastic handcuffs.

All except the Chancellor of the Exchequer. As a former soldier, he was familiar with stun grenades and, at the precise moment that the door had been flung open, he had dived for the floor, shutting his eyes and clapping his hands to his ears. Now he jumped to his feet and drew a pistol before moving towards one of the soldiers. 'I think you should know—' he began.

One of the soldiers levelled a machine pistol at him. 'Stand still!' he shouted.

But the Chancellor advanced on the soldier, his pistol held in the relaxed way that only those confident in the use of firearms display. 'Look, you don't understand ...' he said, but those were the last words he ever uttered. The soldier, whose friend had been killed at Putney, responded by shooting him dead.

The shot concentrated the attention of the rest of the Cabinet as one man, and they struggled, from their prone positions, to twist their heads round, but before any of them could focus on what had happened the soldiers dragged them to their feet, hustled them out through the French windows and hurried them across the garden. As the handcuffed ministers were led away over the rubble that was all that remained of the garden-gate entrance, they were aware of the sudden noise of three giant Chinook helicopters touching down on Horse Guards Parade. With the minimum of delay, Robert Fairley was placed in one of them and his colleagues in the other two.

As the Cabinet was being placed aboard the helicopters, the blast of a whistle summoned the remainder of the raiding party and, leaving most of their bemused captives, they seized the Prime Minister's two detectives and ran through the house to join the rest of the detachment now climbing into the Chinooks. Seconds later, the three giant helicopters lifted off.

The entire operation had taken less than ten minutes, but the arrival of the helicopters, and the sight of the wrecked wall of Number Ten, had alerted a policeman as he turned into Horse Guards Approach Road from The Mall just in time to see the Cabinet being herded aboard the aircraft.

The policeman promptly sent a radio message to Charing Cross Police Station. Minutes later police vehicles, creating a galaxy of blue lights, began converging on Downing Street and Horse Guards as white area-cars and Traffic Division units were joined by flame-red carriers of the Diplomatic Protection Group.

But the response was too late. The police vehicles slowed down and stopped; there was nothing that they could do about the departing helicopters. All that remained for them to investigate was two abandoned armoured personnel carriers in Downing Street and two more on Horse Guards Parade. Seconds later they found the dead body of the Chancellor of the Exchequer sprawled on the floor of the Cabinet Room.

The Royal Air Force was eventually alerted but, ironically, Strike Command had been so weakened by the government's Options for Change that they were unable immediately to scramble any of their depleted force of Tornados. By the time they were airborne, the Chinooks, flying beneath the radar shield, had disappeared.

Later that day, amid great secrecy, two of the helicopters touched down on the parade ground of Blücher Barracks at Sennelager in North Rhine-Westphalia. The surviving members of the Cabinet were installed in a barrack block and surrounded by a strong guard of the 27th Hussars, the vanguard of which had arrived at Paderborn in a military transporter under the guise of replacing an unspecified unit of the British Army.

But some time before that, the third helicopter, carrying the Prime Minister and his two detectives, had landed on the lawn outside the rose garden to the south of Chequers.

In Germany, and in Buckinghamshire, the helicopters

were immediately placed under cover and camouflaged from aerial view. The Army Air Corps crews, who had been misled into believing that they were taking part in a highly secret exercise, were placed in secure accommodation and guarded closely.

Lieutenant-General Sir Roger Tinwall was standing at his window, staring diagonally across Whitehall at the entrance to Downing Street and thinking about where he would go for lunch, when he saw the armoured cars. His soldier's eye noted that all their distinguishing marks, including their registration numbers, had been obscured. Reaching for his binoculars, he witnessed the police being disarmed. Turning quickly to the telephone, he rang the General Officer Commanding London District and the Household Division.

'Tom,' said Tinwall, 'there's something bloody strange going on in Downing Street. I've just seen a couple of armoured cars go in there at a hell of a pace. I don't know what it's all about, but whoever they are, they've disarmed the police. What? No, it doesn't look like an exercise. Any idea what's happening?'

The GOC London District, whose office actually over-looked Horse Guards, had been in the lavatory at the moment of the attack and, having only returned in time to see the helicopters take off, was unable to shed any light on these strange events. However he did hazard an uninspired guess that it was probably an escalation of the more bizarre happenings of recent weeks.

Tinwall next telephoned New Scotland Yard and asked to speak to the Commissioner. After a delay of some minutes, he was put through to the staff officer and, following a further delay, eventually spoke to Sir Lionel Cork. 'What on earth's going on in Whitehall, Lionel?' Tinwall demanded.

'I'm afraid that things are a bit confused at the moment,

Roger,' said Cork calmly. 'Reports are still coming in, but I understand that Downing Street's been attacked. I'm told that the Chancellor of the Exchequer's been killed and the Cabinet's been seized.'

'Good God Almighty!' said Tinwall.

'I'm sorry, Roger,' said Cork, 'but I've got to go.'

'Yes, of course.' Tinwall replaced the receiver, but after a moment's thought he rang the guardroom at Buckingham Palace and spoke to the guard commander. 'Put the Palace on full alert,' he said crisply and briefly outlined what he knew of the attack on Downing Street.

Sharply dismissing the guard commander's initial disbelief, Tinwall spoke once more to the GOC London District and ordered him to send additional troops from Wellington Barracks to safeguard the Royal Family. Then he walked down the corridor to the office of the Chief of the General Staff, General Sir Simon Macey.

'Yes, I've heard, Roger.' Macey spoke calmly in the face of Tinwall's excited outburst.

Tinwall was astounded. 'You know about it, sir?' he said. 'This isn't some sort of huge joke, is it?'

'There's nothing funny about it, Roger,' said Macey. 'Elements of the armed forces appear to have taken over the government.'

'Good God!' said Tinwall. 'Well, who was it? I mean what regiment?'

'At this stage, I have no idea, Roger.' Macey covered his lie with an easy confidence.

'But that's treason, for God's sake.'

'Too bloody right it is,' said Macey, his anger a masterpiece of play-acting. 'But clearly our first priority is to protect the Crown, in case there's further trouble.'

'But I had no idea this was going to happen, sir.' It was a stupid statement to make, but Tinwall was aghast at the enormity of what the Chief of the General Staff was telling him. 'Did you know that the Chancellor of the Exchequer was shot in the attack? I'm told he's dead.'

'What?' For the first time, Macey showed some signs of being genuinely disconcerted. 'Dead, you say?'

'Yes, sir. I've just spoken to the Commissioner at Scotland Yard and he said that Crisp was killed by one of the raiding party.'

'The bloody fools.' Macey stood up and walked to the window where, briefly, he stared down into the street below. 'Have they gone completely mad?' Recovering himself, he turned again. 'Find out which unit was responsible for this outrage, Roger,' he said.

'I've already instituted urgent enquiries to identify it, sir.'

'Make it your top priority,' said Macey, 'and I'll see the bastards hanged if it's the last thing I do.' He sat down behind his desk and looked up, an expression of contrived fury on his face. 'My God, Roger,' he continued, 'I never thought in all my service that I would one day preside over an army that would take the law into its own hands. What have we come to?' He looked up. 'Anything else?' he asked wearily.

Tinwall outlined the provisions he had made for the protection of the Queen and the Royal Family.

Macey nodded. 'Good. I'm glad you chased that up.' He stood up again. 'Well, Roger, it looks as if we're being forced into taking some positive action.' The red telephone on his desk buzzed briefly and Macey snatched at the handset. 'Yes?' he barked. For a moment or two he listened before replacing the receiver. 'It seems that the 27th Royal Hussars were responsible,' he said. 'The police found some documents in one of the abandoned armoured cars.'

At about the time that the Cabinet were being seized from Downing Street, the inspector in charge of the Richmond Park police, having at last received an official written order from the Secretary of State for National Heritage, attempted to serve it on the commanding officer of the 27th Royal Hussars. However, as the inspector's office was near the Kingston Gate, he had not seen the soldiers departing earlier by the Sheen Gate. Consequently when he arrived at the encampment, all he found were empty tents and a mountain of black plastic sacks containing the last of the regiment's rubbish. He returned to his office and, with great attention to detail, marked the order 'Not served', and sent it back to the Department of National Heritage at Horse Guards Road in Westminster.

Shortly before lunch time on the day of the attack on Downing Street, Diana Fairley was in her beloved garden at Drapers. An early-morning shower had accentuated the delicate perfume of lilies of the valley, wafting across a bed of brightly coloured primulas, and she had spent the two hours since the rain had stopped weeding and hoeing.

But as she walked across the freshly mown grass towards the delphiniums, wondering if their new shoots needed staking yet, the superintendent of the local police approached from the direction of the house.

'Good morning, Mrs Fairley.' The superintendent saluted.

Diana dropped her trowel into the trug, stood up and peeled off her gardening gloves. 'Hello, Mr Cross.' Despite the headscarf she always wore while at work in the garden, a lock of hair had escaped and she brushed it out of her eyes with the back of her hand. 'What brings you here?'

'I'm afraid there's bad news, ma'am,' said Cross, uncertain how to tell the Prime Minister's wife of the day's momentous events.

'It's Robert, isn't it?' Diana felt the panic rising and laid a hand on the policeman's arm. 'He's dead, isn't he?'

'No, ma'am—'

'Well what then?'

'I'm afraid he's been abducted . . .' And Cross went on to

explain what he knew of the army's seizure of the Cabinet.

'Good God! Are you sure?' At once Diana realised it was a silly question.

'I'll let you know the moment we hear more.' Cross hesitated. 'In the circumstances, I have arranged to increase the security here.' He smiled, half apologetically, before resorting to a policeman's usual panacea for such crises. 'Can I make you a cup of tea, Mrs Fairley?' he asked.

'No, Mr Cross,' said Diana, 'but you can pour me a stiff gin and tonic.'

Sir James Arbuthnot, the Queen's private secretary, entered her study on the principal floor of Buckingham Palace and bowed.

Her Majesty was standing at the window above Queen's Entrance looking across at the high wall that ran the length of Constitution Hill.

'General Ryder is here to see you, ma'am,' said Arbuthnot. 'He apologises for not having made an appointment, but he says that it is a matter of some urgency.'

'I imagine it is, James.' The Queen turned and smiled. 'Show him in,' she said.

Major-General Thomas Ryder, who enjoyed the cumbersome title of General Officer Commanding London District and Major-General Commanding the Household Division, appeared in the doorway of the Queen's study and bowed. 'Your Majesty,' he murmured.

'General Ryder.' The Queen advanced on the tall guardsman and held out her hand. She was mildly surprised to see that he was in uniform.

'I'm afraid that I bring disturbing news, ma'am,' said Ryder.

'I rather thought so.' The Queen gestured for Ryder to take a seat.

Ryder lowered his frame into one of the gilt armchairs and related, as briefly as possible, what had occurred at 10

Downing Street only an hour previously.

The Queen nodded. 'Yes, General,' she said. 'I've heard.'
The crux of what Ryder had told her had already been
relayed to her by her private secretary. In the absence of
any communication from Downing Street, the disturbing
information had come direct from the Commissioner of
Police at New Scotland Yard to the Queen's private
secretary and finally to the Queen herself. 'How widespread
does this trouble seem to be?' she asked.

'Reports are confused at present, ma'am,' said Ryder,
'but the one thing that is coming out very strongly is that
the troops remain loyal to Your Majesty. There is absolutely
no question of their disaffection to the Crown.'

'Well that's something, I suppose,' said the Queen. 'But
if that is the case, why are there so many more soldiers
than usual around the palace?'

Not for the first time, Ryder appreciated that there was
very little that the Queen missed. 'It's a precaution,
ma'am,' he said. 'There is always a possibility of civil
disturbance and—'

'But the Prime Minister has assured me that the police
are more than capable of containing that.'

'Under normal circumstances, ma'am, yes, they would
be able to,' said Ryder, surprised that the Queen appeared
not to know that the police were finding it increasingly
difficult to cope with public disorder. 'But these are not
normal circumstances, as I'm sure Your Majesty is aware.
The latest report I have is that the Chancellor of the
Exchequer is dead and that the Cabinet have been
removed. No one knows where.'

'Which regiment carried out this disgraceful attack?'
For the first time since Ryder had entered the room, the
Queen displayed a hint of irritation.

'The Chief of the General Staff advises me that it was the
27th Royal Hussars, ma'am,' said Ryder stiffly. 'They are
shortly to be disbanded,' he added.

'I should hope so,' said the Queen and then paused in thought for some moments. 'I suppose there is no doubt about the identity of the regiment involved?'

'None whatever, ma'am.'

'Perhaps then, General Ryder,' continued the Queen, 'you would convey a message to the Chief of the General Staff.'

'Of course, ma'am.'

'Kindly inform him that it is my command that, before they are disbanded, the 27th Hussars be deprived of the "Royal" prefix.'

'Yes, ma'am,' said Ryder, not in the least surprised at the Queen's swift condemnation of a regiment that had, as its colonel-in-chief, a member of her own family.

'Is this matter to be resolved, General?' The Queen reverted to the subject of the Cabinet's seizure.

Ryder looked his sovereign straight in the eye. 'One hopes so, ma'am,' he said, 'but until it is, it is the feeling that Your Majesty should move to a place of safety.'

'Is it indeed?' There was a peremptory tone in the Queen's voice. 'My parents, the late king and queen, remained here in Buckingham Palace throughout the Second World War, General Ryder,' she said tartly. 'And I see no reason not to follow their example.'

'With respect, ma'am, the situation is different now. During the war the nation was behind Their Majesties one hundred per cent.' Ryder looked down at his feet. 'I'm sorry to have to say that we can by no means be certain that that is the case today.'

The Queen nodded. She was only too aware of the extent to which public esteem for the Royal Family had declined in recent years. 'What have you in mind?' she asked.

'New Zealand, ma'am?' Ryder floated the idea tentatively. It was really Arbuthnot's job to tender advice of that nature, but the Queen had asked him.

'Well, at least no one's suggested that I go to Brussels.'

She glanced across at her private secretary. 'James?'

'It would seem a sensible precaution, ma'am,' said Arbuthnot.

'And the rest of the family?' The Queen surveyed her two courtiers with an imperious glance. 'Have you made decisions about them, too?'

'I was hoping that Your Majesty could offer some advice,' said Arbuthnot, conscious that he had just been mildly reproached.

The Queen nodded. 'As you know, James, I have always regarded myself as dispensable,' she said, 'but we must secure the succession. At all costs.' There was a short pause. 'The Prince of Wales, together with Wills and Henry, will go to New Zealand. However, gentlemen, I am not going anywhere.'

CHAPTER THIRTEEN

The Right Honourable Sir William Headley, QC, the Attorney-General, rose from his seat on the front bench and turned towards the Chair. 'I am sure, Mr Speaker,' he began, gripping the despatch box, 'that I do not have to tell the House of the dreadful events of this morning. In fact, Mr Speaker, there is precious little that I can tell them that they do not know already. The Chancellor is dead, murdered during this scurrilous attack, and the Cabinet . . .' He spread his hands in a gesture of hopelessness. 'God knows what has happened to them,' he said, his voice falling to a desperate whisper, 'other than to say that they have been kidnapped.'

The Leader of the Opposition rose, and Headley gave way. 'Mr Speaker,' he began, 'it is not often that this side of the chamber is at one with Honourable Members opposite, but clearly the whole House will be appalled at the outrage that occurred this morning. We do not have time to pay tribute to the late Chancellor of the Exchequer – that will come later – but our immediate task is to decide what steps to take in the face of what is almost certainly an armed rebellion.'

The Attorney-General rose again. 'As the senior law officer of the Crown,' he began, 'I have taken it upon myself, with the agreement of my Right Honourable and Honourable friends' – he glanced back at the government benches – 'to act in what we all hope will be the temporary absence of the Prime Minister—' There were murmurs of agreement from the House and one or two moderated cries of 'Hear, hear!' before he continued. 'And to try to formulate some sort of policy to cater for this—'

'We want action not policy,' shouted an opposition MP, and his leader turned and frowned at him.

'I propose, Mr Speaker,' Headley went on, 'to declare a state of emergency and to put the army on full alert.'

The Leader of the Opposition rose again, almost apologetically. 'Is that a good idea, Mr Speaker?' he asked. 'In view of the fact that it appears to have been the army who have carried out this desperate and audacious crime.'

The Minister of State for the Armed Forces, Peter Garrard, now stood up. 'Mr Speaker,' he said, 'my enquiries indicate that soldiers of the 27th Hussars undertook this attack.' Garrard, a slave to protocol, had already been made aware of the Queen's deprivation of the regiment's 'Royal' prefix. 'But there is no reason to suppose that the rest of the army is disloyal. I have arranged, with my Right Honourable and Learned friend' – he nodded towards the Attorney-General – 'to convene an urgent conference with the Chief of the Defence Staff and the leaders of the three armed services in order that we may formulate a plan of action. From what little information that is available,' he went on, 'I have reason to believe that the 27th Hussars mutinied at their encampment in Richmond Park early this morning. I understand, however, that it was not a mutiny by troops against their officers. More a mutiny of the entire regiment against the Crown. It would seem, Mr Speaker, that the 27th Hussars have become military mavericks.'

But Garrard had not got it quite right. The mutiny, if such it could be called, was against the government not against their Commander-in-Chief.

*

At about the time that the Minister of State for the Armed Forces was addressing the House of Commons, Imogen walked into Macey's office. He was sitting behind his desk, staring into space.

'Ah, Imogen!' Macey looked up as though surprised to see his ADC standing there. 'Sorry, I was daydreaming.'

'Were you?' Imogen stood just inside the door, holding a file. 'Are you all right, sir?'

'Yes, of course,' said Macey. 'Why do you ask?'

'You look preoccupied, that's all.'

'I'm thinking about what happened this morning.'

Imogen closed the door before crossing the room to place the file on the corner of Macey's desk. 'Did you know it was going to happen?' she asked.

'Good God no!' Macey managed to look horrified at Imogen's suggestion. 'Of course not.'

'But last night you said that we were on the verge of exciting things. What did you mean by that?'

Macey waved a weary hand towards the chair in front of his desk and Imogen sat down. 'I had hoped that we, the other chiefs of staff and me, had at last convinced the Prime Minister to deploy the military in aid of the civil power,' he said. He became slowly more compelling as he warmed to the fiction. 'But now this bloody regiment, and Colonel Crosby in particular, have destroyed everything. Until now, the army had behaved impeccably. Then in a moment of madness our whole reputation, our professional standing, has been swept away.' For some time he stared at a solid silver model of the very first tank, which had been presented to him by the officers of the Royal Tank Regiment when he had been appointed CGS.

'Is there anything I can do, sir?' Imogen was completely deceived by Macey's masterful performance.

'I'm afraid that events are getting on top of me a bit. I do apologise.'

'Can I pour you a drink, General?' asked Imogen. She supposed that what had occurred in Downing Street that morning had had a greater effect on Macey than she had visualised possible, and she began to realise just how onerous the responsibilities of the Chief of the General Staff were. In the absence of his wife, who preferred not to share his flat in Central London, Macey had no one with whom to talk over the day's events and, given the advanced state of the army's alertness, he would have been unwise to travel even the comparatively short distance to Esher.

'No thanks, Imogen.' Macey shook his head again. 'There was something I wanted, but I'm damned if I can remember what it was now. I'll buzz for you when it comes back to me.' He smiled ruefully and continued to stare into space once Imogen had left his office.

As Imogen reached her desk, the secure line telephone was ringing. Quickly, she opened the cabinet and snatched up the receiver.

'It's Tim Crosby,' said the voice. 'Is the CGS there?'

'One moment, Colonel,' said Imogen as calmly as she could. She pressed the buzzer on the base of the phone. 'Call for you on the "secure", sir,' she said.

'Who is it, Imogen?' asked Macey.

Imogen hesitated only for a second. 'He wouldn't say, sir.'

'Put him through then.'

Imogen transferred the call but kept her own receiver pressed closely to her ear.

'Who's that?' she heard Macey ask.

'Tim Crosby, sir.'

'What in hell's name went wrong?'

'Wrong, sir?' Crosby sounded mystified by the CGS's tone. 'It went like clockwork.'

'Then how did the Chancellor get killed?' Macey spoke softly, his voice cold, menacing.

'He came at one of my corporals with a gun, sir. There

was no alternative. It never occurred to any of us that one of them would be armed.'

'The Chancellor was my informant.'

Crosby was aghast, and his voice reflected his incredulousness. 'Your informant, sir?'

'Today was not a normal Cabinet day, Tim, and if the Chancellor hadn't told me that there was to be an extraordinary meeting this morning, I wouldn't have been able to let you know when to go in.'

'But why didn't you tell me, sir? One of my NCOs was faced with a Cabinet minister with a gun. It was only natural that he should assume the worst.'

Macey switched the telephone receiver to his other hand and selected a cigarette from the silver case that was open on his desk. 'I didn't think that the damned fool would react like that,' he said. 'I imagined that he would allow himself to be taken with the rest.'

'I was there, sir,' said Crosby, 'and he looked bloody aggressive to me.'

Macey sounded tired. 'The plan was that the Chancellor would become the head of government, a sort of puppet head, you see—'

'My God!' Crosby could not keep the anguish from his voice. 'But you've—'

'Don't interrupt,' snapped Macey and immediately apologised. 'He was fully behind us in all that we were doing. He could see that Sinclair and Kent were merely using the public order situation to unseat Fairley. Then they would have fought over the Prime Minister's chair. But the Chancellor was concerned, really concerned, about what was going on. With him on our side, it would have been easy. Well, easier than it's going to be.'

There was a long pause before Crosby spoke again. 'You conned me, sir,' he said at last. 'This is a bloody coup d'état, isn't it? *You're* intending to take over the government.'

'Of course not. We were faced with a government whose

ineptitude amounted to treason, and one of their number knew it. Unfortunately your soldiers assassinated the one man who might have saved the country from perdition.'

'I'm going to release them, sir. I want no part of this,' said Crosby.

'You can't do that, Tim.' Macey spoke soothingly. 'You see everyone thinks that you acted independently, and if you let them go, you'll be arrested for treason. And complicity in the murder of the Chancellor.' He paused to give emphasis to that chilling statement. 'Stay where you are and I'll make sure that you're all right. We need time to get this thing properly organised and there'll be no recriminations. You have my word on that. And under no circumstances are you to call me here again. Is that clear?'

Proficient soldier he might be, but a simple one, and Crosby was no politician. Too late he realised that his only hope of salvation was to go along with Macey's mad plan. He let the receiver drop on to its rest.

In the anteroom, Imogen Cresswell silently replaced the handset of the secure-line extension phone and spun the combination lock of the cabinet in which it was kept. Then, disregarding security because of the urgency of her information, she turned to her other phone and rang Alec Shepherd at the headquarters of the Secret Intelligence Service.

'I don't care how important it is,' said Shepherd cutting off her unguarded outburst, 'I'm not prepared to let you be caught talking to me. Just find out anything else you can, but for God's sake be careful.'

The Chief of the Defence Staff glanced up and sighed as Macey walked into his office. Bristow was appalled at what had happened. His life had been spent with ships and seafarers, and despite his long experience in the upper echelons of the command system, the army still left him faintly bemused. He often found that the way in which soldiers conducted their affairs was something of a mystery to him.

'My appreciation of the situation is, very simply, this, sir,' said Macey. 'The 27th Hussars have seized the Cabinet. Those responsible will face charges of treason, but that will take time. Not least because we have no idea where they are. Our immediate concern is to safeguard the country. It is almost certain that the riots will escalate in view of what has happened, and I see it as our responsibility to re-establish some sort of order while we locate the Cabinet and restore it to office. That must be our first priority.'

'What are you driving at, Simon?' asked Bristow.

'Frankly, sir, I think that we will have to persuade the Attorney-General to impose martial law. Appeal for calm and insist that the population complies with military directions. He must be made to see that he needs us to secure a semblance of order while he organises some sort of administration, and he must give us the time to locate the Cabinet. One regiment running amok shouldn't infect the entire armed forces. The least we can do is make amends by enabling what's left of the government to get on with governing.'

Bristow stood up. Despite the fact that he was wearing a suit, there was no doubting that he had spent his life in the navy. There was a certain cut to his jib, as sailors say, that implied he was not really at home in an office in Whitehall. 'Do you know, Simon,' he said, 'I read my first Hornblower novels when I was a youngster at Harrow, and all I ever wanted to be was captain of a frigate. And when I achieved that rare station in life, I thought that I'd really arrived. It was certainly the happiest period of my life.' He looked down at his desk, and at the piles of paper on it, before glancing up again at the Chief of the General Staff. 'And I wish to God that I'd made a decision then to stay where I was.'

He sighed. 'We'd better see the Attorney-General.'

*

Ten Downing Street was surrounded by troops. An entire regiment of the Household Cavalry – its only regiment, in fact – was deployed in combat gear and with armoured cars. Inside the house more soldiers stood guard on the Cabinet Room, on each floor, outside in the garden and beyond it on Horse Guards Parade.

The Attorney-General and Peter Garrard, the Minister of State for the Armed Forces, had decided to hold their meeting with the Chiefs of Staff in the Prime Minister's study on the west side of the house.

But the Attorney-General demurred from occupying the PM's seat behind the desk. 'Well, gentlemen,' he began. 'This is a pretty kettle of fish.'

Sir Godfrey Bristow regarded Headley with a sour expression. He did not like politicians and 'a pretty kettle of fish' was not exactly the phrase he would have chosen to describe the momentous events that had occurred on the floor below only a matter of hours previously. It was evident to him that the Attorney-General had not grasped the full impact of what was taking place.

'Are we to be subjected to a full-scale revolt on the part of the army, Sir Simon?' Headley gazed arrogantly at the CGS.

'There is no reason to suppose that the rest of the army has been influenced by the actions of the 27th Hussars, Attorney,' said Macey. 'Both the Aldershot and Catterick garrisons are said to be loyal to the general officers commanding them and, of course, to Her Majesty.' Macey did not regard loyalty to the government as a part of the soldier's duty, and the fact that he failed to mention it was not lost on the Attorney-General.

'And were the whereabouts of the Cabinet included in this sparse information that filtered into the Ministry of Defence, Sir Simon?' Headley raised an eyebrow and surveyed the Chief of the General Staff suspiciously.

'No, they were not, Sir William.' Macey spoke with the bare minimum of courtesy.

'I see. And what, might I ask, is the cause of the hussars' disaffection, General?' asked Headley. 'Do we know that?'

Macey paused before replying. 'If you want the unvarnished truth, Attorney, they're sick to the back teeth of the way they've been treated by the government. Regiment after regiment has been disbanded, and more are scheduled to be. And the navy and the air force are in no better shape. We have done our best, from the chiefs of staff right down to the poor sod who was killed in Putney, to do what's best for the country. But have we had any support? Have we hell.'

'They shouldn't have interfered, General,' said Headley taken aback by Macey's outburst.

'They had no alternative.' Macey snapped the reply. 'And you know it.'

'There is no great profit in reiterating old arguments and opening old sores,' said Bristow. He was concerned at the way the discussion was going and feared that it might degenerate into a slanging match. 'What's past is past. What we have to do now, all of us, is determine what to do next.'

'I should have thought that that was perfectly obvious, Sir Godfrey,' said the Attorney icily. 'Find the Cabinet.' He turned on Macey. 'It might be a good idea if your soldiers, who have been so ready to rush about previously, now turned their attentions to that, General.'

'It's already in hand, Sir William,' said Macey, calmly deflecting the Attorney's sarcasm. 'I have issued orders to all units to liaise with the police and conduct a detailed search of the entire country. And I have asked the Minister of State at the Home Office to arrange for the Security Service to deploy all its resources. I need hardly say that the army is as keen as you that the government is restored to office as soon as possible.'

'But good grief, man, that could take days.' The Attorney's voice rose. 'Perhaps we could appeal to the population to search their own area,' he suggested hopelessly. 'That would speed things up, surely?'

Macey chuckled at that. 'I suspect that there are some people, Attorney, who don't particularly want the government found. Don't forget that half the population voted against you at the last election.'

'But what are we to do in the meantime?' demanded the anguished Attorney-General.

'Perhaps you have something in mind,' said Bristow. 'We have been reminded, frequently, that the running of the country is nothing to do with the armed forces. It's rather a matter for you as the *de facto* head of government.'

The Attorney-General glanced at the Minister of State, but Garrard remained silent. 'I suggest, gentlemen,' he said, 'that we continue to govern the country as though nothing had happened.'

Macey laughed outright. 'It's a bit late for that,' he said. 'I think the people are well aware of what has occurred.'

'I didn't mean that,' snapped the Attorney. 'Of course they know what's happened.'

'If you want my opinion,' said Macey, 'the mobs that have been running riot over the past few weeks will merely take advantage of the situation. They'll sense they've got you on the run. They'll be telling themselves that there was good reason for the army to seize the Cabinet and although you and I know it was one maverick regiment—'

'Do we know that, General?' demanded the Attorney.

'I've already told you that the rest of the army remains loyal—'

'How do you know that?' The Attorney spat the question. 'If you're so well versed in the army's mood, why didn't you know that this Crosby man was going to kidnap the Cabinet, eh?'

'I don't know what's in the mind of every one of my

officers,' responded Macey angrily.

'Exactly so.' Headley smirked at having scored a point.

'Gentlemen, gentlemen,' said Bristow soothingly. 'There are important issues to be discussed here. Now, if I may suggest deploying the army to suppress the riots, to get the country back to a peaceable norm—'

'To use the army will only exacerbate the situation,' said Headley, repeating the Prime Minister's policy on the matter. 'These riots, as you call them, consist of no more than a few hotheads determined to make trouble.' And then, warming to his subject, he added, 'We could swear in special constables as was done during the General Strike.'

'Oh, come, Attorney,' said Macey. 'That was a trade dispute, this is a bloody revolution. You'll be talking about resuscitating the Home Guard next.' He paused, wondering whether the Attorney-General really thought that the situation was not serious or whether he was being deliberately obtuse. 'We are faced with widespread rioting,' he said. 'And if you're looking for causes, you don't have to look far. The trouble seems to stem from dissatisfaction with the government, so far as we can tell.' He lifted his head to stare directly at Headley. 'Your weak government has allowed this country to sink into a slough. And allowed it to be run by an unelected president of the EU and thirty unelected commissioners. So much for democracy,' he scoffed. 'The introduction of the European Currency Unit as a replacement for the pound sterling was the last straw. People have seen their life savings whittled away by unscrupulous business practices. Profiteers have deliberately falsified the valuation rate between the two and made huge sums of money as a result. And I don't exclude the Stock Exchange from that, either. The people are not stupid. They've noted the inability of the government to stem such practices. In addition to that, crime has been allowed to run rife and absolutely nothing has been done about it. All they see are weak responses to violence and

Home Office officials who go around saying that the prisons aren't comfortable enough. The government's only solutions have been to reduce the budget for the police and to decimate the armed forces and a hell of a lot of other things. You can push the British people so far, Attorney, but there comes a point when they will turn and bite.'

'How very prosaic,' said Headley sarcastically.

'But that aside,' Macey continued, ignoring the Attorney's feeble intervention, 'it is now of paramount importance, as I'm sure you will agree, that order is restored to this country as soon as possible. There will undoubtedly be further rioting now that the government is seen to have ceased to govern, so to speak.' He paused. 'And the military are the only people capable of doing that. You must authorise the proper use of the military on the streets.'

The Attorney-General seemed nonplussed by Macey's diatribe. 'Perhaps using the navy would be less provocative, given that it was the army who seized the Cabinet,' he said. 'I mean, what would the people think?'

'Most of the navy is at sea,' said Admiral Ainsworth tersely, and restrained himself from suggesting that the Attorney seemed to be as well.

'Maybe the European Union could help,' mumbled Headley, half to himself. As the country's temporary leader, he was thrashing about trying to take the lead in a discussion that was being progressively dominated by the chiefs of staff.

'Only if you want to make things worse,' said Macey drily. 'Look what happened after the Prime Minister's brainwave of bringing French police over here.'

Headley stared pathetically at the Chief of the General Staff but was saved from making an inane or embarrassing reply – both of which he was quite good at – by Garrard.

'Is it really your view, General,' the Minister of State asked, 'that this situation has arisen because of the failings of the government?' He sounded as though he were taking part in a debate at the Oxford Union.

'I do not have views on political matters,' said Macey tartly. 'I am merely stating the obvious.'

'Well what the hell are we going to do about it?' Garrard asked, half to himself. 'We have no idea where the Cabinet is.' He glanced across at the Chief of the Defence Staff. 'Do we, Sir Godfrey?'

'General Macey has already said that we don't,' said Bristow curtly. 'But to return to the general state of affairs, a decision has to be taken about the present situation.' He stared at Headley. 'There is no excuse for what occurred this morning and I hold no brief for those responsible.' He was being careful both to preserve his independence as Chief of the Defence Staff and to distance himself from Colonel Crosby's audacious actions.

'This is not getting us anywhere,' said Headley impatiently. 'We still have to resolve what we are to do.'

'You, sir, are the acting Prime Minister,' said Bristow coldly, 'and I'm afraid that that decision is yours.'

For several moments, Headley stared at the opposite wall before realigning his gaze on the Chief of the Defence Staff. Finally he acknowledged that Bristow's plan presented the only viable solution to the crisis that now beset him. 'I think that the military must be deployed on proper lines to resolve this bloody awful mess,' he said. He glanced sideways at Garrard, who nodded. 'You are authorised, Sir Godfrey, to do what is necessary.'

'It has gone beyond simply deploying the military, Attorney,' said Macey softly. 'The Cabinet is incommunicado, and firm action is required. If that action is not taken, then we shall find ourselves facing even greater trouble, revolution even. Unless we are given the powers that are needed to put down serious disorder, I am disinclined to risk the lives of my soldiers.'

The Attorney-General appeared bemused by Macey's statement. 'But you were all for using troops to suppress the present disquiet, Sir Simon,' he said. 'And only a matter of days ago you were telling the Secretary of State for Defence that they could not be prevented from taking action independently. Are you now telling me that you will somehow restrain them unless you are granted a state of martial law?'

'That's it exactly, Attorney.' Macey crossed his legs and gently eased the cloth from his knee.

'But, good God, man, we've not had martial law in this country since the Protectorate in the seventeenth century.' Already Headley was having visions of his reputation being laid in ruins by some future critical biographer.

'And we've never had riots like this before in our history,' said Macey.

For what seemed an eternity, the Attorney-General gazed out of the window of the quiet room. Then he turned to the Chief of the Defence Staff. 'Very well, Sir Godfrey,' he said. 'Do what must be done to restore order. Even if it means a declaration of martial law.'

'Very good, Attorney.' Bristow nodded and then waited.

'Was there something else, Sir Godfrey?'

'Yes, Sir William, I would like that in writing, please.'

The joint chiefs of staff reconvened in Admiral of the Fleet Sir Godfrey Bristow's office at the Ministry of Defence.

'Well?' Bristow surveyed his service colleagues and then stirred his tea.

'Headley seems a bit of a political lightweight, sir,' said Air Chief Marshal Sir John Gilbert.

'Maybe,' said Bristow, 'but he's not to be under-estimated. Garrard's the one to watch, however. He's been a Minister of State here at Defence for three years now, and he's looking for advancement. He's a spiteful man and there might just be a power struggle between him and Headley now that the Cabinet's out of the way, if only temporarily.'

'But his decision to use the military, which we know was contrary to the Prime Minister's policy, can hardly improve his chances, surely, sir. I mean not once the Prime Minister is returned to power.'

'If he is,' said Macey.

'There can't be any doubt of that, surely?' Bristow glanced at Macey. 'Incidentally, Simon, do you really not know where the PM is? Or where Crosby is?'

'No idea, sir.' For a moment, Macey concentrated on the toe of his shoe. Then he looked up. 'You don't honestly think that if I knew what had happened to the Cabinet I would keep it to myself, do you?'

'I would hope not, Simon.' The Chief of the Defence Staff inclined his head. 'But does no one have any idea where this Crosby chap is holding the Cabinet? Is there nothing from intelligence about it?'

'No, sir.' Macey shifted slightly in his seat and wondered whether the Chief of the Defence Staff knew more than he was telling; he was certainly labouring the point. 'I have taken the precaution of placing the Aldershot and Catterick garrisons on full alert, but we are unlikely to have enough troops if the disorder gets any worse. Once the civilian population realises what is happening, they may seek to take advantage of the situation by looting and so forth. I have little doubt that things will deteriorate before they get better. And we don't have time on our side. At least not until we can take charge of the television and radio stations. In the interests of public order, of course. Can't have the BBC undermining a delicate situation,' he added with a bleak smile.

'Can't make omelettes without breaking eggs,' said the airman pointlessly.

'What do you propose to do about it, Simon?' Bristow ignored the RAF chief.

'There are ten thousand troops in Germany and a small garrison in the Falklands. And there's a brigade in Kuwait and one in Northern Ireland. Elsewhere around the world, I suppose there are another two or three thousand. As we all know, sir, we just haven't got enough soldiers.'

Bristow nodded. That was exactly one of the crises that was causing discontent in an army still receiving redundancy notices. 'Peter?' He glanced at the naval chief of staff.

'We've got a few ships languishing at Portsmouth and Rosyth, sir, but most of them, as you know, are committed to the Gulf and the Adriatic. And, of course, Hong Kong.' The sabre-rattling of an impatient China had been causing great concern in the approach to the colony's return to the communists. 'Added to which, of course,' Ainsworth continued, 'we've had to increase the Fishery Protection Fleet to stop open warfare breaking out between our fishermen and the rest of the EU.'

Bristow swivelled round in his chair to face the air force chief. 'Air cover, John?'

'Much the same, sir,' said Gilbert. 'Most of our squadrons are in Germany, the Middle East or the Falklands.'

Although all this information was available on the Ministry of Defence computers, Bristow had been making notes on his pad while the others had been talking. 'It looks like your chaps are going to have to bear the brunt of this, Simon,' he said to the Chief of the General Staff. 'What do you suggest?'

'I propose that we bring everything back from Germany, sir.'

'Yes, good,' said Bristow.

Macey paused. 'And the Northern Ireland brigade too, sir.'

Bristow gently tapped his blotter with the end of his silver propelling pencil and gazed mildly at the soldier. 'Is that wise, Simon?'

'It's only a token force,' said Macey dismissively. 'And it's all gone quiet there now.'

Bristow looked pensive. 'Well, Simon, you'd know more about it than me. You served there, after all. All right, withdraw them,' he said.

Imogen Cresswell had been greatly disturbed by the conversation between Macey and Crosby. It was now apparent to her that Macey was involved in the seizure of the Cabinet but she hoped that he had, perhaps, been prompted by an innate desire to do the best for his country. At least as he saw it. Although she could muster no sympathy for him, she still found herself questioning her motives in informing on him to the Secret Intelligence Service. But more than that, she doubted herself, unsure now that she had actually heard what she thought she had heard. There was only one way to resolve it.

Having been excluded from the meeting of the joint chiefs of staff and told by Macey that she need not stay, Imogen left the Ministry of Defence building intent on getting away from its disturbing atmosphere and trying to find some solitude in which to think. As soon as she reached the street, she found that a joint army and police operation had closed the Whitehall area and excluded all but essential workers and transport from it.

As she walked aimlessly eastwards she found herself frequently stopped by soldiers or policemen and obliged to produce her military identity document. In the Strand the home-going crowds constantly jostled her in their hurry to catch trains and buses and seemed oblivious to the grave crisis now gripping the country, even though things appeared far from normal. In particular, the patrolling soldiers looked strangely out of place in their combat gear with SA80 automatic rifles slung over their shoulders.

Imogen's mind was in turmoil. Alec Shepherd had implied that the SIS knew much more of Macey's activities than she did, but that could be a ruse to persuade her to keep informing on him.

Macey's habitual arrogance towards her was becoming more bearable as she got to know him better, in fact she was even beginning to feel slightly sorry for him. She had begun to realise also that his attitude towards her was not singular, but largely a pose born of a long career of commanding soldiers. During the long, chaotic day she'd observed his concern and determination to re-establish law and order. Surely that was his duty? Had she misinterpreted his conversation with Crosby?

Imogen found herself outside a small City restaurant and realised that she'd been walking for over an hour and was hungry. Yet when she sat down her appetite had disappeared and she ordered a chicken salad and a cup of black coffee. As she ate her meal, her muddled thoughts vied with each other until she knew she had to take some definite action. Glancing at her watch she saw that it was gone eight. She was sure that Macey had no dinner engagement, and anyway in the current crisis he'd probably been firmly tied to his desk. She knew the only way she could come to any decision about what was really happening was to confront him directly, and the only way to get him to confide in her would be to seduce him.

Relieved to be taking some action, she settled her bill and took a taxi back to Whitehall. Lights were ablaze in all the government buildings and, once in her office, she heard Macey deep in conversation with a visitor, their voices muffled by the closed communicating door. She settled down to wait and to tackle the mountain of paper that had covered her desk in her absence.

It was close to midnight before Macey was alone. Her decision to seduce him had preoccupied her since her return, and there as now no more waiting to be done. Although her pulse was racing, she controlled her breathing and, tapping lightly on his door, entered without waiting for a response. He was sitting at his desk, his less than immaculate appearance showing the trauma of the day.

'Imogen, I thought you'd gone hours ago.'

'Thought I ought to be here, sir.' She held his gaze, smiling slowly as she gestured vaguely at his littered desk.

Macey stared at her, tired and puzzled. 'It's been an absolute bugger of a day,' he said, 'but there's not much more to be done tonight. Let's have a drink; we deserve a large one.' He crossed to his drinks cabinet and began to mix her a gin and tonic. 'Not stood your diplomat up, I hope.' He grinned, something that Imogen had not seen him do for some time.

'There is no diplomat ... Simon.' Imogen hesitated before using his first name, something he had invited her to do at that first dinner that seemed, now, light years away. 'Not any more. He wanted me to go out to India and marry him.' She sighed gently and moved across the room until she was standing close behind him, almost touching.

'You should have gone.' Macey's voice trailed as he turned, surprised to find her so near to him. He handed her a glass, acutely aware of her perfume.

'I don't think I loved him enough,' Imogen whispered. Macey took a long pull at his Scotch. 'I kept up the pretence of an engagement as a ploy,' she continued, 'until I knew you well enough to be sure of my feelings towards you, *sir*.' This time she used the term coquettishly. She was still standing close to him and now lifted her hand to run the cool backs of her fingers along his cheek.

Absent-mindedly Macey removed her hand and took a step backwards. Astounded, she watched him drain his glass, turn off his desk light and shrug into his tunic. 'Time for me to get some sleep,' he said. 'I'll see you at eight; we'll have a lot to do.' He was so preoccupied with the unfolding drama that he had not even noticed Imogen's attempts to seduce him.

Imogen stood transfixed as the door swung to behind him. Then, in fury, she hurled the crystal glass at the opposite wall and stormed out of the building. At the first phone box she came to, she wrenched open the door and angrily punched out Alec Shepherd's telephone number.

'Alec, I've got to see you.'

'Can you grab a taxi and come round now?'

Minutes later Imogen was relaxing in one of Shepherd's armchairs and taking a sip of the very welcome gin and tonic he had just poured for her. 'Macey took a telephone call from Colonel Crosby late this afternoon,' she began.

'He did what?' exclaimed Shepherd.

Calmly, Imogen repeated herself.

'Presumably he's reported it to the Chief of the Defence Staff?'

Imogen shook her head. 'No, he hasn't,' she said quietly. 'Not as far as I know.'

'What the hell's he playing at then?' For a moment Shepherd sat contemplating the stupidity of Crosby in making the call and Macey for laying himself open by not telling his immediate superior about it. 'Did you hear all the conversation?' He carefully avoided asking Imogen how she had managed to know about the call. In the SIS there was nothing immoral about the acquisition of intelligence, or the means used to gather it.

'Yes, I did.' Imogen wanted Shepherd to know that she was taking risks, so she added, 'There were people in and out of my office all the time. I share it with two other officers, you see. But I managed to hear it all.'

Shepherd nodded. 'Do you know where he was calling from?'

'No idea, I'm afraid.'

'Go on.'

Slowly, trying to recall the conversation as accurately as she could, Imogen recited all she had heard.

'Good God Almighty! The man's mad.' Shepherd exclaimed when she had finished, staggered by the enormity of what Imogen had just told him. 'Did either he or

Crosby give any indication of where the Cabinet was being held captive?'

'None.'

'I see.' Shepherd's mind was assessing the information as Imogen spoke. 'Anything else?'

'Only that the 27th Hussars have disappeared from the order of battle. There's no trace of them anywhere on the computer.'

'You do realise that Macey mustn't learn that you know about this?' Shepherd looked at the girl with a serious expression on his face. 'You could be putting yourself in danger.'

'Yes.' Imogen nodded slowly and felt a little sick.

'Imogen, I assure you that we know a lot more than you do about your man's activities.'

'So you've said, Alec.' Imogen spoke in an undertone. But Shepherd's reiteration of the claim that his service knew more only served to revive her uncertainties.

'You're not alone in all this,' continued Shepherd, attempting to reassure her, 'and it is essential that you supply us with all the information you can.' He paused briefly. 'I cannot put it any better than the old cliché: it is vitally important to the security of the state.'

Leaving her drink untouched, Imogen stood up and crossed to where Shepherd was standing. She put her arms around him and held on tightly. 'Alec, I do know how important all of this is,' she said.

'I know, Imogen, I know. But it is a difficult time ... for all of us.'

'I tried to seduce him,' she confessed, her voice muffled against Shepherd's chest.

Shepherd pushed her away slightly. 'You did what?'

'I thought it was the only way to make him talk, and I failed.' She paused and then added, 'I've never failed before.'

'Listen ...' Shepherd was shrewd enough to appreciate

the torment that she was going through. But he also knew, from previous experience of running agents, that if the relationship between target and informant became an intimate one, a point was reached when doubt crept in and loyalty became the dominant factor, when sex, which was often mistaken for love, superseded duty. 'I know this is serious, but I won't have you giving yourself to that lecher, even if he is a general ...' He paused. 'And a traitor,' he whispered. 'Anyway, apart from anything else, I'm—'

Imogen put her arms around Shepherd's neck and kissed him, cutting off what he was about to say next.

CHAPTER FOURTEEN

Within twenty-four hours, the military had taken firm control. Although the blockade had been lifted and the air-traffic controllers had returned to work, the Channel Tunnel, the airports and the ferry terminals remained closed. And three army brigades had been airlifted from Germany to Aldershot. Already units of that division were moving to take over key points in the capital while others were sent further afield to guard government installations in the provinces.

Although the Cabinet had been abducted and the military had been deployed to suppress disorder, Sir Richard Dancer saw no reason to change his routine. As usual, he sat at his desk, a cup of black coffee to one side, while examining the contents of his in-tray.

With a cluck of annoyance he noticed that it was almost filled with telegrams from SIS officers in various parts of the world.

The signals reported the reaction of heads of state and heads of government to the imposition of martial law in Britain. The SIS man at the British Embassy in Washington – where he masqueraded as a First Secretary – mistakenly believed that he should send as much information as possible, and was particularly fulsome. He repeated just about everything that had been said by the President and the United States government, and by America's other leading politicians. He went on to summarise the innermost views of those who formulated the foreign policy of the United States and thus established the balance of world power. Then, for good measure, he reiterated what had been said by political commentators in the United States press and on its multifarious television channels.

In summary, the President was disturbed that the British should have found it necessary to bring in the army – forgetting how often the USA had mobilised its own National Guard – but made the usual comments about not wishing to interfere in the internal affairs of another country. Dancer smiled wryly at that; it seemed to him to be a radical change of policy. In his experience the Americans did little else but interfere in the affairs of other nations.

The other signals, from places as far apart as Jakarta, Canberra, Tokyo, Delhi, Beijing and, of course, the European Union countries, said much the same. In short, the nations of the world were keeping a watching brief. But already there were signs of nervousness about foreign investments in the United Kingdom and indications that much of the international insurance market was likely to be lost. Dancer sighed at the fickleness of foreign governments and of their financial masters.

In normal circumstances, Dancer would have briefed the Foreign Secretary with the information, but he had no idea where he was, even though his agents were working overtime to discover just where the 27th Hussars had put him and the other members of the Cabinet. After all, that is what the SIS existed for: to find things out. And, in certain circumstances, to rectify and change things. And what Dancer had in mind was probably best not discussed with the politicians anyway.

Irritably, he tossed the signals into the out-tray and, with a sigh, finished his coffee and turned to the tedious task of vetting and authorising 'gratuities to certain highly placed persons who have assisted the Service'.

A uniformed constable of the Diplomatic Protection Group stood impassively at the main entrance to New Scotland Yard and watched as the staff car drew to a standstill. The driver, a military police corporal, leaped from his seat, swung open the rear door and saluted, all in one flowing movement. The officer who alighted – the Provost Marshal of the British Army – wore the rank badges of a brigadier. He paused briefly to look around and then flicked his swagger cane under his left arm.

'Good morning, sir,' said the PC. The brigadier nodded as the automatic doors opened to admit him.

Inside the building the Commissioner's staff officer hovered near the reception desk. 'Good morning, Brigadier,' he said. 'Please come this way. We'll have to take the lift. The Commissioner's office is on the eighth floor.'

'I know,' snapped the brigadier, unhappy at the responsibility just placed upon him by the Chief of the General Staff.

In the face of this response, the pair rode up in the lift in silence and walked through the office occupied by the Commissioner's three secretaries, quietly dealing with mountains of paperwork. The staff officer pushed open the door of Sir Lionel Cork's office. 'Brigadier Passmore, sir,' he said.

'Good morning, Nicholas.' Cork stood up as the Provost Marshal entered, and held out his hand.

'Morning, Lionel.'

'I hope none of your chaps was hurt in that disgraceful business in Downing Street the other day,' said Passmore, accepting Cork's invitation to sit down.

'No, fortunately not,' said Cork. 'The officers on duty

were merely disarmed, and the rest arrived too late. I am concerned about the safety of the two protection officers though. Detective Superintendent Whitmore and Detective Chief Inspector Enderby were abducted along with the Cabinet.'

'So I gather.' Passmore took the cup of coffee handed to him. 'Thank you,' he said and waited until the staff officer, carrying the brigadier's cap, cane and gloves, had closed the door behind him. 'I can only apologise on behalf of the army for what occurred that day, Lionel,' he went on.

'Is there any indication of the Cabinet's whereabouts?' Cork dropped a sweetener into his coffee and stirred it.

'None at all, I'm afraid. How are you coping? With the riots, I mean.'

'Badly,' said Cork. He had given up trying to pretend that the police were in control. He waved a hand towards a pile of computer print-outs. 'And that doesn't help. Another wave of resignations this morning.' He leaned back in his chair, an expression of expectation on his face. The Provost Marshal had not given a reason for his visit, but Cork thought he knew what it was.

'You'll be aware that the acting Prime Minister has authorised the army to restore order, I suppose, Lionel.'

'Yes, thank God.' The Commissioner nodded wearily. 'I got a letter from Headley.'

'The imposition of martial law puts the Chief of the Defence Staff in charge of things, but to all intents and purposes he has delegated the day-to-day running to the Chief of the General Staff.'

'What's he like, this General Macey? I've met him a couple of times, at state banquets and the like, but I've never really had a long conversation with him.'

'Very much a soldier's soldier, if you know what I mean,' said Passmore. 'He certainly doesn't stand any nonsense.'

'Well he can rely upon us to give him all the help we can,' said Cork.

'That's more or less why I'm here, Lionel. General Macey has given me the responsibility of overseeing all police operations in the UK, apart from Northern Ireland, that is.'

Cork laughed. 'Has he indeed? Well I can only wish you luck. It's not a job I'd care for.'

'What it means, Lionel,' said Passmore hesitantly, 'is that I shall take an office here, and all chief officers will be answerable to me for police operations throughout the mainland.'

'What?' Cork sat up sharply. He had expected some changes as a result of the crisis, but not this. 'I'm not sure that I can go along with that. The army has no power to—'

'I'm afraid they have, Lionel, under the provisions of martial law.' Passmore sounded apologetic. 'But General Macey has authorised me to say that if you feel that you can't stay on in those circumstances, he'll quite understand.'

Cork smiled bleakly. 'Go on what you chaps call "gardening leave", you mean, Nicholas?'

'Something like that, yes,' said Passmore. 'Incidentally, I'm to be promoted to major-general for the task,' he added, and was a little surprised that the Commissioner seemed unimpressed.

The following day Major-General Nicholas Passmore entered the conference room at New Scotland Yard and, indicating that the assembled army officers should sit down, took a seat at the head of the table immediately beneath the portrait of the stern Sir Richard Mayne, one of London's first two police chiefs. 'First of all, gentlemen,' he began, 'let me outline the current situation. As you know, the Attorney-General, who is acting Prime Minister, has authorised the use of troops to quell the serious public disorder that has been occurring, virtually unchecked, for the past six weeks. I need not tell you that the law is somewhat confused regarding the precise definition of our role, but in general terms, I can safely say that a state of martial law exists.'

'Will there be specific instructions, sir?' asked a colonel. 'Sort of rules of engagement, as it were. Like Ulster?'

Passmore laid his hand on a copy of the *Manual of Military Law*. 'Suffice it to say,' he said, 'that the common law gives the army fairly generous powers in dealing with the present emergency. Added to which there is almost certain to be an Act of Indemnity passed once the civil government is restored. But that does not give officers and soldiers licence to do as they please.' He smiled bleakly at the assembled officers. 'There are ten of you to take command of the fifty or so police forces around the country, and the chief constables of those forces will be answerable to you. My staff officer has drawn up details of the new arrangements and copies are on the table in front of you. Police forces have not been amalgamated and you will, therefore, find that you are responsible for several forces each. As officers who have attended the Staff College, I don't have to lecture you on the inefficiency of the small units that the police seem to find acceptable. Apart from being a disgraceful duplication of resources, the endemic lack of co-operation is quite ludicrous in this day and age. Consequently you will use all the police under your command as if they were one force.' He glanced down the table at one of the Metropolitan Police commanders who was attending the conference. 'You will be aware,' Passmore went on, 'that the control of all the police forces of the United Kingdom, except for Northern Ireland, has been vested in me. Just to emphasise that, when you return to your respective headquarters you will inform police authorities that they are dissolved for the duration of the present emergency and will play no further part in the policing of the counties they purport to represent.' He stood up. 'That is all, gentlemen. Good afternoon.'

'Imogen?'

'Yes.' Imogen Cresswell thought she recognised the voice on the phone.

'It's Tim Crosby. Is General Macey there?'

'Yes, he is, Colonel. Where are you phoning from?' Imogen made it sound like an offhand and innocent question.

Crosby paused only briefly. 'Germany.' Following his last conversation with Macey, Colonel Crosby had realised, somewhat belatedly, that if the CGS's plan failed, then he, Crosby, was likely to get all the blame. His once great faith in Macey was beginning to waver rapidly and he knew that soon it would be a case of every man for himself. In the circumstances, he thought it might be as well if Imogen Cresswell knew where he was. 'And guess who's with me?'

Macey was not at all pleased that the hussar colonel had telephoned him at the MOD. 'I told you not to communicate with me again, Tim. I made it perfectly clear that you should wait for a coded sentence in the arranged broadcast before releasing your merchandise.'

But Crosby insisted that Macey should hear him out. 'I'm not going to apologise, sir. I've been listening to the radio and watching the television and they're all saying that I acted alone, that the regiment took the action it did without the knowledge or approval of the rest of the army. In fact, several broadcasts have quoted you as saying you don't know what happened. But you ordered me to take the Cabinet into custody for their own safety. So what the hell's going on?'

'For Christ's sake, Tim. I'm ordering you to stop discussing these matters over the phone. There is much, much more to this than you understand. You did tactics at the

Staff College and you know perfectly well that subordinate commanders are rarely aware of the overall situation or the strategy. Just carry on and await further orders.'

There was a pause before Crosby spoke again. 'I think I'm going to have to release them, sir,' he said, almost apologetically.

'I've explained that you can't do that, Tim,' began Macey. Although he had pressed the switch on the sophisticated scrambling system before speaking, he was extremely annoyed by Crosby's total disregard for security, but he was beginning to realise that when he gave illegal orders, there was no redress against officers who declined to comply with them.

Crosby went on, rambling almost, as if he were debating the issue with himself. 'I shall discuss it with my field officers and explain the situation to them. If they agree that the Cabinet should be set free, then that's what I'll do. You see, sir, I was acting under your orders and that, in my view, exonerates me—'

'I'm afraid it doesn't,' said Macey angrily. 'You were given no orders and I shall deny, must deny, that I ever issued such orders.'

But Crosby had already replaced the receiver.

Imogen had begun to get concerned about her own safety. 'I took a taxi to Victoria Station and walked from there,' she said as Alec Shepherd let her into his flat. 'I stopped from time to time to look in shop windows, just to make sure that no one was following me. Am I being too melodramatic?'

Shepherd took her in his arms and kissed her. 'You can't be too careful, Imogen,' he said. 'Drink?'

'Could I have a whisky?'

'Of course.'

'This is for you.' Imogen handed him a plastic bag with the name of a well-known off-licence on it. 'It's only a bottle of Cognac, but I felt that I'd been sponging too much just lately.'

Shepherd smiled and took the bottle out. 'Only the best,' he said, examining the label. 'You Grenadiers don't mess about, do you?' He kissed her lightly on the forehead. 'Thank you, but there was really no need.'

'I spoke to Tim Crosby on the phone today, Alec.'

Shepherd turned sharply from the drinks table, the bottle of whisky still in his hand. 'Did he tell you where he was?'

'Germany. And he made an enigmatic remark. He said, "Guess who's with me."'

'Were you able to find out anything else?'

'No.'

'Pity,' said Shepherd, handing Imogen a stiff whisky. 'Looks as though we'll just have to make do with what we've got.'

Macey had let it be known that a detachment of military had been stationed at Chequers to safeguard the premises and the staff. The story that soldiers were there to prevent a riotous mob from sacking the old house was a simple ruse to disguise the fact that they were, in fact, preventing anyone from escaping. Principally the Prime Minister.

On the day after the abduction of the Cabinet, Warrant Officer Helen Jackson served soup to the lonely figure of the Prime Minister in the dining room at Chequers and replaced the tureen on the sideboard. Now thirty-nine years of age, she had spent all her adult life in the Royal Navy and had only recently reached her present prestigious rank, the gold-wire insignia of which – the Royal Arms – she now wore on her cuffs.

'Whose side are *you* on, Chief?' Fairley asked suddenly. He did not understand the Royal Navy and, as far as he was concerned, Helen Jackson would always be the chief petty officer she had been when they had first met.

'I beg your pardon, sir?' Helen turned.

'I asked which side you were on.'

'I'm not sure I understand, sir . . .'

'Do you support this coup d'état that the military has imposed on this country?' asked Fairley. 'Because that, clearly, is what it is.'

Helen Jackson approached the table, her hands linked loosely in front of her. 'I'm in the Royal Navy, sir. I just obey orders.'

'But you're only obliged to obey lawful orders, Chief. And the orders that your Admiral of the Fleet Bristow is issuing are hardly that.'

'No, sir, I suppose not.' Helen paused. She was unaware of any order issued by the Chief of the Defence Staff that would affect her personally. 'But I don't really see what I can do about it. My job is to oversee the staff who look after you here at Chequers, sir. And that's what I'm doing. It would serve no useful purpose if I stopped doing that. Anyway, I'm afraid that admirals don't take much notice of what I do or say.'

The Prime Minister smiled grimly. 'No, I suppose not,' he said. 'As a matter of fact, they aren't taking a great deal of notice of what I'm saying at the moment. I'm sorry, Chief, I shouldn't have asked you. It's unfair to involve you.' He picked up his spoon and hesitated. 'Although I suppose we're all involved to a greater or lesser degree.'

'Yes, sir.'

'Thank you, Chief,' said the Prime Minister and then paused again. 'Do you know where Gordon Whitmore is?'

'He's in the staff room, sir. Just about to have lunch.'

'Perhaps you'd ask him to come and see me.'

'Very good, sir.'

A few moments later Fairley's senior detective tapped lightly on the door and entered. 'You wanted me, sir?'

'I was wondering why they brought you down here, Gordon,' said the Prime Minister.

'I don't think they knew what else to do with me, sir.'
Whitmore grinned. 'They said that although you were now
in protective custody – that's how they put it, sir – you still
needed to have protection officers. I get the impression that
the army mean you no harm,' he added.

'Killing the Chancellor in cold blood is a funny way of
showing it,' growled Fairley. For a moment he gazed out of
the window, unseeing and lost in thought as he relived that
horrifying scene in the Cabinet Room. Then he looked back
at Whitmore. 'Have you heard what's happened to Diana?'
He had not spoken to his wife since the day before his
abduction. 'Is she all right, do you know?'

'Yes, she is, sir. She's at your house in Wenham. I'm
assured that she's quite safe, and they've increased the
security.'

'Who have?'

'I presume the army, sir, as the Attorney signed the
order.'

'Huh!' growled Fairley. 'He'll only have done that under
duress. But if he did it voluntarily, I hope he's not looking
to stay. Not that I'm likely to be in a position to fire
anyone.' He turned in his chair to look directly at his
detective. 'I should like to telephone Diana. Do you think
that could be arranged?'

'I don't know, sir. I can enquire.'

'What's the set-up here, Gordon?' Fairley's voice took on
a harder edge.

'Looks like a squadron of cavalry surrounding the place,
sir, but there could be more. There's a major here who
seems to be in charge.'

'Have you heard where the rest of the Cabinet is?'
Fairley glanced up at his detective.

'No, sir. I tried to sound out the military, but they're not
saying. If they know.'

'Have they said anything about this business? I mean
what do they want? What's the point of it all?'

'I gather from talking to one or two of the soldiers, sir,' Whitmore said, 'that the hierarchy of the army decided to intervene because, in their view, the country was bordering on anarchy.' Whitmore did not know whether that was the truth or whether it was the story that the soldiers had been told to tell him.

'But that's ridiculous, Gordon. Anarchy indeed.' Fairley faced the table again and toyed with his soup. 'Extremists will always find an excuse for overthrowing a government, but not in England. What do they think they're going to achieve? Did these soldiers tell you that?'

'No, they didn't, sir, but I doubt if private soldiers would know anyway. They just do as they're told.' Whitmore paused, and was wondering whether to go on when the Prime Minister prompted him.

'What's your personal view about all this, Gordon?' he asked suddenly.

Whitmore mulled over the question and it was some time before he replied. 'If you want my honest opinion, sir,' he said eventually, 'I can sympathise to a certain extent with people who see vicious criminals getting away with their crimes. And as a policeman I know how frustrating it is for my colleagues to see cases founder at court simply because of some petty administrative errors. Or worse still, after months preparing a case, to see the accused receive a laughable sentence.' He waited for a moment to give his statement emphasis. 'Probably the two things that would make more difference than anything else, sir, would be to repeal the Police and Criminal Evidence Act and abolish the Crown Prosecution Service. After all, they're only doing what examining magistrates used to do. And did far more efficiently.'

'But there's more to it than that, surely?' said Fairley.

'Yes, there is, sir. To be frank, I think it's the whole European question. People are sick of it. Back in the seventies they were told it was a trade agreement, and they

voted for it in the referendum. But when they found that
you and your predecessors were giving away the country's
sovereignty, they decided they'd had enough. They didn't
expect to be ruled by Brussels, didn't expect Spanish
fishermen to be trawling British waters and they certainly
didn't expect the pound sterling to be replaced by this ECU.
That was the spark that lit the fire.'

'That was quite a speech, Gordon.' The Prime Minister
laid down his spoon, clearly taken aback by his detective's
vehemence. 'But the government had no option. We were
tied into all manner of treaties,' he said. 'Principally the
Treaty of Rome.'

Having gone so far, Whitmore decided to make his
point. 'If you went to the polls with a firm undertaking that
you'd pull this country out of Europe, you'd win hands
down, sir. In fact you'd need half the opposition benches to
accommodate all your new members.'

'Maybe so,' mumbled the Prime Minister, staring down
at his soup. 'But it would bankrupt the country in the
process. There's no way we could withdraw from Europe
now.' He touched his lips with his napkin and then threw
it on the table. 'In any event, it's a matter for the
democratic process, not the army. The people of this
country will very soon get fed up with the yoke of military
discipline, you mark my words.' But Fairley sounded more
hopeful than convinced. He reached for the carafe and
poured more wine into his glass. Some of it slopped over on
to the tablecloth.

Whitmore said nothing. He recognised that Fairley was
trying to bolster his own spirits, but like all politicians he
had set his face against the possibility that there would
come a time when no one listened to him any more.

'Perhaps we could have a walk later on, Gordon,' said
Fairley by way of dismissal. 'I suppose they won't object to
that.'

*

The major commanding the squadron of hussars that was guarding Chequers raised no objection to the Prime Minister taking a stroll around the grounds. In fact he went so far as to emphasise that it was Fairley's country home and he could, more or less, do as he wished. But he refused to allow the Prime Minister to make a telephone call to his wife, knowing that Fairley would tell her where he was.

Fairley greeted the permission to go for a walk by condemning it as a condescending audacity. Nonetheless he and Whitmore took a turn around the rose garden on the south side of the house before making their way through the grounds towards the gate at Great Kimble.

A sentry with a pistol at his belt was posted there and saluted as the Prime Minister approached. 'Good afternoon, sir,' he said.

'Good afternoon,' said Fairley and glanced through the locked gates. 'I suppose there's no chance of my detective and I going across to the Bernard Arms for a drink, is there?'

The sentry grinned. 'I'm afraid not, sir. My orders are that you're not to leave the grounds. Sorry, sir,' he added apologetically.

Fairley nodded. 'I see. I hope you realise,' he said, 'that to claim you were only obeying orders will not prevent your being brought to trial when this business is all over.'

'But that is what I'm doing, sir.' The sentry was taken aback by Fairley's hostility. 'I am only obeying orders.' He had clearly misunderstood what the Prime Minister was driving at.

'Maybe, but you may care to bear in mind that the Nazis found that it was no defence when they were tried at Nuremberg.'

'Yes, sir,' said the sentry, a bemused expression on his face; he knew nothing whatever of the Nuremberg trials. 'We're protecting you, sir,' he added, repeating what he had been told by his troop commander.

The Prime Minister scoffed. 'Really?' he said sarcastically. 'Well, you should think about it very carefully. Not that it's your fault,' he added. 'I don't suppose you agree with all this anyway.'

The sentry remained silent.

'Well, Gordon,' said the Prime Minister to Whitmore, 'I suppose we'll have to be satisfied with a stroll along the perimeter.' And with a further nod to the sentry, he set off again.

The two walked a further hundred yards or so before Fairley spoke again.

'Do you agree with what the army has done, Gordon?' The Prime Minister looked searchingly at his detective.

'No, sir, I don't.' Whitmore paused. 'But I can understand why all this has happened. The government doesn't seem to listen to what the ordinary people are saying about the things that concern them. Nothing personal, sir,' he said, 'but I think the government's become arrogant. And patronising.' He laughed to soften the censure. 'If it's possible to be both at the same time.'

'I'm not sure you're right, Gordon,' said Fairley, 'but when life gets on to an even keel once more, we can consider such matters and analyse properly why this situation arose.'

'You sound confident that things will return to normal, sir.' Whitmore pulled out his pipe. 'Do you mind?' he asked, holding it up.

'Not at all,' said Fairley and felt in his pockets for his own pipe. 'Things have *got* to return to normal, Gordon. We can't have a military dictatorship, not in Britain.'

Whitmore debated whether to mention Cromwell and the Civil War but thought better of it. 'I don't think that the army will give up control easily, sir.'

'We shall see, Gordon, we shall see,' said Fairley and walked on. After several hundred yards, he broke his own silence by remarking, 'This is a huge estate, you know.'

'Yes, sir, it is.'

'And it's virtually impossible to guard every inch of the boundary, wouldn't you say?' Fairley looked thoughtfully at the high walls. 'It would take a great many more troops than there are here at present.'

Whitmore frowned. 'What are you thinking, sir?'

'I was thinking that we might leave, Gordon.'

'That would take some planning,' said Whitmore, amazed that the Prime Minister, never one for making snap decisions, rash or otherwise, should be contemplating an escape.

'Of course it would,' growled Fairley crossly and started walking again. 'I wasn't intending to go this minute.'

'Of course not, sir.' Whitmore grinned. 'Incidentally, sir, did you know that the Chief of the General Staff is making a broadcast at nine o'clock?'

'So I've heard,' said Fairley and turned back towards the house.

An hour before Macey's broadcast, troops had arrived to safeguard the Television Centre. The Director-General of the BBC, a pathetic socialist, had stood symbolically at the main entrance, his arms folded across his chest as if to bar entry to the building. As the armoured cars drew to a halt, a major strode up to him and said, 'Good evening.'

'You shall not pass,' said the DG who, some years previously, had involved himself in demonstrations protesting against new motorways.

'Don't be such a bloody fool,' said the major and walked round him.

At nine o'clock millions of viewers throughout the United Kingdom saw, at the start of the evening's news bulletin, the face of a familiar announcer on the screen. 'This is the BBC,' he said. 'Before the news, the Chief of the General Staff, Sir Simon Macey.' To the average viewer, Macey was an unknown figure. His name came up from time to time in quiz programmes but most contestants, asked what post he filled, got the answer wrong.

'There has been much unfounded rumour about recent events,' Macey began, 'and the purpose of my talking to you tonight is to explain precisely what has occurred and what will occur in the next few days.

'You will be aware that the Prime Minister and the Cabinet have been abducted by dissident military elements, and although I do not know their present whereabouts, I am certain that they are safe. Except, that is, for the Chancellor of the Exchequer who unfortunately died during the course of the scurrilous attack on 10 Downing Street.' Around thousands of television screens, thousands of people indicated, in one way or another, that they regarded the Chancellor's demise as no great loss.

'I wish to make it clear that I utterly condemn the action of the 27th Hussars ...' Macey plucked a handkerchief from his sleeve and dabbed at his brow. 'But the result of yesterday's action is that the Attorney-General, Sir William Headley, has taken over the government. As acting Prime Minister, he has agreed to the use of troops and to the imposition of certain emergency legislation and Orders in Council that permit the army to take such action as may be required without necessarily having recourse to the civil courts. Among other things, this means that all sports meetings will be suspended, and theatres and cinemas closed. The armed forces of the Crown have been deployed and are already on the streets. Their task is to restore order and with your assistance they will do so soon.' He shuffled his notes together. 'I therefore ask you to obey the ordinances of the military for your own good. The soldiers are there to help you.'

Macey paused before launching into an attack on Robert Fairley and his administration. 'I think it only fair to outline to you the causes of the present crisis. We have witnessed the slow erosion of our sovereignty. The Common Market' – Macey disdained the term European Union – 'is poised to take over this country as a subordinate state in a federation dominated by the French and the Germans, a federation that has been established against the will of the people and with a total disregard for the status of Her Majesty the Queen. You have made it clear that you do not want it, but the government has repeatedly declined to seek your views by way of a referendum that was simple enough for you to understand.

'Much of this would have been accepted, albeit with reluctant resignation,' Macey continued, 'by a country famed for its phlegmatism, but the catalyst, if I may call it that, for the present crisis was created by two things: the introduction of the European Currency Unit and the spiralling crime wave. Not only has your money been devalued, but for some years now the God-fearing and law-abiding of this country have sat in smouldering frustration at a government that has refused to take the obvious, and positive, action that is needed to deal with rising crime. But the government's sympathy seems to lie with the perpe-trators of crime, not with its victims. Time after time violent criminals – robbers, rapists, child molesters, murderers and the like – have received derisory sentences. Or worse, have been released to commit further crimes against the com-munity.

'The result has been that many of you have taken to the streets and, on an ever-increasing number of occasions, you have taken the law into your own hands. But I'm sure you will agree that that cannot be right. Rioting has become endemic, disorder the norm rather than the exception. This clearly is worse than that which it sought to eradicate, but the Prime Minister lacked the resolve to deal with it. The joint chiefs of staff, myself included, repeatedly appealed to him to use the military resources available to him to protect you, your loved ones and your property. And to put down the riots. But the Prime Minister declined to act. As you will know, officers commanding troops in various parts of the country dealt with outbreaks of lawlessness as is their bounden duty at common law. But far from supporting the army in those dangerous actions, the Prime Minister attempted to pass legislation that would have prevented soldiers from carrying out this important role. You will also know that he failed in that attempt, thanks not so much to the Opposition as to his own party.

'The government also took it upon itself to suppress the reporting of extremely serious outbreaks of violence in Central London. This information was kept from you because the Prime Minister knew that its reportage would lead to an irresistible demand for the use of the troops, particularly when an attempt was made to storm the armoury at Wellington Barracks.

'One decision taken by the Prime Minister in this whole sorry affair was to ask the French government to send its police force over here ...' Macey smiled and shook his head. 'The tragic death toll that occurred when the French Embassy was bombed was a direct result of that decision. But it was a catastrophe that could have been avoided had the Prime Minister done what he should have done weeks before. I am happy to be able to tell you that the request to the French government has been withdrawn.' Macey looked directly at the camera. 'As a result, the blockade of ports has been lifted and air-traffic controllers have resumed their duties. Finally, I repeat that the soldiers are there to help you, and I ask you to co-operate with them. Good night.'

The announcer reappeared. 'And now for the news,' he said.

Seated in front of the television set in the Hawtrey Room at Chequers, the Prime Minister had watched Macey's broadcast with mounting anger. Although Macey had told the nation that Sir William Headley was now acting Prime

Minister, Fairley was convinced that the statement was a fiction to cover what was, in reality, a military coup d'état. Why else, the Prime Minister asked himself, would Macey have appeared on television instead of Headley?

CHAPTER FIFTEEN

'I thought you went in a bit strong there, Simon,' said Sir Godfrey Bristow. 'That was damned near a political speech you made last night.'

Macey displayed no signs of remorse. 'We have to get the people on our side, sir. Let them know that we understand what their problems are. I know that there's nothing we can do to help them, not politically, but at least if we show some sympathy, it'll make our job easier.'

Bristow stuck his hands into the side pockets of his jacket and stood, feet astride, staring out of the window, rather as he must have looked on the bridge of his beloved frigate. 'I hope you're right, Simon,' he said.

'It's a bloody outrage.' Sir William Headley, the Attorney-General, was fuming with indignation. 'You'd have thought that the damned man had taken over the country.'

'Well you were the one who acknowledged the need for martial law and granted him the powers he asked for,' said Peter Garrard, who had assumed the role of acting Secretary of State for Defence.

'That's no comfort, Peter,' said Headley.

'Wasn't meant to be,' said Garrard.

'What about the Cabinet? What exactly is the army doing to find them?'

'Macey's given me a report, but it doesn't say very much. The army is conducting what he calls a "blanket search" of the whole of the United Kingdom. Frankly I would have thought it nigh on impossible to keep the entire Cabinet prisoner without someone being alerted, but now that you've given the army virtually unfettered powers, we'll only be told what they want to tell us.'

'What does his report say?' asked Headley, unwilling to accept Garrard's word.

'He says that the area – I suppose that means the UK – has been divided into sectors. The police, with military assistance, are conducting a house by house search—'

'How many sectors?'

'Er, a hundred, I think.'

'A hundred!' Headley's tone expressed disbelief. 'A hundredth part of the UK is an enormous area, and if they're conducting the sort of minute search Macey implies, it'll take forever. We could be without a government for months at that rate, Peter. Can't you order him to speed it up?'

'In all honesty, Bill, I can't think of a better way. And you're right, it could take ages. But when you think about searches that the police have carried out in the past, for missing children or kidnap victims, for instance, this one presents them with an almost impossible task. No, I think we'll just have to leave it to Macey and hope for the best.'

Within seventy-two hours of the capture of the Cabinet and the signing of the order by the Attorney-General giving the army special powers, Sir Godfrey Bristow, in conjunction with Macey, had formalised the army's control of the country and ordered an intensification of the search for the Cabinet. Military governors had been appointed and had taken over the functions of local government in so far as they affected the maintenance of order, and the police were now being directed on a national basis by Major-General Passmore from New Scotland Yard.

Many police officers had welcomed the decisiveness of the new administration and quite a few of them saw it as a move towards restoring authority and discipline to a country that had allowed itself to sink into the sort of chaos more often found in a South American republic. The assistance afforded to local, often hard-pressed police by soldiers, who patrolled the streets with them, had improved the former's morale tremendously. The punitive action of the military tribunals, a natural extension of martial law, had resulted in a dramatic decline in crime. And every day the number of soldiers, sailors, airmen and marines on the streets increased as more troops were brought back from overseas.

'Was banning sports meetings, theatres and cinemas a wise course of action, Simon?' asked Bristow. He was concerned that Macey had started making decisions without recourse to him.

General Sir Simon Macey turned from the huge operations board in the tactical headquarters at Northwood. 'There were quite a few incidents of serious disorder arising out of football matches, athletics meetings and, believe it or not, race meetings, sir. Even before Headley signed the order giving us additional powers. It seemed a sensible precaution to ban anything that might erupt into something we couldn't deal with. The television stations weren't too pleased, mind you.' He smiled, briefly. 'Left them with a lot of blank screens, particularly over the weekends.'

Bristow was not happy about that but forbore from taking issue with the Chief of the General Staff. At least immediately. 'The problem that faces us now, Simon,' he said, 'is deciding what we are to do next.'

Macey regarded the Chief of the Defence Staff with a quizzical expression. 'Do next, sir?' he queried. 'Surely to find the Cabinet?' He made it sound as though it was his top priority.

'Of course it is, but there's no telling how long that will take. I hope to God that it'll be a very short while, but we have to look to the possibility of having to carry on for some time yet. After all, we don't even know if they're still alive. There's really no telling what that madman Crosby has done with them. We can't just carry on forever, Simon. It's not our job to run the country. There must come a day, sooner rather than later, when either the present government resumes power or elections are held. And we have to plan for it.'

'You're not suggesting that we put the old lot back, surely?' Macey sat down on a hard wooden chair opposite the Chief of Defence Staff.

'Put the old lot back?' Bristow raised his eyebrows in surprise. 'It's not our place to decide on the future of this country, Simon.' He had become increasingly apprehensive of late at Macey's outspoken views.

'But there's a danger in putting things back the way they were, sir. We could finish up with the same old faces in the House – and in the government – simply because the electorate, as in most other countries, will work on the basis of better the devil you know.'

Bristow had noticed that Macey had recently started to develop a wild-eyed look whenever he discussed the emergency. It may have been exhaustion induced by the traumatic events of the past few days, but Bristow was more than a little worried that the Chief of the General Staff might just be losing his self-control. 'Our job is to restore order, Simon, and that is all. Whatever you may think, the armed forces are still subordinate to the elected government. That's democracy. We can't interfere with the electoral process just because the government is at present incommunicado. You must know that.'

'Why not? Why don't we announce an election? And

decree that none of the present Members of Parliament will be allowed to stand. So we finish up with an entirely new parliament. And while we're about it, we also rule out any previous members who lost their seats last time. That'll put a stop to the carpetbaggers.' Macey leaned back in his chair and grinned. 'What do you think of that, eh?'

'I think you've taken leave of your senses, General Macey,' said Bristow and wondered what the hell he could do about it. If Macey was close to a mental breakdown, there would undoubtedly be procedures for dealing with it. But this was certainly not the time to invoke them.

'You do know where they are, don't you, sir?'

'Know where who are, Imogen?'

'The Cabinet.' Despite Alec Shepherd's words of caution, Imogen had determined to make another effort to find out what was going on. Had she known the full story, she would also have known that she was taking a desperate risk.

'Whatever makes you think that?' Macey raised his eyes from the file he was studying.

'General, are you in some sort of trouble?'

Macey laughed. 'I would be if the Secretary of State walked through that door right now.'

'I'm serious, sir.' Imogen stood defiantly in front of Macey's desk. 'And I'm worried.'

'What about?'

'I know that Crosby telephoned you yesterday . . .'

'Oh that. Damned fool.'

'He's holding the Cabinet prisoner somewhere, isn't he?'

'Yes, he is.' Macey gave the impression of being relieved that, at last, he was able to share his onerous secret with someone else. 'Imogen, I don't want you to get involved in all this. Believe me.'

'How can I believe you if you won't tell me anything?'

Macey sighed and put his pen down on the desk. For a

moment, he gazed pensively at the girl. 'I suppose I ought to tell someone, just in case anything should happen to me. It's a very delicate situation, Imogen, but as you're my ADC, you should know. And you know that what I tell you will be in the strictest confidence.'

'Of course, sir,' said Imogen, knowing full well that she had no intention of being held by her promise.

'Yes, Crosby *has* got the Cabinet. But he's a maverick, and a dangerous one. In fact I've come to the inescapable conclusion that he's suffering some mental disorder. You know his wife was murdered, I suppose?'

'Yes, of course.'

'I gather that the police have more or less closed the investigation. Crosby was very bitter about it.'

'I'm not surprised, sir. Could it have been that that pushed him over the edge?'

'It's a strong possibility, Imogen, and—' Macey suddenly seemed to notice that his ADC was still standing. 'Oh, for goodness' sake, sit down, girl,' he said. 'Apparently he made a scene at the House of Commons on one occasion. Hardly the conduct of an officer and a gentleman, but I suppose he's been under some mental strain. It should have been picked up, of course, but the army can be very close when it comes to things like that, particularly in a regiment like the 27th Hussars. Anyway, the situation now is that he's trying to barter with the lives of the Cabinet. He wants a firm assurance that his regiment will not be disbanded and that he won't be thrown out of the army.' Macey sighed. 'There's absolutely no chance of his succeeding, of course, but we have to pretend that we're going along with it. He's trigger-happy, you see. And I suspect that half his men are too. Apparently they worship him. As I said, it's a very delicate situation.'

'Does the acting Prime Minister know?'

'Good God, no! Nobody knows except Crosby and me. And now you, of course. But I can trust you, can't I?'

Macey seemed badly to need her confirmation of loyalty.

'Yes, sir, you can,' said Imogen.

When Imogen Cresswell called at Alec Shepherd's flat that evening, she was wearing jeans with a black silk shirt, and her hair was tied back with a black velvet bow at the nape of her neck. She had telephoned Shepherd in advance – from a call box – and told him that it was imperative that she saw him.

Shepherd listened to her near-verbatim account of her conversation with Macey and when she had finished, he said, 'I remember reading about the murder of Virginia Crosby. It must have been a good three months ago. But if what you say is true, about his fury with the Crown Prosecution Service and his outburst at the House of Commons, then it's possible that he's mentally ill.'

'Maybe,' said Imogen slowly. 'Personally, I think it's a case of Macey trying to distance himself from what's happened just in case it doesn't work out the way he wants it to.'

Shepherd grinned at the girl. 'You're becoming almost cynical enough to qualify for my service,' he said.

Imogen wrinkled her nose. 'I don't think I'm really suited for that,' she said. 'I thought regimental duty was bad enough, but I'd rather have that any day.'

Since its completion in 1923, Wembley Stadium had seen many huge crowds, from those attending pop concerts to the dedicated who came to be blessed by the Pope. But it was best known, at least until the middle nineties, as the venue for the annual football cup final. And that made it a world-famous shrine for lovers of sport.

On the Sunday after Headley had authorised the deployment of the military, however, the crowds marching up the famous Olympic Way from Wembley Park tube station were angry and demonstrative. Macey's edict to suspend all sporting activities had proved too much of an imposition for the population and, having nothing to watch on their television screens, they had taken to the streets.

Most of the protesters had made for Wembley, but crowds were also flocking to Highbury, Upton Park, White Hart Lane and several other football grounds, as well as the Oval and Lords. Similar demonstrations had been planned at well-known sports arenas in the provinces.

These apparently spontaneous gatherings were, in fact, highly organised. It had not been possible to use the press to advertise the meetings; such notices had to be cleared by the military before publication, and that would have given the authorities advance notice of the protesters' plans. Consequently the ringleaders of the rallies had made a number of telephone calls, always from public call boxes, to a complex network of supporters, and widespread protests had been arranged for the Sunday.

The first intimation of trouble was the sighting of these rallies by several of the army's surveillance helicopters. The duty officer at the operations centre at Northwood immediately directed troops to the main areas of assembly and advised Sir Simon Macey of the possibility of serious disorder.

The army did not have long to wait and, in retrospect, it might have been better to have let the rallies proceed. At the outset, the meetings had been orderly. Speakers, in typically British style, had spoken to the largely peaceful crowds about the unfairness of closing sports meetings and suggested that letters of protest should be sent to the acting Prime Minister. Had they been allowed to carry on in that vein, there would probably have been no trouble, but the army, much less skilled in the control of large crowds than the police were, decided to break up the meetings. And without further ado, soldiers in riot gear, supported by armoured cars, set about dispersing them.

By nine o'clock that night, three soldiers – including an

officer – had been killed and a hundred and ten others injured badly enough to require long periods in hospital. Of the protesters, seventy-five had been taken to hospital, but the true extent of civilian casualties will probably never be known, many of them having limped away from the riots to be cared for by family, friends and doctors sympathetic to the cause.

On Monday morning the area around Wembley – and, to a lesser extent, the other venues – resembled a battle-field. Burned out armoured cars and police vehicles were littered about, along with civilian cars that had also been set on fire. Some shops in the area had been razed to the ground, others set ablaze, and even the least damaged had lost all their windows.

The civilian population had made their point.

General Sir Simon Macey was not a happy man. The army, which had brought about the imposition of military rule so swiftly and so successfully, was not proving the saviour the civilian population had imagined it would be.

The reason for suspending all sporting activities in the country – the fear of further rioting – had seemed sound to Macey, but it had left a substantial part of the population with idle time on their hands. Never a great follower of sport, Macey had been taken aback by the weekend's violent protest meetings at sports stadia across the country. Only now did he realise that the one thing guaranteed to upset the average Briton is to deprive him of sport.

Consequently the Chief of the General Staff was faced with a delicate problem. Further repression of the law-abiding majority of the public could produce a greater unrest than that which it had been designed to avert, this time against the army, which had been supported – and, indeed, feted – when it had taken over the streets. Although it had only been a few days before, the memories of soldiers being greeted with flowers and being kissed by girls – scenes reminiscent of the liberation of Europe in 1944 – now seemed to be in the distant past. Suddenly the population had turned against the army, and it was Macey's fault.

'We are going to have to do something about this, Simon,' said Sir Godfrey Bristow, 'or we shall have disturbances that we'll be unable to cope with.'

'I know, sir,' said Macey, 'but any indication of weakness now will undermine us. We could lose control altogether.'

With a gesture of impatience, Bristow tossed a sheaf of papers across his desk. 'And then there's this lot,' he said. 'The fire brigade strike has spread right across the country, and the army just can't cope. Ambulance drivers are refusing calls, the Post Office are going slow, and the electricity and gas companies are claiming that they haven't enough money to keep going. Power cuts are becoming more and more frequent.'

'That's the fault of the banks,' said Macey. 'They're refusing to process direct debits, those that haven't gone on strike, that is.'

'I know that,' said Bristow. 'But what are we going to do about it?'

Macey shrugged. 'I'm damned if I know,' he said. 'It's Headley's problem rather than ours, but he says that the government is powerless to act.'

'They can't afford not to.' Bristow glared angrily at the soldier opposite him. 'The point about it all is that if the civilian side of government doesn't maintain a flow of finance, it will ultimately affect the military. In short, they won't get paid. And that would mean real trouble.'

'I'm afraid that the only answer is to keep a firm hold on the people, sir,' said Macey.

'For God's sake how, man?' Bristow seemed exasperated that Macey had failed to grasp the import of what he had just said. 'If we're faced with an uprising, we just haven't got the troops to contain it. The navy's about fifty thousand strong, the army's got something like a hundred thousand and the RAF has sixty thousand. Plus about a hundred thousand police.' Bristow reeled off the figures from memory. 'And the population of this country is something in the order of fifty-five and a half million.' Opening a desk drawer he took out a calculator and jabbed at its buttons with his forefinger. Then he looked up. 'If it all goes wrong, Simon, we're in a minority of nearly two hundred to one.' Putting the calculator away again, he slammed the drawer with more force than was necessary.

'I think you're being much too pessimistic, sir,' said Macey.

Sir Richard Dancer looked up as Barry Rogers appeared in the doorway of his office. 'Good morning, Barry,' he said. 'Sit yourself down.'

'We have received information that Macey knows the whereabouts of the Cabinet, sir.'

'I can't say I'm surprised,' said Dancer. 'How reliable is this?'

Rogers repeated what Imogen Cresswell had told Alec Shepherd only hours previously.

Dancer gave a dry cough. 'It looks as though something is going to have to be done about General Macey,' he said.

'He's got to go, sir,' said Rogers. 'The problem is going to be getting rid of him. No one, least of all Headley, will be prepared to take the risk of sacking him while Fairley's still missing, and by the time he's found it might be too late.'

'Please don't say Catch-22, Barry,' said Dancer with a wry smile and leaned forward, elbows on his desk and fingers steepled. 'Given Macey's acknowledged close liaison with General Strigel and the implications of that association, I'm left in little doubt that he has no intention of releasing the Cabinet until he's established his own power base. And somehow we've got to stop him doing that.'

'You're obviously satisfied that he's behind it then?'
Rogers smiled, pleased that at last C was coming round to
his way of thinking.

'I have to admit that I was sceptical to begin with, Barry,
but Major Cresswell's information has confirmed, to me at
any rate, that Macey is a very dangerous man. However, I
think we'd be as well to wait. Any precipitate action might
jeopardise the safety of the Cabinet and the Prime Minister.
The solution, I think, is to put all our resources to
discovering exactly where in Germany they're likely to be
and then—'

'I suppose the German government wouldn't be agree-
able to the SAS launching a raid, would they, sir?' asked
Rogers.

Dancer pursed his lips. 'Probably not. But they do have
GSG 9.'

'So they do,' said Rogers acidly.

'I think we'll have to use our own resources to locate the
Cabinet before we ask the Germans to do anything. Even
so, the prospect of their dealing with it worries me. I'm old
enough to remember how their people turned the Munich
Olympics into a blood bath in 1972.'

'Still doesn't resolve the problem of what to do with
Macey, sir,' Rogers persisted.

'If we managed to have him removed before the Cabinet
was found, we might never find them. This Colonel . . .'

'Crosby,' prompted Rogers.

'Ah yes, this Colonel Crosby. What do we know about
him?'

'According to Cresswell, sir, Macey is putting it about
that he's mentally deranged and is holding the Cabinet
hostage against the reprieve of his regiment.'

'Do we believe Macey?' asked Dancer mildly.

'No,' said Rogers firmly. 'Cresswell's convinced that
Macey's the architect.' He grinned at the Chief. 'And
Crosby is a cavalry officer,' he added. 'They have a

reputation for being a bit thick.'

Dancer smiled. 'You don't seem to have a very high opinion of the army, Barry.'

'Oh, some of them are all right, sir, but I've never been too impressed with donkey wallopers.'

Dancer glanced at his watch. 'I think we need to formulate some plans about Macey,' he said. 'The man is a liability, and he's clearly working against the interests of the country. We need to go more deeply into his relationship with General Max Strigel of the German Army, but first we need more intelligence about him and any links with foreign powers he may have.' He stared meaningfully at Rogers. 'Then we must consider what to do about his removal.'

Rogers had known the Chief for a long time and knew that he would never commit himself to anything that was even faintly illicit. But he had been given similar arcane briefings in the past, and he thought he knew what the Chief wanted now. He rose from his chair, nodded briefly and made his way to Alec Shepherd's office, two floors below.

Walking in without knocking, he slammed the door behind him before sitting down and taking out his pipe.

'Come in,' said Shepherd with a grin.

'I've just seen C,' said Rogers, ignoring Shepherd's sarcasm, 'and he's agreed that we have to do something about Macey.'

'I suspect that's easier said than done.' Shepherd sighed and closed the file in front of him.

'He's agreed to the mounting of a special operation,' said Rogers, putting a very broad construction on his recent conversation with Dancer.

'What sort of special operation?' Shepherd studied his boss closely.

Rogers gazed thoughtfully at his assistant. 'Normally this sort of information is only shared between C and me,' he said. 'But as you're so closely involved with Major Cresswell, Alec, I think you've got to be told. I need hardly say that what I am about to tell you is Cosmic Top Secret.' Rogers paused. 'We are to eliminate Macey.' He had taken a momentous decision. Dancer had certainly not ordered an assassination – nor would he ever have done so – but merely an intensified gathering of intelligence about Macey. Strictly speaking, such a task was the prerogative of the Security Service, but even before the imposition of martial law, Rogers had convinced the Chief that MI5 were failing in that primary duty.

'Are you serious, Barry?' asked Shepherd, amazed by Rogers' uncharacteristic openness. Although the popular press frequently hinted that the SIS carried out assassinations, the Service had no brief to conduct such operations.

'Never more so, Alec. The information you've received from Major Cresswell clearly indicates that Macey is guilty of high treason.'

'Bloody hell,' said Shepherd, still unable to comprehend this sudden twist in the affair. 'But surely a trial is the answer?'

Rogers laughed caustically. 'Perhaps in Crosby's case,' he said, 'but can you imagine any jury convicting the Chief of the General Staff, particularly now that he's holding himself up as the great saviour? And in some cases being believed.' Rogers stood up and tapped out his pipe in the ashtray on Shepherd's desk. 'And if he's not convicted, he'll still be there to start all over again. If we ever find the Cabinet, that is.'

'Where do I fit into all this, Barry?' Shepherd had stood up too.

'You don't, Alec. Not as far as the operation's concerned. C has directed me to take care of it. Your job is to continue to get as much as you can out of Major Cresswell.'

*

'Colonel Martin's here, ma'am,' said Staff Sergeant-Major Watkins.

Imogen Cresswell stood up. 'Show him in, Mr Watkins,' she said.

The soldier who entered was tall and immaculately turned out; his Sam Browne belt was highly polished and he wore the red gorget patches and rank badges of a full colonel. 'Good afternoon,' he said. 'Julian Martin, Army Legal Service. I understand that the CGS wants to see me.' He laid his cap, gloves and cane on Imogen's desk.

'Come in, Julian,' Macey bellowed through his open office door. 'You too, Imogen. Take a seat, both of you.' He glanced at his ADC. 'Perhaps you'd take a few notes of this meeting,' he said and rubbed his hands together briskly. 'Well, how is it going, Julian?'

Martin smiled. 'I think we're getting the message across, sir,' he began. 'I sat at the Old Bailey yesterday, as a military tribunal, and sentenced one man to two years for robbing an old lady of her pension. I got the impression that he thought it was a bit lenient until I explained that he would serve his time in a military corrective establishment and that he would be doing everything at the double, that there would be no remission for good conduct, no television sets and no time to read.'

A gleam came into Macey's eye. 'Good work, Julian,' he said. 'That'll sort the bastards out.'

Imogen was amazed at the frightening expression that Macey had assumed, almost like someone who was on the threshold of taking over everything.

'And the other courts?' Macey helped himself to a cigarette from the box on his desk and then pushed it towards Martin.

'They're being consolidated in the sense that we're reducing the number of Crown Courts to one for each Military Governor's area.'

'But won't that create a backlog bigger than that which

exists already?' asked Macey mildly.

'I don't think so, sir. We've dispensed with juries and we're not wasting too much time on the fripperies with which civilian barristers seem obsessed. From now on they'll get a flat fee, not the daily rate that encouraged them to spin these things out.'

'Good, good,' said Macey. 'Well, keep it up, Julian. It's essential that we make it clear to the criminal elements of the country that the good times are over. Once you've put a few more away for a bit of sharp military punishment, I think we'll see a further reduction still in the crime wave. What about military corrective establishments? Has the Provost Marshal got that in hand now?'

'I understand that there are a number of disused barracks which will be recommissioned as a matter of urgency and the Military Provost Staff Corps is being augmented by the Guards Division.' Martin smiled briefly. 'The Guards seem ideally suited to the sort of discipline that these tearaways need.'

'Splendid,' said Macey. 'I hope the staff have been told to work these bastards till they drop.'

'I think they've grasped the general idea, sir,' said Martin with a grin.

'Good.' Macey stood up and shook hands with the lawyer colonel. 'You do appreciate what we're trying to do here, Julian, don't you?'

'Yes, sir, I do, and I think you've done very well so far.'

Macey relinquished Martin's hand. 'You'll not lose by this, Julian, I assure you,' he said. 'And if you have any problems, let me know.'

When Martin had left, Macey sat in his high-backed chair and swivelled it round so that he was staring out of the window. 'I think we're beginning to get things right, Imogen,' he said. 'Incidentally,' he added, 'on second thoughts, there's no need to record any of that.'

Later that evening, Imogen called, once more, at Alec

Shepherd's flat and briefed him on this latest turn of events.

'I read about the army taking over the Old Bailey in the paper,' said Shepherd. 'I suppose it's legal. Within the terms of martial law, I mean. You say this colonel's name was Martin?' He handed Imogen a gin and tonic and poured a Scotch for himself.

'He was from the Army Legal Service,' said Imogen, 'but it seemed strange that a colonel should report directly to the Chief of the General Staff on a matter that is not terribly important when you consider all that's happening at the moment. It cuts right across the sort of protocol I've been used to. But Macey said afterwards that he wanted to get a first-hand account of what had happened. I would have thought that the correct procedure was to ask for a report from General Turner, the Director of Army Legal Services.'

'Perhaps Macey doesn't trust him,' said Shepherd thoughtfully. 'As the army's chief lawyer, it does put Turner in a rather difficult position.'

'He may have sacked him,' said Imogen. 'Things are so chaotic at the moment that we probably wouldn't know. It could be that he intends to promote Martin. As I said, he did tell him that he wouldn't lose by it. Whatever "it" is.'

'I don't like the sound of any of this.' Shepherd, his Scotch momentarily forgotten, had been listening intently to what Imogen had been saying.

'It's possible that he's trying to get officers like Martin to join him.'

'To join him?'

'Yes. Perhaps he's trying to create a cabal of like-minded officers whom he can trust. I'm sure that's what he did with Crosby. He saw him at least twice before the abduction of the Cabinet.'

'Is there anyone else who appears to be on his side, in an inner circle as you might say.'

'Me?' said Imogen and smiled innocently.

But Shepherd didn't respond. 'I want you to be very careful,' he said. 'For God's sake don't take any risks, Imogen. I don't want anything to happen to you. If he asks you to do anything illegal try to play for time and let me know immediately.'

'What good will that do?'

'It means that when this whole sorry business is eventually sorted out, the fact that you have been acting as an informant for the SIS will save you from prosecution.'

Imogen had picked up her glass, but set it down again. 'Do you really think it'll come to that, Alec?' she asked.

'You did military law at Sandhurst, Imogen,' said Shepherd. 'Just think about what's happening. Do you honestly imagine that everything that Macey's done in the past few weeks has been lawful?' He paused to take a sip of whisky. 'What about Bristow? Is he involved?'

'No more than he has to be as CDS, I suppose. I'm not allowed to be in on Macey's conversations with him any more.'

'Do you mean that Macey's beginning to have doubts about your trustworthiness?' Shepherd suddenly looked worried at the prospect.

Imogen shook her head. 'No, I don't think so. I think it's Bristow. You know what the navy's like. They're much more rank conscious than the army, and I don't think that Bristow likes the idea of having a mere major listening to all that's going on. After all, I'm only the equivalent of lieutenant-commander in his eyes, and that's pretty far down the scale.'

'I think the old man's planning to escape, David.' Whitmore and Enderby were standing in the centre of the Great Hall at Chequers beneath the huge electrolier that dominated the vast room. In front of them stood the refectory table upon which was the visitors' book, a living testament to the history of the house. Whitmore didn't think that the army had gone to the trouble of installing eavesdropping equipment; in fact he was sure that they hadn't. He had been there for as long as the Prime Minister, and he would have noticed any work of that nature. But he wasn't prepared to take the chance, which is why he and Enderby were standing in the centre of the large room, speaking in low tones.

Enderby nodded. 'Has he suggested how?'

'Not in as many words. It was just a comment he made when we were walking down by Kimble Gate.'

'Is there anything we can do to help him?' asked Enderby.

Whitmore looked his deputy straight in the eye. 'Are you willing to help, Dave?'

'Of course I bloody well am.'

'Sorry. It's just that under the present circumstances you never know who's on which side.'

'Shouldn't have thought you needed to ask,' said Enderby irritably. 'What do you reckon he's got in mind?'

'I don't know, but there's one sure way of finding out. Where is he?'

'Watching television.'

The two detectives walked through into the Hawtrey Room at the front of the house and found the Prime Minister hunched in an armchair watching a wildlife programme.

'Ah, Gordon, David, come in, come in. This is very interesting, if you're interested in meerkats.' Fairley spoke sarcastically and then stood up and made to turn off the television set.

'Leave it on, sir, if you don't mind.'

'You interested in meerkats then?' asked the Prime Minister.

'Not really, sir.' Whitmore smiled and turned up the volume. 'But it prevents us being overheard.'

'Sounds mysterious.' Fairley sat down again in the armchair.

'Can you spare us a moment?'

'Of course,' said the Prime Minister. 'What's on your mind?'

'You mentioned yesterday that you were thinking about leaving here, sir,' said Whitmore. 'Had you got anything specific in mind?'

Fairley looked from one of his detectives to the other. 'Look,' he said, 'this is an uncertain situation, but I *am* the Prime Minister and I don't want to get you chaps involved.'

'And *we* are your protection officers, sir,' said Whitmore with a smile. 'I'm only sorry that we haven't done a very good job so far.'

Fairley waved a hand. 'Hardly your fault, Gordon,' he said. 'Not a great deal you could have done in the face of the attack on Downing Street.'

'Well if we can make up for it by helping now, sir, you know you can count on us.'

For a moment the Prime Minister sat in silence. Then he looked at Enderby. 'David,' he said, 'why don't you pour us all a drink.'

'Right, sir.' Enderby crossed to the drinks table and poured three measures of whisky from the decanter that was always kept full. Adding equal amounts of water, he handed a chunky tumbler to Fairley.

'You both saw Macey's broadcast on television,' said the Prime Minister. Whitmore and Enderby nodded. 'It's obvious that he's taken over the country,' Fairley continued. 'A military coup d'état, in fact. It is therefore imperative that I get away from here.' The Prime Minister spoke quietly and took a sip of whisky. 'Get out of the country, in fact.'

'Any idea where, sir?'

Fairley nodded. 'Yes,' he said, 'but all I propose to tell you at this stage is that I intend to reach the continent.'

'We can be trusted, you know, sir,' said Enderby who was perched on the arm of a chair near the empty fireplace.

'My dear chap, I know that,' said Fairley. 'Point is, the less you know the better. For your own good.'

'Well, wherever you go, sir, we're coming with you.' Whitmore held up a hand as Fairley appeared to be about to speak. 'I'm sorry, sir, no arguments. The Commissioner would never forgive me.'

'That's good of you, Gordon.' Fairley glanced at Enderby. 'You too, David.'

For once Whitmore detected a rare flash of warmth in the Prime Minister's response. But he also remembered the cautionary advice given him by an old and experienced Special Branch officer when he had undertaken his first spell of protection duty more than twenty years previously, that politicians tended to discard people once they had served their purpose. 'Right, sir, leave it to us. We'll put our heads together and formulate a plan.'

Warrant Officer Helen Jackson was enjoying a rare moment of relaxation in front of the television set in the staff room at Chequers. 'Have you seen the news?' she asked when Whitmore and Enderby entered.

'No,' said Whitmore. 'Anything special?'

Helen grinned. 'There was an account of a trial at the Old Bailey yesterday,' she said. 'Apparently a colonel turned up and took over from the judge. Said it was a military tribunal now and promptly weighed some yobbo off with a couple of years in a military detention camp. Told him that once he got there he wouldn't stop running from morning to night. They do everything at the double in those places, you know.'

'About time too,' said Whitmore and turned up the volume of the television set before he and Enderby sat down, one on either side of her. 'Helen, how well do you know Portsmouth?' Whitmore asked quietly.

'What is this, a joke?' asked Helen Jackson and laughed. 'I've spent twenty years in the Andrew and you ask me if I know Pompey.'

'This is serious, Helen.' Whitmore leaned closer to her. 'Are you willing to help the boss to escape from here?'

'Of course.' Helen spoke without hesitation and then looked from Whitmore to Enderby and back again. 'What are you thinking of?'

'We're not quite sure yet, but it's about, what, eighty or ninety miles from here to Portsmouth?'

'About that, I should think, but have you thought this thing through? Firstly, we've got to get out of here. And secondly, we've got to find a way of getting there. How do we do that? And thirdly, we don't know whether there's anyone in Pompey who'd be willing to help us. Don't forget that the army's everywhere.'

Whitmore nodded. 'Yes, I know,' he said, 'but the navy don't seem to be very involved, do they?'

Helen shrugged. 'I've no way of knowing,' she said. 'But there's one sure way of finding out.'

'What's that?'

'By getting down there.'

Enderby laughed. 'Good thinking,' he said.

Helen gave him a withering glance. 'Well we won't find out by sitting here talking about it,' she said sharply. 'But it's no good going off at half-cock. We mustn't fail, otherwise there's no telling what might happen to us, or to the PM. First we must work out how we're going to get away from here.' She turned to face Whitmore. 'Are you two still armed?' she asked.

'No,' said Whitmore. 'They took our weapons away before we left London. Makes a bit of a mockery of suggesting that we're still protecting the old man.'

'In that case, the first priority is to acquire a firearm,' said Helen.

'And that's easier said than done,' said Whitmore.

'Not necessarily,' said Helen, smiling. 'I've got a staff of twenty here. From the navy and the air force. All young single women. And, in case you haven't noticed, soldiers are very attracted to young women.'

'Bloody hell,' said Whitmore, 'you don't play around, do you?'

Helen Jackson gave the Prime Minister's detective a cheeky smile. 'No, I don't,' she said. 'But one of them will.'

CHAPTER SIXTEEN

Peter Garson had been employed by the Chequers Trust for twenty-seven years, the last twelve as head groundsman. It was not a demanding post, consisting mainly of opening the gates for the arrival and departure of the Prime Minister when he came down, usually at the weekends, and doing odd jobs around the house and estate. Among the perks of Garson's job were an allowance for using his car and a tied cottage in the grounds, which he and his wife had lived in for most of their married life.

But since the imposition of martial law, he had had very little to do. The army now guarded the gates, which were opened only to admit the occasional suppliers of necessities, none of whom was aware that the Prime Minister was there and whose goods were unloaded by military personnel.

Garson could not shake off the routine of a lifetime, and each morning at about ten, after a walk of inspection around the grounds, he could be found in the staff room of what he called 'the big house', having a cup of tea and scanning the newspaper.

This particular morning he was joined by Gordon Whitmore and David Enderby.

'Morning,' said Garson in his soft Buckinghamshire

burr, and got on with reading the paper. 'When's the army going to start sports meetings again?' He jabbed at an item in the paper with his finger and then, folding the paper carefully, took a sip of his tea. 'I'm surprised the man's still here,' he said suddenly. Garson always referred to the Prime Minister as 'the man'.

'He hasn't got much option, Peter,' said Whitmore.

'Thought he was made of sterner stuff.' Garson frowned. 'If he'd a mind to go, they'd need the whole bloody army to stop him. More than the handful of donkey wallopers they've got here now.' Garson was not above talking to the soldiers he met on his rounds but had not formed too high an opinion of them.

Whitmore moved his chair closer to the table where Garson was sitting. 'And if you were in his shoes, Peter, how would you go about it?' he asked softly.

'Easy,' said Garson. 'Use the gate.'

Whitmore raised his eyebrows in exasperation. 'What are you talking about? The army are guarding all the gates.'

'I'm not talking about the main gates,' said Garson, 'nor the Kimble Gate. I'm talking about the secret gate between Kimble Gate and Risborough Gate.'

'I've never heard of it,' said Whitmore. He thought that after five years of spending almost every other weekend at Chequers he knew the estate quite well. But he had never heard mention of a secret gate.

Garson poured himself a second cup of tea and drank it down almost immediately. 'Lady Mary Grey was imprisoned here for two years in the sixteenth century,' he said. 'You must know about the Prison Room.'

'Of course,' said Whitmore, wondering why Garson appeared to have changed the subject. He was familiar with the tiny garret on the top floor, had slept there on more than one occasion when his usual room had been taken by some distinguished visitor. But he hadn't realised that Garson was an amateur historian. 'But what's that got to do with this secret gate that no one knows about?' he asked.

'I've been here a long time,' said Garson, 'and I've got to know the estate very well.'

Whitmore held up his hands in a placatory gesture. He knew that Garson was not a man to be hurried. 'Tell me more,' he said.

'When I first came here, the head groundsman was an old boy called Walter Simpson. And when he started, the Prime Minister was Neville Chamberlain. Well, Walter told me about this gate, see.' Garson poured himself a third cup of tea and then wandered out to the kitchen to replenish the empty sugar bowl. When he returned, he continued as though he had not left the room. 'William Hawtrey owned the house in the sixteenth century. And some friends of Lady Mary's husband – he were a sergeant porter in the royal household – got together to try and rescue her. She were allowed the occasional walk round the grounds, see, and they thought that if they could make this hole in the wall what no one never knew about, they could get her out. Seems they spent ages getting through it. Bloody thick it is, just there.' He grinned at the thought. 'They had to work by night, see, and cover it up afore they left, in case anyone spotted it. But just as they'd finished it, in . . .' He paused and stared into the middle distance. 'About 1567, I think it was, Lady Mary was released anyway, so the story goes. So it weren't never used, not to get her out, like.' He paused again. 'It weren't meant to be a gate, not at first, but when Hawtrey discovered it, much later, he decided that rather than brick it up again, he'd have a proper gate made of it.'

'Have you ever seen it, Peter?' asked Enderby.

'Course I have.'

'And can it be used?'

'Don't see why not.'

'I can't understand why I've never seen it,' said Whitmore.

'Well you wouldn't have. It's covered over by thick bushes and bramble now. You wouldn't know it was there, not unless you went looking for it.'

'Is it kept locked, Peter?'

'Happen it is.'

'And is there a key?'

Garson stared at Whitmore and shook his head slowly, as though the detective had lost his reason. 'Course not, not after all these years. It'd need a crowbar to open it now, like as not.'

Whitmore felt let down. 'That would make too much noise,' he said.

Garson stroked the side of his nose with his forefinger. 'I ain't daft,' he said. 'I reckon it could be persuaded. I can have a try if you think it'll be useful.'

'How soon?' Whitmore was not at all optimistic about Garson's secret gate.

'Course, it could be stuck fast, because I've never tried opening it up. Want me to have a go?'

'Yes,' said Whitmore, 'but don't take any chances. If a sentry catches you, that would be an end to it. And there's no telling what might happen to you.'

'Pah!' said Garson. 'Take more 'an a few soldiers to frighten me. Don't make 'em like they did when I was a para.'

'I didn't know you were a para,' said Whitmore.

Garson grinned. 'You might be a detective,' he said, 'but you don't know everything.'

Despite his apparent languor, Garson had wasted no time, and twenty-four hours later he and Gordon Whitmore were standing under one of the box trees on the drive that led to Great Kimble Lodge. To the casual observer, they could have been discussing the weather or the state of the shrubbery, or even talking about the test match in India. But they were not talking about any of those things.

'I got the lock off,' said Garson. 'Much easier than I thought. Went out after dark and done a bit of work on it. Bit of tapping with an old screwdriver and a hammer and away it come. Screws was all rusted and the wood was rotten,' he added.

'Did you open it?' asked Whitmore.

'Only a fraction. After I'd put some oil on the hinges. Bloody amazing, ain't it? After all these years. I thought it'd be stuck fast.'

'What's on the other side, Peter? Any idea?'

'Difficult to say without opening it right up,' said Garson. ''Cept to say it'll be the main road what runs past the Bernard Arms. I shone my torch out, but I couldn't see nothing. Didn't want to be seen. Course if we could get out for a walk round, we could tell straightaway, but I've never thought to look before.' Garson took off his cloth cap and scratched his head. 'Bit late now, ain't it?' he added with a grin.

'I reckon we'll have to take a chance on it then,' said Whitmore and nodded to a passing soldier who was patrolling the grounds. 'Helen's got a plan to divert the inside sentry who comes on duty at ten o'clock. If we can get the old man away from the house to your cottage, can you lead us to the gate?'

'Reckon so,' said Garson.

'Then we might just get away with it.' Whitmore shrugged. 'Any idea how many soldiers there are here altogether, Peter?'

'There's a major in charge, so one of the squaddies told me. That makes it a squadron. Be about a hundred men all up, but they can't all be doing the night stag. Probably no more than twenty-five. But I think they rely on the inside man. If I know soldiers, they'll be holed up somewhere having a crafty drag.'

'We'll be taking a hell of a chance even so, but we can only get caught, I suppose,' said Whitmore.

'Want me to come with you?'

'No, Peter. It's essential that you stay to close the gate after us and camouflage it. We want to keep the bastards guessing for as long as we can. My betting's that they'll search the grounds once they find he's disappeared, but if I didn't know about the gate, it's a racing certainty that the army don't either.'

Garson looked mildly disappointed at the prospect of being left behind but could see the sense of Whitmore's reasoning. 'When are you going to try then?'

'Tomorrow night.'

'Right. Just you and the man, is it?'

Whitmore shook his head. 'No,' he said. 'David Enderby's coming and so's Helen Jackson.'

'Helen Jackson? What are you taking her for?'

Whitmore grinned. 'Because she knows Portsmouth, and that's where we'll be heading, Peter.'

'Bloody hell,' said Garson. 'And who's getting Sunday lunch?' Garson and his wife always joined the rest of the staff for Sunday lunch in the staff room.

'Don't worry, Peter,' said Whitmore, 'we're not taking the chef.'

Lieutenant-Colonel Angus Wilson did not have the appearance of a soldier. His hair was a shade too long, although lancer officers – and he had been one – would tell you it was about right, and his clothes, although well cut, were unpressed and baggy at the knees and the elbows. He had a look of vagueness about him, more fitting, perhaps, to someone whose life was devoted to lecturing in ancient history. It was not entirely an inaccurate analogy. History, both ancient and modern, was more relevant to his trade than people might think. Lieutenant-Colonel Wilson was an officer whose duties were undefined.

He waited now in the entrance hall of Barry Rogers' club. It was not the club with the briefly attired waitresses who so diverted the visiting CIA agents whom Rogers occasionally took there to dine. This was one of the proper, old-established St James's clubs, where gentlemen fore-gathered to discuss all manner of gentlemanly matters, like high finance and horses and shooting, and occasionally other members. But they never discussed other members' wives or, much less, their mistresses for fear that one member's wife might be another's mistress.

Wilson occupied his time examining notices about obscure but very clubbish matters that were arrayed untidily on the noticeboard and watching, with interest, the other men who came and went. He looked around the entrance hall at the chairs, all of good quality but clearly past their prime. And he noted the sycophantic hall porter, who was also past his prime and living in a bygone era, who dealt efficiently with telephone calls and enquiries and managed to identify all the members who came in and went out, addressing them correctly as 'my lord' or 'Sir So-and-so', or just plain 'sir', and occasionally glancing at Wilson, who did not seem to fit into any of the acceptable categories of persons he could reasonably expect to find coming through the portals of his illustrious establish-ment.

'Angus, my apologies.' Rogers swept into the club, acknowledged briefly the porter's greeting and shook hands with Wilson. 'I'm most awfully sorry I'm late, it was one of those—'

'Don't apologise, Barry,' said Wilson. 'Affairs of state can be tricky matters, and I presume that you'll not be making an excuse of anything less.' There was a twinkle in his eye as he spoke, his soft Aberdonian accent sounding a little mocking.

'Oh, to hell with you, Angus Wilson,' said Rogers. 'I forgot the bloody time. There, will that do you?'

'That's much better, Barry. And for that you can buy me a decent lunch.'

Rogers steered Wilson into the bar that was between the hall and the dining room. 'I'm sure that you need a drink before we eat, eh?'

'I'll take a Glenlivet, Barry, thank you,' said Wilson. 'And no ice,' he said to the barman. The barman looked offended.

Persisting in his habit of declining to discuss business while the much more important pastime of eating was under way, Rogers waited until the brandy was poured and the cigars well alight before he broached the subject that had caused him to invite this soldier to lunch.

'One of my people needs some assistance, Angus. Some assistance that has your special brand of professionalism about it.'

'I didn't think I was getting this splendid lunch just for old times' sake,' said Wilson phlegmatically.

The old times to which Wilson alluded went back a long way. To when he was a young subaltern helping, in the arcane way of his regiment, to secure a military solution in a volatile area of the Near East while Rogers, interfering in the way that only his service could, was trying, at the same time, to establish some political sanity and garner intelligence. They had first met in a dusty Arab village, when Wilson, attired in some sketchy attempt at a British Army uniform topped by a kaffiyeh, had reined in his horse and engaged in an acrimonious exchange with Rogers about some now forgotten aspect of policy. The problem, whatever it had been, had eventually been resolved over a bottle of whisky, and they had been firm friends since. From time to time over the years they had been in contact about various aspects of nefarious activity in which they had common interest, and although the association had never been a close one, there had arisen out of it a trust based upon a mutual and grudging admiration for each other's professionalism.

'My colleague's looking for a man with the usual qualities,' said Rogers in a flat tone as he rolled the ash from his cigar.

'Which part of the world?' Wilson did not seem at all surprised at Rogers' statement.

'London.'

'Interesting. I thought you chaps didn't operate in the United Kingdom.'

'We don't.'

'I see,' said Wilson. 'What you mean is mind my own business.'

'Something like that.'

For some minutes neither of them said anything, and then Wilson spoke. 'Sorry, don't think I can help you on this occasion, Barry. Apart from anything else, I think the fee would be more than even your company could afford.'

'I think we could probably run to it,' said Rogers, 'but the arrangements for payment would be the same as usual. In full on completion.'

Wilson appeared to mull over the proposition for a few moments, and then, 'No, sorry, can't help you.'

Rogers shrugged his shoulders. 'Oh dear, my colleague will be disappointed. No harm in asking, I suppose, Angus?'

'None at all, Barry. You know me. Always willing to help if I can. What was the name of your colleague, incidentally?'

Rogers hesitated only briefly before thinking up a suitable name. 'John Silver,' he said.

The remainder of the lunch was spent in exchanging inconsequential gossip about mutual acquaintances. At a quarter past three, Barry Rogers returned to his office.

It was the following day that Rogers' private-line telephone rang and a voice with a Londonderry accent asked to speak to Mr Silver.

'I'm sorry,' said Rogers, 'I think you must have a wrong number.'

Slowly the Irishman quoted the number he claimed he was trying to reach. 'Sorry to have troubled you,' he added, and the line went dead.

Rogers carefully folded the piece of paper on which he had written the number and placed it in one of the inner pockets of his wallet. 'I'm just going out for an hour or so, Sheila,' he said to his secretary, as he walked through the outer office.

Inserting his Phonecard into one of the telephones near Vauxhall Station, Rogers dialled the number.

The same Irish voice answered with the number Rogers had dialled.

'May I speak to Mr Silver,' said Rogers.

'I think you have the wrong number,' said the Irish voice. 'This is 4 Cavalier Place, W9.'

'I'm sorry to have troubled you,' said Rogers, and replaced the handset. He left the phone box and hailed a cab.

The driver dropped him at the Maida Vale Hospital for Nervous Diseases, a short distance from the quiet cul-de-sac of new town houses called Cavalier Place.

Rogers was about to touch the bell push when the door opened; it was obvious that the occupant had been watching. 'Mr Silver?' he asked.

'Come in, sir.'

Rogers estimated that 'Silver' was about thirty-four years of age. He was obviously fit, and spare of build. He had sharp features and prematurely grey hair, and he moved about the room into which he had shown Rogers with a deliberate economy of movement. Accent apart, there was little doubt that Silver was Irish. It was indefinable, but everything about him pointed to an Irish background and upbringing.

Silver had been born in a Loyalist area of Londonderry,

and the sight of British soldiers patrolling the streets, dashing from doorway to doorway, sheltering from some unseen enemy, had been commonplace on his journey to school.

He remembered, too, one such soldier suddenly falling to the ground and staying motionless, and the sudden crackle of small-arms fire that sounded like the jumping crackers he and his friends let off on the Apprentice Boys' March that took place on 12 August every year. Silver knew that the soldier had been killed by a sniper, but it saddened him to see that it provided a new variation on the street games that the neighbourhood children played. Saddened and angered him.

The house in which he was brought up was not very grand – his father being sometimes in work and sometimes not – but it was scrupulously clean. And in the place of honour over the fireplace in the parlour there had always been a picture of the Queen and Prince Philip. The picture hung there still.

His upbringing had been fiercely Protestant, and he had learned to be God-fearing, deeply loyal to his sovereign and an implacable enemy of the Republican cause.

It was no wonder, then, that with the example of soldiers all around him, the spirit of service that had been instilled in him, and a desire to improve upon his impoverished youth that he became a soldier.

To John Silver's mind there would be no greater honour than to be accepted as one of Her Majesty's personal troops but to retain, at once, the essential Irishness of his character. The letter, when eventually it arrived, directing him to join the Irish Guards at somewhere called Pirbright, not far from London, was a cause of great celebration.

And so he set off, feeling quite the hell of a fellow, and swanking a bit to the mates he already regarded as inferior. The one note of regret, though, was that with the Troubles continuing, and threatening to continue, he would never be allowed home on leave in uniform.

Over the next few months he was to have many more moments of regret as the instructors at the Guards Depot started, as one of them put it, 'to take you apart and put you back the way we want you'.

The punishing routine, from dawn to dusk, day in and day out, left him utterly exhausted. Even church parades – long abandoned by the rest of the army – were so demanding in terms of personal appearance that he would almost have been prepared to become an atheist to avoid them, except that the drill staff hinted darkly that what atheists were obliged to undertake as an alternative to church parades was too horrible to contemplate.

At last the moment came when he was a trained guardsman. A general appeared, inspected the recruits, walked down the ranks and spoke to a select few, and finally took the salute.

Over the succeeding years, Silver undertook public duties in London and Windsor, served in Germany and Hong Kong and travelled, with a detached company of the battalion, to Kuwait. But his battalion never served in Northern Ireland, the army considering it too risky for a Loyalist Irish regiment to try to become impartial in the dangerous streets of Belfast, in Silver's home town of Londonderry, or in that graveyard of the British Army, Crossmaglen.

Slowly Silver rose through the ranks: from lance-corporal to lance-sergeant to full sergeant, and finally to colour-sergeant.

At that stage of his career he was sent for. A major of the Irish Guards serving in the Special Air Service had suggested that Silver's talents would be particularly useful to that regiment. Silver travelled to Hereford, undertook the gruelling tests, survived the even more demanding training and finally became a member of that select band of unorthodox soldiers.

Then tragedy wiped out Colour-Sergeant Silver's career. On one highly secret overseas operation, his shoulder was broken while he was abseiling down the side of a building. It healed in time and left him with only the smallest of disabilities, but it was enough to remove him from the active list of the SAS.

The prospect of a return to such mundane duties as Queen's Guard at Buckingham Palace did not appeal to Silver, and he accepted a medical discharge and the pension that went with it. Until that awful day he had been married to the army, but now he felt like a man divorced from a woman who had been unfaithful to him. But the SAS, being a regiment to which esprit de corps is paramount, looked after him. He was found a job with an organisation that took on the sort of dubious tasks that, if not exactly legal, were considered morally acceptable, but that the SAS itself could not undertake officially.

Silver did not enquire if Rogers wanted tea, he just went out to the kitchen and made it. There was nothing genteel about its presentation, and he brought it in on a tin tray, of the sort that are used in public houses. There were no saucers, just large china mugs.

'I don't know your name, sir,' said Silver, handing Rogers a mug of tea and inviting him to help himself to sugar from the packet which he had considerately brought in.

'And I don't know your name, Mr Silver.' Rogers smiled.

'No, sir, and I was about to say that's the way we ought to keep it.'

'Agreed.'

'Right then, sir,' said Silver, hunching himself in the chair and holding his mug of tea in both hands as if warming them, even though the weather was mild. 'And what exactly can I do for you?'

Rogers had the utmost faith in Angus Wilson, and that

extended to anyone he recommended. Consequently he did not hesitate to answer the tall, angular Irishman opposite him and set out his requirements as succinctly as possible. And finally, he named the target.

Silver also had faith in Colonel Wilson, and similarly would trust anyone with whom the colonel had put him in touch. There was not a trace of surprise or demurral when he learned what Rogers wanted of him. 'Well, well. Isn't that irony for you, sir?' For a moment or two he stared into space. 'Very good, sir,' he said. 'When and how?'

'It may well be, Mr Silver,' said Rogers, 'that in the light of current events this operation might not be necessary, but you will know if that is the case, as we all will. If it is to go ahead, the "how" is a matter for you. I wouldn't presume to suggest to an expert how he should go about his trade. And the "when" is something that I shall leave to you also.'

'Of course, sir.' Silver nodded thoughtfully, as though already formulating his plan.

'Is there anything that you need, Mr Silver?'

Silver considered the question for a moment. 'A police warrant card would come in very handy, sir,' he said. 'If you can make it for a detective sergeant, I'd be much obliged.' He gave a wry grin. 'It's the Irish accent, you see, sir. Causes a bit of trouble at times.' He produced a passport-sized photograph of himself and handed it to Rogers without comment.

'Be here in two days' time, Mr Silver. After that we shall not meet again.' Rogers stood up and shook hands with the Irishman. 'Payment will be made through our mutual acquaintance upon completion.'

'Goodbye, sir,' said Silver. 'Until the day after tomorrow, then.'

One of the delights of working for an organisation like the Secret Intelligence Service, thought Rogers, was that no one ever asked questions. The man commissioned to produce an undetectable forgery of a detective sergeant's warrant card didn't want to know why he was doing it, in fact knew better than even to wonder. He just got on with it and when he had finished gave it to Rogers. Both he and Rogers knew that neither of them would ever mention it again. Even to another member of the Service.

At the appointed time, Rogers gave the warrant card to Silver. They never saw each other again.

Brian Kennard had become leader of the Labour Party immediately after his party's defeat at the last general election. And Kennard did not like Robert Fairley, the Prime Minister. It was not just a political animosity, not a staged affair across the floor of the House for the benefit of the voters, but a genuine dislike.

When Fairley had taken his place for Prime Minister's Questions on the day after Kennard's election, he had congratulated him with genuine warmth on becoming leader of the shadow cabinet, making the usual jocular comment that he hoped Kennard would occupy that office for many years to come.

Kennard had responded by informing the House that to be leader of the shadow cabinet was better than being the leader of a Cabinet full of shadows, which was how he saw the Prime Minister's role. From then on, never an opportunity was missed for either one of the party leaders to snipe at the other.

And now, seated in the Prime Minister's room at the House of Commons, Kennard was intent on scoring more political points. Behind the PM's desk was Sir William Headley, Attorney-General and acting leader of the Conservative Party.

'There seems little point, Bill,' said Kennard, 'in continuing to have sittings of the House if all you're going to do is rubber-stamp what the army is doing.'

But Headley chose to ignore the heavy sarcasm that was apparent in Kennard's voice. 'I'm sorry, I don't agree, Brian. It was vitally necessary that the military be deployed, and the irony of it is that if Fairley had done it himself, much earlier, it is unlikely that he and the rest of the Cabinet would have been kidnapped. It is essential to the well-being of the country that Parliament is seen to be there. It would be an awful mistake to seek a prorogation of the House.'

'In that case I hope you'll cancel the Easter recess.'

Headley looked up in surprise. 'But why should I do that, Brian?' he asked. Despite having been in the House for fifteen years, political nuances escaped him much more easily that forensic ones.

'Because, Bill, in the middle of the worst crisis we've seen in years, if not forever, it would not look good for Members to push off on holiday.'

'I suppose you're right,' Headley mumbled grudgingly.

'More to the point, how long is this martial law business going to continue?' Kennard picked up a paperknife from the edge of Fairley's desk and balanced it between his forefingers. 'My party is getting very worked up about it. I would have thought that your first priority would have been to instruct the army to find where the Cabinet's being held. Good God, Bill, there are enough troops in the country now to search every damned building from Land's End to John O'Groats.'

'We've given the army carte blanche to restore order. We cannot now impose conditions or tell them how to do it. And I have Macey's assurance that every effort is being made to find the Cabinet.'

Kennard laughed and dropped the paperknife back on to the desk so that its point was towards Headley. 'What's your majority, Bill?' He knew exactly; the question was a rhetorical one.

'Ten.'

'But there are twenty-two members of your party who are not in a position to vote. Correct?'

'You're not suggesting—?' Headley looked alarmed as the impact of Kennard's statement struck him.

'If we debated a motion of no confidence in the government now, you'd be out, Bill.' Kennard smiled maliciously. 'And I'm reaching a point where I can't hold my people back for much longer. If someone wants to put down an early-day motion and gather enough signatures on it, I'd be hard pressed to stop it. We'd have to allocate time for the debate. And there'd be no pairing for your absent friends.'

'But for Christ's sake, Brian.' Headley looked directly at the Leader of the Opposition, a shocked expression on his face. 'That'd be damned unfair in the circumstances.'

Kennard smiled. 'Whoever said politics were fair? It's all right for you Tories, but in the Labour Party I've got about two-thirds of the political spectrum on my side of the House. From bloody crypto-communists to pink Liberals, all of whom knew that they stood a better chance of getting elected under the Labour banner than under their true colours.' He grinned insolently at the Attorney-General. 'All right, I'll try and hold them off, but only on condition that we continue to act as though these bloody pongos are under parliamentary control. And that means that you've got to make absolutely certain that they don't exceed their brief. Whatever that brief is.'

'It's very easy to be Leader of the Opposition, Brian—' began the Attorney.

'Yes, and Fairley's likely to find out just how easy after the next election,' said Kennard. 'If you ever find him,' he added sarcastically.

'I'm afraid you'll just have to be patient,' said Headley, ignoring Kennard's taunt, 'and let the army do their job.'

'But they've taken over the major installations, they have broadcasting under their control and they're censoring the Press. And, I understand, they've virtually renationalised the utilities: gas, water, electricity and so on.'

Headley laughed, but there was no humour in it. 'That should please you,' he said.

'Under normal circumstances, it would have done,' said Kennard, 'but there are more important things to be considered right now.'

Headley played with his glasses, clicking the arms open and shut. 'It's all very well for you to talk about returning to normal government ...' He glanced at Kennard and paused. 'If that's what you are talking about.'

'Yes.' Kennard nodded.

'You're just playing politics, Brian. The police are working quite amicably with the military, and the people seem reasonably happy with it. All except for the criminals. Order is being restored rapidly.'

'Pity your party didn't think to do it before it needed the imposition of martial law, Bill,' snapped Kennard. 'I was talking to a rather senior policeman a week or two back, and he told me that when I win the next election all I have to do to stay in power forever is to crack down on the law and order situation. Face it, Bill, your lot have got to take responsibility for what's happened.'

Headley shook his head. 'It was Attlee's government who started the rot,' he said weakly.

'Oh come off it. That's history, and you've had long enough in office to put things right. However, this is not getting us very far. What is concerning me right now is the denial of free speech. If anyone holds a meeting, they get arrested and put in clink. Like one of my MPs was the other day. We went straight to the Court of Appeal, naturally, and they said they had no power to intervene. And to add insult to injury, they said that if, after the restoration of normal government, it was found that the military had acted ultra vires, then the soldiers concerned would be dealt with. Well frankly, Bill, that's Alice-in-Wonderland stuff. And, as Attorney, you ought to be doing something about it.'

'I don't think you quite understand constitutional law, Brian,' said Headley. 'What the Court of Appeal said is perfectly correct.'

'Well I say it's a bloody scandal.' Kennard was starting to get angry now. 'And the people won't stand for it. The army have shut down the newspapers – all except for your precious *Daily Telegraph* – and the television stations are only allowed to broadcast what the army tells them to. And stopping sports meetings has created more rioting than it's prevented,' he added.

'The Chief of the General Staff told me that he's not going to risk large gatherings of people. He fears they might cause further outbreaks of rioting.'

'If you don't keep firm control of your General Macey, you'll find that he'll be occupying Number Ten before you know it, Bill.'

'Macey is a responsible officer.' Headley was not wholly convinced of that. In his recent meeting with the joint chiefs of staff, it was Macey who had taken the initiative. Bristow, the Chief of the Defence Staff, had said very little by comparison.

Kennard sensed Headley's doubt. 'I think you're whistling in the dark, Bill,' he said. 'You've got to rein him in. And if you can't do it, why not ask the Queen? Persuade her to talk to Macey and explain that he's alienating the people of the country. He'd listen to her.'

Headley scoffed at the suggestion. 'That's bloody rich, coming from a socialist,' he said. 'Last year you were talking about abolishing the monarchy. Changed your mind, have you? Anyway, you know the rules. The Royal Family does not become involved in politics, and you can't have anything much more political than the present situation.'

'No, perhaps not,' said Kennard, 'but at least you've done us one favour.'

'What's that?' asked Headley innocently.

'You've guaranteed us a thumping majority at the next general election.'

'Don't you be so sure,' said Headley, but deep down he knew that Kennard was right.

CHAPTER SEVENTEEN

'Mr Shepherd?'

Alec Shepherd immediately recognised the businesslike tones of Sir Richard Dancer's secretary and was mildly surprised that she should be ringing him. 'Speaking,' he said.

'The Chief would like to see you as a matter of urgency, Mr Shepherd.'

Shepherd replaced the receiver and took his jacket from the coat rack, slipped it on and checked his tie in the mirror. To him, C was a rather remote figure and although he had passed the time of day with him on many occasions, their conversations had usually been confined to mundane subjects such as the weather or the latest test-match score. Consequently Shepherd wondered why he should be sent for so late in the evening and, in common with many people in similar circumstances, his mind raced through a personal catalogue of the things he might have done wrong. Apart from anything else, C was a stickler for the protocol of the Service and, under normal circumstances, would have conveyed any message through Barry Rogers. Shepherd presumed that Rogers had already left the office.

'You wanted to see me, sir?'

'Ah, Shepherd, come in.' Dancer was seated behind his

desk in a dark-grey suit so immaculate that it made Shepherd feel positively scruffy by comparison. 'Er, sit down, why don't you?'

Shepherd seated himself in the upright armchair in front of C's desk and waited.

C linked his hands together on the desk and gazed at Shepherd. 'I've some bad news, I'm afraid. Barry Rogers died of a heart attack this afternoon.'

'Good God!' said Shepherd and stared at the Chief.

'He collapsed in the street, not far from here. Apparently he had suffered a heart condition for some time, but these things always come as a shock when they happen.'

'I had no idea, sir.' A thousand questions raced through Shepherd's mind. Rogers had been one of those operatives in the Service who tended to be insular in his professional life, a sometimes necessary drawback of working for the SIS. There was no telling how many operations he had been overseeing at the time of his death, the details of which probably had not been committed to paper. And given the secrecy of the Counter-Intelligence and Security Section, it was fairly certain that few other people in the Service would know anything about them either.

'It will be some time before I can appoint a new director,' said Dancer. 'Do you think you can keep things running until then?' His deep-brown eyes concentrated on Shepherd's face.

There was only one answer to that question that anyone looking for advancement could give. 'Yes, sir, of course.'

'I don't want to give you the impression that you are under consideration for Rogers' job, Shepherd,' said Dancer. 'You're much too junior, of course.'

'Of course, sir.'

'You are aware of the operation that Rogers had mounted on General Sir Simon Macey, aren't you?'

'Yes, sir, I am,' said Shepherd. The problem was that he knew none of the details, other than that, to use Rogers' own phrase, Macey was to be 'eliminated'.

'Good. Well I think I can safely leave everything in your hands, Shepherd. If you have any problems, don't hesitate to come and see me.'

'Thank you, sir.'

Dancer nodded and picked up a pen. The interview was over.

Aileen McGregor had joined the Royal Navy to get away from Glasgow. And to find a husband of better quality than the boys who lived in the mean streets of Kelvinside where she had been born. Now twenty-two years of age, she was a good-looking brunette, tall and shapely, and her uniform became her well, accentuating her curves and causing more than one naval officer to cast a lustful eye at her when she had waited at table in the wardroom of HMS *Vernon*.

In her quest for a husband, however, she had been free with her favours and had secured for herself the unfortunate reputation of being an easy lay. It was a reputation of which Warrant Officer Jackson at Chequers had quickly become aware, following Aileen's posting there six months previously.

'I've a job for you, Aileen,' said Helen Jackson.

'Yes, ma'am?'

At first Aileen McGregor was tempted to refuse, not because she objected to the idea but because she was irritated that her easy virtue appeared to be common knowledge. But eventually, when the gravity of the task was explained, she agreed. 'Aye, aye, ma'am,' she said cheerfully, 'I shall lay back and think of Scotland.'

The soldier who had been warned for duty inside Chequers that night had reported sick earlier in the day and, by a lucky coincidence, Trooper Stuart Ferguson was detailed to fill the post. About Aileen MacGregor's age, perhaps a year or two older, he was heartily sick of being stationed in the wilds of Buckinghamshire, patrolling the grounds or guarding the gates. Even during his off-duty periods, he and his colleagues were forbidden to leave the estate for fear that they might have too much to drink and give away the information that Robert Fairley was being held prisoner at Chequers.

By midnight the Prime Minister and the rest of the staff had apparently retired for the night and Ferguson, sitting on a hard-backed chair in the Great Hall, was looking forward, without enthusiasm, to a long night's vigil.

But when he found that the night-duty stewardess was Aileen McGregor, who not only came from Glasgow but was a real bonny lassie too, he felt that things had suddenly taken a turn for the better.

'Would you like a cup of tea?' Aileen McGregor appeared silently beside the soldier, startling him.

Ferguson stood up. 'Aye, that'd be great,' he said.

'You're a Scot,' said Aileen.

'I am that.'

'Where are you from?'

'Paisley,' said Ferguson.

'I'm from Kelvinside.' Aileen smiled seductively at the soldier. 'Come away into the staff room,' she said. 'The tea's made.'

Ferguson glanced around the Great Hall. 'I'm no' supposed to leave my post,' he said.

'Don't worry about that,' said Aileen. 'All the doors are locked and bolted, aren't they?'

'Aye.'

'Well then, that's it. No one can get out and none of your sergeants can get in. Not that they've ever bothered to try so far.'

'Och, what the hell!' said Ferguson and followed the girl through into the staff sitting room.

An hour later, when the naked bodies of Trooper

Ferguson and Aileen McGregor were entwined and engaged in an activity that, under normal circumstances, would have rendered Aileen oblivious to the outside world, she saw David Enderby slip silently into the far end of the staff sitting room. Her shapely legs were already locked around Ferguson's waist and her arms encircled his neck, but now she moved her hands up so that they clasped either side of his head and covered his ears. Pulling his face down to hers and kissing him passionately, she became more active physically and moaned a little, further distracting the already distracted Ferguson while Enderby relieved him of the pistol which Aileen had placed, with their clothing, on a chair near the door. And she kept Ferguson's attention for the next hour, realising, probably for the first time, the meaning of mixing duty with pleasure.

It had not crossed the minds of any of the military that the Prime Minister's detective would carry a key to the house and consequently the front door presented no problems. Fairley, Helen Jackson, Whitmore and Enderby moved silently into the courtyard. Whitmore locked the door again behind him and followed the other three, Enderby being careful to steer the Prime Minister on to the lawn surrounding the statue of Hygeia to avoid crunching the gravel.

Silently the quartet stole between the trees towards Peter Garson's cottage.

Suddenly Whitmore, his eyes by now accustomed to the darkness, froze. 'Stay still.' He whispered the urgent command and put a restraining hand on the Prime Minister's arm. 'There's a sentry moving through the trees just beyond that clump of bushes.'

The little group stood stock-still and waited until the unsuspecting trooper, whistling quietly to himself, had passed across the lawn and disappeared round the other side of the house, doubtless to enjoy an illicit smoke.

'Right, sir,' said Whitmore quietly.

When Fairley's party reached Garson's cottage, the head groundsman was waiting and moved quickly out of the shadows. 'Good evening, sir,' he said.

'Evening, er, Garson.' The Prime Minister nodded, grateful that Whitmore had reminded him of the man's name. 'Very good of you,' he murmured.

Without further delay, Garson led the party through the trees until they reached some thick bushes. 'I've already cut this lot, sir,' he said, 'and tied it up again with twine. It's a bit tricky and you've got to watch out for the brambles.'

The Prime Minister grunted an acknowledgement and waited while Garson cut the twine and pulled open the gate just far enough to allow the party out. Whitmore went out first and found that a dense thicket of gorse and bramble, and some branches from a nearby tree, were barring the outside of the gate. He held them aside as best he could and waited as Fairley squeezed his way out, wishing that he would hurry. He wondered whether the theft of the sentry's pistol had been a good idea. Helen had explained the plan to Whitmore earlier, and he just hoped that Aileen McGregor was sufficiently resourceful to keep Ferguson occupied for long enough to ensure their escape. Once the sentry found his pistol was missing, he would raise the alarm. And if that happened too soon, their escape would be foiled. On the other hand, without Aileen they would never have got out of the house.

'Keep in the shadows, sir,' whispered Whitmore to the Prime Minister, and then helped Enderby and Helen Jackson to free themselves from the entangling bushes.

'That's done my tights no good at all,' muttered Helen.

'I'll buy you a new pair,' said Enderby and looked around. 'Where the hell are we?' he asked.

'That's the Bernard Arms,' said Whitmore, pointing at the pub on the other side of the road. He turned to the Prime Minister. 'If you wait here with David, sir, I'll have a scout round and see what's what.'

Crossing the main road, Whitmore made his way towards the pub. A minute or two later, he returned. 'There's a car in the car park,' he said and, glancing at Enderby, asked, 'You any good at hot-wiring, Dave?'

'I'll give it a shot,' said Enderby. 'Had a lecture from a bloke on the Stolen Motor Vehicle Squad when I did the CID course. Knew it'd come in handy one day.'

Whitmore, the Prime Minister and Helen Jackson waited in the shadow of a large tree until they heard the engine of the car burst into life. Then they moved quickly across to the pub car park.

'How much petrol is there, Dave?' was Whitmore's first question.

'Enough,' said Enderby tersely, 'but let's not hang about. If the landlord of the pub wakes up and sees us pinching a car from his car park, we've had it before we start.'

Whitmore and the Prime Minister sat in the back of the car, and Helen Jackson sat next to Enderby in the front so that she could navigate.

By avoiding the main roads, the party managed also to avoid most of the numerous checkpoints that had been set up by the military.

Until they ran into one about ten miles outside Portsmouth.

A soldier, rifle slung, stepped into the road and waved the car to a standstill with his torch.

'Whatever you do, don't let this chap see your face, sir,' said Whitmore to the Prime Minister.

'And where do you think you're going at this time of the morning?' asked the soldier, shining his torch into the interior of the car.

Enderby produced his warrant card. 'Special escort,' he said. 'Taking a prisoner to Portsmouth for trial.'

'On whose authority?' asked the soldier.

'Mine.' Helen Jackson spoke sharply and leaned across

so that the soldier could not fail to see the Royal Arms of a warrant officer on her cuff.

To the military, a coat of arms meant only one thing: a regimental sergeant-major. And that spelt trouble in any soldier's language. The fact that it was on a member of the Royal Navy – and a woman at that – made little difference. The soldier snapped to attention. 'Yes, ma'am,' he said. 'Carry on. Sorry to have held you up.'

Enderby wound up the window and drove on.

'Bloody pongos!' exclaimed Helen and then turned. 'Oh, I beg your pardon, sir,' she said to the Prime Minister.

Fairley chuckled. 'I wish I had that much authority over the army, Chief,' he said. And then, after a moment or two of silence, 'Gordon, what do we do once we get into Portsmouth? I mean, how do we go about getting a boat?'

'All in hand, sir,' said Helen from the front seat.

Whitmore grinned in the darkness. 'We've had to leave this part to Helen, sir,' he said. 'She claims to have all the answers.'

'I always knew you were resourceful, Chief,' said Fairley, 'but what exactly are you proposing?'

'If you don't mind, sir,' said Helen, 'I'd rather keep that to myself for the time being. I'll need to test the water before I commit us.'

'I hope that's a metaphor,' said the Prime Minister.

They arrived at the outskirts of Portsmouth at about three in the morning. Then, under Helen's directions, Enderby followed a convoluted route until they turned into a long, secluded road. 'Stop there, David,' said Helen and pointed to a patch of grass shielded by a row of trees. She turned to face Whitmore and the Prime Minister. 'I'm taking a chance here, sir,' she said to Fairley. 'This is the house of the Flag Officer, Portsmouth, Rear-Admiral Moore. I used to be his chief stewardess at one time, but I'm not going to risk taking you in with me until I see how the land lies.' She glanced at Whitmore. 'If I'm not out within about twenty minutes, you're on your own,' she said. 'I don't know what to suggest you should do if it all goes wrong, but it'll be up to you to think of something.'

A naval sentry stepped from a small cabin near the closed gates as Helen approached. 'Help you, ma'am?' he asked, catching sight of Helen's insignia. But he unbuttoned the flap of his revolver holster nonetheless. Even in the present emergency, the arrival of a warrant officer at the flag officer's official residence at ten minutes past three in the morning was a little unusual.

'Warrant Officer Jackson to see Admiral Moore.' Helen hoped that the admiral was still in residence. There had been no official notification that he had been posted, but anything could have occurred during her enforced isolation at Chequers.

'What, at this time of the morning?'

'Yes, at this time of the morning.' Helen clearly did not intend to brook any nonsense from an ordinary seaman. 'Now get on with it,' she snapped.

'Yes, ma'am.' Somewhat chastened by Helen's aggressive approach, the sentry stepped back into the cabin and picked up the receiver of a telephone. There seemed to be some delay, but returning after several minutes, he said, 'You're to go up to the house, ma'am. The admiral's expecting you.'

'Thank you.' Helen waited while the sentry swung open a wicket gate, nodded as she passed through and breathed a sigh of relief. At least the first obstacle had been overcome.

Knowing Rear-Admiral Moore as she did, Helen was not at all surprised that the door was opened by a navy stewardess who was immaculately dressed, even at this early hour. The girl looked suspiciously at Helen's torn uniform and snagged stockings. 'Follow me, ma'am,' she said.

Rear-Admiral Dermot Moore was a short, stocky man

with iron-grey hair and a jutting chin. When Helen Jackson had first started to work as one of his stewardesses in Gibraltar, she had been a leading Wren, and he had terrified her. But beneath the bluff exterior, she later learned, there existed a very fair man who would stand no nonsense from anyone, subordinates and superiors alike. Furthermore, he had been impressed by her efficiency, had told her so in a series of bellowed, staccato sentences, and had arranged for her accelerated promotion to petty officer. It had come as no surprise to him when, much later, she had been appointed to head the staff at the Prime Minister's country residence.

'Well, Helen, this is a pleasant surprise.' Moore, wearing trousers and an open-necked shirt, pushed out a hard and rough-skinned hand. 'Sit down and tell me what brings you here.' He glanced across at the young stewardess, still hovering at the door. 'Well, don't stand there, girl,' he barked. 'Get the warrant officer a horse's neck. And one for me. And be quick about it.' He turned to Helen. 'Still partial to 'em, I suppose?'

'Yes, thank you, sir.' Helen smiled, and felt sorry for the scared young girl who had fled to do the admiral's bidding. 'And excuse my rig, sir,' she added.

'Look as though you've been in a fight,' said Moore, taking in Helen's dishevelled appearance. 'Haven't been mixing it in Pompey Town, have you?'

'No, sir, but it's rather a long story,' said Helen, taking the brandy and ginger ale which the stewardess had produced in record time. Waiting until the girl had left the room and closed the door, she said, 'Forgive me for being impertinent, sir, but what do you think of the military seizing power? Are the navy in on it too?'

Moore looked blankly at the warrant officer. 'What on earth are you on about, lass?' he said. 'Don't you read the papers?'

'Yes, sir, but I don't know how much to believe.'

'Well, it's not a coup d'état, if that's what you're suggesting. The army's been granted powers of martial law, and the navy and the air force are helping out, but it's not a damned revolution.' Moore gave Helen an amused glance and took a sip of his brandy. 'And if the Cabinet hadn't been seized at gunpoint by some mutinous bloody colonel, it probably wouldn't have happened anyway.'

Helen was astounded at the admiral's statement. 'Is that true, sir?' she asked.

'Of course it's true,' said Moore. 'Too much spare time, that's your trouble, Helen.' He paused. 'I suppose you've been idling your time away at Chequers ever since Fairley was abducted,' he added.

Helen put her glass down on a side table and stood up. 'As a matter of fact, sir, I've got the Prime Minister outside in a car.'

'Have you, be damned?' Moore did not seem unduly surprised at this startling revelation. 'Well, we'd better have him brought in then.' Swiftly, he crossed the room and grabbed at a telephone.

'No, sir!' Helen shouted.

'What?' Moore replaced the receiver and turned.

'Mr Fairley genuinely believes that there's been a takeover, sir. We escaped from Chequers about three hours ago and stole a car to get here. If the sentry approaches them, they'll drive off.'

Moore grinned at the warrant officer. 'Always knew you had a rebellious, resourceful streak about you, Helen,' he said. 'What d'you want to do?'

'I'll go and fetch him, sir. He'll explain.'

'Right. Bring the car into the drive and I'll get some rooms organised. How many are you?'

'Four altogether, sir. The PM, his two detectives and me.'

'Carry on then, Miss Jackson,' said Moore with a grin and tugged at the velvet cord that would ring a bell in what he called the galley.

When Robert Fairley, Whitmore and Enderby arrived at the front door, Moore was waiting, a huge grin on his face as he stuck out a hand. 'Morning, Prime Minister,' he said shaking Fairley's hand vigorously. Then he shook hands with the two detectives.

'Good morning, Admiral.' Fairley glanced around the large hall of the flag officer's house with a hunted look that implied that he could be in greater danger here than he had been at Chequers. He was by no means certain that Helen Jackson had done the right thing in bringing him to the house of a senior naval officer. 'I'm sorry to impose upon you at this hour.' It was a formal statement with little warmth in it.

'Not at all, sir, not at all,' said Moore heartily, and led the group into the sitting room. 'Where's that damned girl gone now, Helen?' he said. 'Need you back here to sort the staff out.'

'I think you'd have a hard job getting Helen away from Chequers, Admiral,' said Whitmore with a grin.

The stewardess appeared in the doorway and waited. 'Sir?'

'You can get us some drinks, girl,' said Moore and glanced at the Prime Minister. 'What would you like, sir?' he asked.

'I'll have a small whisky, if I may, Admiral,' said Fairley.

'And if I know coppers, you two'll have *large* whiskies,' said Moore to the two detectives. 'Is that right?'

'Absolutely,' said Whitmore. 'Thank you.'

'Oh and another round of horse's necks for Miss Jackson and me,' said Moore.

Once the drinks were served, Moore stood in front of the fireplace, legs apart, clutching his glass of brandy and ginger in his huge fist. 'Now, sir,' he said, addressing Fairley. 'I'm having the rooms sorted out right now and you're welcome to stay for as long as you want.'

'I'm not thinking of staying at all, Admiral,' said Fairley.

'But you must be very tired, sir.'

'That is of no importance to me at this precise moment, Admiral,' said Fairley. 'I have been held captive at Chequers by the army, and my priority now is to break this military coup d'état as soon as is humanly possible.'

'Coup d'état, sir? There's been no military coup d'état.' The fact that Moore had been briefed by Helen Jackson on the Prime Minister's views and responded mildly to the Prime Minister's outburst did not help to reassure Fairley.

'Really?' Fairley reacted sharply, the sarcasm clear in his voice. 'Then why has the Royal Family been exiled?'

'I gather from Miss Jackson that you've been held incommunicado at Chequers, but I assure you that all that has happened is that the acting Prime Minister, Sir William Headley, has authorised the imposition of martial law. As for the Royal Family, the Queen is at Windsor and the Prince of Wales and his two sons are on a private visit to New Zealand.'

For several moments the Prime Minister stared at Moore, as if attempting to gauge the man's probity. 'Frankly, Admiral,' he said at last, 'I don't believe that.'

'You have my word on it, sir,' said Moore. 'And it only came to that when you and the Cabinet were abducted.'

'Really? Have you considered the possibility that you yourself have been deceived by the military?' The Prime Minister spoke in level, noncommittal tones.

'I think that unlikely, sir.' Moore was beginning to get just a little annoyed by the Prime Minister's hostile attitude but made allowances for the fact that he had just undergone a traumatic experience.

'Be that as it may,' continued Fairley, 'I have to get to Brussels as soon as possible.'

'Brussels, sir?' Moore raised his eyebrows.

Fairley took a sip of his whisky. 'Yes, Admiral.' He debated whether to tell Moore what he had in mind but decided against it. The Cabinet was still being held somewhere, and it was difficult to believe that the army had been unable to find them. The inescapable conclusion was that they were not really trying. And as the Chief of the Defence Staff was an Admiral of the Fleet, Fairley felt disinclined to trust one of his subordinate officers.

'What can I do to help then, sir?' asked Moore.

For a few moments, Fairley looked pensively into his whisky before speaking. Then he glanced up. 'I want you to get me to Cherbourg,' he said. 'In the utmost secrecy. Is that understood, Admiral?'

'Of course, sir. When and how?'

'As soon as possible. The means I leave to you.'

Moore grinned. 'Aye, aye, sir.' He finished his horse's neck in a single swallow. 'God!' he said. 'Haven't had this much fun since we chased the bloody Iraqis out of Kuwait.'

It was almost five in the morning when Aileen McGregor next glanced at her wristwatch, the only thing she was still wearing. Then she switched her gaze to the retreating figure of Private Stuart Ferguson as he walked towards his clothing. He had a fine body, muscular and athletic. And he was a good lover, of that she had proof. She had kept him occupied for as long as possible and reckoned that the Prime Minister, his two detectives and Helen Jackson must be in Portsmouth by now.

'Stuart, will ye no bide a while longer?'

Ferguson turned, the early light that filtered through the curtains dappling his naked body. 'I canna, hen,' he said. 'I'm to be relieved at oh-five-forty-five hours. If the sergeant sees me like this, I'm for the guardroom.' He laughed and started to sort through his clothes.

Aileen sighed. Her one regret about this whole deception was that Stuart Ferguson was on the point of making a discovery guaranteed to result in him being court-martialled.

'Jesus, no!'

Aileen sat up. 'What is it, Stuart?'

'It's my pistol. It's no' here.'

'It must be.' Aileen stood up and walked towards the soldier, putting her arms around him and flattening her breasts against his back.

But Ferguson was no longer in a mood for dalliance. He turned, his face white with panic. 'It's no' here, I tell you. Look for yourself. It's bloody gone.' Quickly, he pulled apart the neat pile of clothing, his own and Aileen's, tossing it on to the floor in his fevered search for his firearm. 'See, here's the holster. It's empty.'

'Are you sure you had it when you came?' Aileen knew it was a silly question to ask a sentry. There was no way he could be posted without an inspection, and the sergeant of the guard would have ensured that he was properly equipped. But the Scots girl was doing her best to delay the inevitable discovery of the Prime Minister's disappearance.

'Of course I am. The bloody thing's gone.'

Still attempting to delay him, Aileen pulled the soldier towards her and gave him a passionate kiss. 'It'll turn up,' she lied.

'There's no time for more of that, hen.' The anguished Ferguson pushed the girl away. 'Oh God, I've had it,' he said and started to pull on his clothes.

Moore had insisted upon the Prime Minister and his party having a meal, and it was nearly five o'clock in the morning by the time the flag officer's two official cars, containing Moore and the Prime Minister's party, arrived at the dockyard gates.

The docks police had been replaced by an armed naval sentry who bent down and peered into the lead car, but the moment he sighted the Flag Officer, Portsmouth, in the back, he took a pace back, snapped to attention and saluted with a rattle of musketry.

Leaving Fairley in the car, Moore strode into the duty office. The officer of the day was a lieutenant-commander long passed over for further advancement, who had found for himself what, until now, had seemed like a comfortable post. He was a good fifty years of age, and his uniform had a tired and worn look about it. He was not altogether surprised to see Rear-Admiral Moore enter his office at five o'clock in the morning, but then he was surprised at very little these days. 'Good morning, sir,' he said, rising from behind his desk.

'Good morning, Jenkins.' Moore glared around the office as though he had arrived to carry out an inspection.

'Anything I can do to assist, sir?' The lieutenant-commander's question was a formal one, but the tone of his voice implied that he did not really want to be bothered with a rear-admiral who was apparently suffering from insomnia.

'Yes,' said Moore. 'Make ready with a vessel.'

The lieutenant-commander looked unhappy. 'What sort of vessel, sir?' he asked.

Moore looked at the officer of the day as though he were being deliberately obstructive. 'One that will get to Cherbourg as quickly as possible,' he said.

'The crew'll have to be mustered, sir, and—'

'Well muster the bloody crew, man, but don't stand there looking like a wet Wren,' said Moore. 'This *is* Portsmouth Dockyard, isn't it?' he added sarcastically. 'I haven't come to the wrong bloody place, have I?'

'Aye, aye, sir,' said the lieutenant-commander wearily. 'I'll get it organised immediately.' He turned away, having been given no reason to revise his opinion of the bloody-minded attitude of the average senior naval officer.

'Thank you,' said Moore with icy politeness.

The corporal who arrived to relieve Ferguson was known, in military parlance, as the NCO marching reliefs. He was accompanied by a trooper whose duty would be to stand guard in the Great Hall until eight o'clock. Thereafter, this day-duty man would be withdrawn, and only the perimeter of the Chequers estate would be guarded.

Realising the awkwardness of his situation, and realising also that he could hardly excuse the loss of his pistol by explaining that he had spent most of the night making love to a naval stewardess, Ferguson had stuffed his revolver holster with newspaper. It had been Aileen's idea. She had said that Ferguson could more easily explain the loss of his firearm by suggesting that it had been taken from, or even misplaced in, the temporary tented accommodation that had been set up in the grounds for the troops guarding Robert Fairley. But there were other reasons, too. Not only would such a stratagem delay further the discovery of the Prime Minister's absence but it would also safeguard Aileen herself. As a serving Wren, she was just as likely to be court-martialled as Ferguson was, it being an offence against the Naval Discipline Act to spend a tour of duty naked and in the arms of a soldier. The fact that she was carrying out the orders of Warrant Officer Jackson would be unlikely to be believed. But Ferguson was a simple soul. It did not cross his mind that the theft of his firearm might be connected with something far more serious.

Consequently it was not until a quarter past eight that the orderly officer, a young cornet, made the horrifying discovery that the Prime Minister had disappeared. Making the daily routine visit to the house, he casually enquired the whereabouts of Fairley, only to be told by an unsuspecting woman member of the Royal Air Force that he had not been in his room when morning tea had been taken in.

The squadron leader was informed immediately and ordered a thorough search of the grounds. At ten o'clock, he telephoned Lieutenant-Colonel Crosby in Germany. Minutes later General Sir Simon Macey was made aware that his star prisoner had escaped.

*

It was five-thirty in the morning before the vessel that Moore had demanded was made ready for sea. Fortunately HMS *Leicester*, a Class 42 destroyer, was at Portsmouth engaged in training exercises. Its grumbling crew had been roused from their quarters and, harried by the captain, a stern-faced commander, had prepared to set sail for France. Doing his best to shield his face, the Prime Minister had been hurried aboard, placed in the captain's cabin and requested to stay there.

Rear-Admiral Moore had issued a string of terse orders to the ship's captain, telling him that he would make for Cherbourg, maintain radio silence, and under no circumstances discuss his mission with anyone, either now or later. And he was to obey any instructions that the Prime Minister might give.

HMS *Leicester*'s two Rolls-Royce Olympus TM3B gas turbines, pounding all-out at 50,000 shaft horsepower, thrust the ship across the Channel at its maximum speed of 29 knots and at twenty-eight minutes past ten, it came in sight of the port of Cherbourg. By then, the troops at Chequers knew that the Prime Minister had escaped.

Within minutes an offshore patrol boat of the French Navy approached and ordered the British vessel to heave to. Ever since the imposition of martial law in Britain, the French government had mounted a Channel patrol, mainly to prevent British refugees, who had been making for the mainland of Europe in increasing numbers, from landing.

'So much for the European Union and the single market,' said Whitmore as he watched the French come alongside.

'Looks like the French want a chat,' said *Leicester*'s captain.

After seeking the customary permission, a French lieutenant came aboard and saluted. 'What is your business in these waters, Captain?' he enquired in perfect

English, realising that addressing a British naval officer in French would be unlikely to elicit a response.

Whitmore stepped between the captain and the French officer. 'I have the British Prime Minister aboard,' he said quietly.

'Is that what is called the English joke?' asked the Frenchman. As sensitive to ridicule as most members of his race, he was obviously not amused at what he took to be levity on Whitmore's part.

'He's below,' said Whitmore. 'You may see for yourself if you wish.' Then he laid a hand on the lieutenant's arm. 'Apart from the captain, none of the crew of this vessel knows who he is. He has escaped from military custody.'

'Really?' The lieutenant spoke sarcastically, clearly disbelieving Whitmore's statement. 'And who, may I ask, are you, m'sieur?'

'I'm a Scotland Yard officer and so is that gentleman there.' Whitmore nodded towards Enderby. 'And the lady in naval uniform is the Prime Minister's wife.' He decided that making the story sound even more bizarre than it really was would ensure that the French would take them ashore for questioning.

'I see,' said the French officer with a look on his face that implied he did not relish being made fun of. 'So you are both policemen and you have the British Prime Minister aboard with a wife who appears to be a lady sailor.' He lifted his shoulders in a typical Gallic shrug. 'Do I have this right?'

'Absolutely, old boy,' said Whitmore.

The French naval lieutenant cast a suspicious glance around the deck of *Leicester*. 'I do not believe any of this,' he said, 'and I am placing this vessel under arrest. You will accompany me to Cherbourg.'

'Excellent,' said Whitmore, 'but perhaps you would be so good as to transfer the Prime Minister and the three of us to your vessel before we move.'

'Naturally,' said the lieutenant. 'I do not want you making a run for it.'

Shepherd walked into his office, his mind still in turmoil as he wondered how he was to fill the void left by Barry Rogers' death. He sat down behind his desk and looked at the ashtray that he had kept solely to cater for the pipe-smoking Rogers' visits. It still contained some shreds of burnt tobacco, and he realised just how much he would miss his gruff, often aggressive boss. With a sigh, he emptied the tobacco into the wastepaper basket and put the ashtray into a drawer before going next door to Rogers' office.

In the outer office, he came across Sheila, Rogers' secretary. She was sitting at her desk, her eyes red, staring into space.

'Isn't it terrible, Mr Shepherd?'

'Yes, it is, Sheila. But we've got to carry on, haven't we?' It was a trite comment, but Shepherd never quite knew what to say in circumstances such as these.

Sheila assumed her professional mask. 'Can I help you at all, Mr Shepherd?' she asked.

'The Chief's asked me to look after things until a successor's appointed, Sheila. I'm just going in to sort through Barry's papers. See if I can make sense of anything.' Shepherd grinned at the girl as if to imply that there was very little chance of anyone making sense of Rogers' paperwork.

Sheila smiled wanly back at him. 'That could be difficult,' she said, 'but if there's anything I can do, let me know.'

General Sir Simon Macey's retribution was swift and merciless. Following the withdrawal of the squadron of the 27th Hussars from Chequers – there was no point in leaving it there any longer – the major commanding it was

relieved of his duties and placed in close arrest at Chelsea
Barracks, charged with conspiring with others unlawfully
to detain the British Prime Minister.

'Is there any indication of where Fairley might be,
Simon?' Sir Godfrey Bristow spoke in a tired voice. The
news that Fairley had been detained at Chequers all along
had come as a revelation to him and he was beginning to
think, somewhat belatedly, that Macey perhaps had known
more than he had revealed. And that worried him.

'At the moment, sir, none,' said Macey smoothly.

'Well, no doubt we shall find out soon enough,' said
Bristow.

Macey shrugged. 'I imagine so, sir, but it is rather
strange that he's just disappeared. I'd've thought that he
would have made a triumphal return to Downing Street.'

'I think our best bet is to start planning for the future,
Simon,' said Bristow. 'If Fairley cancels the order giving us
the powers we're exercising, we could well be faced with
the same problems as before. If troops are withdrawn, there
could be an uprising. I know we've discussed this before,
but if it happens, we just won't be able to contain it. And
if Fairley takes it into his head to take action against us for
withdrawing troops from abroad, it's just possible that we'll
be facing serious charges.' He pinched the bridge of his
nose and looked up at Macey with tired eyes. 'We should
have let the navy guard him,' he said.

'What do you mean, sir?' asked Macey suspiciously.

'If we'd surrounded 10 Downing Street with Royal
Marines at the start of this wretched business, your
damned maverick cavalry colonel wouldn't have got near
him.'

'You've heard then, sir?' Imogen Cresswell had entered
the room clutching a signal.

'Heard what, Imogen?'

'About Portsmouth, sir.'

'What about it? For God's sake spit it out, woman.'

Even though she was accustomed to Macey's frequent displays of bad temper, Imogen hesitated before going on. 'The Prime Minister's just arrived in Cherbourg, sir.'

The two chiefs of staff listened in silence. Then Macey spoke. 'How did he get to Cherbourg, for God's sake?' he asked.

'The Royal Navy took him, sir,' said Imogen and smiled at Sir Godfrey Bristow.

CHAPTER EIGHTEEN

After placing HMS *Leicester* under guard in the *port militaire* at Cherbourg, the French lieutenant and a party of sailors escorted the Prime Minister, Whitmore, Enderby and Helen Jackson to the gendarmerie in the rue du Val de Saire.

None of the party had a passport, and Robert Fairley carried no form of identification whatsoever. The two policemen's warrant cards, and Helen Jackson's naval identification document, which showed her to be Helen Jackson and not the Mrs Fairley whom Whitmore had said she was, merely served to deepen the scepticism of *Officier de la Paix Principal* Raoul Desfarges as he listened to the French naval officer's interpretation of Whitmore's account of their escape.

Desfarges shrugged his shoulders and spoke rapidly in his native tongue.

The French lieutenant turned to Whitmore. 'M'sieur Desfarges says that he finds the whole story inconceivable, m'sieur,' he said. He indicated Fairley, now sitting in an armchair. 'He does not believe that this is the British Prime Minister.'

Whitmore could understand the French police officer's doubts. Fairley looked extremely unlike a prime minister.

Although he had washed and shaved at the flag officer's house, his suit was torn in places and still bore the dirty marks that it had acquired in penetrating the thick gorse and brambles outside the gate at Chequers. 'Well I can assure you that it is.'

'I'm afraid that your assurances are not sufficient, m'sieur,' said the French lieutenant, 'but in any case M'sieur Desfarges is uncertain what you want of him.'

Whitmore turned to the Prime Minister. 'What exactly are your plans, sir?' he asked.

'I've got to get to Brussels, Gordon,' said Fairley. 'To seek help from the European Union.'

Whitmore nodded and turned to the French lieutenant. 'Perhaps you would convey the Prime Minister's wishes to the officer,' he said, indicating Desfarges.

The French naval officer looked doubtful but translated what Fairley had said.

After a further conversation with the French lieutenant, Desfarges, in desperation, despatched a *brigadier* to the *hotel de ville* to find a reference book containing a photograph of the British Prime Minister.

When the *brigadier* returned, clutching a large volume, Desfarges still appeared dissatisfied and, holding the book in front of him, walked round Fairley several times, making comparisons. Finally he snapped the book shut and indulged in yet another rapid exchange of French with the naval lieutenant.

'The captain,' said the lieutenant, using a rough equivalent for Desfarges's rank, 'says that there is a similarity, but he believes this man to be an impostor. However, m'sieur, he is rinsing his hands of him and has instructed me to take you all to the *sous-prefet*. His office is in the rue Emmanuel Liais.' He seemed to think it important that they should know exactly where they were going. 'It is little more than one kilometre.'

The party was ushered out of the gendarmerie and into

a small white Renault bus that was normally used to convey riot police.

The *sous-prefet* was a huge man, almost bald, with a flowing black moustache. He seemed quite unperturbed when a woman in naval uniform and a trio of motley civilians, one of whom looked vaguely familiar, were ushered into his office. He listened intently to the French lieutenant's story, occasionally glancing at Fairley and nodding. Then he strode across the room and shook the Prime Minister's hand. 'I 'ave 'eard, m'sieur,' he said, 'on the radio this morning that you 'ave escape.' He gestured towards armchairs on one side of his office. 'Please, you sit.' And then he marched to the door of his office and ordered coffee. 'Presumably you will wish for me to contact the British Ambassador in Paris. He will assist, *non?*' he said, turning once more to face the Prime Minister.

'Certainly not,' said Fairley brusquely. During the voyage Whitmore had raised this same point, but Fairley, unconvinced by Rear-Admiral Moore's assurances that there had not been a coup d'état, had no intention of trusting any member of the Foreign Office. 'I want to get to Brussels, to the European Union.'

'*Pas de probleme, m'sieur,*' said the *sous-prefet* and grinned broadly. Being a shrewd politician, he was of the view that the sooner the British Prime Minister went to Belgium the better it would be for France.

The *sous-prefet* had telephoned the *Prefet* of Manche in St Lo, his immediate superior, who in turn contacted the Elysee Palace in Paris and, within minutes, spoke to the President himself. From then on, events proceeded with a giddy swiftness. The Prime Minister and his party were taken to the Liberte, a three-star hotel in the rue Georges Sorel in Cherbourg, where they bathed, ate and changed into fresh clothes provided by the French government.

An army helicopter arrived at three o'clock in the

afternoon and took the party, now increased to seven by
the presence of three heavily armed members of the
gendarmerie, directly to the military enclave of Brussels
National Airport. It was almost six o'clock that evening
when they touched down, to be taken immediately to the
Brussels Hilton, where a complete floor had been allocated
to them, guarded by a strong detachment of the Belgian
gendarmerie. After nearly thirty-four hours without sleep
they promptly took to their beds.

At the Elysee Palace, the President of France sighed with
relief when he heard that his embarrassing visitor was now
out of his jurisdiction.

Pieter van Ostade had been President of the European
Commission for three years and, until this very moment,
had been thoroughly enjoying the job. But then the British
Prime Minister arrived. He had known he was coming, of
course – cable traffic had been flashing backwards and
forwards between Paris and Brussels all the previous day –
but faced with the reality, van Ostade knew that he was
going to have to make a decision. Even if it was a decision
not to make a decision. He had taken the precaution of
asking Sir Jeremy Sands, the British Ambassador to the
European Union, to be present also, even though his
contribution was unlikely to be helpful. Van Ostade did not
have a very high opinion of British diplomats.

'Prime Minister, what a pleasure,' said van Ostade. With
hand outstretched, he moved rapidly across his large
office.

'Mr President,' murmured Fairley as he shook hands
with van Ostade and then, after a moment's hesitation,
with the British Ambassador. 'How is it that you're here?'
he asked curtly.

'I was invited by the President, Prime Minister.' Sands,
unaware of the reasons for Fairley's suspicions, was
somewhat taken aback by his hostile attitude but attrib-

uted it to fatigue. 'Welcome to Brussels,' he said jovially. 'I only wish it were under better circumstances, though.' He beamed confidently.

'Er, please sit down, Prime Minister.' Van Ostade ushered Fairley towards a large settee. 'The coffee is coming very soon.'

'It's Dutch coffee, too, Prime Minister,' said Sands. 'The very best, of course.'

Fairley searched his pockets and produced his pipe. 'I don't suppose you've any tobacco, Mr President?' he said.

'Of course, of course.' Van Ostade opened a cupboard and produced a jar with a three-legged brass clamp that held the lid firmly in place. 'It's Dutch too, of course.' He switched on a fan that stood on a table near his desk. 'I don't smoke myself but I'm told by the experts that it's very good,' he added, placing the jar on an occasional table near Fairley's right hand.

Now that he was back in a political environment, Fairley seemed much happier. The escape from Chequers and the crossing to Cherbourg had involved him in an unfamiliar world, one over which he had no control, but now, in the office of the European President, he was much more relaxed. 'You will know, Mr President,' he said, as he started to fill his pipe, 'that after I was kidnapped, along with the rest of the Cabinet, my acting successor, Sir William Headley, declared martial law.' He replaced the lid of the tobacco jar and carefully screwed down the clamp. 'The Cabinet are still held prisoner, and I believe that Headley was imposed upon by dissident elements in the army to give them unfettered power. In my view it amounts to a coup d'état.'

Van Ostade nodded sympathetically. 'Tragic, tragic,' he murmured.

'Oh, surely not, Prime Minister,' murmured Sands vaguely.

Fairley ignored the British Ambassador's inane remark.

'I managed to escape from Chequers yesterday,' he said, 'with the aid of my two detectives and the Chief—'

'Chief? What is that?' asked van Ostade glancing at Sir Jeremy Sands for guidance.

'She's a lady sailor, Mr President,' said Sands. 'A warrant officer, I think.'

'Ah, yes, of course.' Van Ostade nodded. 'My apologies for the interruption, Prime Minister.'

'The purpose of my coming to Brussels is to seek the help of the European Union in restoring the lawfully elected government of my country.' Fairley took the box of matches that the President had been toying with and lit his pipe, puffing great clouds of smoke into the air.

Van Ostade wrinkled his nose slightly and moved his chair back an inch or two. 'Exactly what do you want me to do, Prime Minister?' He posed the question diffidently, hoping that the Prime Minister would give him an indeterminate reply.

Fairley sighed and leaned back against the cushions of the settee. 'The answer would seem to be the imposition of economic sanctions,' he said. 'I appreciate that the long-term effects of that could be disastrous, but allowing an army junta to remain in control would be even worse. Blockading the country and stopping imports and exports is a swingeing solution to the problem, and undoubtedly the people will suffer, but I can see no other way.'

Van Ostade glanced at the impassive face of Sir Jeremy Sands, but seeing no sign of encouragement from that quarter, breathed out with a lengthy sigh. 'The Treaty of Rome,' he said, 'makes no provision for such interference in the domestic affairs of another member state.'

Fairley was tempted to say that that was news to him, as they seemed quite prepared to interfere in just about everything else. 'I'm aware of that,' he said, 'but if its signatories had ever foreseen such a thing happening, it probably would have done.'

'Ah, good,' said van Ostade with some relief as a raven-haired girl came through the door pushing a trolley. 'Just leave it here, Gerde.' He smiled at the secretary and busied himself with pouring the coffee. 'I'm sure that I don't have to explain the function of the Commission, Prime Minister,' he said smoothly, 'but it is only empowered to issue directives which must then be approved by the Council of Ministers and passed by the European Parliament.'

'I know that,' said Fairley tersely. He felt like adding that in the past Commission presidents had not been so reluctant to meddle. 'So you could start by issuing a directive, couldn't you?' He had been exhausted by the events of the preceding forty-eight hours or so and the last thing he wanted now was a Dutch functionary explaining to him how the European Union worked.

'It is unprecedented,' said van Ostade.

'I know that too,' said Fairley, 'but so is a military takeover of a member state, and something has to be done.'

'I think . . .' said van Ostade slowly, 'that the Council of Ministers would have to take the initiative in a case so, so . . .' He searched for a suitable word. 'So original as this, yes?'

'Are you saying that the Commission does not wish to be involved, Mr President?'

Van Ostade spread his hands in a gesture that was somewhere between hopelessness and uncertainty. 'I think that would be the best course,' he said. 'I do not think that the Council would like the Commission issuing such a directive.' He got more confident. 'It is outside the scope of their remit.'

'It's outside *everybody's* remit, I should think,' growled Fairley.

'It would mean convening such a meeting, of course. All there is at present is COREPER.'

'Is what?' Fairley half turned in his seat to glare at the

ambassador. He had a grave dislike of European acronyms.

'The Committee of Permanent Representatives, Prime Minister,' said Sands, unabashed by Fairley's abrupt question. 'The ambassadors of the fifteen.'

'Well, they won't decide anything, will they?' Fairley was no stranger to diplomatic intransigence.

'I imagine that they'll have to refer to their own foreign ministers,' said Sands. 'Except me, of course, given that the Foreign Secretary is, um, unavailable.' He laughed nervously.

'That would certainly be difficult,' said Fairley sharply, who did not see the funny side of either the ambassador's comment or the Foreign Secretary's predicament. 'It would all take time, wouldn't it?' He was beginning to get impatient. 'However, I do not intend to be put off by such things. I have travelled here at no little risk to myself and I do not intend to allow the army to rule over Britain for an hour longer than is absolutely necessary.' He stood up. 'I think you had better arrange for this Council to be convened forthwith, Sir Jeremy.'

'Ah, well, yes, of course.' Sands stood up too, less confident now that responsibility for the next phase of Fairley's plan seemed to have shifted from van Ostade to himself. 'It won't be easy though,' he muttered, half to himself.

'Thank you for the coffee, Mr President,' said Fairley, shaking hands once more with van Ostade. 'And for your assistance and advice.' But the sarcasm in his last remark escaped the Dutchman.

'The Prime Minister's reached Brussels, sir,' said General Sir Simon Macey. He laid a cablegram on Admiral of the Fleet Sir Godfrey Bristow's desk.

'What's he doing there? Do we know, Simon?' Bristow stood up and drew the message towards him.

'I understand that he's visited the President of the

European Commission, sir.' Macey's voice sounded tired. 'Perhaps it was a courtesy call.'

'I don't somehow think that Robert Fairley is in the business of making courtesy calls, not at the moment,' said Bristow. 'There will have been a purpose in it.'

'I just hope that Crosby sees sense and releases the Cabinet,' said Macey. 'Now that the Prime Minister's free, there'll be little point in his holding them any longer.'

Bristow looked up sharply. 'You *don't* know where they are, do you, Simon?'

Macey looked pained. 'You don't think for one moment that I would keep that sort of information to myself, sir, surely?' he asked.

'No, of course not. I'm sorry, Simon.' Since the seizure of the Cabinet, the dual responsibility of overseeing martial law and trying to explain to Headley why the Cabinet had not been found was beginning to take its toll on Bristow.

'Have you heard from the Prime Minister yet, sir?' Macey steered the CDS away from his doubts.

'Nothing,' said Bristow sinking back into his chair, 'but I've no doubt that we'll be hearing very soon. And that will spell trouble, I think. I just hope that we'll not be accused of plotting to kidnap him. We do have some vicarious responsibility, I suppose.'

'It has been a difficult week, sir, but I don't see that any blame can be attached to us.' Macey was nervous that if Crosby was arrested, he would not hesitate to accuse the Chief of the General Staff of complicity in the plot. And now that Crosby knew of the Prime Minister's escape, he would almost certainly be considering the release of the remainder of the Cabinet. But even at this late stage Macey, as a general, was sufficient of an egotist to believe that he could talk his way out of anything a mere lieutenant-colonel might allege against him which, he was sure, would be seen as a desperate attempt at vindication for his treason.

'Crosby's mad, of course,' said Bristow, 'and one can

only hope that the authorities will deal with him in that
light. If they don't, all that he can look forward to now is
a charge of treason.' Suddenly he felt quite deflated and
began to wonder how he could extricate himself from what
was rapidly becoming a living nightmare. 'I just hope that
Fairley sticks by the government's standing instruction,
that if terrorists seize any ministers and hold them hostage,
no negotiations are to be entered into with terrorists. And
there is no doubt that Crosby, by his actions, has declared
himself to be a terrorist.'

Unable to avoid knowing of the escape of the British Prime
Minister – every television newscast for the preceding two
days had led with the story – the foreign ministers of the
other fourteen countries of the European Union were not
surprised to receive lengthy cablegrams from their representatives in Brussels. In each of their capitals, discussions
took place at a hastily convened conference over which the
head of government himself presided. The discussions
included long debates about whether the European Parliament should be consulted. But as it was pointed out, that
assembly met for only one week in four, and as the last
occasion had been last week, the parliament would need to
be reconvened. And that would take time. And time was at
a premium. In any event, the matter to be discussed was
generally regarded as too important for the parliament.

Within hours, Brussels National Airport was ringed
with police and soldiers as the heads of government flew in
for their crisis meeting. Traffic in the centre of the city was
disrupted as motorcades, marshalled by whistle-blowing
outriders, were brought to the headquarters of the European Union.

Robert Fairley was excluded from the conference, but
Pieter van Ostade reported what the British Prime Minister
had told him and repeated the suggestions he had made.
Meanwhile Fairley waited impatiently at the Brussels

Hilton for the outcome of the delegates' deliberations.

As was increasingly the case these days, the President of France and the Chancellor of Germany played leading roles, confirming the belief that an unofficial Franco-German alliance existed, and dominated the discussions which went on all day and half the night.

Early on, the conference vetoed Fairley's hopeful suggestion that the impasse could be resolved by economic sanctions, and they concentrated on faster ways of securing the restoration of civil government in Britain. The leaders of the Union's member states had wisely concluded that sanctions against one of their number could only result in long-term damage to their own economies, and that was a price they were not prepared to pay.

At last the German Chancellor put into words what many of his colleagues had been thinking. 'There is only one solution, ladies and gentlemen,' he said and outlined his plan. When he had finished, there was silence around the vast, ornate, chandeliered room.

The Danish Prime Minister – Denmark held the presidency that half-year and was, therefore, chairing the meeting – put it to the vote. All were in favour.

'That leaves only one matter to be resolved,' said the Dane. 'I shall see the British Prime Minister this afternoon and inform him of the Union's decision.'

'The Danish Prime Minister has arrived, sir,' said Whitmore who, since their arrival in Brussels, had assumed the role of unofficial private secretary to Robert Fairley, who was still unprepared to accept the offer of administrative assistance made by the British diplomatic mission in Brussels.

'Ah!' Fairley stood up. 'Perhaps a decision has been made at last,' he said as Whitmore opened the door wide and then closed it behind him to leave the two prime ministers alone.

'I'm sorry, Robert, that we meet under such distressing circumstances.' Grethe Andersen held out her hand as she walked confidently towards Robert Fairley. In her late forties, she was a tall, elegant woman with neat short blonde hair and piercing blue eyes.

'Grethe, a pleasure to see you again,' said Fairley, clasping her outstretched hand with both of his. 'Please sit down. May I get you a drink?'

'A mineral water if you have it. Thank you.'

'I take it that a decision has been reached,' said Fairley when they had settled in armchairs.

'Yes.' Grethe Andersen looked momentarily sad, wistful almost. 'But I think it is a decision that you will not like, Robert. The Union has decided that the situation in your country is too serious for anything but strong action.' In common with many of her compatriots, Grethe Andersen spoke perfect English.

'It sounds as though you are about to tell me something rather unpalatable, Grethe.'

Grethe Andersen made a little gesture of regret with her graceful and exquisitely manicured hands. 'I am sorry, Robert, but the heads of government decided that the damage to the economy of the Union that is being caused by your country's plight cannot be allowed to continue any longer than is absolutely necessary. As for sanctions, they would merely make the situation worse. And having in mind the attempts that were made to bring Rhodesia, South Africa, Iraq and the former Yugoslavia to heel, we were by no means convinced that sanctions would work. Except against those who imposed them.' She shrugged and reached out for her glass, the sun glinting on the diamonds of her engagement ring as she did so. 'They all dragged on for much too long and if we were to do the same with your country, it would take forever and probably damage us as much as it would damage you. Also the British are resourceful people. I'm sure that they would manage to overcome the problem of short supplies.' She paused briefly. 'After all, you are a nation of smugglers.' As she smiled to soften what otherwise might have been taken as an insult, Fairley thought what a handsome woman she was.

'So what are you proposing, Grethe?'

'I'm afraid that a decision has been made to wrest power from your army by the use of military force.'

Fairley was stunned. He had expected some alternative to the idea of sanctions, knowing that what Grethe Andersen had just said about their past lack of effect was true, but this ... 'Did the Union consider that the people of my country could be put in great danger by such an act?' he asked.

'We do not think so, Robert. I can assure you that the decision was not made lightly. There are fourteen nations in the Union apart from Britain, and they can muster a large number of troops between them. Far, far more than the British Army. I think that your generals, and particularly your General Macey, would realise that there would be little point in attempting to resist such overwhelming odds.'

'I sincerely hope so, but Macey is a stubborn man.' Fairley's chin had sunk on to his chest as he considered the ramifications of an invasion of Britain. 'Is there no other way?' he asked, looking up at the Danish woman opposite him.

'There is, of course,' said Grethe Andersen. 'The Union recognised that our decision might be unacceptable to you. But if you disagree, your only alternative would be to face expulsion from the European Union forthwith.' She paused and glanced down at the floor. 'But that would not solve your immediate problem,' she added softly.

Fairley nodded slowly. If only the Cabinet were available to be consulted, the Foreign Secretary in particular. But in the end it would be Fairley's own decision, no matter how many advisers he consulted. When it came down to it, the stark choice facing him was a simple one: agree to an invasion or be forced out of the European Union with its resultant economic disaster. 'Might I make one request?' he said. 'That our army be advised of the Union's intentions so that they are given the chance of conceding.'

Grethe Andersen rose from her chair. 'I will convey your wishes to the Union,' she said, 'but I cannot offer any assurances. You do understand that, don't you, Robert?'

'Yes, Grethe, I do,' said Fairley.

The European Union's solution to 'the British problem', as they called it, had come as a terrible shock to Fairley, and for some time after Grethe Andersen's departure, he sat contemplating its implications. His pusillanimous attitude over the preceding months, years even, had brought the country to this. Within hours of his arrival in Brussels the SIS officer at the British Embassy had been in touch with C, and Fairley had soon been receiving secret cables detailing what had been happening during his enforced absence. They had confirmed that his refusal to deploy troops had resulted in a military takeover led by General Macey. That, in turn, had been responsible for the force that was now preparing to invade the United Kingdom. With a sinking heart, he realised that he had lost all control, even before his abduction. And he knew that the European Force would stay in the United Kingdom for as long as the Union decided.

When Whitmore entered the room, the Prime Minister was slumped in his chair, head in hands. 'Are you all right, sir?' he asked.

St Augustin, just outside Bonn in the west of Germany, is the home of *Grenzschutzgruppe 9*, Germany's crack anti-terrorist assault unit, which is a part of the Federal Border Police.

In the operations room of its highly protected barracks,

GSG 9's commander, Colonel Wilhelm Gropius, was contemplating a large-scale map of North Rhine-Westphalia.
After a moment or two of deliberation, he switched his gaze
to an even larger-scale map of Paderborn and its surrounding area, which showed in detail the disused Blücher
Barracks at Sennelager.

It was only a short time since his unit had been put on
stand-by. In Munich the head of the *Bund Nachrichtendienst*
– the SIS's opposite number – had received a telephone call
direct from Sir Richard Dancer telling him the whereabouts
of the Cabinet. The BND chief had demanded an immediate
interview with his Foreign Minister and from then on
events had moved rapidly towards the point where GSG 9
had been alerted.

Gropius had deployed every resource available to him –
and they were considerable – to gather further information
about the target. Detailed plans had been obtained. Local
residents, including the handful of people who until
recently had been employed in the barracks themselves,
had augmented those plans with descriptions of the
interior of the buildings and had spoken of the arrival of a
unit of the British Army. Sources at the German Defence
Ministry had received no notification of this arrival, and
the fact that the British tommies were not allowed out to
frequent the local *gasthofs* and drink the local beer had all
served to heighten Gropius's suspicions. Consequently he
had deployed all three strike units of GSG 9 for the attack
which now was only an hour away.

Gropius turned to his deputy, Major Manfred Stern.
'Everything is ready, Manfred?' he asked.

'Yes, sir, but are you sure that we have enough men?'

Gropius grinned. 'Ninety men. Of course it will be
enough.'

'But according to our information there are five squadrons of this hussar regiment, sir. That's almost six hundred
men.' Stern looked distinctly unhappy at the prospect of

being outnumbered by nearly seven to one.

'They are soft, Manfred, and they are not infantry. They ride around in armoured cars all day, which they don't have with them at the moment.' Gropius grinned. 'And they are not the SAS. We have the element of surprise. They will not be expecting an attack. We will be in and out before they have had time to put their socks on.'

The three strike units of GSG 9 approached Blücher Barracks in Sennelager from different directions, two by road in their specially equipped Mercedes, and the third in BO 105 helicopters. But the helicopters had been ordered to stand well clear of the target until they were advised that the first phase of the attack had been successful.

One of the motorised units, consisting of three Special Tactical Sections, drew up at the gates of the barracks on Paderborner Strasse, and an officer alighted. He strolled up to the sentry and flicked the peak of his cap. 'Good evening,' he said.

'Evening, sir,' said the unsuspecting sentry.

'I wonder if you can direct me—' The officer suddenly chopped at the side of the sentry's neck with a swift and devastating karate blow, catching the unconscious man as he sank to the ground. Quickly dragging his body to a spot behind the sentry box, he signalled to his men.

Within seconds twelve black-clad members of GSG 9 spilled out of their cars at top speed and raced silently through the night to surround the guardroom. Inside, the sergeant was playing cards with the corporal while three of the four off-duty troopers dozed on wooden benches; the other was making tea. The sergeant looked up as the door opened but leaped up in alarm as he saw the black figure levelling a Heckler and Koch MP5 submachine gun at him.

'Just stand up slowly and do not attempt to reach for your weapons,' said the border-guard officer. 'That way you won't get killed.'

'What the bloody hell's this all about?' asked the sergeant nervously as other GSG men flooded into the small room.

'What this is about, sergeant,' said the officer, 'is that we are here to release your government. We are acting on the express orders of the German Chancellor and we shall not hesitate to kill anyone who resists. Is that understood?' He turned to two or three of his men. 'Lock them up. All of them,' he said. The other members of the guard were now fully awake, and with the corporal, were hustled down the passageway leading to the cells. Two more GSG men appeared in the doorway of the guardroom, dragging the semiconscious sentry with them. He too was locked in the cells. 'How many other men do you have on patrol, sergeant?' asked the officer.

'Find out.' The sergeant of the guard spat the words.

The German officer shrugged. 'Very well,' he said and picked up the guard report from the table. Running an expert eye down the disposition of sentries, he nodded before throwing the report down again. 'Just the one?' He raised a sceptical eyebrow. 'You have just the one sentry to look after the British Cabinet? Surely not.'

'Don't know what you're talking about,' said the sergeant. In fact the Cabinet were being held in a block at least a mile away on the far side of the huge barracks.

'Well, we shall have to find this one before we go looking for the others,' said the German. 'He will probably do something stupid and die for it. Unless . . .'

'Unless what?' asked the sergeant.

'Unless you go to the door and call him. I daresay he's not far away, seeing that you have just made tea.' The young German officer glanced at the teapot.

The sergeant moved slowly towards the door. 'I'll see if he's about,' he said sullenly.

'And don't forget that I have an H and K pointing at your back, Sergeant.'

The sergeant opened the door. 'Carter!' he shouted.

'What is it, Sarge?' The other sentry materialised from out of the darkness.

'Tea's up.'

'Right. Ta.' The sentry walked straight into the guard-room and was promptly disarmed.

On the other side of the barracks the main body of the GSG assault team, led by Colonel Gropius himself, moved silently through the night, closing on the accommodation block that the colonel's earlier enquiries had indicated housed the twenty captive members of the British Cabinet.

A sentry, armed with only a pistol and smoking a cigarette, strolled nonchalantly along the roadway in front of the barrack block. As he turned at the limit of his patrol and yawned, a black-clad GSG man appeared silently out of the darkness and struck him down. At the rear of the block, another sentry met a similar fate.

The group of attackers now stealthily approached the wooden double doors only to find them locked.

'Call in the helicopters and the units at Bad Lippspringe and the Paderborner Strasse,' whispered Gropius to his radio operator. 'We're going to make a lot of noise getting in, so we'll need all the support we've got.'

Minutes later the sound of rotors disturbed the night and the black shadows of the BO 105 helicopters hovered overhead. Within seconds the airborne detachment of GSG 9 were swinging down ropes as fast as firefighters descending greasy poles.

The explosives expert stood back from the doors and shouted to his colleagues to take cover. A dull crump followed, and splinters of wood flew through the air. Where the stout wooden doors had stood for nigh on seventy years there now appeared a smoking gap. Lights started to go on in the block. Somewhere a man's voice shouted a warning, and elsewhere a siren began to wail.

The GSG vanguard, led by Colonel Gropius, was

through the doorway in an instant. A corporal, drawing his pistol, ran towards Gropius, but a staccato burst of machine-gun fire from the colonel's Heckler and Koch stitched a red line across his chest and he fell dead, blood pumping out on to the stone floor as his pistol clattered noisily away and struck the wall.

Major Manfred Stern kicked open the door of the makeshift guardroom and sprayed it with a full magazine.

Jumping over the dead corporal's body, Gropius fired again as another soldier came at him, assault knife in hand. The soldier hit the wall, leaving a bloody smear to mark the spot as he crashed to the ground. Not pausing for a single moment, Gropius led his men from room to room, throwing open doors and shouting to the British ministers to lie down. There was smoke and confusion everywhere. From time to time the dull thud of a stun grenade flattened the air, and there were cries from different parts of the building.

Outside, the bulk of the GSG attack force formed a defensive ring around the barrack block as soldiers of the 27th Hussars, roused from their beds by the siren, the commotion, the explosions and the exhortations of their officers, struggled quickly into their one-piece combat uniforms and grabbed their weapons. Then they ran, in a disorderly rabble, towards the neighbouring block.

Colonel Tim Crosby, who had insisted that the officers billet with the men, and had stayed with them himself, rolled out of his bed, thrust his feet into his combat boots and made for the door of his room, seizing an SA80 rifle as he did so.

As the British troopers approached, the GSG men opened fire with their Mauser .66 sniper rifles. Carefully aiming at the foremost soldiers, and aided by their infrared sights and light intensifiers, they had picked off about ten troopers before the British decided it would be politic to withdraw and regroup.

Crosby, believing at first that Macey had sent British troops to arrest him and release the Cabinet, was determined not to let his prize prisoners be taken. 'Come on, lads, they're only bloody Krauts,' he yelled, suddenly recognising the attackers for what they were. And he ran towards the GSG men, his gun blazing.

A GSG sergeant took careful aim at Crosby and when he was about a hundred yards off, gently depressed the trigger. For a moment Crosby faltered before flinging up his arms, involuntarily abandoning his rifle. Then he swerved to his left and crashed into a flowerbed, dead before he hit the ground.

'The bastards have got the colonel,' shouted a disembodied voice.

'Hit the deck and stay there, Two-Sevens,' shouted a major, the A Squadron leader. 'There's no sense in getting killed.' The major twisted round. 'Sarn't Hennessey, take a troop and try to get round behind them.'

'I'll try, sir,' said the sergeant, 'but they seem to have formed a circle round the sodding place. Just like bloody Red Indians, sir,' he added before wriggling away on belly and elbows.

Suddenly the withering and spasmodic fire of the GSG attackers increased in intensity as the Germans started edging towards the British.

'What the hell's happening now, sarn't-major?' yelled the squadron leader.

'They've landed the choppers, sir,' said the squadron sergeant-major. 'They're going to lift the bastards off.'

Sure enough, even though they were being pinned down at a distance of at least a hundred and fifty yards, the hussars could see the Cabinet being bundled into the waiting GSG helicopters in a seizure reminiscent of their own operation such a short while ago.

'I knew we should have copyrighted that,' muttered the SSM.

A sudden rattle of submachine-gun fire rent the air, and the British tried to bury themselves in the concrete roadway where they were pinned down.

'Cease firing,' shouted the squadron leader, 'or you might hit a member of the Cabinet.'

'What's wrong with that?' asked an anonymous voice, and the squadron leader smiled in the darkness.

At about the time of the GSG assault, Imogen was sitting in one of Shepherd's armchairs, her legs crossed, sipping a gin and tonic. 'I know I said I didn't like Barry, but I'm sorry to hear that he's dead,' she said. 'Mainly because it will probably have left you with a lot of problems.'

'It's not too bad.' Shepherd thought that Imogen looked particularly attractive this evening and gave her an admiring glance. He already knew that her legs, now encased in black stockings, were long and extremely shapely, and her black dress had a simple elegance. 'What was Macey's reaction to the Prime Minister's escape from Chequers?'

Imogen smiled. 'I must give him his due, Alec, he gave the impression of being pleased. Almost the first thing he did was to put the major who was in charge at Chequers in close arrest at Chelsea Barracks. But what happens now?'

Shepherd paused briefly before speaking, wondering whether to tell her of the attack in Germany. But, despite the fact that the awful saga of the past week or so was almost over, he still held back. 'We've started sending cables to the PM giving him a complete rundown on everything we've learned. And most of the information came from you. You should be very pleased.' He smiled at her. 'Fairley will probably make you a dame,' he said.

'I am a dame, or hadn't you noticed?' said Imogen drily. 'Do you think he'll take action on the information? Positive action, I mean.'

'He's mad if he doesn't get rid of Macey,' said Shepherd. 'I think,' he added mysteriously, 'that the Cabinet will be free very soon.'

Imogen gazed at him quizzically. 'What do you know that you're not telling me?' she asked.

'Wait and see, young lady,' said Shepherd and stood up to refill her glass. 'But your information that the Cabinet was in Germany has been very helpful in deciding on a course of action.'

'Oh, for goodness' sake stop talking in riddles, Alec. What do you mean, the SAS?'

Shepherd grinned. 'Like I said, wait and see.' Even now, he was loathe to tell Imogen that the SIS had informed the German government of the Cabinet's exact location and that the operation to liberate its members was probably under way at this very moment.

Imogen stood up and put her drink on the table before crossing to the settee and sitting down beside Shepherd. 'Do you think that Bristow discovered that Macey knew where the Cabinet was?' she asked.

'I don't know, Imogen. And presumably he never gave a hint.' Shepherd put his arm around the girl's shoulders and pulled her close.

Imogen scoffed. 'Bristow doesn't like me,' she said. 'Probably because I'm a soldier. He could hardly bring himself to talk to me, let alone drop a hint. Still, I don't think I shall be one for much longer.' She moved her head slightly so that it rested more firmly against Shepherd's chest, her hair lightly brushing his cheek. 'Funny, that,' she said.

'What's funny about it?'

'Because now I'm sick of the whole bloody business. The battalion was bad enough, but this has been ten times worse. I'm sick of that womanising, arrogant bastard Macey, and sick of the intrigue and the deceit. And above all, I'm sick of what that sod's done to this country. I don't think he gives a fuck about anything but himself.'

Alec tightened his grip on the girl's shoulder. He had never heard her swear before, always imagined that, Guards officer or not, she was too demure to use coarse language. But somehow it endeared her to him. 'Let me get you another drink,' he said and started to move.

Imogen stood up and held out both her hands towards him. 'Later,' she said.

CHAPTER NINETEEN

Sir Richard Dancer pressed down the switch on his intercom. 'Yes?'

'Mr Shepherd to see you, sir,' said the disembodied voice of C's secretary.

'Send him in.'

Shepherd was through the door before C had switched the intercom off. 'Our liaison in Brussels, sir,' he said, using the customary euphemism for the SIS officer who was stationed at the British Embassy there, 'has informed us that the Prime Minister failed to persuade the European Union to impose sanctions on the United Kingdom. Instead it's been decided to mount an invasion force to regain control of the country. This country.'

'Interesting.' C gazed at Shepherd with his usual bland expression. 'And when Fairley regains power, as he undoubtedly will, I imagine that General Macey will be arrested and tried. In which case the intelligence we've acquired will be extremely useful to the prosecution, although I will be loathe to use Rogers' informant as a witness. Or any informant for that matter.'

'Er, yes, I suppose so, sir.' Shepherd was somewhat taken aback by the Chief's presumption that Macey would still be alive to stand trial.

'But politics are a strange business,' continued C, 'and it may be that Macey will manage to talk his way out of a charge of treason. In that event, even though the Prime Minister has persuaded the European Union to restore him to power, albeit by the use of force, the CGS would still pose a threat and might try again. It just means that we shall have to continue to keep a close watch on him.'

That was not what Shepherd had expected to hear. 'I think I'm labouring under a misapprehension, sir,' he said. He actually thought that C was but had not the courage to say so.

C raised his eyebrows. 'You'd better sit down, Shepherd, and explain what you mean.'

'Before he died, sir, Barry Rogers told me—'

'It would have been,' said C drily.

'I'm sorry, sir . . .?'

'He could hardly have told you after he died,' said C, who abhorred sloppy English.

'Of course, sir.' Shepherd always found it difficult to talk to the aloof Dancer. 'However, Barry said that you had sanctioned the elimination of General Sir Simon Macey.' He spoke softly, as if the words should not have been uttered at all.

'What?' The surprise in Dancer's voice and the unchar-acteristic expression of shock on his face alarmed Shep-herd. 'What do you mean by elimination, man?' he asked, hoping that he had either misheard or misunderstood.

For a brief moment there was absolute silence in the office; not even the noise of traffic on Albert Embankment penetrated the thick glass of windows designed to resist long-distance eavesdropping devices.

With awful suddenness it came to Shepherd that Rogers had been acting entirely alone, that perhaps he had known that he was going to die and had decided on one last act of misplaced loyalty. 'I understood from Barry that you had sanctioned the assassination of the Chief of the General

Staff, sir,' he said, tentatively almost, as if fearing that he would be blamed for a plan about which C, it was now apparent, knew absolutely nothing. If it was true that Rogers had devised the plan himself, without reference to C, it would undoubtedly destroy Dancer's career, and possibly the SIS too, unless it could be prevented or contained in such a way that no stigma would attach to the Service.

'Good God Almighty!' Dancer stood up and started to pace around his large office, his face betraying his awareness of impending calamity. For the first time, Shepherd appreciated that the Chief was as vulnerable to emotion as anyone else in the Service. Eventually C sat down again. 'Tell me all you know about this,' he said.

'I'm afraid I don't know a great deal, sir.' Shepherd tried to recall all that Rogers had said to him, but the truth of the matter was that he did not know very much. His late director had not been in the habit of detailing the more sensitive of the SIS operations with which he had been involved, and Shepherd knew, from his search of Rogers' office, that nothing had been written down. But then he would not have expected to find anything. Nevertheless, he told Dancer as much as he could remember of their conversations.

'Do you know if Rogers had taken any steps to implement this . . . this . . .?' Dancer broke off, unwilling to repeat the chilling words that Shepherd had just used.

'I don't, sir, no.'

'Ye Gods! What a bloody mess.' Dancer stared censoriously at his subordinate. 'How could Rogers possibly have thought that I had given my blessing to such lunacy? Did he actually say that, in as many words?'

Shepherd struggled to recall the exact conversation. 'I'm sure he said that you'd sanctioned an elimination, sir.'

'But we never do that, despite what you might read in the newspapers. You must have known that, Shepherd.'

'It was hardly my place to . . .'

For a moment or two, Dancer stared at his subordinate. 'No, of course not. I'm sorry.'

'Should we warn General Macey, sir?' Shepherd asked.

'How the hell can we do that? What do we say to the man? I'm sorry, General, but due to some administrative cockup in SIS, it appears that you're likely to be assassinated. So keep a sharp lookout. If we were to do that . . .' Dancer left the sentence unfinished. He knew that to reveal the existence of a plan to kill the CGS would result, at best, in his own dismissal and an everlasting distrust of the service that he had done so much to defend in the face of politicians who were all for dragging its operations into the open. For some time he remained deep in thought. 'I shall make enquiries, through sources,' he said eventually, 'to see whether any moves have been made to implement this madness. I'm certain that I know who Rogers would have approached. If that source knows nothing, then I think it's safe to assume that the idea never got beyond the planning stage.' Dancer seemed to recover his composure. 'Thank you, Shepherd, that's all,' he said. 'Naturally, if you learn of anything you will report it to me urgently, at any time of the night or day.'

'Yes, sir,' said Shepherd, relieved to escape the nightmare that was now occupying Dancer's mind.

Sir Richard Dancer gazed thoughtfully at Shepherd's retreating figure and when the door had closed behind him, he picked up the handset of his telephone and tapped out the number of Angus Wilson. He knew Wilson quite well and had met him on several occasions. He also knew that if Barry Rogers had consulted anyone with a view to having the Chief of the General Staff assassinated, it would have been Wilson. But because the call was on an open line, Dancer was more guarded than usual and did not announce himself by name, hoping that Wilson would recognise his voice. He did, but it was no help.

'Angus, I believe you recently put Barry in touch with an operative,' said Dancer.

'I didn't put him in touch with anyone,' said Wilson. He knew the SIS of old, and they were risky people to do business with. Even if Rogers had telephoned him and referred to their meeting at Rogers' club, that was precisely the reply he would have received. Wilson was a man who knew how to protect himself.

'For God's sake, Angus, this is important. Desperately important. Rogers is dead.'

'Sorry to hear that,' said Wilson drily.

Dancer deliberately slowed down his delivery, lowering the pitch of his voice at the same time. 'I have got to get in touch with whoever it was that you introduced him to,' he said portentously. 'It really is terribly urgent.'

There was a longish pause. 'Look,' said Wilson eventually, 'I don't know how best to convince you, but I put Barry in touch with no one.' He knew damned well that the SIS always worked in watertight compartments, and it worried him at times; if ever they were infiltrated by a mole, such a spy could do a lot of damage before anyone challenged him. Many of their operations, independent as well as those carried out in conjunction with the Special Air Service, bordered on the fringes of illegality, and there was no way that Wilson would tell anyone, even C, what arrangements he had made on Rogers' behalf.

'Thanks,' said Dancer, and replaced the handset, convinced that his late Director of Counter-intelligence and Security had done no more than merely talk about assassinating General Sir Simon Macey.

'We shouldn't be here much longer,' said Fairley, 'now that the die is cast.' He sounded depressed and gave the appearance of having aged years since his arrival in Brussels. The decision of the European heads of government to use troops to break the military hold on the United

Kingdom was one that had shocked the Prime Minister beyond measure. It was, in part, his own fault. When he had seen Pieter van Ostade, Fairley had thought that he had argued convincingly, whatever information may have come out of the United Kingdom, that the country had been subjected to a military coup.

Now, while he waited for the next stage in the unfolding drama of restoring him to power – a power that he felt instinctively would be less than he had enjoyed before – Fairley was doing his best to relax over a drink in his suite at the Brussels Hilton, together with Whitmore, Enderby and Helen Jackson.

'I suppose there's no point in asking how long it's likely to be before things start happening, sir,' said Whitmore.

'It's anybody's guess, Gordon. But I tremor to think what will happen if the army – our army, that is – decides to put up a fight.'

'Do you think there's a chance they will, sir?' asked Whitmore.

'Difficult to say,' said the Prime Minister. 'If Mrs Andersen has succeeded in persuading the Union to give our army advance notice of its intentions, it might avoid bloodshed, but the mere fact of an invasion force arriving might well be construed by some of our more hidebound generals as an attempt against the Crown. I just hope that they see reason rather than looking upon it as an opportunity to break what some of them see as the stranglehold of Europe.' He stood up and walked around the large room, his hands clenched firmly behind him. 'Oh God,' he said, 'why in hell's name did we ever get mixed up with this damned Common Market thing?' Then, realising that he had betrayed too much of his inner feelings, he glanced at Helen Jackson. 'I can't get used to seeing you out of uniform, Chief,' he said.

'Find it a bit odd myself, sir,' said Helen.

'What have you being doing while I've been arguing

with the EU?' It seemed that Fairley wanted to talk about anything but the impending invasion of Britain.

'Wandered around Brussels and did a bit of shopping, sir. The embassy was very good; they lent me some money.'

'I hadn't thought of that,' said Fairley. 'Of course, you wouldn't have had any, I suppose?'

Whitmore was not surprised that the Prime Minister had given no thought to the question of money. When he had first been assigned to protect Fairley, he had found himself paying bills on all sorts of occasions and was out of pocket until Fairley's House of Commons secretary had tackled him about it and started to reimburse him. 'We took it in turns to take Helen round, sir,' he said. The presence of the Belgian gendarmes, who had surrounded Fairley on every occasion that he had moved, had made it unnecessary for more than one of the Scotland Yard officers to be on duty at any one time.

'Incidentally, I, er, haven't said thank you for all that you did.' Fairley glanced at each of the small party in turn and hesitated. He was not very good at thanking people. 'But I can assure you that it will not go unmarked.'

There was a light tap on the door and Whitmore strode swiftly across the room. After a brief and hushed conversation with the Belgian gendarme outside, he turned to the Prime Minister. 'The British Ambassador is here to see you, sir,' he said.

'Which one?' asked Fairley. There were two in Brussels: one accredited to the Belgian nation, the other to the European Union.

'It's a Mr Keane, sir,' said Whitmore. 'Our ambassador to Belgium.'

'Ask him to come in, Gordon.' Fairley spoke wearily, as though the ambassador was the last person in the world he wanted to see right now.

The august figure of James Keane walked in through the

door. 'Prime Minister,' he murmured, 'I do apologise for interrupting, but I have just heard that the Cabinet has been rescued.' He glanced at the two detectives and Helen Jackson, wondering who they were and why he had not been accorded the usual custom of a private interview.

'Thank God!' said Fairley. 'Where were they?' He waved a hand, inviting the ambassador to sit down.

'They had been imprisoned in an army barracks in Germany, Prime Minister. They were rescued by GSG 9.' The ambassador paused. 'I understand from first reports that Colonel Crosby was killed in the attack.'

'Serve him bloody right,' muttered the Prime Minister.

The ambassador looked shocked at such an unstatesmanlike reaction. 'I have been given to understand, Prime Minister,' he said, 'that the Cabinet are to be brought here to Brussels with all due despatch.'

'Thank you, Ambassador,' said Fairley.

General Max Strigel was surprised to be called urgently to the office of the Chancellor in Berlin. And he was even more surprised to be told that he had been appointed to command a force consisting of seventeen divisions, some 85,000 troops, from the German and French armies. 'And the purpose of this force, *Herr Kanzler?*'

'To invade England and restore the lawfully elected government, General Strigel.'

Strigel expressed no emotion at the task he had just been assigned. 'Do you have any specific instructions, *Herr Kanzler?*' he asked.

'No. You are the soldier, General. You must do as you think fit. The timing of the invasion is entirely your decision, other than to say it must be carried out as soon as possible and that your preparations must be as secret as you can make them.'

'Of course,' said Strigel, wondering how he was expected to keep an invasion force of 85,000 soldiers and their tanks, vehicles and equipment secret.

'But remember,' the Chancellor continued, 'you are at the head of a European Union force, not a German one and not a French one. And your mission must be executed with the minimum of bloodshed. You understand that?'

'Naturally, *Herr Kanzler.*'

A light breeze whispered along the Calais coastline as the invasion fleet prepared to set sail. The English Channel was as calm as it had been on that day nearly sixty years previously when a bedraggled and defeated British Army had embarked on the greatest retreat in its history.

The German Chancellor's injunction, that there must be as little bloodshed as possible, had led General Strigel to deploy orthodox infantry and light armour rather than to make use of the arsenal of more sophisticated, some nuclear, weapons available to him.

Now, fidgeting with the zip fastener on the front of his combat uniform, he was seated in the command landing craft, the slight swell moving the vessel against its moorings with a gentle motion, while he waited impatiently for the succession of signals that would tell him that the embarkation was going according to plan.

Two hours had been allowed for the crossing to Shakespeare Beach, which lay between Dover and Folkestone. The plan then was for the invasion force to advance on London – a blitzkrieg, Strigel had called it in his briefings – and, once they were there, one airborne division – a German one – to drop on Hyde Park. Strigel knew it was a calculated risk, but not as much of a risk as if he had acceded to the views of his deputy, the French Lieutenant-General Paul Braque. Braque had been in favour of dropping the division at the same time as the combined force went ashore at Shakespeare Beach in the hope that those ground troops would not be needed at all. There had been a heated argument between the two, during which

Strigel had suggested that Braque would not have been so keen to risk a French airborne division. But that aside, Braque had been unable to offer a strategic plan that would resolve the problem of the airborne division being cut off if the invasion force met with heavy resistance.

Strigel had been encouraged by intelligence reports that indicated that there had been no massing of British troops on the Kent coast. Either they did not believe that Strigel's force would land near Dover or they did not intend to resist. Strigel hoped fervently that the latter would be the case, even though Fairley's request that the British Army should be advised of the impending invasion had been rejected by the European Union.

'It's under way, sir,' said Macey. He ran a hand through his hair. 'I never thought they would.'

Admiral of the Fleet Sir Godfrey Bristow stood up and walked towards the large-scale map of the south of England that covered almost the whole of one wall in the operations centre at Northwood. 'It looks like Dover then,' he said wearily. He turned to look at Macey. 'You realise that there's nothing we can do, Simon, don't you? We dare not mobilise our forces to resist a landing.'

'Why not? The British Army is not in the business of surrendering.'

'Don't be such a damned fool, Simon. It's not a question of superiority,' said Bristow. 'It's a question of politics. The Prime Minister has been released, and that will almost certainly result in the rescinding of martial law. All right, perhaps we are in a position to give seventeen divisions of German and French troops a bloody nose, but there'll be more where they came from. Just think about it. If we give the first wave a mauling, there'll be an outcry in the European Union – throughout the world, in fact – and the initial assault will be followed by troops from Belgium, Holland, Italy, Spain . . .' He stopped, unable to remember all the countries in the Union. 'There are fourteen member nations apart from ourselves, don't forget, and they've all got armies, navies and air forces.'

Macey did not see this as a propitious moment to discuss the relative merits of the European armies, and changed the subject. 'I've just heard that the Cabinet has been rescued by GSG 9,' he said. 'Seems they took the 27th Hussars completely by surprise.' There was grudging admiration in Macey's voice for a skilfully planned and well-executed military operation.

'Yes, I know. I suppose that the SIS somehow got wind of where they were being held, or the German intelligence people did.' Bristow sat down heavily in his chair. 'I'm only sorry that it was not the armed forces that came up with the answer. It makes it look as though we were dragging our heels, and that is something that will certainly come out in the enquiry. There will be an enquiry, of course, a Royal Commission probably, and I have no doubt that in the search for a scapegoat we'll head the list. I can see it now: failure to control the army, allowing them to suppress civil disorder without restraint. And, in giving them their head, not seeing that a maverick element like the 27th Hussars would take the law into their own hands. Sooner or later we could finish up in a prison cell somewhere.'

'We only did our duty to the Crown,' said Macey as he stood up, 'and that's as good a reason as any for making a fight of it.' His eyes flashed and he tugged at the hem of his service dress tunic; he had worn uniform ever since the imposition of martial law.

Bristow rose to his feet again, a look of determination on his face. 'That's up to you, Simon,' he said, 'but if you do decide to meet this invasion head on, you'll be on your own. You can no longer look to me for support.' Slowly, like a man who had aged ten years, he walked back to his own office in the command complex.

For some time, Macey stood in silence mulling over

what the Chief of the Defence Staff had said. Bristow was
right, of course; the British Army could not win. Macey
was still confident that he could talk his way out of what
had happened so far, but any resistance now would most
certainly be seen as rebellion.

'Issue a general order, Imogen,' he said, and started to
pace backwards and forwards.

Imogen flicked her fingers at a sergeant and demanded
a notepad but at once regretted her rudeness. 'I'm sorry,
Sergeant,' she said. 'It's getting to all of us, I suppose.'

'Yes, ma'am,' said the sergeant impassively and handed
Imogen a pad.

'To all units of the British Army ...' Macey began
dictating. 'European forces have now effected a landing in
the Dover and Folkestone areas and have established a
bridgehead inland. In view of the potential for defeat at the
hands of overwhelming odds, units will not attempt to
resist and will remain in barracks to await further orders.
Signed Simon Macey, General, Chief of the General Staff.'
Then he sighed. 'Get that off as a Flash signal, Imogen. It's
all over.'

It was twenty minutes or so before Imogen Cresswell
returned to the operations centre and looked around.
'Excuse me, sir,' she said as she sighted her chief.

'What is it, Imogen?' Macey lent only half an ear to his
aide. For the most part he was concentrating on the huge
map as a corporal started placing magnetic tabs on it
showing the disposition of the invading European forces.

'Sir Godfrey Bristow, sir.'

Macey glanced around the room. 'He's not here, Imogen.'

'I know, sir. A military policeman has just found him in
the basement garage. Apparently he'd locked himself in his
car and ...' Imogen hesitated. 'He's shot himself, sir.'

'What?' Macey swung round, his concentration now
fully on what his ADC was saying. 'But I was talking to him

only minutes ago.' It was a ridiculous thing to say, but even generals are apt to say stupid things in moments of anguish. Then the gravity of what had happened sunk in. Bristow had taken the easy option and left Macey, as the senior chief of staff, to bear the responsibility for a rebellion that had all but been crushed. 'The bastard,' he said.

'I beg your pardon, sir?' Imogen looked quizzically at Macey. Although the CGS had always been arrogant and brusque, the pressure of the last few days had turned him into a bad-tempered and strained individual far worse than anything she had known before.

Suddenly Macey brightened as his fertile brain alighted on a face-saving option. 'Well,' he said, 'that relieves me of the need to go along with his mad plan any longer.'

The chartered Lufthansa Boeing 737 that touched down at Brussels National was quickly marshalled to the area usually set aside for the isolation of hijacked aircraft and surrounded by units of the Belgian Army. After a brief but formal greeting by the President of the Belgian Senate, the twenty surviving members of the British Cabinet were hurried to a fleet of waiting cars and escorted to the Brussels Hilton by a team of police motorcyclists.

Within half an hour, Robert Fairley was welcoming his Cabinet colleagues as they were installed in rooms on the floor that had been assigned to the Prime Minister.

Fairley dismissed the champagne reception that had been arranged by the general manager – he was in no mood to waste time on niceties – and promptly convened a Cabinet meeting in the conference room at the top of the building. 'It is quite evident, gentlemen,' he began without delay, 'from the reports I have received from the head of the Secret Intelligence Service that the Chief of the General Staff was behind our abduction and that Colonel Crosby was acting specifically under his orders.' He paused to smile wryly. 'Some of you may have heard that Crosby was killed during the attack on the barracks where you were being held, and I have just been advised that Admiral of the Fleet Sir Godfrey Bristow has committed suicide.'

There were surprised gasps from around the table and Graeme Kent, the Defence Secretary, said, 'Good God!'

'I would have thought,' said Fairley, directing his steely gaze in Kent's direction, 'that from your conversations with Macey immediately before the outrageous attack on Downing Street you might have detected what he was planning.'

There was heavy sarcasm in the Prime Minister's voice, but it was an unfair comment. Kent had, after all, kept the Prime Minister fully briefed, but Fairley had declined to take the matter seriously. Kent's – and the Home Secretary's – vain attempts to delude him over the matter of the Whitehall riot casualties had only served to deepen his suspicion of their motives.

'I have been in discussion with the other heads of government of the European Union,' Fairley went on, 'and I now have to tell you that a force, a considerable force, of German and French troops has already landed in Kent with a view to securing our return to Britain.'

'I don't believe it,' said Usher, the Foreign Secretary. 'That will destroy our credibility forever. How could you let them—?'

'You got a better idea?' snarled the Prime Minister with an uncharacteristic lapse into what he would normally have regarded as the vernacular. 'While you were being rescued from Germany, I was trying, without any success I may add, to persuade them to impose sanctions . . .'

'Just as bad,' murmured the President of the Board of Trade and received a frown.

'But I was faced with the stark choice of agreeing to the use of military force or being expelled from the European Union. However . . .' Fairley was determined that he would brook no discussion about something he regarded as a *fait accompli* and moved on to the next point on his agenda. 'I have received several cables from Headley' – he spoke the name with evident distaste – 'and a number of matters arise. Firstly, despite what I have learned from the SIS, there is no substantial evidence to warrant a prosecution of Macey, but I shall dismiss him the moment I arrive on British soil. To that end, I have issued orders that, once I am informed that it is safe for us to return, he and others will be at the airport to meet us. There will be adequate notice – it's been suggested that we should wait for at least a week after the European force has secured the country – and I intend that our return will receive full publicity.'

'Military bands and guards of honour? That sort of thing?' asked Kent innocently.

'Military nothing,' snapped Fairley. 'A band, yes, but it will be a police band. And there will be no guards of honour. The last thing I want is a triumphal return organised by the bloody army. And neither, I should think, would any of you,' he added.

Several members of the Cabinet studied the Prime Minister as he spoke, wondering where this new steel had come from, but they remained silent.

'Furthermore,' Fairley continued, 'to teach them the lesson that they do not interfere in politics, I now intend to go ahead with what, until now, has been a provisional plan for a substantial reduction in the strength of the army.' He grinned owlishly at the Cabinet. 'I have decided that in addition to the English and Scottish regiments already earmarked for disbandment, the remaining Irish ones will go as well, starting with the Irish Guards. That, of course, implements the agreement reached by John Major and the Taoiseach when the Irish peace plan was finally thrashed out.'

'But, Prime Minister—' Kent started to speak, but did not get very far.

Fairley turned on him. 'I don't think that your views on

the army are too valid at the moment, Secretary of State for Defence,' he said caustically.

'I was not thinking of my views so much as those of the Queen,' said Kent. 'The Irish Guards are part of Her Majesty's personal troops, after all.'

'You leave that to me,' said Fairley. 'Right now, I shouldn't imagine that the Queen is too enamoured of the army. I have already cabled her with my intentions, and she has raised no objections.' The Diplomatic Wireless Service had established a secure facsimile link to the Prime Minister's suite, but Fairley continued to refer to its transmissions as cablegrams. 'It will be announced shortly before our return.' He smiled at the shocked faces around the table. 'And widely announced. I do not intend to let the army think that they've emerged victorious. They haven't. The European Union is in the process of releasing the British people from the heavy and intolerable yoke of unwarranted military tyranny.'

There were inaudible groans from one or two Cabinet ministers at the Prime Minister's reversion to extravagant language.

It was more like a day out than an invasion. Agreeably surprised that there had been no opposition, apart from a few shouted insults from lorry drivers and the occasional pedestrian, the combined German and French forces had joined the M20 motorway at Folkestone and made for London at full speed. Strigel knew that once the capital had been secured, any pockets of resistance that might be encountered in other parts of the country could be quelled.

In Park Lane traffic was brought to a standstill as drivers stopped to watch the spectacle of a brigade of German paratroopers descending on Hyde Park but, generally speaking, it elicited no greater interest than the periodical appearance of the Royal Horse Artillery firing salutes.

Within twenty-four hours of their landing, thanks

largely to Macey's signal forbidding military action, the European task force had occupied London and key points in other principal cities. The so-called invasion, General Max Strigel thought ruefully to himself, would not even warrant the award of any battle honours. But it had, indeed, been a blitzkrieg.

General Sir Simon Macey had asked Imogen to help him shred and then burn the last of the incriminating papers at Northwood and later at the Ministry of Defence in London. The only exceptions to his orgy of administrative destruction were those documents wherein Bristow had issued him with orders that Macey hoped would prove that the Chief of the Defence Staff had been the prime mover in the military takeover. But he was unaware of the information that the Secret Intelligence Service had received from his own ADC and, indeed, from Sir Lawrence Dane, the Adjutant-General.

In his anxiety to absolve himself, Macey did not notice that Imogen, while appearing to assist him, was actually secreting papers that she thought might be useful to Alec Shepherd.

By lunch time the task was completed and Macey invited Imogen into his office and poured drinks for them both. 'Not much to celebrate, really,' he said. 'But the outcome was inevitable, I suppose.'

'I suppose so, sir,' said Imogen, accepting the glass of whisky that Macey handed her. She was amazed at his composure. She had been convinced, by her own discoveries and from what Shepherd had told her, that Macey was the architect of a military takeover that had almost succeeded. And yet here he was, calmly relaxing over a drink in his office awaiting whatever fate, in the shape of the Prime Minister, had in store for him. Not for the first time, she felt almost sorry for the man. Perhaps he was so smugly self-confident that it had not occurred to him that the intelligence services had been monitoring his every move, or maybe he firmly believed he could talk his way out of any allegations that were made against him. Conversely, he might just think that he had acted properly. It seemed to Imogen that he was deluding himself into believing that he could lay the blame on the dead Chief of the Defence Staff and the luckless Colonel Crosby.

Staff Sergeant-Major Watkins tapped lightly on Macey's door and stepped in. 'Signal from CINCEF, sir,' he said, proffering a message form.

'From *where?*' demanded Macey.

'Commander-in-Chief, European Force, sir,' said Watkins. 'A General Strigel.'

Macey snatched the signal and scanned it. 'Good God! So soon?' he said. He looked up at Imogen, a shocked expression on his face. 'Strigel's coming here to relieve me of command of the army.' He was obviously wounded by, what in his view, was a quite unnecessary, and deliberately demeaning, formality. But he was unaware that Strigel was acting on the specific orders of the British Prime Minister.

At six o'clock that evening, General Max Strigel walked confidently into Macey's office and saluted before removing his cap. He was a tall, spare man with thinning grey hair, most unlike the popular image of a German general. But then Macey was not much like the stock depictions of British generals either.

'Max, you old warhorse. Good to see you again.' Macey moved rapidly across his office, his hand outstretched.

'General.' Strigel shook hands and then glanced in Imogen's direction.

'Oh, this is my ADC, Major the Honourable Imogen Cresswell.' It was the first time that Imogen had ever heard Macey describe her in that way, but she sensed that he had done so merely to impress the German general.

'Major.' Strigel took Imogen's hand and accorded her a

small bow before turning back to Macey. 'I am ordered to relieve you of command of the army, General,' he said stiffly. 'Your Prime Minister Fairley has ordered it, but he has asked me to tell you two things.' Strigel's attitude seemed strangely cold, not like the old Max Strigel that Macey had known. 'That you remain Chief of the General Staff and that, in that capacity, he expects you to be at the airport tomorrow morning when he returns from Brussels.'

Macey mustered a smile and nodded. 'Understood, Max,' he said. 'Won't stop you having a drink though, will it?'

Strigel paused momentarily and glanced at his watch. 'Of course not, but I'm dining with a friend of mine this evening, Charles Spain. You know him, perhaps?'

Macey shook his head. 'Name doesn't mean anything,' he said.

'An industrialist,' said Strigel. 'He has many interests in Germany.'

Macey poured Strigel a large whisky and invited the German general to sit down. Imogen paused, expecting to be dismissed, but Macey merely indicated another chair with a brief wave and handed her a drink.

'Good health, Max,' said Macey, relaxing into the chair opposite him.

'Thank you. Yours also,' said Strigel as he took a sip of whisky, but there seemed little sincerity in his response. 'This is good.'

'It's a malt called Laphroaig,' said Macey. 'Comes from the Isle of Islay.'

'I'm sorry that I had to be the one to lead the invasion force.' There was a trace of contrition in Strigel's voice but no smile to accompany the apology.

Macey waved a deprecating hand. 'Quite understood,' he said. 'Soldiers do understand that sort of thing. It's the interfering bloody politicians who cause the problems.'

Strigel nodded. '*Ja*, always the same, in my country too.

But now things will get back to normal, I think.'

'I'm not too sure about that, Max.' Macey leaned forward, placing his elbows on his knees and holding his glass in both hands. He seemed not to have noticed Strigel's restrained attitude or if he had, had put it down to the embarrassment of being an invader.

'Oh?'

'From what I hear, the Prime Minister seems to think that everything will be all right again now. Unfortunately for him, this country is like a powder keg at the present time. The European Currency Unit – the ECU – started it, of course, but there is still unemployment, too much unemployment. And crime is running unchecked. Or it was until I, er, that is to say we, took command of the situation. And there's still widespread dissatisfaction with the present government.' Macey leaned back and sipped at his whisky. 'I think we might find ourselves in exactly the same situation as before in two or three months' time.'

'Is that so?' Strigel shook his head slowly and looked genuinely surprised at Macey's statement.

'Oh yes. It's far from over, you mark my words.' Macey appeared suddenly to change the subject. 'How long do you think you'll be staying here, Max?' he asked.

Strigel shrugged. 'I have no idea. It depends on the European Union and your Prime Minister, I suppose. I have received no orders for departure yet.'

'Well as far as I'm concerned, the longer you stay the better.' Macey stood up and carried the whisky bottle towards Strigel.

'No, really, no more,' said Strigel, moving to put his hand over his glass. 'I have to go very soon.'

'Another drop won't hurt you,' said Macey with a smile as he poured more whisky into Strigel's glass. Then he topped up his own drink and, as an apparent afterthought, Imogen's as well, before sitting down again. 'I think we ought to keep closely in touch, Max,' he went on, a serious expression on his face. 'If we were to work as one, there would be little that the government could do if we decided that the situation required further military intervention.'

'I don't think I quite understand,' said Strigel. 'What are you proposing?'

'This government is finished,' said Macey. 'We need new blood. A fresh approach. The alternatives, the Labour Party and the Liberal-Democrats, are a worse proposition than the Tories, and they're bloody awful. They've lost all control and credibility. Unless the army takes a firm stand, we'll be back where we were a few months ago. The army has to be prepared to act again, if necessary. And for that, your help would be invaluable. Next time we must succeed.' Macey stared at his companion with a disconcerting gleam in his eyes. Then he leaned across to take a cigarette box from the side table and offered it to the German.

'No thank you,' said Strigel.

Macey lit himself a cigarette. 'You know, I suppose, Max, that after all that's happened they'll probably sack me. Politicians are very good at finding a scapegoat.' He paused, a cynical smile on his face. Secretly he had no fear of dismissal, firmly believing that the Prime Minister would not dare do such a thing.

'I think that Germans know more about that sort of thing than anyone else. And they also know that for a soldier to get involved in politics is a very dangerous thing.' Strigel put his glass down carefully and stood up. 'I think I know what you're suggesting, General,' he said, 'but you are wrong.'

'What about the long conversations we had when I was in Germany, about the NPD? I thought that you were in favour—'

One side of Strigel's mouth lifted in a sardonic smile that was almost a sneer. 'I was acting as an informant for the head of military intelligence at that time,' he said. 'I had learned some very disconcerting things about the NPD, particularly about their attempts to recruit a few of my brother officers. And I must say that your own interest in it did not go unnoticed. For myself, I have to tell you that I am implacably opposed to any resurgence of Naziism.' He paused and absent-mindedly checked the buttons on his tunic pockets. 'But now I am here in command of the European Force. My job is not to interfere in the domestic affairs of this country any more than is necessary to secure the reinstatement of your government, and if you'll take my advice, as one old soldier to another, you'll stay out of it too.' He made a point of peering closely at his watch. 'And now I must go. Thank you for the whisky.'

Macey was clearly disconcerted at Strigel's revelation about the real reason for his interest in the NPD, which explained, in part, his formality and the hostility that had accompanied it. Nevertheless, Macey persisted. 'But this is of vital importance, Max. If this country ceases to be strong it could damage Germany. In the long run it could have a devastating effect on the whole of the European Union.' He was now quite excited, his fists opening and closing.

Strigel turned at the door, a malevolent expression on his face. 'I think that it's time I made my position clear, General,' he said and, glancing at Imogen, added, 'You might wish for your ADC to leave us.'

'I have no secrets from Major Cresswell,' said Macey stiffly. He was beginning to get angry at this animosity from one he believed to be a friend. A friend and, indeed, an ally. 'All I am saying, Max—'

'Even if what you have been saying was a tenable proposition, the last person I would trust is you. And that is not a professional mistrust, it is personal.' Strigel was standing in the centre of Macey's office now, perfectly composed, his hands clasped behind his back. 'It is only very recently I learned that when you were in Germany and I thought we were friends, you were abusing my friendship. It took many years, but I have now discovered that, at that time, you were having an affair with my daughter. She is more than twenty years younger than you, but that didn't worry you, did it? When you had tired of her – and found someone else to share your bed – you just abandoned her, cruelly and without a word. Only recently has she told me about it. Well, not her exactly. She gave her psychiatrist permission to tell me. After you had finished with her, she had a mental breakdown and now she is in an institution in Garmisch-Partenkirchen. They say she will never recover.' Strigel picked up his cap and sketched a stiff bow in Imogen's direction before opening the door and casting one last glance over his shoulder. 'Goodbye, General,' he said, and closed the door quietly behind him.

For some minutes after General Strigel's departure, Macey sat in the armchair nursing his whisky glass but saying nothing.

Imogen also remained in her seat, too embarrassed by the German general's accusations to move or to say anything. There was little that she could say.

At last Macey spoke. 'It's all lies, you know, Imogen,' he said. 'The man's quite deranged.' He took a sip of whisky.

Imogen was not surprised by Macey's effrontery, only at his belief that she would be taken in by it. He surely could not have forgotten his blunt attempt to inveigle her into an affair, something he was aware that Elizabeth Macey had warned her against. But, in any event, Shepherd had already told her of Macey's involvement with Annelise Strigel. 'Why should he make up a story like that?' she asked.

Macey shrugged. 'I suppose his daughter's problems have had an effect on him, and he wants to find someone he can blame.' He smiled and reached out for a cigarette.

In view of the momentous events of the past twenty-four hours, Imogen sensed that her career as Macey's ADC was near its end and she no longer cared what she said. 'Did you have an affair with his daughter?' she asked.

Macey gave Imogen a tolerant smile. 'Annelise Strigel was a striking girl,' he said, 'but she hadn't the maturity of her mother. Or the beauty that goes with that maturity. I was kind to her, of course. Max Strigel was my friend, or so I thought.' He shook his head as he recalled their recent conversation. 'Perhaps she mistook my felicitousness for something deeper. Looking back, she certainly gave the impression that she was attracted to me.' Macey gazed, unseeing, into the middle distance as though he had just come to that conclusion.

Imogen was astounded at the arrogant and self-deluding ease with which Macey lied and wondered if he was trying to convince himself rather than her. She stood up and glanced at her watch, tiring of his conceit in thinking that she was to be so easily taken in. 'You won't forget, sir, will you, that you are due at the airport tomorrow for the arrival of the Prime Minister? We had a signal saying that he would arrive at eleven hundred hours.'

'I don't think I'll go,' said Macey flatly.

'Is that wise, sir? The Cabinet will be there.' Details of the Prime Minister's impending arrival had been fully publicised on television and in the national press, and the Cabinet were scheduled to arrive on a slightly earlier flight so that they could be seen to greet Fairley's triumphal return. Fairley certainly knew how to stage-manage his political career, even though many would see it as coming too late. 'People might get the wrong impression if you weren't to go.'

Macey stood up and gave his ADC a tired smile. 'You're a good girl, Imogen,' he said and walked round his desk. For a moment he toyed with a few pieces of paper and then looked up. 'You believed in what I was trying to do, didn't you?'

'No, sir, I didn't.' After Macey's recent performance, she

saw no reason to lie any more. There were no longer any doubts in her mind about the propriety of having informed on him to the Secret Intelligence Service. She now knew, with a certainty that surprised even her, that she hated this pompous, vain womaniser. Oddly, it was more that he had treated Elizabeth so badly that offended her. 'I think that you'll be reviled for everything you've done in these last weeks,' she said.

Macey appeared stunned. 'You mean that I—?'

'What I mean, sir,' said Imogen spiritedly, 'is that you've destroyed everything I held on to, everything I admired and supported. But you've brought disgrace on yourself and discredit to the British Army, and I no longer wish to be a part of it, any of it. I intend to resign my commission at the earliest opportunity.' She turned on her heel, half expecting Macey to place her in open arrest for insubordination, or at best rebuke her, but he said nothing. Leaving the communicating door open, she strode through her office, pausing only to pick up her service cap and shoulder bag. At the door of her own office, she paused and looked back. The morose figure of General Macey was sitting slumped in his chair, staring moodily at his half-empty glass of whisky.

CHAPTER TWENTY

Major Hans Kampf stood proudly in the front of his black open-topped Mercedes as it drove slowly under Admiralty Arch and into The Mall. His gloved hands rested lightly on the top of the windscreen as he surveyed the silent crowds, undoubtedly brought out by the announcement on radio and television that morning that the German Army was to take over the guard at Buckingham Palace.

The earlier rain had left the air smelling fresh, and the trees lining the famous processional route seemed greener for their wash. All in all, Kampf felt very pleased with himself at having been selected for so prestigious a duty. Behind him, a military band, complete with glockenspiel, played 'Glorious Prussia' as it led a company of infantry in rubber-soled boots towards the Victoria Memorial in the centre of Queen's Gardens.

'I imagine that this is what it must have been like when the German Army entered Paris in 1940,' said Kampf to his driver.

'Exactly so, *Herr Major*,' said the driver, his eyes on the road.

'That Admiralty Arch is very like the Arc de Triomphe, you know.'

'I imagine it is, *Herr Major*.' The driver wondered why he

had to be saddled with a talkative officer.

For a moment or two Kampf beat time on the top of the windscreen with his swagger cane and hummed the tune that the band was playing. 'Did you know that my grandfather was in the *Afrika Korps?*' he asked.

'Was he indeed, *Herr Major?*'

'And he was killed in the battle of Alamein.'

'A tragedy, *Herr Major.*' The driver nodded gravely but still kept his eyes on the road.

'He would have been very proud to know that one day I would be commanding the guard at Buckingham Palace.'

'I am sure he would, *Herr Major.*'

'Do you have any military connections, *Gefreite?*'

'Oh yes, *Herr Major*. My father was a lieutenant-colonel.'

'Was he really?' Kampf frowned. 'You had better keep your eyes on the road,' he said. And then, apparently countermanding his last order, he added, 'That is Clarence House on your right, *Gefreite*, where the Queen Mother used to live.'

But then Kampf's urbanity and good humour was shattered. Unguarded by police, the crowds on either side of The Mall began to move into the roadway, leaving only the narrowest of passageways for the German Army's procession.

'Drive on,' said Kampf. 'There is nothing to worry about. It is typical of the British. They are pleased to see us. Any minute now they will start to cheer.' Nonetheless, he was unconvinced by his own assurances, and looked nervously at the silent crowds pressing ever nearer to his car.

Suddenly Kampf was struck on the side of the head by a rotten tomato. Two eggs followed, staining his immaculate uniform. But that was only the opening salvo of the barrage of missiles that followed. Kampf's driver, protected in part by the windscreen, hunched over his wheel as tomatoes, eggs, cabbages and a variety of other rotting foodstuffs rained down on the car, most of it striking the luckless German officer beside him. Kampf sat down quickly, attempting to shield his face with his hands. '*Donner und Blitzen*,' he said. 'As fast as you can, *Gefreite*!' He shouted at his driver as though the entire débâcle was the soldier's fault.

Behind Kampf, the music stopped abruptly as the band fell victim to the onslaught and musicians clasped their instruments to their chests and ran. A tuba was abandoned by its player, clattering loudly as it struck the road. And Kampf heard an excited German voice complaining that someone had stolen his glockenspiel.

But when Kampf's sorry gaggle of soldiers reached Buckingham Palace, a further indignity awaited. The guard commander had refused to parade his guard, despite an order from the GOC London District, and Kampf found that the gates were closed. The guard commander, a tall bearskinned major in the Coldstream Guards, stood impassively behind the South Centre Gate and saluted with a languor that only a Guards officer could muster. 'Good morning, Major,' he said, a half-smile on his face.

The police who were habitually on duty at the Palace for a guard change formed a cordon across Queen's Gardens in front of the Victoria Memorial, and the crowd that had followed the Germans down The Mall dutifully stopped behind it; they had no argument with the London bobby. But then they started whistling. Most of them had seen *The Bridge on the River Kwai* on television, but the rest knew the tune anyway. And now the strains of 'Colonel Bogey' filled the mid-morning air as the huge crowd gave vent to a peculiarly British sort of insult.

'We have come to take over the guard,' said Kampf in impeccable English, attempting to wipe egg yolk from his uniform.

'What, dressed like that?' The Guardsman's enquiry was posed with a straight face.

'You have received orders to that effect, I believe,' persisted Kampf. 'We are here to mount the Queen's Guard.'

'Over my dead body, old boy,' said the British major.

Imogen threw her arms around Alec Shepherd's neck and kissed him. He responded hungrily to her passionate embrace, putting his arms around her waist and holding her close as he felt her body mould to his.

'Thank God it's all over.' Imogen slackened her hold and leaned back against Shepherd's arms, which were still encircling her waist. 'What d'you think will happen now?'

Releasing his hold on her, Shepherd took Imogen's hand and led her into the sitting room before pouring drinks for them both. 'I don't know. It's rather up to the Prime Minister now, I suppose.' He handed her the whisky that she had asked for and raised his own glass in salute. 'Here's to you, and thank you for all your help,' he said.

Imogen took a chance. 'Here's to *us*,' she said.

For some moments, Shepherd appraised the slender blonde for whom he had developed an attachment that surprised even him. 'Yes,' he said softly, 'here's to us.'

Imogen took a sip of her drink and felt an inner excitement that Shepherd had responded to her toast, but she had got to know him well over the preceding weeks and knew that he was not a man to be rushed, either in his profession or in matters removed from it. She knew it would take time, but she had decided that Alec Shepherd was her sort of man. 'I've got some more stuff for you,' she said. She placed her drink on the side table and picked up her handbag. 'I had to be careful, but Macey embarked on a damage-limitation exercise this morning. He and I spent an hour or two destroying papers. As he was with me for most of the time, I could only lay hands on a few bits and pieces.' She handed over a sheaf of documents. 'I don't know whether they'll be of any value.'

'Thank you.' Shepherd took the proffered papers and quickly scanned them before locking them in his bureau. Then he took her hand once more and led her to the settee and when she had sat down seated himself beside her. 'What you've done has been of inestimable value to my service, and to the government,' he began, rather stiffly. But then he paused, the old question of trust besetting him once more.

Imogen sensed his doubt immediately. 'I am to be trusted, Alec,' she said softly. 'I would have thought that you'd had proof enough of that by now.'

'I'm sorry, Imogen, of course you are.' Shepherd half turned to smile at her. 'Much of what you've told us has been forwarded to the Prime Minister in Brussels and no doubt he will act on it. I'm not a lawyer, and I don't know whether it amounts to a case of treason or whatever against Macey, but I should think that it will almost certainly result in his dismissal.'

A frown clouded Imogen's face. 'Will the Prime Minister know that it was me?' she asked.

Shepherd smiled and shook his head. 'No,' he said. 'Not even the PM is told the identity of our informants.' But he was by no means sure that it was true in this case; her contribution had been so valuable that Dancer might think she merited some recognition.

'I told Macey this evening that I was resigning my commission.'

'Good heavens, why on earth – ?'

'I don't want to stay where I am, and I don't want to go back to the battalion.' Imogen stared wistfully into her glass. 'I just can't take any more, Alec. Can't take any more of the deceit, and I certainly can't take any more of Macey.' She glanced sideways at Shepherd. 'There was an unbelievable confrontation between him and Strigel this evening. It seems it was true what you told me about him and Annelise Strigel.' And she proceeded to tell Shepherd about the extraordinary scene in Macey's office.

When she had finished, Shepherd remained thought-fully silent for the few moments it took him to digest the information. 'I never doubted it,' he said eventually, 'but I'm pleased to hear you confirm it.'

Imogen had noted his sudden silence. 'Drafting another signal for the Prime Minister?' she asked playfully.

The sight of French and German soldiers patrolling the streets was a discomfiting one, but Macey was relieved that none of his own men had become victims of the invasion. Although he had been sorry to hear of the death of Tim Crosby, he realised that the hussar colonel, by his own demise, had become a useful scapegoat for all that had gone wrong in the last days of the failed coup d'état, in particular the seizure and imprisonment of the Prime Minister and the Cabinet but, more importantly, the death of the Chancellor of the Exchequer.

A detachment of the French Foreign Legion guarded the approaches to Heathrow Airport, but the sight of Macey's uniform was sufficient to allow him through unhindered. Casually, he returned the salute of a tough-looking Legion sergeant.

The VIP lounge was crowded. The Cabinet, having arrived from Brussels thirty minutes earlier, were there, along with the naval and air force chiefs of staff, the Commissioner of Police – undertaking his first official engagement since returning to duty – the Lord Lieutenant of Greater London and the Lord Mayors of London and Westminster among others. Diana Fairley, the Prime Minister's wife, was in the centre of the room, a gin and tonic in her hand, holding court to a small knot of younger officials, some making polite conversation, others furtively eyeing her low-cut neckline and recalling the saying about good tunes being played on old fiddles.

There was a coldly polite acknowledgement of Macey's

arrival from a few of those present, but most ignored him. There had already been a whispering campaign among the less important officials suggesting that he must have been responsible in some way for the dastardly events of the preceding weeks.

Macey stood looking out of the window and wondered what the outcome of the inevitable interview with the Prime Minister would be. He gazed at the cars that were parked some way off on the edge of the tarmac, the drivers giving their vehicles a last-minute flick over with feather dusters. The two cars nearest the VIP suite were armour-plated Jaguars, and several obvious Special Branch detectives stood around, trying to look inconspicuous as they occasionally scanned the rooftops of nearby buildings. Airport policemen mingled with legionnaires, two customs officers stood to one side of the doorway sharing a joke, and Foreign Office and airport officials conversed and fussed over inconsequential pieces of paper. Alongside the VIP suite, the Metropolitan Police band stood at ease sorting their music and talking quietly among themselves. Fairley's order that no military bands or guards of honour should be present had been obeyed.

Then an A340 Airbus of the Royal Belgian Air Force taxied into view and stopped opposite the VIP lounge, its screaming jets suddenly running down.

Led by Diana Fairley, the waiting crowd of dignitaries filed out, instinctively assuming the precedence that their Cabinet and civil posts dictated. They walked slowly down the narrow pathway and across the tarmac apron. Then they stood, waiting uncertainly, as the steps were driven into position and the door of the aircraft opened. There was a slight breeze in the air, sufficient, occasionally, to waft kerosene fumes in the direction of the reception party. The police band came to attention and, competing with an ascending Concorde, began to play Zehle's 'Wellington'.

First off the aircraft was Gordon Whitmore, followed by

Enderby and Warrant Officer Helen Jackson. Then, after a moment's delay, the figure of Robert Fairley appeared at the top of the steps, paused and slowly descended. Spontaneously, the small crowd of well-wishers broke into applause.

Then, for a second or two, the crowd's activity was stilled as Diana Fairley ran towards her husband and embraced him while the meeters and greeters shuffled their feet and pretended not to watch. Moments later it all became formal as Cabinet ministers and other notables vied with each other to shake the Prime Minister's hand for the benefit of the television cameras, which were there in abundance. Finally, Fairley led the group in a slow procession towards the VIP lounge. After a suitable interval for refreshments, they would get into the waiting cars, and the motorcade would set off for Downing Street.

After careful thought, ex-Colour-Sergeant John Silver had decided on the Center Super 14 version of the Thompson Contender pistol. It was, in his view, the best weapon for the task he had been given by Colonel Wilson's mysterious associate. He knew that reassembling a sniper rifle – an act so beloved of film-makers – would entail zeroing the weapon again and he had neither the time nor the facilities for doing so.

The source which had supplied the pistol had also supplied a standard executive briefcase adapted to accommodate the weapon which, with a length of nearly eighteen inches, lay diagonally in its sculpted bed of foam rubber. At an indoor range made available to him, he had zeroed the weapon and then spent hours practising until he was satisfied that his skill, already of a high standard, could not be improved upon.

Silver was an intelligent man, which is why Wilson had steered him in Barry Rogers' direction. He read the newspapers thoroughly and rarely missed the late-evening television news. As a result, he had kept himself fully informed about the events leading up to the release of the Prime Minister and the Cabinet, and when it had been announced that they would arrive at Heathrow, he began a detailed survey of the airport. If that failed to provide a suitable site, or was too difficult a place from which to mount the assassination, he would have to wait.

On three successive days, Silver had journeyed to the airport by underground train and walked around the huge complex. He had studied the VIP area on the south side and had wandered into places normally closed to the public. Whenever he had been challenged, he had produced the skilfully forged warrant card – showing him to be Detective Sergeant Wainwright of the Metropolitan Police – with which Barry Rogers had provided him. But he had avoided the many genuine police officers on the airport for fear that, simply out of friendship, they might have asked questions he could not answer. At last he was reasonably satisfied with his plan. Silver was a man who was never more than reasonably satisfied.

Today Silver had again been challenged several times as he moved through the airport but again had produced the fake warrant card. And he had produced it each time he had been asked to pass through an electronic screening frame, exercising his right as a police officer, albeit a bogus one, not to undergo body checks anywhere on the airport.

At last he entered the deserted office that he had selected. It was some distance from the VIP lounge but Silver was an expert sniper. On his first visit he had taken a press of the door key in cuttlefish and made a copy, just in case the original key was missing later. But the copy was not needed. Now he locked the door and pocketed the key before moving the escutcheon back into place and securing it with a piece of sticky tape.

As quietly as possible, he moved a desk close to the window and opened his briefcase. With a skill that would have enabled him to do it in pitch darkness, he quickly checked over the Thompson before placing it gently on the desk.

He turned his attention to the window. Taking two pieces of thin steel rod from his case, he squatted down out of sight and used them slowly to push the bottom half of the frame upwards a distance of ten inches, sufficient to give him a clear view. He just hoped that some inquisitive policeman on the roof of one of the terminal buildings was not, at that moment, training his binoculars on that particular office. He leaned across and took the Burris telescopic sight from its resting place in the briefcase. Slowly, to avoid any sudden movement that might attract unwelcome attention, he scanned the VIP area and the doorway from which he knew the reception party would emerge. Then he attached the sight to the pistol.

Macey had remained in the VIP suite, declining to join in the unrestrained but, he suspected, slightly hypocritical enthusiasm with which Fairley had been greeted.

'Ah, General Macey. Good morning.' The Prime Minister strode towards the Chief of the General Staff but made no attempt to shake hands.

'Good morning, Prime Minister. Welcome home.' Macey glanced at Graeme Kent, now standing beside Fairley. 'Secretary of State,' he murmured and nodded a brief acknowledgement to his political boss.

'General Macey, I wonder if you would spare me a moment.' The Prime Minister looked around the room until his eyes alighted on the airport special facilities officer. 'Is there a private room somewhere, where the Defence Secretary and I can talk to General Macey?'

'Of course, Prime Minister.' The official, half bowing as though in the presence of royalty, led the way to a small room off the main VIP lounge.

'I shall not be long, my dear,' said Fairley to his wife. He walked towards the room followed by the Defence Secretary and Macey. He intended that this should be a very formal interview. And a very short one.

Having asked Gordon Whitmore to ensure that he was not interrupted, Fairley closed the door behind him and moved into the centre of the room, but he did not invite either Macey or Kent to sit down. Fairley stood behind an armchair, his hands lightly clasping its back. 'I wanted to see you as soon as possible to give you the opportunity of excusing your actions, General,' he said.

'I'm not quite sure what you mean, Prime Minister.' Macey had moved so that he was grasping the back of the chair opposite Fairley. Kent stood to one side, hands locked tightly together in front of him.

'Let's not pussyfoot around, Sir Simon,' snapped Fairley with a show of anger that surprised even the Defence Secretary. 'It is two weeks to the day since elements of the British Army launched an assault on the government and murdered the Chancellor of the Exchequer.'

'I assure you, sir,' said Macey, 'that I had no knowledge that that was going to happen. It came as a complete surprise to me.'

'And to me, General,' said the Prime Minister drily. 'But you are adamant that you had no prior knowledge of the attack?'

'None, sir,' said Macey, his gaze unwavering.

'I see.' Fairley smiled cynically. 'Are you suggesting that it was entirely the brainchild of this ...' He paused and turned to the Secretary of State for Defence. 'What was his name?'

'Colonel Crosby, Prime Minister.'

'Yes, this Colonel Crosby?'

'I'm afraid that the evidence points towards that being the case, sir,' said Macey.

'I find that very difficult to believe, General,' said Fairley. 'I would have thought that, as Chief of the General Staff, control of the army was something you would have exercised very closely.'

'One cannot always get inside the minds of one's officers, Prime Minister.' Macey appeared quite unruffled by Fairley's innuendoes and continued to lie confidently. 'But I think that Admiral of the Fleet Sir Godfrey Bristow may have known. I understand that it was he who advised the German government of the Cabinet's whereabouts, even though he claimed it was the SIS who found them.'

'It was,' said Fairley tartly. 'But how interesting that neither he nor Colonel Crosby is here to defend himself. But I suppose that, working on the principle of vicarious responsibility, Sir Godfrey cannot entirely escape some of the blame. Actually,' he continued, 'it is more likely that Sir Godfrey had no knowledge of the Cabinet's whereabouts.' The Prime Minister gazed at Macey sternly. 'Or mine.'

'Once I learned that you and the Cabinet had been abducted, sir,' Macey went on, 'I did what I thought was best for the country in what, I'm sure you will agree, were very difficult circumstances. After consultation with Sir Godfrey, of course.'

'Of course,' murmured the Prime Minister. Beside him, Kent silently applauded Fairley's ability to inject so much sarcasm into two words.

'After Colonel Crosby had seized the Cabinet, Sir Godfrey and I immediately discussed the matter with Sir William Headley, who became convinced that the imposition of martial law was the only solution to the grave crisis that faced us all. It was my impression that the Attorney concurred wholeheartedly with the view that something had got to be done or anarchy would prevail. It seemed a sensible precaution and in the interests of the safety of the nation. It was a difficult time.'

'For all of us,' said the Prime Minister quietly.

'I must emphasise, sir, that I had no knowledge that it

was Bristow's intention to supplant the lawfully elected government, and I can only thank God that you have been returned unharmed.'

Fairley ignored Macey's excessive blandishments. 'Now that the government has been restored to power, General Macey, it is not my intention to create further disharmony. No doubt the Attorney-General and the Director of Public Prosecutions could find a number of charges to bring against you, but I am loathe to drag this thing on any longer than is necessary. I want to see a unified society bringing peace and prosperity to this country once more. We have all been through trying times, and I do not wish to prolong the agony of the past few weeks.' As Fairley had told the Cabinet in Brussels, the Attorney's opinion was that the evidence was far too tenuous to hold out any hope of convicting Macey. Apart from that such action might further damage the Conservative Party's standing, such as it was, in the eyes of the electorate.

Macey breathed an inaudible sigh of relief. 'I quite agree, sir,' he said.

'However, General, I have decided that Air Chief Marshal Sir John Gilbert will be promoted to Marshal of the RAF and appointed Chief of the Defence Staff. In those circumstances, I think it is only fair that he has a new Chief of the General Staff with whom to work, and I am sure you will quite understand when I ask for your immediate resignation as CGS.' He paused. 'And from the army also.'

Macey was staggered. Not only had he been certain that he had covered his tracks sufficiently to escape prosecution, but he had confidently expected to get the job – and the field marshal's baton that went with it – that the Prime Minister now proposed to give to Gilbert. 'But Sir John Gilbert is very junior, sir,' he said.

'I know,' said Fairley, 'but perhaps a more youthful and less entrenched attitude is what we need at the Ministry of

Defence.' He smiled at Macey and nodded. 'Thank you, General.'

'Very well, sir,' said Macey coldly, stunned by his summary dismissal. It required all his self-control to appear unruffled when inwardly he was seething at the way in which he had been outmanoeuvred by the astute politician opposite him. He had almost hoped for a trial at the Old Bailey where, under the cloak of forensic privilege, he could have lambasted the Prime Minister for his incompetence.

Fairley waited until the door had closed behind Macey before turning to the Secretary of State for Defence. 'Well, Graeme, that's disposed of that little problem, I think,' he said as he lowered himself into an armchair.

Kent shook his head. 'You should have had him charged with treason, Prime Minister. I'm certain that there's ample evidence.'

'That's not the advice I was given,' said Fairley quietly and waved a limp hand over the file of reports that was now open on his knee. But even if it had favoured a prosecution, he would have dismissed it as being impolitic. 'According to the Secret Intelligence Service, their informant' – he glanced at Kent – 'whom they don't name, talks of a deterioration in Macey's mental stability.' In fact, Fairley had been told in a top-secret despatch that the informant was Imogen Cresswell, whose father he had known as a respected Labour peer, and he had already determined that her name would appear high on the next honours list. 'There's talk of him developing a gleam in his eye when deploying troops, and maniacal behaviour, whatever that means, but there is nothing concrete.' There was more, of course, much more, but Fairley had no intention of sharing it with Kent. 'Quite frankly, Graeme, you can't convict a man on that sort of stuff, any more than you can bring him to trial for his extramarital peccadilloes. According to this' – again Fairley tapped the report – 'he's been screwing any woman who came within yards of him.'

'Really?' Graeme Kent raised his eyebrows and wondered what changes had been wrought in Fairley as a result of his enforced incarceration.

'Including, it seems, the daughter of General Strigel.' The Prime Minister sighed. 'I thought that adultery was the preserve of Cabinet ministers,' he added, in a sly reference to the Home Secretary's recent affair which, fortunately for both Sinclair and the government, had by some miracle been kept from the popular press. 'As a matter of interest, Graeme,' said Fairley, changing the subject slightly, 'have you any idea why all this information came to me from the SIS, who are supposed only to operate abroad, rather than the Security Service, who have been strangely silent throughout? Why is that, do you suppose?'

Kent suspected that the Prime Minister was playing devil's advocate but could not resist scoring a point against the Home Secretary, his arch rival for Fairley's job. 'I really have no idea, Prime Minister. But Ken Sinclair is the political head of the Security Service. Perhaps the question would be better posed to him.'

'Maybe,' growled Fairley, adamant that he was going to ask a lot of questions once he was back in Downing Street, and adamant also that the Right Honourable Kenneth Sinclair would shortly become a backbencher.

'But I'm sure that all that stuff about Bristow being the prime mover was rubbish,' said Kent, switching the conversation back to the main subject again. 'Macey planned the takeover and the seizure of the Cabinet. And all you've done is to award him a fat pension.'

'I wish it was as simple as that, Graeme. But you see we have to preserve the integrity of the Cabinet.'

'What does that mean?' Kent was beginning to tire of Robert Fairley's cat-and-mouse posturings.

'It means that I have information from the Secret Intelligence Service that points to Alexander Crisp being just as culpable as Macey in all this. In fact, given that he was a member of the government, probably more so.'

'I don't believe it.' The Defence Secretary sank down into a chair. 'Surely not.'

'But Crisp is dead now. And so are Bristow and Crosby. All that remains is to solve the last of what Harold Macmillan used to call a few little local difficulties.' The Prime Minister smiled. 'There is more than one way of killing a cat, Graeme,' he said and closed the file containing the SIS reports, the last of which had been handed to him as he boarded the aircraft. 'And to remove Macey from office, to discard him as though he were of no importance, will not make a martyr of him.'

But Graeme Kent was not satisfied with that and immediately offered his resignation. Which saved the Prime Minister from the distasteful task of sacking him too.

At last there was movement. The fleet of cars that was to carry the Prime Minister, the Cabinet and the other dignitaries back to London lined up on the roadway opposite the entrance to the VIP lounge. Then two policemen opened the doors.

Minutes later the party began to emerge, milling about in the May sunshine and waiting for the Prime Minister. Robert Fairley came into view and another round of hand-shaking began. Finally, the Prime Minister walked away from the main crowd towards the Metropolitan Police band and shook hands with the director of music. 'What was that piece you played when I arrived?' he asked.

'It was called "Wellington", sir,' said the director of music, preening himself slightly. 'I thought it particularly apposite – a famous general who later became Prime Minister.'

'Quite so,' said Fairley stiffly and turned away.

The director of music was surprised at the Prime Minister's reaction and was thankful that he had not mentioned that the composer was German.

As he waited, Silver recalled the moment two days before when it had been announced that, as a part of the reduction of the armed forces, the Irish Guards were to be disbanded along with all the other Irish regiments. Stunned by the news that had appeared on his television screen, Silver could only recall the catechism of battle honours that he and the other recruits had been obliged to learn at the depot. Mons, Marne, Aisne and Ypres ran through his mind like credits on a silent film, stretching on through Cambrai, Boulogne and Nijmegen to Anzio. Then there were the names of the VCs, which were engraved on the mind of every Irish Guardsman: O'Leary, Moyney, Woodcock, Kenneally and Charlton. And now, for the sake of some political vendetta, they were to be swept away, another disbanded regiment whose files would grow dusty in the archives, to be remembered only by a fading band of old soldiers. Ex-Colour-Sergeant Silver was a very angry man, but he tried to suppress his anger; he knew that anger would impede the task he had to perform.

Slowly and carefully he loaded the Thompson with a single round of .223 Remington and brought it up. His right hand grasped the butt; his left hand, holding a second round of ammunition between his second and third fingers, was curled gently around the walnut and rubber stock beneath the centre of the barrel. His elbows were rock steady on the desk.

Silver spotted Macey almost immediately but he relaxed his eye until the cross sight centred perfectly on his target. The eye clouded over and he closed it for a moment before realigning his aim. With a steadily increasing pressure he drew the trigger towards him.

The Prime Minister's body jerked once, as if in spasm, and Silver fired his second round exactly two seconds later, the time it had taken him to reload.

Whitmore was not watching the Prime Minister when it happened. Protection officers rarely spend too much time looking at their principal. That, after all, is not the place from which an attack might be expected. But there was a sudden cry, and he spun round in time to see the Prime Minister fall and Diana Fairley throwing herself on his lifeless body. Then she looked up, an expression of the most frightening anguish on her face. She looked very old, the costly cosmetics mocking her for trying too hard. To his dying day, Whitmore would never forget that reproachful glance as she said, 'They've killed him, Mr Whitmore.'

Quickly but calmly, and with his usual economy of movement, Silver closed the window. He removed the sight from the pistol and packed both in the briefcase. He picked up the two cartridge cases and, looking around to check that he had left nothing, moved swiftly across the room. He stripped the tape from the escutcheon, unlocked the door and, leaving the key in the keyhole, stepped into the corridor.

The last thing his brain ever registered was the sight of a uniformed policeman levelling a Heckler and Koch at him. Instinct made Silver's right hand move rapidly towards the Browning automatic at his waist, just before a blow like a steam hammer smashed him back against the wall.

Author's Note

For reasons of security, many of the actions described in *Division* are deliberately misleading. For instance, it would not be possible to mount an assault on 10 Downing Street in the comparatively simple way that the 27th Royal Hussars did, and the Secret Intelligence Service would most certainly shrink from arranging an assassination of any sort, despite what investigative journalists might like you to believe. My description of the assassination at Heathrow Airport is pure fiction. It is not possible for anyone, even police officers, to pass through airport checkpoints as easily as the bogus Detective Sergeant Wainwright did, neither is there an unguarded building that affords a suitably commanding view of the exterior of the VIP Suite. And because of the air-conditioning system, all windows in the airport buildings are sealed and incapable of being opened.

The Eagle and the Snake

Douglas Boyd

Branded on the soul of every Foreign Legionnaire is an unbreakable code of loyalty – to the Legion and to each other. But then Raoul Duvalier betrayed that code ...

Already crippled, tortured and starved by the Viet Minh, he is court-martialled by the Legion, disgraced, and repatriated to France with no job and no prospects. Except the prospect of revenge ...

For twenty years he has known of, and not betrayed, the whereabouts of the Foreign Legion's gold. Now, recruiting a private army from the Legion itself, he sets out to claim it for himself. But this time, one of his men has betrayed *him*.

Imprisoned in his own dungeon, Raoul reviews the lives of recruits, relatives and lovers – two decades of action and adventure from Algeria to Idaho, Belfast to Vientiane, the Dordogne to Dien Bien Phu – as he tries to identify the traitor. A traitor on whose unmasking depends not just his gold but his life, and other lives barely yet begun ...

FICTION

The Honour and the Glory

Douglas Boyd

Basic training in the Foreign Legion is brutally tough. Its aim is to forge bonds of loyalty that stand the test of modern combat and last a lifetime.

Fifteen years after he took off his white kepi for the last time, Peter Bergman is a No Release prisoner in a Gulag camp that officially no longer exists. The man he blames for putting him there is his old Legion comrade, Jack Roscoe. For such treachery, Bergman swears bloody revenge, if he ever gets free.

In St Petersburg during the autumn of 1992, Roscoe learns that Bergman is still alive and decides to rescue him. The plan is brilliant but the chance of success is small.

Roscoe's only ally is the beautiful woman over whom he and Bergman fell out. She warns that the price of failure is death. That doesn't stop Jack Roscoe. To him, something far more important is at stake: a man's honour, without which life is not worth living.

FICTION

<u>Firefox</u>

Craig Thomas

The Soviet Mig-31 is the deadliest warplane ever built. Codenamed Firefox by NATO, it can fly at over 4,000 mph, is invulnerable to radar – and has a lethally sophisticated weapons system that its pilot can control by thought impulses.

There's only one way for the West to fight the greatest threat since the Second World War – hijack the Firefox!

'In a class by itself – a chilling, superbly researched thriller'
Jack Higgins

FICTION

☐ The Eagle and the Snake	Douglas Boyd	£5.99
☐ The Honour and the Glory	Douglas Boyd	£5.99
☐ Firefox	Craig Thomas	£5.99

Warner Books now offers an exciting range of quality titles by both established and new authors which can be ordered from the following address:

> Little, Brown & Company (UK),
> P.O. Box 11,
> Falmouth,
> Cornwall TR10 9EN.

Alternatively you may fax your order to the above address.
Fax No. 01326 317444.

Payments can be made as follows: cheque, postal order (payable to Little, Brown and Company) or by credit cards, Visa/Access. Do not send cash or currency. UK customers and B.F.P.O. please allow £1.00 for postage and packing for the first book, plus 50p for the second book, plus 30p for each additional book up to a maximum charge of £3.00 (7 books plus). Overseas customers including Ireland, please allow £2.00 for the first book plus £1.00 for the second book, plus 50p for each additional book.

NAME (Block Letters) _____

ADDRESS _____

_____

☐ I enclose my remittance for £ _____
☐ I wish to pay by Access/Visa Card

Number ⬜⬜⬜⬜⬜⬜⬜⬜⬜⬜⬜⬜⬜⬜⬜⬜

Card Expiry Date _____